About the author

Graham John Lowe 31 May 1955 – 19 July 2020

He was a man of intrigue, integrity and compassion. He lived his life helping others, whether it be as a father or working for Queen and Country with the Military of Defense Police Department in the United Kingdom. He was also a computer specialist but his love for adventure came out in his writings which came to fruition when his first book was published, *Mountjoy: The Reluctant Recruit*.

Telling his stories captivated his audience as he spoke the words with eloquence and intrigue, depicting the voices of his characters in true form. Graham was never in one place too long, and was always challenging the change.

Graham was the story, and is sadly missed by his family and his readers.

MOUNTJOY: TO CATCH A SPY

GRAHAM LOWE

MOUNTJOY: TO CATCH A SPY

Vanguard Press

VANGUARD PAPERBACK

© Copyright 2022
Graham Lowe

The right of Graham Lowe to be identified as author of
this work has been asserted by him in accordance with the
Copyright, Designs and Patents Act 1988.

All Rights Reserved

No reproduction, copy or transmission of this publication
may be made without written permission.
No paragraph of this publication may be reproduced,
copied or transmitted save with the written permission of the publisher, or in
accordance with the provisions
of the Copyright Act 1956 (as amended).

Any person who commits any unauthorised act in relation to
this publication may be liable to criminal
prosecution and civil claims for damages.

A CIP catalogue record for this title is
available from the British Library.

ISBN 978 1 80016 242 6

*Vanguard Press is an imprint of
Pegasus Elliot MacKenzie Publishers Ltd.*
www.pegasuspublishers.com

First Published in 2022

**Vanguard Press
Sheraton House Castle Park
Cambridge England**

Printed & Bound in Great Britain

Dedication

This book is dedicated to all those who love life, and live for adventure.

Take the risk to succeed.

"May your waves roll with the tide, and fall gently on the shores of tomorrow."

Diana Lowe

Chapter One
The Colossus

The smoke-filled deck hung heavy in the damp atmosphere. The rain almost horizontal kept Sylvian's face from the gun port; with his back to the main mast, he gave way to exhaustion. His tired legs gave way to the muscles that trembled and screamed at two days of constant use and he slumped slowly down to the wet deck.

The ship heaved sharply to starboard and caught the wind which drove hard through the port side gun ports and bulkhead holes created by French cannon fire. It forced its way through the gun deck relentlessly carrying the cold drops of salty rain into the faces of the exhausted crew. The blast of cold air picked up the smoke and sent it whirling like a tornado caught in such a confined space, continuing on and out through the starboard gun ports and ripped out bulkhead.

Two days had seen this battle fought with neither ship giving quarter as they danced around one another and stirred the ocean to a foamy frenzy. Bodies of men lay around and across the cannons, some dead, some so exhausted with fatigue that they lay to sleep wherever they could.

The powder monkey came around during this lull and carried a bucket of water and bread which he gave to those who were conscious to receive it, leaving bread on the wet salty, bloodied deck at the feet of those who were not.

It was a sad and lonely sight which beheld First Lieutenant Sylvian Mountjoy this day. He had hit the Colossus in every place he thought he should find her powder store, and yet there she still floated and was now coming about.

The Antelope had steadied her course dead ahead and to the stern of the mighty double hulled French man of war. They were severely out gunned and out manoeuvred but had fought bravely to keep this ship from good escape. The Colossus had taken much damage to sail and bulkhead by the fine gunnery of the Antelope crew and was disabled enough to be slowed to their own speed.

On the approach of the Antelope the Colossus tacked hard to starboard, momentarily catching Captain Andrew Young off guard. Captain Young was a fine looking fellow and stood short and stout in his silver buckled shoes. His face unshaven after two days of constant hunt and chase with the Colossus, but distinguished in looks though he bore one, now more prominent slight scar to his left cheek. This he had earned when a young midshipman given to easy challenge to a duel for honour on the Plymouth Ho. He turned to the wheel man and commanded to hold course dead ahead. He knew well his First Lieutenant Sylvian Mountjoy who commanded the gun decks, he knew that he would take chance at a shot to the stern of the fleeing Colossus. He hoped that this was the case and not that the Colossus should come fully about to yet be broadside to the Antelope. He was not disappointed.

Sylvian heard the cry from above that the Colossus had tacked to starboard. He pushed his complaining muscles and came to his feet on the wet slippery deck. He moved to the splintered hole where cannon three had once stood and through the cold driving rain that stung his face could just see the Colossus still coming about to starboard. "Mr Fitzwalter," he cried as he turned to face the gun crews.

"Aye, sir," said Fitzwalter as he pulled his large bulky frame to his feet.

"All guns ready and await my command if you please," he replied.

The deck came to life as Fitzwalter called command after command to ready all guns to firing positions. All gun commanders reported back that all guns available and crewed were ready to fire. Fitzwalter reported to Sylvian that all guns were ready and waiting command. Sylvian thanked Fitzwalter and instructed all gun commanders to fire at his command and dispatched the powder monkey to the lower gun deck to repeat the order.

Sylvian positioned himself at the foot of cannon one on the starboard side of the ship, his view to sea greatly enhanced by the fact that the bulkhead had been ripped away where the cannon faced out to sea. The Colossus's starboard side was now just starting to come into view as the ship continued on its starboard tack. The Antelope had continued dead ahead and the stern of the French ship was now coming full to the starboard side of the Antelope.

"All lower deck guns and upper deck guns shall fire in sequence on my command," shouted Sylvian as loud as the whole ship should hear his voice. The distance to the Frenchy was less than five hundred yards. His chin rested on the back end of cannon one as he gazed along the barrel. They were making good speed and the Frenchy soon came in line, he waited. The point of the barrel moved slowly across the stern; he could clearly see the vessel's name in high gold letters to the stern. A flash and the bang of a shot from the stern guns of the Frenchy cleared the Antelope and found only water on her port side. The cannon barrel had now found the centre of the French stern.

"Sir…" said Fitzwalter impatiently.

"On my command, Mr Fitzwalter… if you please," replied Sylvian, not wavering from his sighting down the cannon. Three quarters past the stern, he stood upright.

"Cannon one… Fire!" the deafening roar of the cannon as she sent her ball on its way.

"Cannon two… Fire." The first shot found its target and passed through the windows of the stern cabin.

"Cannon three…. Fire!" Cannon two's shot found its target taking out the bulkhead between the windows of the stern cabin.

"Cannon four… Fire." An enormous explosion ripped through the stern of the Colossus raising her many feet out of the water and sending timber into the air as cannon three's ball had found the powder store. The force of the blast could be seen as it distorted the air and headed at massive speed towards them like a clear bubble of air. It sent the air from their lungs and threw the crew back across the gun deck. Sylvian found himself back against the mast sitting in almost the same position. The dullness of sound put eeriness to the deck as he looked around at his men, the whistling in his ears slowly abating as sound was coming back to him, the awareness of his surroundings as if he had just awoken from a deep sleep in a foreign place. Startled, he pulled himself to his feet, regaining his composure as he set eyes on the familiar faces that surrounded him.

"You've done it, sir... they are surrendering, sir, look, sir..." said Fitzwalter as he took the arm of his lieutenant and led him back to cannon one.

Sylvian watched through the gun port as the Antelope moved towards and then alongside the Colossus. He could clearly see the extent of the damage to this great ship that his cannon had inflicted. The ocean was strewn with bodies and debris rising and falling with the swell as they approached. The stern cabins had all but been destroyed and had taken the upper deck and steerage with them. Looking up at the stern of the ship now called Col as the rest of her name had disappeared with the stern bulkhead, the sky was clearly visible through the stern cabin and what was the poop deck.

The men sat silently upon cannon as the ship made way slowly alongside. The damage and carnage had quelled their brief excitement at the cessation of the battle. The lower gun deck crew were bringing up their dead and injured. Ship's surgeon, Jack Mountjoy, was busy to his task when Midshipman Jamison made his way to the gun deck and saluted Sylvian as he approached.

"Captain's compliments, sir. He asks that you join him on the Colossus, sir," he said as he looked around at the carnage of bodies, splinters of wood and upturned cannon. His face slowly paled.

"Thank you, Mr Jamison, I shall attend him immediately and I believe you should accompany me with some haste," replied Sylvian as he took young Jamison's arm and led him to the stairway to the upper deck.

"Lieutenant Gant," he called behind him.

"Aye, sir," said Steven Gant as he helped two injured men from the lower gun deck to the surgeon's makeshift table.

"You are in command of the gun deck, sir. Please report when all is well and secured."

"Aye, sir," said Steven to the back of his lieutenant.

The Colossus was still afloat, but drifting. Captain Young had brought the Antelope to the port side of the Colossus and men were starting to board her. The senior officer left alive after the explosion was a lieutenant who had introduced himself as Lieutenant Pierre Sanquin from St Malo. He formally surrendered himself, his crew and of course his ship to Captain Young.

Sylvian made his way in company with Mr Jamison on to the main deck of the Colossus and found Captain Young at the foot of the main mast with Mr Sanquin. Sylvian found Mr Sanquin unshaven and with his uniform in a poor condition. He was young, around twenty-two or twenty-three and gave quite a handsome presence. He saluted Sylvian on his approach and was introduced by Captain Young. Sylvian returned the salute and then looked about him at the busy deck. Men, both French and British were busying themselves to the task of clearing the deck of the debris of battle. The sun was high in the sky and a cool breeze drifted among them. The damaged sails flapped wildly in the breeze and failed to catch the energy it provided.

"I am pleased to make your acquaintance, sir," said Sylvian. "Although somewhat in unfortunate circumstances, your captain and your first officer have succumbed to the battle, sir, I assume."

"Indeed, sir," replied Pierre in excellent English. "My captain was killed on the second day of our engagement when your shot caught one of our skiffs as he was passing." He pointed to the centre of the ship just past the main mast where lay the poor remains of the skiff. "We have yet to commit him to the sea, as with all of my fellow officers, or what is left of them after your shot took our powder store and of course the poop deck where my officers were gathered," he explained. "Sir." He turned to address Captain Young. "By your leave I would like to request the service of some of my men to gather together the captain and officers and men of this ship that have found their way to God, and prepare them for burial?" he requested and took a bow of his head in respect.

"Indeed," replied Captain Young. "Mr Mountjoy, please see to it that Lt Sanquin receives what he needs if you please." As he turned to depart, he paused and looked back to Sylvian. "And please arrange for a report on any damage that may preclude us from returning this prize to Portsmouth," he said looking about him at the vast damage that surrounded them.

"Sir," replied Sylvian as he saluted his captain.

Sylvian took a long look about him at this once fine ship. Four masts and foresail would give her good speed in a fair wind. Two of the masts stood fine with just the crow taken out on the main mast. The mizzen stood at only half her size and the foremast was hanging to the port side.

"Mr Jamison, if you please," called Sylvian to the young midshipman who was assisting Mr Sanquin to move some mast debris from an unconscious soul.

"Aye, sir," he replied as he dropped the end of the large timber safely away from the unconscious man.

Sylvian made his way through the rubble of broken mast and ripped sail, and groaning men stepping over bodies on the blood swilled slippery deck to join Mr Jamison who was looking totally exhausted and ill at ease with his surroundings. "Please leave the task of clear up to the French prisoners and attend with Mr Fitzwalter and Mr Stubbings to the more important task of securing the ship to the Antelope, we shall then attend an inspection of the damage and assess whether she is fit to repair and sail," said Sylvian.

"Aye, sir," replied the young midshipman who saluted his officer and turned to his duties.

"Mr Sanquin, sir, if I may trouble you to escort me about your ship so that I may inspect the damage, Mr Hardcastle here will assist and direct your men in your absence to their task," Sylvian requested.

The young lieutenant looked as exhausted as Mr Jamison. He saluted Sylvian and turned to his men and in his own language instructed them to obey the orders of Mr Hardcastle. Sylvian instructed Juno to organise the French to the task of clear up and salvage in case the ship may be saved and not scuttled. She would make a fine prize as a double hulled four mast ship in the service of His Majesty's Royal Navy.

***

The full moon of the night gave light to the French frigate as she slowed without sail to be carried on the current. The command went out to aweigh anchor and to lower the longboat. The officer of the watch looked to port and could see the land and the flickering lights on the distant beach. The sea was calm as a pond without so much of the sound of water that lapped to the side of the vessel. The ship dragged to her anchor until she caught on the sea bed and brought the ship slightly to starboard and to a stop. The officer of the watch sent his midshipman down below to tell their distinguished passenger that it was time. A seagull took to the top of the main mast and screeched its greetings to the crew and breaking the silence of the still night. The sound sent shivers to the very depth of their souls as they lowered the sailors to the longboat in silence.

They were off the coast of Dorset in southern England and in the shipping lanes used by His Majesty's navy to gain access to Portsmouth. The man in the crow had been briefed to be aware should he not lose his life to the presence of any approaching vessel without warning.

The moonlit deck was pierced with the harsh light that came from the hatch below as it was slid slowly back. The dark figure with large brimmed hat and long black cloak slowly emerged and closed the hatch behind him. He passed a small bag to the seaman on the deck and made his way to the port side of the ship. He paused and looked towards the poop deck and raised a hand to the officer of the watch who acknowledged with a salute. He threw his cloak over his left shoulder and slid over the deck rail and down the side of the ship to the longboat, followed by the seaman with the bag.

The officer of the watch waited until he could hear the oars slap to the water before moving to the side rail. The longboat made good ground on the calm moonlit sea. The distinguished guest sat to the stern with tiller in hand identifiable only by the large brimmed hat, slowly they disappeared from sight.

The longboat cut almost silently through the water; the brimmed hat steered her towards the flickering beach light which took on more brightness as they approached. The rolling gentle waves took the boat onto the shingle beach and the men deftly disembarked and pulled the boat to shore.

They stood all around the boat facing out to observe whilst brimmed hat made his way from the boat and onto the shore, he paused looked around and without a word made his way towards the light at the top of the beach. By the time he arrived the longboat was already on its journey back to the ship. There stood a man with a candle lantern and a horse which was very nervous at the approach of this strange man. Brimmed hat took a watch from his pocket and opened it in the light of the lantern, one fifteen a.m. He lifted the small bag and tied it to the saddle of the horse that moved away to his touch.

"Steady," he commanded harshly.

"He's a good steed, sir, and should see thee off to Portsmouth in no time I'll be bound," said the lantern man nervously.

"Silent," commanded the brimmed hat as he spun to face the lantern man, who in turn lifted the lantern in fright and caught sight of the face before him. He drew a breath of shock as he spied the patched eye and the scar that ran through it. In stepping back, he caught his foot on a rock and fell back to the ground. The lantern fell down the rock slope and clattered noisily on its journey, he watched it fall then turned back to the brimmed hat just in time to see the moon for the last time as it glinted on the steel of the blade that found his heart. Brimmed hat wiped the blade slowly across the sleeve of the dead man's tattered woolen coat and replaced it to his scabbard. Looking down at the dead man he sneered and said, "Nathaniel Billings at your service," and took a slight bow before lifting himself into the saddle and turning his horse eastwards.

***

Sylvian in company with Lt Sanquin was making his way topside having examined the three decks of this vessel and what was left of her aft cabins. He was met by Jacko at the top of the gangway who reported that the vessel had taken damage to the wheel and steering mechanism and would take at least a day to make her seaworthy. Sylvian instructed Jacko to go ahead with the repairs and to oversee them to a satisfactory state to see them safe back to Portsmouth. He returned Jacko's salute and turned to the young Lieutenant Sanquin and instructed him to arrange for the burial of his crew later this day. There would be a service aboard the French vessel upon which all crew would attend and pay their respects before committal to the deep. The young lieutenant thanked Sylvian and with a salute he turned to his duties.

Sylvian spied Jack on the far side of the vessel amongst the rubble of what had been once a fine poop deck. On his approach Sylvian could see that Jack was removing a man's hand with a saw, thankfully the man had long since lost consciousness through his pain. Jack looked up at his brother and smiled through his blood-spattered lips and very tired eyes. He wiped the sweat from his forehead with his sleeve and continued to his task. Sylvian made his way to the plank that now bridged the two ships and onto the deck of the Antelope where as much work was being carried out as he had just left. Mr Gant reported that the gun decks had been secured and the dead and dying taken care of. He reported that half the crew had been dismissed for some well-earned rest with the other half making good the ship. Sylvian thanked Steven for his report and dismissed him to his quarters. Steven saluted his officer and thanked him for his relief. His bloodied powder blacked face lit up with a smile as he turned towards the mess deck.

Sylvian made his way to the captain's cabin and stood before the door, brushed down his coat which was filthy and took a knock to the door. There was a slight pause before the command to enter found the captain sat behind his desk with brandy bottle and glasses on top. "Ah, Sylvian," he said as he looked up. "Sit down and take a glass with me if you please."

Sylvian removed his hat and sat down in front of his captain. Andrew filled a glass with the brandy and topped his own up before sliding the full glass to Sylvian. "Fine shooting Mr Mountjoy has brought us success this day, and of course a prize I hope?" he said inquisitively.

"Indeed, sir," said Sylvian as he raised his glass to his captain and then took a rather large mouthful to burn his parched throat. "The prize has damage to steerage but my team are on to repairs so that we may take her back to Portsmouth, however I fear the repairs will take a day at least to make her seaworthy."

"Then so be it," replied Andrew. "For a good ship of the fleet I think she will make; do you not agree," replied Andrew

"Again, indeed, sir, although I feel we may have to tow her into the harbour at Portsmouth as she may not respond so well to her damaged steerage," said Sylvian as he took another large mouthful of the rather fine brandy and drained the glass in doing so.

"Jolly good, then please give my compliments to Mr Fitzwalter and instruct him to take first watch, I think then young Sylvian you should take some well-earned rest so that you may oversee the repairs and take command of the prize on the morrow. What say you, sir," announced the captain.

Sylvian thanked his captain and stood, saluted him and set off to find Fitzwalter.

***

The brightness of the moon lit Nathaniel's way as he made his way up the cliff path on this boisterous beast. He reined him in as they approached the top and took time to see that the cliff top was clear. The man had come alone as instructed for not a soul was about. He edged the horse up onto the cliff top and away towards the east finding first a canter then a gallop as the spirited beast found his heart.

It was less than an hour before he came across a small village, the place was dead as not a soul stirred. He walked the horse through the main street and past the thatched houses set in darkness, keeping his weary good eye to each as he passed. Once on the other side of the village he set his horse to a gallop along the lonely road only slowing when a cloud passed across the moon to no longer light his way. His determination to his journey's end kept him to his task until the faint light of dawn came from the east. The forest had given him some shelter but he now needed to find somewhere to rest his horse. The journey had been long and he was beginning to feel hunger and the slowing of his ride confirmed his mount needed to rest.

After some time riding through the lonely forest in the dappled first light of day, he came across a forester's cottage that seemed abandoned with little roof and broken windows. A small broken fence leaned into the front garden and was consumed with weeds and long grass. He guided the horse to the back of the cottage and slipped from his back and stretched his tired muscles. He removed the bag from the saddle and placed it by the back door.

Having removed the saddle from the horse and guided it into a small covered stable, he returned to the cottage picked up his bag and took a look at his surroundings in the early English light. Surrounded by trees he found himself in the perfect secluded place to rest. The horse had grass and was settled, now it was time for him to feed.

The door to the cottage gave way to his push and he found himself in a small room, a scullery with makeshift sink of stone and little else but a broken chair and table rested against the peeling wall. He took water, cheese and bread from his bag and sat to the table rather unsteadily, pushing the broken chair at the wall gave it a little more stability for him to unpack his cheese from the wax paper that the ship's cook had wrapped it in. His one eye scanned the small scullery, the walls had peeled their whitewash to reveal the uneven wattle and daub surface. Parts had fallen away and lay like chalk upon the flagstone floor leaving the wattle exposed. The window above the makeshift sink had not a pane of glass unbroken and had let the weather and some plant life enter the room. He broke a piece of cheese from the newly unwrapped chunk, wrenched a chunk of bread sending crumbs to the ground and his lap to be latter enjoyed by the mice and rats that were now quite evident, but hidden during his presence.

Having consumed his meal, he rested his head back against the wall and closed his eye, the sound of the woodland with birds singing and the light rain tapping its sound upon the leaves and debris outside of the now open scullery door lulled him into a short but deep sleep.

The sight of Mary came to him, standing before him, naked. Her fair long hair swept down over her shoulders and reached her ample breasts, her slender waist led down to her warm milky white thighs where between he could see… voices raised him from his sleep, he stood up fast and sent crumbs and the remainder of his bread across the room. He pulled his knife from its scabbard and moved slowly towards the open door. There in the distance between the trees he spied two men. Woodcutters by what he could see, young and large in size. Both carried an axe and one had what seemed a large tree saw over his shoulder. Billings edged back into the protection of the door so that his movement may not be seen. They were coming down a small path some five hundred feet from him and directly towards the cottage. There was a small deviation to the path where it parted by a large oak and would take the two men from the view of the cottage and in amongst some small foliage and scrub before coming back into plain view. They were yet some twenty feet from this point so Billings quickly gathered his belongings and made ready to move, again glancing through the door at a distance so as not to be seen. Billings noticed that the two men had stopped just before the large oak, he could not hear what they were saying but could see that they were removing the sacks from their backs and were preparing their axes in what seemed preparedness to remove the great oak from its roots.

The rain had long since stopped and the early morning sun was dappling through the trees creating a light mist to the ground as it warmed the dew. The men had taken axe to the tree in unison and had created what appeared to be a chip to the bark of this mighty oak. Billings moved closer to the door with his back pressed firmly to the wall. He could see the hindquarters of his mount in the small shed some ten feet from his lookout. He looked back to the two woodcutters and could now see that they had tree saw in hand. It was a two man saw with handles to both ends now held firmly and were making slow drawing across the base of the tree. Both men had their backs to him and gave him ideal opportunity to make good his escape. He moved swiftly through the doorway and out into the yard not once taking his eyes from the men, he had not been seen. The horse whinnied lightly to his arrival but the sound had been muffled to the noise of the saw drawn on oak. He quickly saddled the beast and packed his meagre meal in the saddlebag and raised himself onto the beast. With bent head to miss the shed door he kicked his mount into the open yard, both men startled by the sudden movement and noise behind them stood to see the horse move through the yard and down the side of the cottage. It had made good its escape before they had realised what had taken place.

Once clear of the cottage Billings gave the horse his head and pushed him along the cart track and away, looking back over his right shoulder once to see if he was pursued. Having a clear road and now some distance to the cottage he slowed the horse to a canter and continued on his journey.

***

Sylvian was woken by the loud knock to his door to which he sleepily called, "Enter."

Fitzwalter stood in the doorway and saluted his officer. "So sorry to disturbs you, sir," he said apologetically, "only I as to report, sir, that we have made repairs to the Colossus, sir, well her steerage that is… as best as we can, sir."

Sylvian slipped from his cot and drew his feet into his shoes, the cold of which sent a shiver to his spine. He stood and moved to the water bowl in the corner and dispensed water from the jug into the bowl and threw it onto his face, rubbing with his hands as he did so. The refreshing feeling of the cold water and the rub of his hands sent him to stand straight and stretch his back. He took the towel from the hook by the bowl and dried his hands and face. "Very good, Mr Fitzwalter," he said as he returned the towel to the hook by the bowl. "What say you to the damage we have caused to the Colossus, do you think her sailable to Portsmouth?"

Fitzwalter shifted from one foot to the other and wringed his hat firmly between his ham sized fists. "Well, beggin yer pardons, sirs, but she as had a good bashin that's for sure. She is held firms with rope and tar and one or two nails, sir… but I is sure, sir, that she will make the journey well in your hands, sir, although I thinks we shall have to tow her behind dingy to portside, sir," he concluded.

Sylvian moved over towards Fitzwalter and slapped him on the shoulder. "Have you slept at all?" he asked.

"'Fraid not, sir, as I as needed to make sure those slovenly layabouts had made good such repairs as I as been given to oversee, sir," he replied with a large grin of brown and broken teeth.

"Well away now, Mr Fitzwalter, to your bed and I thank you for your diligence this day, you are not to report for duty until such time as I send for you. Understand?"

"Aye, sir," said Fitzwalter continuing to smile. He saluted his officer and made good his way to a well-earned rest. Sylvian slipped his tail coat about his shoulders and with his hat firmly to his head made his way to Jack's quarters and the surgery. He found the good surgeon just rising from his cot and sitting to the side. He looked about the surgery and found blood-soaked cloths on the floor and a French officer asleep in the corner complete with bloodstained bandage to head.

"Don't ask, brother," said Jack raising himself from his cot and seeing to his ablutions as Sylvian had done.

The French officer stirred from his rest at the noise about him, he looked up at the new arrival and started to raise himself to his feet. Sylvian brought his sword from its scabbard and had it to the man's chest in a trice.

"Hold fast, brother," shouted Jack. "He is the surgeon of the ship Colossus; he has helped me with the many wounded this night." Jack moved over to Sylvian and rested his hand to the sword hand of his brother.

Sylvian looked at his brother and returned his sword to its scabbard. "Well why did you not tell me, brother?" said Sylvian as he moved forward and helped the shocked Frenchman to his feet. Sylvian brushed down his jacket and proffered his hand. "Sylvian Mountjoy, first officer of this fine ship, my apologies, sir, for scaring you half to death."

The French doctor took Sylvian's hand and bowed his head. "Lieutenant Marcel Phillipe Cherade of the ship Colossus, I am pleased, sir, to make your acquaintance as I have heard much of your exploits against my country, and may I say… our unfortunate luck to find ourselves engaged in battle with you these days past," he stated.

"I thank you, sir, for your comment, your English is quite fine, sir," replied Sylvian as he took a step back. "How so have you heard of my exploits may I ask, sir."

"Ah, Monsieur Mountjoy. Our papers repeat also what is printed in the English press… although with some editing I am sure. My English has been learnt through my mother who was of fine English birth and my attendance at your fine English medical schools completed my education and finds me here today as doctor of the Colossus. I hope that we shall sail to Portsmouth as my mother's family is from Hampshire, sir, it will be good to spend some time with them," he concluded with a bow of his head and a queried look to his face.

"Indeed," said Sylvian, "Well, by your leave, sir, Jack I shall be away to my duties, brother, I see you are well and we shall catch some time together later," said Sylvian as he gave a nod to Marcel and headed for the door.

He found Lt Gant on the poop deck who reported all was well and that the Colossus was being readied to make sail with her surviving masts. He told Sylvian that the captain had requested his presence at his convenience. Sylvian took a look across at the Colossus and saw that she had been fitted with a makeshift rudder and tiller that would take at least two men to control. Matelots were up in the rigging preparing sail and Jacko could be heard barking his orders at the men. Sylvian excused himself from the poop deck returning a salute to Mr Gant's and made his way to the captain's quarters.

He was bid enter to his knock to the door and found Andrew at his desk. "Ah, Sylvian, do come in and take a seat," he commanded. Sylvian removed his hat and took the chair in front of his desk. "I am going through the charts and estimate we are some seventy miles from the southern coast of Ireland," he said indicating the chart spread out across his desk. "Mr Gant informs me that the prize is ready to sail and maybe somewhat of a devil to control. I think we should sail within the hour and the Antelope shall take the rear in case we need to come forth to tow the prize in. What say you?" he asked.

"Indeed, sir, she appears to have rudder and tiller as her makeshift steerage, I believe that will take at least two men to hold in a calm sea," said Sylvian. "Let alone the lack of sail to push us more easily through the water, nonetheless, sir, I believe we shall make it back to Portsmouth with some luck and the wind behind us."

"I agree, Sylvian, so let us to it and see that prize in the safe custody of our carpenters in Portsmouth," concluded Andrew.

***

The sun was setting to the rear of the horseman as he made his way along the road towards Portsmouth. He was now only five miles from his destination and would make it by early evening.

The journey had been clear with just a few wagons and some farm workers along his route. He had stopped only once to take some cheese and water and allow his mount to drink from the stream at the ford and then move onto the grass at the roadside. The weather had held well and the warmth had caused him to remove his cloak, but now as evening was setting in the chill of the night air, he pulled his cloak out and around his shoulders whilst not stopping his beast from its path. He knew where he wanted to be and the road that led to Fratton was his current path. He soon found himself in the road of the Crown and Anchor Inn, people were moving around but paid him no heed as the heavy rain was now filling the early evening streets. He dismounted and tied his steed firmly to a lamp at the corner of the street. He made his way slowly with hat pulled firmly down and covering his face, his collar pulled up allowed only his eye to be seen. The house had but one light as he moved up to the doorway, it was the kitchen that had the oil lamp burning and curtains closed to the night. He put a knock to the door and took a step back and made ready to leap forward as the door was opened. He had to steel himself to a stop when an old woman appeared at the door and asked him his business. He stated that he was looking for the Mountjoys keeping his head bowed low. The woman told him that they no longer lived here and she had no idea as to their new address, somewhere in Portsmouth she believed as her husband was a naval man and was away to sea a lot. Billings touched the brim of his hat and thanked the woman as he retired from the doorstep. He made his way back to his horse under the now lit lamp, glanced at his watch which told him five thirty, he untied the horse and swung into the saddle and headed the beast towards the dockyard.

With the beast now tethered and secluded in a side street, Billings now made his way to the dockyard. The rain was heavier now that he was close to the sea so he moved in close to the twelve-foot dockyard wall to wait for his quarry. He heard the bell in the dockyard sound and echoed in the cool wet night. He could hear doors slam and hobnailed boots upon the cobbles on the other side of the wall. The street was soon full of dockyard Mateys making their way home. He remained unseen as the workers had covered their heads to the rain each calling their goodbyes as they moved off in separate directions. The street soon emptied with just a few that were delayed to their task. He knew that key holders would be the last as they secured their buildings and made their way to out muster to hand in their keys. A few drifted by and then he saw his quarry, that woolen cloak and brown suit, he now wore a hat against the rain and his head was low and looking to the ground. He did not see Billings as he walked past him but the spy was not slow in his movement.

Billings had his man around the throat and up against the wall in a trice. With musket rammed firmly into his ribs and his mouth close to his quarry's ears, water dripping from his hat and down the neck and cheek of his captive; he slowly growled his menacing voice into action. "Hello, Collins, Remember me," he snarled.

"You... it can't be you," whined Simon on his realisation of who had him pinned so firmly to the wall.

"Missed me have ya!" said Billings mockingly and purposely spitting into his ear.

"What do you want, Mr Billings?" said Simon with still a little of that subservience to his voice and the rest as fear to his predicament. "I don't have anything."

"Oh, but you do, old friend, you do," he said grinding the barrel of his musket harder into Simon's ribs causing Simon to squirm in pain. "You know where my Mary is don't you, so let's have it before I pull this trigger and have your insides spread nicely over this wall."

"No... no I will not tell you, she is safe and is happy with her child... please leave her be," Simon pleaded.

"Child, what child?" questioned Billings in surprise at this news.

"She has a boy, a baby, not yet a year," replied Simon as he tried to turn to see the shock on Billings' face. He just pushed him harder at the wall in his anger to the news.

"Where is she, scum, you tell me now or so help me I shall pull this trigger," he sneered.

"No... no I will not tell you. I will never tell you, you are the scum your shot will bring the rounders and perhaps this time they will hang you, you're evil, Billings, pure evil," retorted Simon.

Billings took a moment to think of his predicament and within a split second he had stowed his pistol and had his knife to Simon's neck all in the time it took to turn him to his front and grab his chin with his free hand. The knife started its sorry journey at Simon's left ear and sunk deep into his neck severing his windpipe and arteries on its way to his right ear. His legs collapsed and he fell to the ground with his head twisted almost all the way round and resting against the wall. His eyes looked sightless up into the rain filled sky. Billings bent over and cleaned his blade and wiped his bloodied hands, on Simon's cloak. He kicked his feet from his path and made his way back to the side street and to his mount leaving the blood to mix with the rain as it followed its path amongst the cobbles.

He headed his mount back towards Fratton and the Crown and Anchor Inn where he again tied his mount to a lamppost and waited. His wait was not long but the first man he asked did not know of the Mountjoys. After asking three people without success an elderly couple who had just crossed the cobbled street were a little more helpful, they discussed between them about young Mary and the baby until eventually the man had remembered his brother had taken some furniture up to George Road on his cart number seventy-four he thought and was corrected by his wife. "Seventy-six, you dumb old fool," she said. Billings thanked them kindly and was now pleased he could get this parcel to them as he tapped the bag he had taken from his saddle.

Seventy-six George Road was indeed a fine Georgian double fronted detached house with a brick and stone wall to the front and a wrought iron gate set to the center and in line with the front door. George Road was set at the top of a hill and would have views of all Portsmouth. A street lamp burned at the corner of the cobblestoned road. Billings had left his horse at the back of the gardens of these fine houses on a small service alley. He had found the back gate to seventy-six but had walked on and around the streets to get his bearings and now found himself in a dark alley between two houses across the street from seventy-six. He had seen Mary draw the curtains at the upstairs left-hand window after pausing to look out on the rain filled night. Billings had sunk back into the shadows when it seemed that she was looking directly at him. He was filled with longing when his one eye had fell on the sight of his one true love.

As night fell and each of the houses in the street fell into darkness then Billings moved from his seclusion in the alley and made his way slowly and unseen to the service alley where he had left his mount. The beast was happy and chewing on the ample grass that was around and in his reach. Billings moved to the back gate of seventy-six and clicked down the latch and found the gate unlocked. He slowly opened the gate and looked up at the darkened house. The large rear garden sloped up towards the house and supported many trees and bushes. He moved stealthily towards the house and found a cobbled area to the rear. He tried the back door and found it locked, he moved towards the large window of the sitting room which was just a foot above the floor, it was a latch window and his knife soon found the latch and released it. Billings climbed in to the sitting room and stood his ground and waited for his eye to adjust to the darkness. The place was silent, not a sound other than the mantle clock with its loud tick, the room felt warm and welcoming, although not for this visitor. He could see a door to his left at the far end of the sitting room. This gave way to a hallway and the stairs. He moved over to the stairs and placed his foot firmly on the first step to see if it squeaked, it was firm. He then moved slowly up the stairs trying each step as he went. He could feel the sweat run down his back. Each step stayed firm to his foot, except for the second to last when he thought he was safe. The noise to him was deafening as the wood gave way to his weight and groaned. He stopped. He waited for a sound. All was silent. He moved onto the top step and looked about at the hallway. There were several doors, all closed except one. His count was five and the end of the landing had a slightly open door, this he thought would be the baby's room so logically, the next door, would be Mary's room. He moved slowly towards the door and but just a foot away a light came on below the door. He stopped. The door opened and a candle lit the face of an old woman, Mary's mother. She screamed and Billings took a well aimed punch to her face and she collapsed onto the floor in her room. The door next to this opened and there stood Mary in a long white nightgown. Billings moved fast and clasped his hand to Mary's mouth before she could scream, forcing her back into the darkened room and onto the bed. She punched and kicked at her assailant catching his bad eye twice. Billings could feel the blood trickle down his cheek and brought his fist firmly to Mary's chin sending her into a deeper darkness. Billings rose up from the unconscious form of Mary and looked about the room. An oil lamp stood on the bedside table. He took a match from the base and lit the lamp. He looked back at Mary lying on the bed with her legs slightly apart and her nightdress above her knees. Her arms were raised and her hands lay above her head. He thought she looked beautiful with her fair long hair now free and spread across the bed. He removed his cloak and his jacket and took his large handkerchief from his top pocket and folded it before pushing it tightly into her mouth. He took string from his pocket and tied her hands firmly above her head.

Mary slowly came to as her body rocked backwards and forwards, she looked up to see the sickening sight of this beast lying on top of her. His one eye was closed and blood trickled from under the leather patch of the other eye and into his beard. He was inside of her and she wanted to be sick but her mouth was full of cloth, she struggled to move but his weight kept her in place. Her hands were tied behind her back and tears were streaming from her eyes, his one eye opened at the moment he released himself inside of her. She was sick into her mouth and started to choke on the vomit. He lifted himself off of her and stood in front before removing the handkerchief from her mouth and allowing the vomit free passage. Whilst she took care of herself, he removed a case from the pillow and folded into a long band. He took the handkerchief and wiped her face, she turned her head away to his touch, he forced the movement again and then turned her head to face him. "You have got what you want, now get out," said Mary angrily.

"Oh, Mary, my sweet, I have only just started," he said teasingly.

"Nathaniel…" she cried, now realising who this beast was. "What are you… I thought they had sent you to the colonies, how…" she said astonished at her realisation whilst sitting herself to the side of the bed.

"Hard to keep a good man down, Mary, and I did it all for you," he replied.

"You bastard… you evil bastard, don't you know by now that I hate you and now you are ugly on the outside to match what is within," she cursed.

"Ah the eye… yes well I have your husband to thank for that and now I have you to return the favour. A good start I think I have made; you are just as sweet as I thought you would be, so much better than those squaws in Canada." She aimed a kick at his shin which brought his hand to her face with such force that she fell from the bed. He picked her up and tied the case from the pillow across her mouth. "Enough talk for now, we have a long way to go." He pushed her on the bed and turned to the wardrobe and took a long thick cloak with a hood from the rail and put it about her shoulders. He lifted her roughly over his shoulder and with kicking legs he made his way from the house and back to his horse. He threw Mary across the saddle and climbed on behind her, the horse startled at the extra weight reared up and was soon brought under control by Billings. He headed the beast out of the alley and found the road out of Portsmouth.

Chapter Two
Portsmouth

The Colossus handled fairly well against all expectations. Chris and Boots had taken the tiller and had set a competition between the two at who could hold her straight to course the best. With no poop deck other than what Chris and Boots called their steerage platform, there was nowhere for Sylvian to go. He positioned Jacko on the main deck just in front of the poop and took himself to the forecastle deck which gave him an elevated position. He could see the Antelope some five hundred feet to their starboard stern. The sea was calm and they were making fairly good pace along the English Channel. They had passed the south coast of Ireland late yesterday and had seen the needles this morning at daybreak. At this pace they should see Portsmouth harbour by tea time.

Andrew instructed Mr Gant to bring the Antelope to full sail and pass the Colossus as they closed into the Isle of Wight and passage into Portsmouth harbour by Southampton. Steven called the monkeys aloft and brought full sail to the Antelope and with good wind was easily able to pass the Colossus on her starboard side. Sylvian waved across to Andrew who returned his acknowledgement. The two ships entered the harbour with the Antelope making straight to port and dock three as instructed by the harbour flagman.

Sylvian instructed Jacko to bring in all sail and bring the vessel to a stop. The matelots manned the rigging in quick time and had what few sails they had raised, stowed. The Colossus slowed to a drift on the current and row boats were lowered to the side. With the row boats manned and attached to the bow by ropes, the Colossus slowly moved into her berth at repair dock three. The dock yard mateys had taken the ropes of the stricken ship and pulled her nicely into the dock and tied her up. Sylvian called his thanks to Chris and Boots and asked Jacko to secure the ship and make ready for the prisoners to be brought up and handed over.

Sylvian noticed that the admiral's carriage sat on the jetty between the Antelope and the Colossus, an officer stood at the side of the ship and waited for the gang plank to be lowered. He requested permission to come aboard which was granted, upon which he immediately presented himself as Lieutenant William Ward of the admiral's staff to Sylvian and requested on behalf of Admiral Lethbridge that Sylvian attend the captain's quarters on the Antelope at his earliest convenience.

The two officers saluted one another and Lieutenant Ward left the ship. Sylvian tasked Mr Selway to assume command and with a quick brushing down of his coat and a dust off to his hat saw himself piped off the ship and piped onto the Antelope. Mr Fitzwalter welcomed him aboard and reminded him that he was to report to the captain's cabin immediately. Sylvian thanked Mr Fitzwalter and having looked around at the familiar harbour now bathed in sunlight and the gulls calling their cackled retorts to one another, made his way somewhat apprehensively to the captain's cabin.

Andrew called enter to his knock and Sylvian found an array of familiar faces on his entry. He saluted both his captain and the admiral who was sat beside the captain at the rear of the desk. On their left stood Mr John Scott who immediately approached Sylvian and shook a familiar and friendly handshake. "So good to see you again, Sylvian, so glad you were successful in your endeavours... of which I had no doubt, sir," said John

"Thank you, sir, my men acquitted themselves admirably, sir, and of course with your help I find myself here today," replied Sylvian. John waved his hand dismissively and moved back to his place by the admiral.

"Please sit down, Sylvian," said the admiral, which, immediately put Sylvian on his guard as he had never referred to him in the personal tense of Christian names before. Sylvian removed his hat and took the chair in front of the admiral and Andrew.

"I do not really know how to say this, but well... Mr Scott arrived two weeks ago on a merchant vessel and acquainted me of your dilemma concerning the rogue Billings. We immediately attended the home of your good lady to find that your wife... er... Mary had been abducted during the previous evening. Her mother was being attended to by the physician as she had been attacked also. It would appear from her description of the assailant that it was indeed Billings as confirmed by Mr Scott here."

Sylvian stood to his feet in a shocked panic, he didn't know which way to turn or what to do, all his training, his experiences gained during his skirmishes, all gone, and he felt so alone. John Scott moved to his side and urged him to retake his seat and to listen to the admiral. Sylvian just wanted to be out of this room and find his Mary but he retook his seat under the pressure of John's hand. He looked at the admiral and his friend Andrew who both had saddened expressions to their faces.

"Now listen to me, Mountjoy," shouted the admiral. "We know of this shock to you and that you will wish to find your good lady and we are here to help. Please listen to us as much thought has been put to this, and then you may be away to your child."

"The boy... William is he okay?" asked Sylvian, searching for some reality to this madness.

"He is fine," said the admiral. "He is with your mother-in-law and mother at your home; they are under military guard and quite safe. Now there is more that I must share with you. Do you feel ready, Lieutenant?"

"What more, sir," asked Sylvian resignedly.

"Whilst you were away, your father and Mary's father have passed away these past two months since, I am so sorry to be the bearer of all this sadness to you who have been through so much and having served your country so well. My carriage sits on the dock, Sylvian, and is ready to take you and Mr Scott to the admiralty in Whitehall as the first sea lord wishes to see you with much haste I shall state. The intelligence service has and is indeed working very hard to find your dear lady, now you must ready yourself for this journey. Captain Young will deal with your crew and make all necessary arrangements on your behalf so that you need have no concern for what takes place here. My driver has been told to take you to your home for a brief visit with your family and then you must be away. Is that clear, dear boy?"

"Yes, sir," said Sylvian, as still in shock he stood and saluted the officers as he was helped to the door by John.

"Before you go, Lieutenant, one final thing," said the admiral as the two men stopped and turned to face the now standing Admiral Lethbridge. "Your friend Simon Collins also sadly fell victim to the man

Billings; he was found against the wall of these very dockyards where a knife had been taken to his throat. It was our belief that Billings had tried to gain your wife's address without success as it is understood that he then travelled to Fratton and gained that information from other parties. I am again sorry to bring you this sad news."

Sylvian's legs buckled and he was caught by John who pushed him towards the door and out into the corridor. "Pull yourself together, man, tis much sad news that you have had this day, but you are Sylvian Mountjoy and you must now find Mary and find this rogue for which I will gladly stand by your side. Now come on," said John as he pulled Sylvian towards the wooden stairs and up onto the main deck.

They were met by Fitzwalter who was shocked to see his lieutenant in such a poor state. He took Sylvian's arm and was asked by John to help him to the carriage. John told Fitzwalter that Captain Young would inform him of what had taken his officer's mind so bad. Fitzwalter almost carried the silent Sylvian to the carriage. All of the ship's company of both ships stood as they watched in horror their first officer being carried so. Jacko called to Fitzwalter and was greeted by a look that said wait. With Sylvian and John in the carriage and it moving away from the dock with Fitzwalter and now joined by Jacko watching as it pulled away. Even the prisoners being unloaded from the ships had stopped to watch the spectacle as there was an air to the crowd of great sadness and shock.

The carriage headed out of the dock and made its way towards upper Fratton at quite a pace as to cause people to move rapidly from its path. The rounders had cleared the gate to give the admiral's carriage clear passage. Sylvian did not see any of this as his mind fought hard to process what he had known as home, the people he had known as family and friends had all changed. His Mary, oh what of his Mary, her sweet blue eyes and her slender waist that he had so looked forward to slipping his arms around and kissing her tender full lips.

The carriage bumped and jolted as it made its way up the hill towards George Road. John Scott looked at his charge and never let go of his arm as they raced on. He knew he must bring Sylvian round somehow, but he knew not how. Suddenly he pulled him towards him and slapped his face hard twice. Sylvian responded and released his anger at the pain of the slap and the hurt from inside. He punched John hard to the face and caused him to almost fall from the carriage at the force of such a punch. John caught himself and grabbed at both of Sylvian's arms and shook him hard whilst shouting his name and telling him it was John, John Scott. Sylvian's rage stopped as he looked at the man before him and saw the same man as he had seen in the fire lit clearing, the man that had saved his life. He stopped; tears rolled from his eyes as he apologised for his actions. John just held him fast and told him all was well.

They arrived at seventy-six, the carriage stopped on the cobbled road and John turned to Sylvian. "Are you okay… we are here at your house?" asked John.

Sylvian looked around him at the houses that spread down the road. The nice houses with gardens, and walls, and hedges. "This is not my home, John," he stated

"It is, Sylvian, this is the home Mary had bought before William was born. Come on now, your family and son are inside. Come now." John helped him from the carriage, he picked up his hat from the seat and brushed down his fine coat with his hands and placed the hat on Sylvian's head. "There… you will do," he said as they walked through the gate and up the path to the door.

The door was opened as they approached and Sylvian's mum rushed out and threw her arms around her son's neck and hugged him tight. Jack came out of the house and took Sylvian's arm, and with John, they led him through to the parlour where Wendy sat with the baby in her arms. Sylvia left for the kitchen and some much-needed tea. Sylvian walked slowly over to the now standing, Wendy. She had tears in her eyes and a soft look to her face. Sylvian took the baby from her arms and looked down into Mary's eyes. He was beautiful and looked up at his father and smiled a Sylvian smile. The bond was struck!

***

The rain had started again as the horse made its way at a trot towards Southampton harbour. Billings could see some movement down by the fishing boats. He pulled his mount to a walk and slowly moved down towards the dock where he could see by the dock oil lamps a small ketch being readied by its owner for a day's fishing. Dawn was yet an hour away and would be slow to come with the darkened cloudy rain filled sky. Billings coached the horse to a rail by the end of the dock. He dismounted and pulled the struggling Mary from across the saddle. He faced her to him and smiled before punching her jaw and feeling the unconscious weight fall into his arms. He then neatly swept her across his shoulder, patted the horse and made his way onto the jetty. There was not a soul about on this side, save the one man preparing his ketch. Billings walked past the protesting man and placed the unconscious Mary on the boat. The fisherman came up behind protesting loudly at his conduct wherein Billings swung deftly around to face the man and place his blade neatly into his heart. He then pushed the body from the boat and into the water. Two jetties to his right he could see that he had caused some activity by his actions as men started to run up that jetty. He calmly left the boat and untied both fore and aft ropes, gave the boat a push and jumped back on. He immediately started to lower the sails and headed the boat out of port and was some way away when he looked back from the helm and saw some men dragging the body from the water. Another had a flintlock that sent a ball whistling past his head. He pointed the ketch out of the harbour and into the sea at the head of the port and keeping the Isle of Wight to his port. He had good wind to take him out into the open sea of the English Channel.

The rain was harder out here and the wind was gusting, he tied the helm and moved over to the still unconscious Mary. He pulled a tarp over her and headed back to the helm as the sea was becoming quite rough.

An hour into their journey and a tired Billings allowing his eye to close for a second whilst nestled down against the wind nearly brought him to an end. One of His Majesty's navy ships narrowly missed the stern of the ketch with sailors calling abuse at his seamanship. The shock brought him to his senses and he called out his apologies to the crew as they passed. Nervous and still shocked from the close encounter he glanced into the boat where he saw movement from beneath the tarp. Billings again tied the helm and moved over to the tarp. The ship had well passed and nothing could be seen except by spyglass, so, he chanced a look. Mary was coming to and struggling at the weight of the canvass tarp. He replaced the tarp and picked up a wooden spike and brought it down upon her head. The tarp stopped moving so he returned to the helm. It did not move again for the rest of their journey.

After six hours the wind had calmed and the sun was now high in the sky with not a cloud in sight. Billings had spotted the French coast and knew where he was. He had sailed down the coast and was just coming around the headland that led to the inlet of St Malo. They were passing Mont Saint-Michel when he was challenged from the shore battery emplacement at the head of the river. He called out his French password and was waved to continue. The ketch made good ground through the sand banks and to a small dock area outside of the walled city. Having tied up the ketch he sat and waited as he had called to the lookout to have a cart meet him.

He did not wait long as a high-backed cart pulled by a mule came along the riverside track. The driver gave over the cart to Billings and made his way on foot towards the lookout. Billings loaded the still unconscious Mary into the back of the cart and headed back the way the cart had come.

***

After a very welcome cup of tea and some sandwiches Sylvian was feeling much back to his old self. William lay on his lap where he had been since his arrival and was being such a happy child. Sylvian looked across at Jack who had sat with his arm about their mother's shoulders. She had herself aged much since last they had seen her, as had Wendy who was as she explained really in fear of her daughter's safety. Sylvian had explained all that had gone on to bring them to this situation and Wendy was certain that the man Billings had all intention of taking the life of her precious daughter. Jack, John and Sylvian comforted her with their own plans to get Mary back home and into the bosom of her family. Sylvia was distraught to think that both of her boys were to leave her again and place themselves in more danger, more than they had already faced.

John brought calm back to the room when he stated that it was time for him and Sylvian to make their way to London. The carriage was waiting and the first sea lord was not well known for his patience. Sylvian reluctantly passed the baby back to Wendy and hugged his mother before shaking hands with Jack. In company with John, he made his way to the carriage with his mind full of what he was leaving and just how he was to get his Mary back. He wanted Nathaniel to die slowly at his hands, so slowly that he could watch his own suffering and feel all his life slowly and painfully ebb from his sorry body and then feel his soul descend to the depths of hell, for all eternity.

The carriage was quick to pull away as Sylvian waved to those of his family that had gathered on the step of his fine new home. John gathered a blanket and wrapped it about their knees as the dusk was descending and it would be a long journey. They would stop at Petersfield at the inn for the night and rest the horses and would leave at dawn to complete their journey.

The carriage had made good time and had passed without issue into the city and on to Westminster Bridge before passing parliament and heading down Whitehall to the admiralty building. They were greeted by a midshipman who escorted them up three floors and showed them to an ante room where they were provided with tea. The building was very impressive and relatively new as it had been completed in 1788. The walls were lined with oak paneling in the not so small ante room where they found themselves in quite comfortable chairs.

It was not long before the midshipman reappeared and asked the men to accompany him as the first sea lord would see them now. They followed the midshipman down the impressive corridors and up to some very large beautiful wooden double doors, whereupon the midshipman opened the doors and entered. John held Sylvian back as he moved forward to follow and they both waited outside.

"My Lord, if it please," he announced, "First Lieutenant Mountjoy of the Antelope and Mr John Scott of the admiralty intelligence, My Lord."

"Send them in if you please," the unsighted voice came from within. There was an echo to the room which gave Sylvian the shivers as he felt so out of place. The midshipman stood back to one door and bowed his head and raised his right arm and hand. John grabbed Sylvian's sleeve and they both moved forward and into the large and very impressive room. They marched smartly to the front of the large desk and Sylvian saluted Admiral James Gambier whilst John bowed his head. The admiral stood and moved around his desk and took John's hand. "So good to see you again, John, sounds like fun has been had yet again at the admiralty's expense."

"Indeed, sir," said John as he gave a very firm handshake.

"And this must be Mountjoy, good to meet you at last, my boy," he said as he took Sylvian's hand in a very firm grip which was returned. "Do sit down, both of you, he said as he pointed to a long table that pointed from the end of his desk.

Sylvian glanced around the table where he saw several people he did not know albeit one he did. Avery Simpson stood and moved over to Sylvian and took his hand. "Dear boy," he said. "So good to see you safely back and such a good job you have made of such an arduous task going by the reports."

"Thank you, sir," said Sylvian. "My men accounted well for themselves."

"Now come. sir, do not be modest," said the first sea lord as he took his seat at the end of the table. "We have all read the reports... both official and unofficial," he said whilst looking at the only lady that sat to the table. "May I introduce the Countess Alice Stockwell of Swinderby whose son, Henry, I believe you know?"

"Indeed, sir, it is a great pleasure to finally meet you, Countess, Henry speaks very affectionately about you," he replied bowing perfectly to the countess.

"Nonsense," she said with a wave of her handkerchief. "Henry knows not of affection... although I do miss the little scallywag so. The pleasure is all mine," she said as she stood and proffered her white gloved hand, which Sylvian took and kissed. "I do so hope you do not mind that I have taken to write your exploits so in the *Times* newspaper. It has so garnered the nation's interest and has seen a marked upturn in our recruitment to the service," she concluded with a face contort in concern.

"Not at all, Countess," Sylvian lied. "Although I do find some embarrassment at the approaches I have received from perfect strangers."

"Such notoriety I think is deserving for you, young man, do you not all agree," she said looking about the table and finally releasing Sylvian's hand.

"Indeed," said the admiral. "Do all sit down, please, my neck is starting to take an ache looking up at you all," he smiled. "Now to business," he continued. "It is indeed with a sad heart that we have all learned of the taking of Mrs Mountjoy against her obvious will, and of course of the tragic loss of one of our well-regarded dockyard managers and young Mountjoy's lifelong friend, which is what has brought us to this table now. So, without further ado… Mr Simpson if you please bring us all squarely up to date."

Avery stood up and looked about the table. "My Lord. Firstly may I state for the record my congratulations to Lieutenant Mountjoy in what has turned out to be a remarkable endurance for him and his team, however, with determination they had completed what I thought to be an impossible task. This country owes a great deal to them for ensuring that we are indeed, now prepared for any conflict that may arise with the union states." The table erupted into a round of applause and more than one, hear, hear. "Which brings me to our current dilemma, having served us so well Lieutenant Mountjoy has returned home to his family and country to find not only has his wife been taken against her will, by this… this madman and traitor Billings, but to also learn of the murder of his childhood friend and the loss of his father and father-in-law. My deepest condolences to him as I am sure you will all concur, however I do find myself in an awkward place that I must also turn once again to Countess Stockwell's well published hero and ask yet again for him to step into the breach of danger. Lieutenant Mountjoy," he said as he walked to the end of the now silent table who had all proffered their condolences to Sylvian. "Two weeks ago, one of our ships returning to Portsmouth from patrol encountered a fishing ketch out of Southampton, damn nearly collided with the thing in heavy rain, wind and high seas. The crew gave a good description of the man at the helm which uncannily fits that of the cad Billings. They reported only him on the vessel but two of the older ratings on watch that night stated that a tarpaulin was spread rather unusually across the center of the vessel. This could have concealed the possibly unconscious form of your good lady." He moved over towards the large map set and framed upon the wall at the rear of Admiral Gambier's desk. Sylvian pulled himself and his chair around to face where Mr Simpson now stood in order to better see what had now totally consumed him. "His heading was due south west so we can assume that he was heading for the protection of the French coast. and eventually on to St Malo right here," he said pointing to the map and turning back to the room.

"What makes you think St Malo, sir," asked Sylvian.

"Avery, please Sylvian, I am sure that you and I have passed that point," he replied with a bow of his head. He turned back to the map and continued. "We have intelligence men in this area and we now know that a small band of traitors to the king are working for the French and are billeted at a chateau just outside of the small town of Dinan, here," he said pointing again to the map. "Where I am certain the man Billings is heading for. This area is still under the control of Napoleon's army but we are in the west of Brittany and are making good ground." He paused again and headed back to the table where he stood directly opposite to Sylvian. "My friend, we need you to get in there and rescue your wife and deal with this man Billings however you think fit. Of course, you cannot do this alone, I would ask that you make room for John Scott within your team if you please? He shall remain at Portsmouth and will provide some training and map briefing to your team."

"Indeed, sir, I would welcome his expertise," said Sylvian. "How would we get even close to Dinan as none of us know this terrain, and to get lost within the area of Napoleon's troops would indeed put us to a disadvantage?"

"I concur, Sylvian, we are waiting the return of Bill Mitchell from the colonies, I believe you are acquainted somewhat?" he asked.

"Indeed, Avery, another fine man," replied Sylvian.

"Good… good, you see Bill is well acquainted with this area and speaks fluent French, as indeed does John. Our army is currently in the small city of Saint-Brieuc some fifty miles from Dinan," he said as he moved back to the map and pointed out the two positions. "Your team will be landed at Binic to the north, which is some seven miles from your rendezvous with an army captain who with his platoon, which is as your team, Sylvian, and will join you on this mission. Are there any questions so far?" he asked.

"When do we leave?" asked Sylvian eagerly.

"Well, there is much yet in support of your endeavour that we need to prepare, however we have initially set the date at Friday next, this should see you in Dinan on the evening of the Sunday when most of the French troops will be at rest. The place is not heavily guarded we are informed. However, we should be ready for all developing circumstances; your team will be disguised as French peasants so as not to be out of place should you be challenged. Papers are being prepared as we speak. There will be a full briefing at the admiralty building in Portsmouth on Wednesday which shall give you two days to return," he concluded.

"May I then beg your leave to return and prepare my men, sir," said Sylvian to the admiral.

"Hold fast, young Mountjoy, I shall need words with you and Mr Scott before you travel back," said Mr Gambier as he stood to his feet and looked at the members sat at the table. "My Lady and gentlemen I thank you for attending this meeting at such short notice, now I will request that you are back to your positions, you know what needs to be prepared for young Mountjoy's task."

The members of the meeting all raised and bowed their heads to Mr Gambier and one at a time took to shaking Sylvian's hand and wishing him well. The countess singled him out as the last to leave and took his hand.

"Sylvian... may I call you that?" she said with such a distinguished voice and such countenance to her stance that Sylvian felt very humbled.

"Indeed, My Lady, I shall be honoured," replied Sylvian.

"Then, Sylvian, you may have wondered why I am here so. Well, it is incumbent upon me to kill you orf, young man," she replied, very matter of factly.

"My Lady!" said Sylvian dropping the countess's grip.

"Not literally you understand. I shall publish in my column in the *Times* the sad loss of Lieutenant Mountjoy on the capturing of the French ship Colossus, you see," she said as she dragged Sylvian towards the door. "The admiral, my second cousin, knows that this paper is also read by the traitors to the king." She gave him a wink and a nod which he was totally not expecting. "Gives you something of an advantage you see... he is such a sly old dog, was like that when we were children. Now when this is all over you must promise me that you and your good lady shall join us at the house for the weekend and allow me the pleasure of really getting to know my Sylvian Mountjoy," she shook his arm gently and kindly. Sylvian liked her immensely and would tell Henry such when next they meet.

"It would indeed be our pleasure, My Lady, and it has been an honour to finally meet you, now I must ask you to excuse me as I see my admiral grows impatient," he replied as he bowed his head and moved back into the room and joined John in a seat at the front of the admiral's desk. "My apologies, sir," said Sylvian as he took his seat.

"Not at all Mountjoy, always been the same she has. So now down to our business, this captain chappy from the army that you shall be working with has only been at it for a short time so you will need to be on your fettle, you will have overall command of the mission so here are your papers," he said, picking up a sealed parchment from the top of his desk and passing it over to Sylvian. "Open it on your way, young Mountjoy, and make sure you give good account of yourselves, and mark me! Leave no man standing of these traitors, will you see to that?" he asked.

"Indeed, sir, I will," replied Sylvian.

"Then good luck to you all… and I shall see you for a debrief on your return, now away the pair of you," he concluded.

Sylvian stood and saluted the first sea lord and they both turned and left his office. The building was vast but they found their way easily to the exit and found a carriage waiting for them outside. The sun was now high in the sky and it was quite warm. They climbed into the carriage which set off down Whitehall at a good pace.

When they were some way from the town, John Scott looked across at his compatriot and said, "Are you not going to open your orders, Sylvian?"

"Oh god yes, I had forgotten about them." He reached inside his pocket and pulled out the parchment, broke the seal and unfolded it. It was headed with the admiralty seal and was dated. This day of Monday 13th of July 1807 and was signed by the first sea lord. Within, it prescribed the promotion of one First Lieutenant Sylvian Mountjoy to the rank of commander in His Majesty's Royal Navy and a commendation for services to His Majesty King George III. Sylvian lowered the parchment slowly to try and take in what he had read. He lifted it again and read aloud through the contents for a second time. It also stated that he was to be awarded the naval medal for gallantry and his men were to receive the commendation and medals for bravery. He lowered the paper again and turned to John. "Did you know of this?" he asked.

"No, Sylvian, I did not, very rightfully deserved I might add, that is for you and your team. Congratulations, friend, if I may call you that," said John holding out his hand which Sylvian accepted and confirmed their friendship. They spent the rest of their trip to the inn at Petersfield discussing what needed to be put in place for the upcoming mission. This discussion continued through their evening meal and again on their trip to Portsmouth early next morning. The carriage stopped outside of Sylvian's house and John gave his goodbyes and they arranged to meet first thing at the admiralty. Sylvian had written a note to Mr Gant the previous evening and passed that on to John who said that he would deliver it as soon as he arrived at the dockyard.

The door was opened by his mother as he moved up the pathway, she was smiling as she ushered him inside and took his coat. "Jack has gone off to medical school in London, Sylvian, I am so proud of you boys, but I worry so much about you. Have you any news of Mary?" she asked.

"Jack's gone, oh," said Sylvian. "I may have need of him, never mind... no there is no news of Mary. Sorry, Mother, I am so tired after my journey. Some news though, I am to leave this Friday in search of Mary, and I will find her I assure you," he said as he headed towards the sitting room and a very comfortable chair.

"I'll get some tea, son," she said as she patted his shoulder lovingly.

Wendy entered the room with William and put him on Sylvian's lap, he sat the boy in the crook of his knee and William smiled up at his father and wriggled to turn himself over. Sylvian lifted him up and held him to his shoulder and cuddled him hard before kissing him and placing him back on his lap. He felt so exhausted after all that had gone before. His eyes felt so heavy and were starting to close when Wendy took William from Sylvian's lap and ordered him off to bed just as Sylvia came in with the tea. Sylvian apologised to his mother and she took him by the arm and up to the bedroom where Mary was taken.

***

Sylvia woke early and was greeted by the rising of the summer sun through the bedroom window as it spread its warm light throughout the room. The English birds were enjoying their dawn chorus, a sound Sylvian had so missed during his time in Canada. He looked about the room that spoke of Mary everywhere he glanced, the comfortable bed that he had shared many nights with Mary, and yet still some of her clothes lying round about. Sylvian marveled at how she had been able to find such a beautiful home for them all to share as a family.

He reluctantly gave up the comfort of the bed and rose up and filled the rose decorated bowl on the night stand with water. He washed and dressed and made his way down the stairs to find the kitchen already occupied with his mother. He kissed her on the forehead as she busied herself by the range preparing some breakfast. Tea was already poured and on the table. The same table as they had at the old house. Sylvian found himself running his hand across the wood and remembering Mary sitting on his lap at this table and wondering if she ever would do so again.

After a good breakfast and two good mugs of tea Sylvian prepared to leave the house when a sharp knock to the front door brought Sylvian's attention. On opening he found Mr Gant on his doorstep who immediately saluted his officer and reported that he had brought the carriage for the commander as Admiral Lethbridge had asked that he attend him at Sylvian's convenience. Sylvian smiled at Mr Gant and told him to wait whilst he retrieved his hat.

The trip from North Fratton to the dockyard would indeed have been a fair stretch of the legs on such a morning Sylvian thought as the carriage made its merry way down the hill. The cobbles to the road made quite a bumpy ride but caused more grief to shod horses, as they noticed on their journey. Sylvian thought that the cost of a carriage may be found from his share of the prize or maybe the use of the new Portsmouth handsome cab service would fair him with much more favour to his pocket.

On their arrival at the headquarters building Sylvian asked Steven to muster the crew together in the training shed by pier three in an hour's time. He brushed down his uniform and moved up the five steps and through the door to this fine brick building. He made his way to the third floor and to the admiral's clerk who asked him to wait whilst he checked with the admiral. He was back in a trice and bid Sylvian to follow him whereupon they soon found themselves at the admiral's door. The clerk knocked and the voice boomed from within. "Come in, Mr Mountjoy, if you please." Sylvian opened the door and found the admiral and Captain Young along with Mr Scott pondering over maps on the conference table. He marched up to the table and saluted the two officers. "At ease, Sylvian," commanded the admiral. "Your journey to London was a good one I trust?"

"Indeed, sir, thank you," said Sylvian.

"Then why, sir, do you appear before me out of uniform," he barked.

"Sir," said Sylvian as he looked down at his coat and raised his hat to see what was amiss.

"Congratulations, young man, and may I say well deserved," said Admiral Lethbridge as he offered Sylvian his hand. "Need to get you into a commander's uniform as soon as we can."

"Oh indeed, sir," said Sylvian as he took the admiral's hand in a firm shake.

"Now young John here has informed me of His Lordship's request," he said as he made his way back to the table and resumed looking down at the maps. "This is quite some task he has laid before you and in such short notice from your previous campaign." He looked up at Sylvian. "Are you ready for this, young Mountjoy?" he asked kindly.

"Sir, if I may, my wife has been taken from me, one of my closest friends has been taken from me and I need to get my wife back and deal with this rogue once and for all, let alone the other traitors he has with him," He replied moving towards the table and standing beside Andrew.

Andrew put his hand on his friend's arm. "We are all with you on this one, Sylvian," he said whilst squeezing his arm. "Now getting you in is quite easy but getting you out again will be something more of a trial I fear," he continued. "We shall sail you and your team as far down as Binic where we shall anchor and you shall take the small fishing ketch that we shall tow, into the small harbour. We cannot remain too long as I have already instruction to sail onto the Canadas and Halifax."

"I see," said Sylvian. "I think that such shall not be an issue for us to gain a good escape if we shall not be captured. We shall have the ketch still in the harbour and if it is so then we shall second another if needed." He paused and looked at the three faces about the table. "Sir, our army does still hold Binic and some land down to Saint-Brieuc so I fear that we should be quite safe in making our escape count," he concluded.

"Very well, Commander, then I shall wish you well for this Friday and what follows, you too, Mr Scott, and get my young officer back to me in one piece if you please," said the admiral, as he dismissed them all to their duties.

Andrew congratulated Sylvian on his promotion as they left the building and arranged to meet with them later this afternoon aboard the Antelope. He told Sylvian that the prize had been taken into service and the major repairs required to her had already started. John and Sylvian made their way through the busy dockyard to pier three and the training shed. The sun was well into the sky and would provide a warm dry day. The training shed as it was called was made available to ships companies for general seamanship training and Sylvian found on his arrival that they had been given sole use of the building.

John entered the small wicket door of a much larger door that would enable larger equipment access to the building. As Sylvian came into the building that was served well by windows all around and a high ceiling, he was somewhat embarrassed by a huge cheer and a round of applause from his men. Mr Gant and Mr Selway approached him and saluted their officer. Mr Gant was first to speak when he said, "Sir, your ship's company are mustered and ready for your instruction. And, sir, if I may be so bold as to offer my congratulations on your well-earned promotion."

"I thank you, Mr Gant," said Sylvian returning his two officers' salutes. "At ease, gentlemen," he shouted to his men as he made his way to the end of the building and onto a small command rostrum. "Gentlemen, we again find ourselves so tasked with yet another campaign and I feel that I shall have need of all of you to ensure our success, however... and as is usual. This shall be a campaign whereby I will ask you all if you wish to take part. It is one where we are required to enter within enemy territory at great risk to our lives and freedom." He paused and took stock of the faces that looked up at him. He felt a pride in each and every one of them. They had given their all when called upon in Canada and when in action at sea.

"Sir… if I may be so bold, sir," said Fitzwalter stepping forward and looking at the faces of the men gathered around him. "I thinks as is how I talks for all of us, sir, when I says how we as all been devastated at the news of Mrs Mountjoy's takin, sir," his head had dropped and his large hands were making a terrible mess of his hat. "We as all taken to feeling… well as family, sir, and I as no doubt as to hows I feels about this man Billings and wot he as brought upon our little family, and of course, sir, wot we is ready to do about it. Sir, we stands behind you now and will always stands wiv you, so, sir, there is no needs for you to askin us again as to wever we wants to volunteer, sir." He paused. "And, sir, we is all so proud that you as been made up to commander, sir."

Sylvian looked at this man and all the others who had nodded and grunted approval during Fitzwalter's speech. "I thank you, Mr Fitzwalter, as I thank all of you," he said with just the smidgen of a tear to his eye. "My God, man… I do not think I have heard you speak so much." He laughed as all the men did with Jacko taking Fitzwalter a slap to his back. Fitzwalter took a humble step back. "It is with the hope that you would all join me that I have asked for the use of this building as we must prepare and be ready, this Friday gentleman, we shall set sail on the Antelope and shall find ourselves on French soil by sundown. We shall arrive at a fisherman's port of Binic in north western France and will liaise with an army captain and his team, we shall then march as French peasants to Saint-Brieuc where we shall then move past enemy lines and onto the outskirts of the French town of Dinan. There, gentlemen, is the house that gives shelter to these traitors of King George." Sylvian paused and looked at the faces before him.

Jacob Stubbings raised his arm and Sylvian indicated for him to talk. "Beggin yer pardon, sir, do we know if this here house is heavily with guard, sir?" he asked.

"Good question, Mr Stubbings… we do not, we have some intelligence as provided by the good Mr Scott here and his team that there is a garrison of French troops not too far distant from the location, but that is all. We shall almost certainly encounter some patrols as we move deeper into enemy territory, these must be dispatched silently and without gunfire, that may not be possible when we reach our destination as these men are well armed and well trained. That is why we are here now. We have two days to be ready so I will now handover to your officers, Mr Gant and Mr Selway to organise you into groups, we must have hand to hand fighting down to a fine art using only sword and knife. Tomorrow we shall make some sort of range where we practice our pistol work, I will leave that to Mr Gant. Mr Osborne and Mr Fitzwalter," he said looking down at the two men. "I shall have need of your services tomorrow as you are both experienced pistol men. You will need to travel to Gosport and acquire us a fishing ketch to look as French as is possible, and of sufficient size as to convey us all," he concluded

"Aye, sir," said the two men as they raised their hands to their forelocks.

Sylvian dismissed the men to their duties and made his way over to Mr Scott. "John, I shall away to the Antelope as I have much to discuss with Captain Young, do you wish to join me?' he asked.

"No, my friend," he said as he looked about the group as they started to get themselves organised to train. "I think I shall stay with your men… maybe I shall learn something, if not then maybe I can impart some knowledge."

"Then I shall see you for some supper in the officer's mess?" asked Sylvian.

John nodded and the two men parted. Sylvian left the building and took a pause and rather a deep intake of air as he reached the sunlit day. The seagulls found their way around the dockyard calling cackles of greeting and the dockyard mateys and matelots busied themselves to their duties. Sylvian had to pass the rope shed on his way to the Antelope and could not help but climb the stairs out of curiosity. The door at the top gave way to his pull and he found himself on the boarded walkway that he had last felt himself upon some two years past almost. The noise from the shed below brought back those days that now felt so foreign to him. He felt out of place and foolish for finding himself so, he was about to turn and leave when a voice called his name. "Sylvian," called the voice a second time. Sylvian looked down the corridor and saw Bryn Llewellyn with his arm raised and walking towards him. "My god," he said as he approached with hand outstretched. "An officer no less, lieutenant is it," he said in his Welsh accent.

"Commander," said Sylvian as he took Bryn's hand in a firm shake. "How fares you, Bryn?"

"My God, boyo, commander is it, wellll," Said Bryn. "So good to see you, do you want to take a look at the old office see?"

"No, no, thank you, Bryn, I was just curious as I passed. Are you now chief clerk?" he asked.

"Well yes, these past two weeks see, well ever since poor Simon… well you know," he answered

"Yes, yes, Bryn," he said feeling the pain again at the loss of his friend. "Well, I must now be about my duties and shall not keep the chief clerk from his, farewell, Bryn, it has been good to see you."

Sylvian made his way down the stairs and continued on his way to the Antelope. Thoughts of Simon now filled his mind.

The Antelope was a hive of activity with men in the rigging retarring the ropes and the mainstay to the foot of the foremast; new blocks were being added where the old blocks had worn thin with use. The seagulls beat their cackle at the men who waved them away from their perch. Such activity was now home to Sylvian, and it was good to be home. A new seaman stood guard at the gangplank and came to attention on Sylvian's approach and saluted the officer. Sylvian returned the salute and looked aboard where a new midshipman stood at the top. He saluted and Sylvian again returned the salute. "First Officer, Sylvian Mountjoy," he announced. "Permission to come aboard, sir."

The young midshipman looked pleased and moved to one side as Sylvian came aboard. The pipe man sounded the officer on board and the ship's company came to attention.

"As you were, gentleman," shouted Sylvian and the ship again came to life. "And you are?" said Sylvian to the young midshipman who looked well in his fresh new uniform and hat. He was but seventeen years in age and had yet not taken a razor to his chin, being there was no need.

"Midshipman Arthur Seaward, sir, new to the Antelope this day, sir," He replied.

"Then I am pleased to make your acquaintance, Mr Seaward, be so good as to make your report if you please," commanded Sylvian with a wry grin to his face.

"Yes, sir, sorry, sir," said Arthur in somewhat a panic. "Indeed, sir, it is my duty to report all is correct, sir, the men have been laid to duty as instructed by the new first officer, sir. Lieutenant Coombes, sir."

"Thank you, Mr Seaward, is the captain aboard, sir?" asked Sylvian.

"Sir, yes, sir, he is in his cabin, sir," replied the young officer indicating with his hand the direction of the captain's cabin.

Sylvian smiled, "I am aware of where it is Mr Seaward, thank you."

Sylvian found his way to the captain's cabin and passed many familiar faces on his way. It seems that word had spread quickly of his promotion as all of the men had heartily congratulated him. A knock to the door brought the usual response of "Come," and Sylvian found Andrew at his desk with another. Sylvian saluted the captain and the other stood to attention and saluted Sylvian.

"Ah, Sylvian, good to see you, this is Martin Coombes my new first lieutenant, Mr Coombes served on the Indefatigable and has seen much action against the French." Sylvian shook hands with the young officer who was indeed well presented and spoke with an educated accent.

"An honour, sir, to meet such a decorated officer, my congratulations on your promotion, and indeed my thanks for doing so as it has given me this opportunity as I find myself here and now, sir," he said.

"Well glad to have been of some service, Mr Coombes, she is a fine ship with an excellent captain and I hope that you shall enjoy your time on her as I have had," replied Sylvian.

"Please sit down, gentlemen," Andrew instructed. The two men took their seats across the table from Andrew. "Whilst I welcome Martin aboard it is with great sadness that I lose Mr Mountjoy to my ship's company, you have indeed, some shoes to fill, sir."

"Indeed, sir," said Martin as he looked down at his hat. "For I have heard all the stories and indeed at gunnery school they use Commander Mountjoy's methods which I found very useful and informative. Indeed, it is well spoken of the man who was pressed and became a hero is one that I feel all young seamen should aspire."

"Well now we have yet again to send Commander Mountjoy out to face danger as only he knows how to deal with. We shall sail on the evening tide this Friday, gentleman, which should give us time to get you as close as we can to Binic and set you and your men on your campaign, Sylvian. It will of course be the dark hours that should see you arrive at your destination and you should therefore not be too troubled by any French vessels to hamper your way. Does this give you suitable time with your men to be ready?" asked Andrew.

"Yes, sir, my men are just now honing their skills, they are always ready to face the odds that are against them." Sylvian glanced at Martin who was taking great notice of their conversation.

"I wish, sir, that I was joining you on this adventure as I am skilled with sword, close combat with knife and marksman with pistol, sir," said Martin.

"Maybe next time, Mr Coombes, I have need of you for the Canadas as much seems to be building there. Have you been briefed on dispatches, Sylvian?" asked Andrew.

"No, sir, what is this you speak of?" replied Sylvian as he moved about on the uncomfortable chair. A knock came to the door and Tom announced that he had tea for all and would it be a good time to serve. Andrew bid him enter and tea was served.

"Well, Sylvian, back to where we were," continued Andrew. "It would appear that there is indeed a build of union ships in the area of Sacketts Harbour on the Great Lake and in the Port of York. Our prize when completed shall be sailed to Halifax and will join with Admiral Albright's flotilla."

"Admiral Albright," said Sylvian with his head cocked to one side. "Well not a better man is there than to hold such title. Well I hope that after France that I may be sent back to the colonies to join with you all."

"Indeed," said Andrew. "Firstly, let's get you safely away this Friday and to your duty and of course the rescue of Mary which must take priority, Commander, she is important to us all I can assure you."

They finished their tea and shared some ideas on Friday's evening sail. Andrew passed to Sylvian some orders he had received from the admiral's office this morning and dismissed both the officers to their duties. Sylvian retrieved his belongings from the first lieutenant's quarters and made his way, somewhat sadly from the ship and up to the officer's mess where he would billet until departure.

Chapter Three
Le Chateau

It was a fine evening as Sylvian and his crew mustered alongside the Antelope. Mr Selway was absent and enjoying the attention at the naval sick quarters where he had been taken with his arm now damaged by Fitzwalter's over arduous demonstration of unarmed combative techniques. Although he had protested quite harshly, Sylvian had told him that this trip would not be his. He was to get fit and quickly as he would be needed when they all returned.

Sylvian had requested the services of Martin to replace Peter and although Andrew was somewhat perturbed at the request, he did with a great deal of jiggery pokery manage to get a replacement at the last minute. Martin had been sent to the shed and the men were looking forward to seeing if he could really look after himself as he had boasted. He was put up against Fitzwalter and Sylvian was worried that yet another young lieutenant would end up in the naval sick quarters. Fitzwalter had put him to his back in rather a short time. Mr Coombes had seemed somewhat winded but stood to his feet and asked Mr Fitzwalter whether he should like to land on his head or his arse. He landed squarely on his rear and with such a shocked look to his face that brought a huge round of laughter to the men. Mr Coombes helped him to his feet and they shook hands firmly.

The ketch that had been acquired by Fitzwalter and Jacko had been checked over by the dockyard boys and was given a French flag and identity numbers. It was now tied firmly to the stern of the Antelope as the *Fawn* had been when they sailed to Kingston. With all his crew and materials aboard the Antelope the order was given to give way fore and aft. The Antelope moved gently into the Solent. The evening light was giving way to a clear night and the sea was calm. The wind picked up as they rounded the Isle of Wight and headed out into the channel. The sea was a little more excited and gave the ship a good rise and fall to the swell. Sylvian had joined Andrew on the poop deck and they found themselves reliving some memories with Mary. She had been such a fine host and a good friend to all during the trial of Billings. They spoke of Captain Strong and had wondered where William had found himself now. Sean was also mentioned in the conversation as they had all become such good friends. Jack was missed as he was now attending medical school in London, and would probably be so for the next two years. Sylvian spoke of how he would hate being confined to a classroom after his adventures at sea. He wondered if Jack would stick to his training, he was not so sure.

With the French coast clearly in sight and the Antelope in total darkness, Sylvian and his men prepared the ketch with all that they needed. They were dressed such as French peasants and had been given some fish to complete their ruse. The ketch pushed away with Chris Thompson at the helm as the Antelope moved away into the night. They sailed in close to the coast with Jacko fore and keeping watch. The boat was in silence and was only illuminated by good seaman's eyes and a half moon. The sea was calmer this close in and the tips of the waves glistened like diamonds in the half light. Sylvian had studied his charts before leaving the Antelope and felt that with this wind and pace they should round the estuary at Binic in around two hours.

After an hour's sailing and most of the crew hidden below the tarps voices were heard seaward. A large fishing vessel had crept up to their starboard stern. Sylvian called out a warning in his limited French and the boat took evasive action. The captain called to them and asked where they were from. Just before Sylvian could attempt an answer, Mr Coombes blurted out in fluent French that they were out of Binic, and had not enjoyed much luck this evening. The boat they could see was out of St Malo and the captain wished them well as he sailed on.

When they were at a safe distance Sylvian called out to Mr Coombes to come aft. "You continue to astound me, Mr Coombes, I am somewhat glad to have you aboard, sir. Where did you learn such fine French?" he asked.

"Well, sir, my mother was intent on making sure that my education was not lacking so I was given over to languages such as I have just spoken, and of course Spanish which I have rarely used. It was not as I can assure you, my choice. But right now, I am quite pleased that she pushed me so," he answered.

"As am I, Mr Coombes, as am I," said Sylvian.

"Me bleedin too," said Chris Thompson as he smiled at his two officers.

The rest of the sailing went without occurrence and they arrived into the estuary of Binic and with steady sail made it through to the port whereupon they were challenged by an English voice as they came up to the small jetty. The tide was in and they were able to get right up and close to the jetty. They had arrived in northern France in the Provence of Brittany. Sylvian announced who he was and the soldier came to attention and saluted the officer. He helped tie the boat and with the men he gave good help to unload their equipment. By this time a fusilier sergeant arrived and dispatched the man to wake the captain. The sergeant escorted Sylvian and his men to a small house at the end of the jetty. All was quiet and the night was still with them. Some oil lamps had lit their way and was also illuminating the inside of the house.

Sylvian glanced at the sergeant and thanked him for his help and then realised who it was. "Sergeant Strong, if my eyes do not deceive me," he exclaimed.

"Staff Sergeant now, sir," he said pointing to his crown above his stripes.

"Well, congratulations, Staff Sergeant Strong, how on earth do you find yourself here, man," continued Sylvian. Before he had a chance to answer the door opened and in came his captain with a lieutenant behind him. The room came to attention.

"Hello, Sylvian, old chap, so good to see you again," said the captain.

"Robert," said Sylvian as he moved over to the red coat and took his hand. "So good to see you, and of course Sergeant Strong, what on earth are you doing here, sir, and with an extra pip to weigh you down from when last we met."

"Indeed," said Robert, "and of course yourself, Commander, no less and well deserved I might add, so sad to hear that your wife has been taken but that, sir, is why we are here. I was given to persuade Colonel

Gage that the army needed such as Mountjoy's guerrillas and such was granted and I find myself here with my good men."

"Excellent," said Sylvian. "Let's sit and plan what is to be done to destroy this nest of vipers and gain the release of my good lady. Mr Coombes could you be so kind as to see that the men are bedded down for a few hours, I am sure that Staff Sergeant Strong will aid you in this endeavour."

The men gathered their belongings and moved through a back door and closed the door behind them, leaving the two men to discuss their tactics. Captain Sinclair had already checked out a good route and had already been close to the house where the men were. He had not seen sign of Mary or any women near to the chateau. From what he had seen it was indeed one small part of the house that most of the men seemed to confine their living. It was fairly well guarded but not something that would be too difficult to overcome.

It being four thirty by Sylvian's watch and the fact that the two groups would move out at ten a.m. both men decided to get some rest. They had enjoyed a glass of whisky and were now easily soothed into a rest.

Sylvian was woken by Mr Gant at nine and with all the men now fed and watered they were soon joined by Robert and his ten-man unit. Introductions were made and the men all now dressed in peasant clothes set off in groups of two and three, at ten-minute intervals. Each group comprised one of Robert's men who knew the route that they would take. Sylvian, Mr Coombes and Robert had a cart and one mule to pull it. The cart was loaded with hay which concealed all the weapons to complete the task. They left thirty minutes after the last group and made steady on the cart track road that led towards Saint-Brieuc.

They passed some units of British soldiers who were heading back towards Binic and looked quite battle scarred and in some degree of disarray. Sylvian was told by a sergeant that they had been part of an intense battle which had pushed the front line some two miles this side of Saint-Brieuc. The day was sunny and warm but had a definite feel of storm in the air. Robert felt that it would be necessary to go around the town now that French troops had made good in pushing the British line. He had found a farm track that led around the town and would bring them back to where they would need to be for Dinan. Once they had reached the meeting point on the west of Saint-Brieuc then he would arrange that his men lead the party using the alternative route. This would need to be at night so that they would remain undetected. They would then need to find a suitable hiding place for the day so that they should be ready to storm the chateau on Sunday night.

Evening came quickly as they arrived at Plérin just west of Saint-Brieuc. They found the men sheltered in a small side road and were resting having taken water and hard tack for sustenance. Robert explained to his men that they would need to forge their way south of the town and onto the cart track they had found. It was dusk and they would move when darkness had fallen. British troops were around them and they could hear cannon fire towards Saint-Brieuc.

Night came in rapidly as well as lightning in the distance to the south west just where they were heading. Sylvian, Robert and Martin set off with the cart and a few of the men on the back, the rest of the men had already left with instructions to meet up at Plestan towards morning. They would shelter there and then head on towards the chateau at Trélivan west of Dinan.

Halfway through the night the sky decided to open and drench the team with cold hard rain. the sky also favoured them by lighting their way briefly with bright flashes that saw them on the right path.

They arrived in Plestan just before dawn and again the group were together, the rain had not subsided but the storm had long since passed. They had not encountered a single soul on their route which was of no surprise in this weather. The group hid themselves well in an old barn and got some well-earned sleep, the straw in the barn worked well to dry them through. Some had discarded their clothes and spread them across the straw to dry. They had given themselves six hours to rest, then eat and then resume their fragmented journey.

Sylvian could feel that Mary was nearby, it was as though her soul called to him. He tried to dismiss from his mind what torment she had been subjected to, the anguish she had suffered at the hands of this mad man, and all of it was his fault, if he had not chosen this life and returned to the rope shed, all would now be well. Mary would be at home already preparing his supper, singing and floating around the kitchen as she always did, almost dancing through chairs and waving her cloth like a feather boa around her beautiful shoulders. Oh, how he missed her and longed to sweep her into his arms and feel her full soft lips on his. He drifted into sleep with her warmth all around him.

***

The cart track proved easy for the old cart and the mule that pulled her. Mary had not stirred in the back and was firmly wrapped in the tarp from the boat. The day was warm and the sun was high in the afternoon sky. Billings brought his whip to the rear of the mule and goaded him into a faster pace. With St Malo behind him the journey was short to Dinan and then on to Trélivan, he should be there well before night had settled on them, that is, if this damn lazy mule would keep to his pace. He again brought the whip to his rear and caste some ugly words in its direction. The mule's ears were back and he was not best pleased at his treatment, however he did pick up his pace as he did not wish to feel the sting again.

The house at Trélivan was almost a chateau, large and imposing set within a walled perimeter and with fine gardens. The gate guards waved Billings through without him stopping, such lax security that he would need to talk with the captain of the guards yet again. The cart pulled up to the front of the house and Billings called out to the servants to give him help. Two men came at his call and helped to remove the still unconscious Mary from the cart and carry her in. Billings told them to take her upstairs and to the room next to his, and to make sure the door was locked. He called the matron of the house and asked her to look Mary over to see if she was badly hurt and he would be up shortly after giving his report.

Billings found himself in the large library amongst seven other men who all shared his betrayal of Britain and her king. A large desk sat at the end of the room whereupon a man sat with his back to the tall windows. The shutters were open and the sun drenched the room and blinded Billings' one eye when he approached. He moved his head to one side so that his wide brimmed hat would shield the sun. Billings made his report to his superior and gave over all that had happened from the time he had been dropped by the French ship off the coast of England.

All of the men in the room stopped their reading or talking and listened to the report. When Billings had concluded his superior stood and moved around the desk, Billings held out his hand and received a sharp slap across his face, momentarily dislodging his leather eye patch. Nathaniel put the patch back in place as he staggered back to his feet and moved towards his assailant, his superior stood his ground and Billings stopped in front of him, always the coward.

"You brought her here," said the assailant. "You were meant to kill her and then move into the dockyard and take care of the powder store, what were you thinking, man?" said the assailant.

"I couldn't leave her; I knew it would hurt Mountjoy more and I would be keeping my word… you said we were to drive terror into the hearts of our countrymen," said Billings as he backed away and lowered himself into a seat in front of the desk. The assailant retook his seat and looked glaringly at Billings who could not hold his stare.

"You fool, you damn fool, and you may have endangered us all. A dead wife sends a man to grief before he looks to vengeance, a taken wife… well that is different altogether, don't think for a minute that he will not try to redeem what is his, we are talking of Mountjoy here. What were you thinking, sir?" said the assailant.

"That, sir, is exactly what I was thinking," said Billings with a little more confidence. "He will come, of that you can be sure and then we shall have him. The great Sylvian Mountjoy who has done much harm to our French brothers, whose praises are sung in the national newspapers, the hero of the king's navy, yes, sir, that's exactly what I have done, with the hero killed by the French on French soil, yes, sir, indeed, and it will drive terror into the hearts of our countrymen," said Billings as he had risen from his chair and was now leaning over the desk of his superior with that clear and unmistakable snarling Billings' glare. The face of a mad man.

***

Sylvian was woken by Juno who had his hand firmly across Sylvian's mouth and had his index finger raised to his lips to indicate silence. Juno removed his hand and moved away from Sylvian towards the other men and started to wake them in the same way. Sylvian raised himself to his knees and could hear voices, voices all around the barn, French voices. Sylvian glanced around him and saw Robert with Sergeant Strong; they nodded to one another in the acceptance of what was now happening around them. Sylvian saw that his men and those of Robert's were now secluding themselves into the crevices of the barn. Some had started to cover themselves and their armaments with straw, within minutes Sylvian could only see what looked like an empty barn. He too then set to the task of concealment. He moved closer into the corner of the small stable area that he found for himself and pulled the surrounding straw up and over his head. A piece of straw was too close to his nose and was giving a tickling sensation. He dared not move as French voices had now come into the barn. He had told his men that if they were to be discovered then they should take to hiding and under no circumstances were they to attack. Any missing French soldiers would arouse suspicion and could jeopardise the whole mission.

They remained so as a cursory search of the barn was carried out by the French fusiliers. There had been some poking in the hay and straw with bayonet but none of the men had been found at the point of such. Sylvian's straw had brought him close to the sneeze but he had held still and with tears rolling down his cheeks had wondered how so.

As the voices slowly faded away with the departure of the French fusiliers, who had now continued on their patrol, the men slowly emerged from their hiding. Albert had to be woken as he had fallen fast asleep, which was a sign of just how brave Sylvian's men had become, that they could actually sleep in the face of such danger of discovery. Sylvian after indulging his sneezing fit, much to the joy of his men, called them all forward to his location and bid them sit. He looked about at the twenty-two faces that looked back at him and wondered how many would return with him, or if indeed he would return himself.

Robert sat beside Sylvian and asked if he had completed his episode of sneezing. Sylvian smiled and elbowed Robert playfully. "Gentlemen, this has been a reminder that we are indeed in the heart of enemy territory. We are now quite close to our target and our walk this afternoon shall bring us to it. We shall find a suitable place to conceal ourselves when we get there," said Sylvian.

"We have already found such," said Robert. "About one quarter mile from the chateau there is an old church ruin, the walls and part of the roof remain, but it should give us some concealment until we move. Now the chateau is surrounded by a wall of some ten feet in height so we shall have to scale the walls and take out what guards patrol the interior of such. We have rope and hook that should enable us to scale the wall."

"Now we must not assume that we shall take them off their guard for it is my firm belief that they will be expecting us." There was a small gasp as Sylvian looked about at the men who were now taking glances at one another. "Billings would know that I would come for Mary, he would also know that our intelligence would have some idea as to where they were in France," continued Sylvian. "My thought is that he is actually hoping this will happen as there would be no greater satisfaction for Nathaniel Billings other than to lure me into a trap whereby my life and unfortunate notoriety could be used to best effect," he concluded.

"That, gentlemen, is why we must proceed as if we were expected, albeit they do not know when and may have already relaxed themselves as it has been three weeks since the taking of Mary Mountjoy," said Robert.

"So," continued Sylvian, "when we arrive at the next point of meeting at the old church, Captain Sinclair, Lieutenant Coombes and I will do some reconnaissance on the chateau to try to establish what security has indeed been put in place. I believe that our best time will be around midnight as the guard would have changed around eight and the men will be more prone to fatigue as it is Sunday and all French like to enjoy wine after mass."

"Now we must be away, we shall leave in groups of three and shall give ten minutes between each group. Sergeant Strong, you shall leave first with your group, when you are near to the little lane that leads down to the old church, leave a marker so that the other men who do not know of its location, may follow."

"Very good, sir," said Strong as he gathered his farming tools of rake and fork poking from a canvas sack which also contained his knife, sword, musket along with powder and ball. Each man moved off and started to do the same in preparation to move.

The cart wobbled along the track with its big solid wooden wheels stirring a little dust to add to that produced by the mule. Last night's heavy rain had soon been dried by the hot sunny day and the tree lined avenue that they moved slowly down gave respite to the heat of the sun with each tree that gave them shadow, then sun, then shadow. Sylvian had the reigns with Martin at his side, Robert and Mr Gant sat on the rear of the cart each with one sliver of straw in their mouths. They blended so well that passing French soldiers paid them no attention whatsoever. Sylvian looked resplendent in his straw woven hat which was so badly frayed there was little left of it. He had untied his hair which was now straggled and full of straw and hung down past his shoulders. They did not speak for the whole journey and were each totally engrossed in thought. For Sylvian that meant Mary. He worried that she might be dead already, a thought he had quickly dismissed but kept coming back. His worse thought was what Billings may have done to her; a couple of times tears had come to his eyes to be wiped away quickly lest they be seen.

Evening was coming on and the sun was low in the sky when they arrived at the church. The cart was left in the field to the side as any farmer would do. The mule had been taken into the church and given hay and water. He was quite happy and contented. It had been a long walk for most of the men and a very uncomfortable ride for the others, so they had taken to rest. The open part of the church roof gave vision first to dusk and then to the darkness of night with stars glistening so brightly.

Sylvian, Robert and Mr Coombes made ready to leave the men. Mr Gant was given charge during their absence and should they be caught, he was told by Sylvian to make sure that if they had not returned by midnight, he was to send all the men individually to make their way back to Saint-Brieuc.

The three men slipped out of the church and across the fields staying well clear of the road. Mr Sinclair took the lead and led them through hedgerows and more fields. After fifteen minutes they came upon a wall that sat atop a rise. A mighty oak tree was close to the wall and gave good view to Sylvian once it was climbed. He took his spy glass and trained it on the chateau. It was indeed a large building having three floors. Lights were to be seen on the first floor in one window. The window was open to a small balcony and light curtains blew in the breeze. Sylvian could see a woman sat to a mirror to the left of the window. The curtain was not allowing him full view but at one point blew into the room causing the person at the table to turn, it was not Mary. Sylvian trained the glass to the ground floor and could see three rooms had light; they also had doors open to the terrace and curtains that blew in the breeze. In the room to his right, he could see several men drinking and enjoying cigars. In the room to his left, he could see a man in the candlelight sat to a desk. He was talking, or what looked like arguing with another that he could not see. The man at the desk brought his fist down hard and stood up just as the other man came into view, he could not see him properly and then as luck would have it he turned and walked to the open window. It was Billings, an angry look to his face and he was looking directly at Sylvian. Sylvian wobbled a bit on his branch and then realised that he could not see him at this distance. He raised the glass again to his eye. Billings was throwing a newspaper onto the desk. The other man picked it up and threw it back to Billings. A loud 'pssst' came from below the tree where Sylvian could see Robert beckoning for him to come down. Sylvian looked to his left and could see in the distance four soldiers coming his way. He was out of the tree in a trice and the three men were through the hedge and away before the soldiers arrived.

They made it back to the church without further incidence. Sylvian told all of the men what he had seen, getting access to the chateau would not be a problem, as the windows were each doors, that gave access to the house from the terrace. Once in the building was a different matter altogether. A lot of it would be luck but under no circumstances were they to leave from this chateau with any man left alive inside. Mr Fitzwalter was given charge of the gunpowder that they had carried and four kegs were made up with fuses. Each would be placed within the house to cause maximum damage. They would be secluded in areas not easily found, if the house had a basement Fitzwalter and Chris Thompson would make sure they were in place and lit. Each barrel had a thirty-minute fuse which should be ample for their needs. They gathered together and checked all of their arms. Pistols were loaded and the soldiers charged their muskets, the officers strapped on their swords, placed knives into their belts along with their pistols powder and ball.

The time soon came for them to leave, the plan was set and they all knew their tasks. Sylvian and Robert checked their watches, Sylvian smiled at the portrait he had done of Mary before closing his watch. Albert called the men to silence and they all said a prayer. Mr Strong stood to his feet and raised his sword and said, "God save the king," after which all of the men left the church.

***

Mary sat quietly by the wall of the south garden. The stone bench she sat upon was cool on this hot day. Beside her was a newspaper, the *Times*. The front page was emblazoned with the news for once not of Wellington's victories. Just a short piece, a meaningful piece that she just could not come to terms with. 'Lieutenant Sylvian Mountjoy Dead' was the title. The story told of his bravado in the taking of a French vessel the Colossus on his return to Britain. He had been hit by a sniper from the enemy vessel which had already surrendered. The sniper was captured and he was hung from the yardarm and had taken minutes to die. Her eyes were red with having cried for days since receiving this news, her heart was broken her whole life destroyed. She was so distraught at first her kidnap, then the physical and sexual abuse by Billings and the loss of her child, now this was all just too much to bear. She rolled her handkerchief around in her hands and just looked down at the gravel path wondering how she was going to end this nightmare that she now lived. She could not imagine her life without Sylvian or her son William, the new home she had created for Sylvian's homecoming that now he would never get to see. He knew of his son but would never get to hold him and love him as she had. It was all too much, she had not eaten or taken cloth and water to her body, she felt dirty at the hands of a man she despised who had used her incessantly and without care.

She was disturbed from her thoughts as the housekeeper approached calling her name. She told her that she would need to get ready as there was to be a visit this evening and she would need to be presented to someone very important. Mary had long been resigned to these events when French high-ranking officials wanted to see and be with the people they were at war with. It had been Napoleon himself who had started this exhibitionism so that his high society would be pleased to spend time with and experience why they were at war with these poor British people. She rose slowly and gathered up her paper and pushed her handkerchief into her sleeve before moving along the gravel path being followed by her jailer the housekeeper who had beaten her more than once when she had disobeyed her commands.

"We are to marry," said the voice as she walked through the door from the terrace. "Tonight, Mary, a priest will come and we shall be married."

"No," said Mary. "I will not marry you, I will not," she protested.

"You will do as you are commanded, woman, we shall marry this night." Mary started to protest. "And there shall be no more on the matter, Mary, it is done, with Mountjoy gone we shall be together at last as I have always foreseen," he concluded as he lowered his arm and turned and walked from the room.

Mary stood in despair; this was the final insult, the one she could not take. She ran from the room and up the stairs, first floor, second floor and then on up to the roof closely followed by her jailer. She slammed the door behind her and hit the housekeeper square in the face as she followed sending her backwards and down the stairs breaking her neck as she fell. Mary heard the scream and she ran across the lead of the roof until she had no more roof, she landed on her back across the wall of the terrace, blood trickled from her beautiful full mouth. Her body gave one last tremble as it fell into death. Billings rushed out of the room and onto the terrace at the sound of the scream, he looked down at Mary and took in all that he could see, his one eye closed briefly before he said, "What a waste," then turned and walked back into the room he had come from. The newspaper floated gently down on the warm breeze and landed on Mary's legs. It was Friday and Sylvian had just sailed from Portsmouth.

***

The men made their way across the fields in groups of four led by Sylvian, Robert, Martin and Steven Gant. Mr Strong had teamed up with Fitzwalter being of similar size and strength, they were accompanied by two of Robert's men who were particularly skilled in gunpowder demolition. Each had a barrel strapped to their backs and would be the last to enter the compound. Albert and Juno were also joined by two of Robert's men and would be the first to throw the hook and ropes and make their way over the wall. They would then approach the back gate, disable the guard and let the group into the compound.

It was not long before the group arrived at the outer wall of the chateau, the men had the rope and hooks and themselves over the wall in a trice. They pulled down the hooks and hid them behind rock and grass. The rest of the party had made good time to the back gate and waited silently. The wait was not long as the gate was opened and Juno's face came to the end of the musket held by Chris Thompson. Colin Bates was first through the gate rapidly followed by the rest of the men who made good use of the bushes to the right of the path. Last through were Fitzwalter's group who closed the gate and stood to guard as the French fellows had that now lay motionless in the bushes.

The men moved out silently and split up as planned. Each group made their way to their assigned tasks. Sylvian, Robert and Martin watched as all the groups moved and when the last group had gone from sight then they too moved towards the terrace. The chateau remained in darkness and was silent, no guards to patrol the grounds. As they made their way onto the terrace Sylvian noticed something white by the terrace wall. He picked it up and held it so that what light they had from the night sky was able to show him that it was the *Times* newspaper with the announcement of his death. He showed the paper to the other officers all of whom now knew why there was no guard and they had not yet been challenged. They made their way silently towards the door of the library and with a quick movement of Sylvian's knife the lock slipped up and gave them easy entrance.

The library was in total darkness so they waited within for their eyes to adjust. Scuffling noises came from above as Sylvian and Robert's men moved through the rooms gathering up the occupants. Sylvian could see an oil lamp on the table and took a taper from the embers of the fire and lit the lamp. The room came to life just as the first of the prisoners started to come through the door. They had been bound and gagged as instructed and were unceremoniously thrown into the chairs that filled the room. Jacob Stubbings was the last to enter the room with three ladies that he had found sharing the beds with the traitors. Sylvian recognised one of them from his spy glass.

Sylvian approached the woman and asked her if she spoke English. She nodded her head He lifted the gag from her mouth and kept his index finger to his lips.

"Where is the man Billings?" he asked. She looked around the room and one of the men was shaking his head which Jacob immediately punched and sent the man to the floor. Sylvian grabbed the woman's chin and pulled her back to face him. She could see he meant her harm.

"He went with Mr Scrubbs, they had a meeting with the French commander in Dinan," she said as tears filled her eyes.

"And the woman?" asked Sylvian.

"What woman?" replied the very scared lady before him.

"The woman he brought back from England," he asked scowling at the girl.

"Do you mean Mary?" she asked

"Yes... I mean Mary, has she gone with him?" he continued.

"No sir... Mary she's dead, sir," was her reply.

"No, no she is not, Billings took her as prisoner, now tell me where she is," he shouted as he brought his hand hard to her cheek. He was feeling pain run right through his very core and out through anger that anyone should suggest that his Mary was dead. The woman screamed and fell to the floor. Robert picked her up and pushed her blond hair from her blue eyes and wiped the small trickle of blood from her lips.

"My friend asked you where is Mary, do you know where she is?" he asked kindly. The scared and crying woman looked at Sylvian in total fear and looked back to Robert. He pulled her to one side as all of the occupants of the room were consumed with what had just happened.

"What's your name, miss?" asked Robert.

"Jane, sir, Jane Godwin from London, sir," she replied to his kindly asked question.

"So, Jane, where is Mary Mountjoy?" he asked again.

"She, she... fell from the roof, sir, just this last Friday," she replied.

Sylvian moved fast at the woman but was caught by Martin's grip and held back. Jane took a step back in fear as Robert moved between them and had Jane's arm firmly gripped.

"Now, Jane," he said looking back at Sylvian and shaking his head. "Just tell me slowly what happened." Sylvian stood and stared and felt nothing, it was as though he was not there, that he was witnessing this as a play on the stage. It was not real, just somebody acting this part.

"She had seen in the newspaper from Mr Billings that her husband had died and it fairly destroyed her, sir," she replied.

"Carry on," said Robert encouragingly.

"Well, sir," she said as she wiped away a tear, "Mr Billings did not leave her alone and taunted her with this news, he had changed, sir, he was like a cock that should crow in the first sign of daylight, sir. She spent all day in the garden with the newspaper and cried so badly, sir, that we all were so concerned. Then Friday, sir, Madge that is the housekeeper who had been giving her such a bad time brought her back to the house and Mr Billings well he...."

"He what?" shouted Sylvian menacingly.

"He told her that they would be married that very evening by a priest, sir," cried Jane in fear. "She couldn't take no more, sir, she just upped and ran for the stairs and the roof, Madge tried to stop her and was pushed down the stairs and to her death for her trouble. Mary ran the roof and fell to her death just outside these doors, sir."

Sylvian looked at the newspaper in his hand and screwed it tightly in a ball and threw it at the dying fire in the grate. He was numb throughout, two days ago, just two days ago and his Mary had given up all hope. "Where is she, Jane?" he growled.

Jane paused and looked at his ashen face. "She is buried, sir, in the graveyard by the church, sir, we marked her grave, sir, and tried to give..." Robert put his fingers to her lips and shook his head. Jacob and Albert moved to the side of Sylvian and took him by the arms just before his legs gave way. They carried him to a chair as Colin Bates poured a large brandy from the decanter on the table and pushed it into Sylvian's hand. Sylvian dispatched the contents with expert ease and with calmness stood to his feet and looked at all of those around him.

"Gentleman... you have a job to do, see that it's done, no prisoners, and I mean, no prisoners," he said as he threw the glass into the fire grate and marched towards the door and out into the hallway.

He was stopped by Robert from his exit who spun him round and looked straight into his eyes. "Think what you are doing, man," he said. "There are women in that room!" he pleaded.

Sylvian looked long into the eyes of Robert with his empty soulless eyes.

"When you asked Colonel Gage to set up your team to be like mine, then you set yourself to be like me. No prisoners, sir, means no prisoners," he said emphatically.

Robert stood back and let go of Sylvian's arm as he knew there was no point. This man had just lost a huge part of himself and now looked for vengeance, and he would have it whatever.

Sylvian turned and continued his way and found himself in the large entrance hall with its black and white tiled floor and large staircase. Mr Fitzwalter approached him and reported that all barrels had been placed in the four corners of the cellar. Sylvian ordered him to light all the thirty-minute fuses and get himself and all of the men clear of the building. Robert caught up with Sylvian and asked what was to be done about the man Billings and the other man Scrubbs. Sylvian told him to get all of his men clear of the building and through the wall to safety. Robert again asked Sylvian about the two men.

"Robert, please take the men to safety it is now my task to search for Billings and bring him to account, for Mary's sake," he replied.

"You cannot do that alone, Sylvian, you risk capture and torture, and after this even death," he replied.

"Do not make me pull rank, Captain Sinclair, you will do as I have asked, do not question me, sir, now set to your duties and have these men out and through the back gate before this place goes up. I will remain outside of the wall as I am sure Billings will be back when they hear of the explosion. You will get the men to a safe distance and do not stop for rest until you are back past Saint-Brieuc, that, sir, is an order." Sylvian slipped the leather pouch crammed with documents that he had found in the library, over his shoulder and headed for the front door.

There was not a sound outside or any sight of guards. Sylvian now joined by some of the men made his way down the side of the house along the terrace and waited for the rest of the men. It was not long before he was joined by his officers, Fitzwalter and Sergeant Strong. They were soon at the gate and Sylvian moved through the gate and saw just blackness as his legs gave way and his consciousness slipped into darkness. Robert instructed Fitzwalter to pick up his officer and start with the rest of the men back to the church. Whilst they had been back in the chateau Robert had told Fitzwalter of Sylvian's intentions of planning to remain on his own to confront the men Billings and Scrubbs.

The men arrived in good time back at the church. Fitzwalter loaded his officer into the back of the cart and with the horses that Juno had stolen from the chateau stables all loaded with men they set off for Binic using just the local farm tracks to avoid detection. Almost to the minute of thirty they were brought to a stop by the loudest of explosions. They looked back to the way they had come and could see a large fireball ascending into the sky. Sergeant Strong looked at his officer and said, "Good lord, sir, and all that brandy... such a waste." They all started again on their journey with determination in mind, to get back to safety.

Chapter Four
Home

The group had split up shortly after leaving the church, the men, two to a horse had arranged to meet up at Binic. The cart with Robert, Martin, Mr Strong, Fitzwalter and of course Sylvian had made good time as the cart rumbled and wobbled on the uneven farm track. It was now late afternoon and they were approaching the small settlement of Lamballe. Sylvian had regained his consciousness a couple of hours ago and was quite aggravated at his situation, so much so that Mr Strong and Fitzwalter had to bind and gag him. This was a difficult task for Fitzwalter as his level of respect for his officer was indeed very high. But he was not himself and had threatened Fitzwalter that he would be keel hauled for his actions. This was not how all of the men had come to know Sylvian, he was always fair and could be quite firm, but never cruel. Fitzwalter had noticed an absence in Sylvian's eyes which, given the past days' circumstances was only to be expected. All of Sylvian's men had taken a great sadness to the revelation of Mary's death, especially Juno who had been given to shed a tear or two. The frustration of the men at not having the guilty party Billings to hand for some old-fashioned naval punishment was very evident. The men had discussed this before they had left the church. Robert had brought sense to their eagerness to continue until Billings was captured and dealt with. His words were of no sense at first but the men soon came around and could see the sensibility that by waiting they would have a much better chance of success without the loss of lives that they may encounter, should they act now.

It was Martin who now held the reigns of the cart had noticed the soldiers ahead. There were four of them and they appeared to be blocking the track. He nudged Robert who was at his side and had taken a nap from the rocking and rolling of the cart. Robert sat upright and said nothing as they approached.

A corporal held up his hand as the cart closed in on the quartet and indicated for them to stop. "Where are you going and where have you come from?" asked the corporal in his own language.

"Please keep back," said Martin in his fluent French. "We have, well, we think we have measles amongst us and do not wish to infect our glorious and triumphant heroes."

The two men walking towards the back of the cart stopped at this news and started to back away. Fitzwalter and Strong who could also speak some French started to pinch at their faces to cause red marks to appear.

"We are seeking the good doctor in Lamballe to help us, I have already lost my wife and daughter to this and our neighbour too, and he thought it was the plague, caught from his nephew who has just returned from Paris."

"Move on, move on you scabs," commanded the corporal as he lifted his musket and waved his arm. "Move on," he repeated as Martin and Robert touched the brims of their tattered hats in recognition. As the cart moved past them the soldiers moved well back off the road and when they spied the red marked faces of Strong and Fitzwalter they covered their faces with their hands and turned from the sight.

They continued on and through the night and did not encounter any more soldiers and thought that this must have been the new lines. The British must have advanced further in the last few days. They had come upon a contingent of British who had taken quite some convincing that they were who they said. Fitzwalter had convinced them when they realised that it was almost impossible to put on such a southern English naval drawl. Mr Strong had also strengthened their case when he went up one side of one soldier and firmly down the other when he reminded the man on king's regulations regarding dress, the man had stood to attention throughout being berated by the staff sergeant about his two top buttons being undone.

Sylvian had remained asleep under the canvass and hay throughout the journey, he had taken no food nor water during the entire trip. They arrived in Binic as dawn was coming up in the east. It was a beautiful night with clear skies filled with the most amazing stars. The dawn now chased the stars away and illuminated the small port from across the sea.

They were back at the old house and the men, apart from Sylvian who remained curled up in the cart refreshed themselves and changed back into their uniforms. The other men had all arrived back safely and some were still asleep in makeshift cots and beds in the long back room of the house. The smell was indeed not pleasant as some of the men had not seen water and a cloth for many days. Some had also taken to using horse dung as a disguise at being a real French farm worker.

Robert instructed Mr Strong to have the men woken and to avail themselves of the sea and some soap to make themselves presentable as the king's men, and of course, back in uniform. Fitzwalter and Juno had attended their officer and carried Sylvian down to the small sandy beach where they stripped him of his clothes and cleaned him down with soap. They carried him back to the house and now dried, dressed him back in his uniform. Robert came to see Sylvian who now back in uniform and with a brandy or two inside of him was a little more back to himself.

"How fare's you, my friend?" asked Robert.

Sylvian looked up from the table at this fine officer and now friend, smiled and looked back at the table. Robert pulled out the chair on the opposite side and poured himself a brandy.

"We have secured a boat for you to sail back to England with your crew, my colonel said that you must return and report to the admiralty," he continued.

"Report what, Robert, my failure at securing the man Billings, it even makes me sick to say the man's name," replied Sylvian.

"For God's sake, man, we took down a den of traitors, yes we missed Billings and Scrubbs but their day will come. This whole thing that we do is patience, and taking what triumphs we can. And if you don't mind me saying my friend, and not feeling sorry for ourselves afterwards," replied Robert.

"Damn it, man," retorted Sylvian as he stood to his feet. "My wife is dead, the mother of my son and a woman no man could have loved more than I." He paused and walked to the small window that looked out onto the harbour. "I have to live with that, I have to live with that." Tears had filled his eyes.

Robert joined Sylvian at the window and they both looked upon the harbour for a minute. "I am sorry, friend, I cannot know what pain you feel, but I do know that your day will come, and I praise God that I am there to see it. It is your son you must now think of, his future now rests in your hands, he will need your strength as do your men for each one suffers this bad news and even more so, those that had known her." He paused and looked back out of the window. His men were outside and were preparing horse and their readiness to move on as ordered. "I have to leave, Sylvian, as do you. We must both look upon our first mission as a success and I take from it much that I and my men have learnt from you and yours. We shall meet again of that I am sure; I hate to leave you to your grief but I must be away."

Sylvian turned to Robert and the two men shook hands firmly. Sylvian saw Robert and Sergeant Strong and his men away from the pier. Mr Gant reported that the vessel had been loaded and they were ready to put to sea on the tide. Sylvian gathered up his belongings from the house and made his way to the rather nice ketch that had been found for their journey home. He was piped aboard by Albert and stood and took in his men. "Gentlemen, we have come this far and survived each and every one of us, we have triumphed in our mission and we have triumphed in ourselves that we live. I have great pride in you all and save for Mr Baker's cooking feel privileged to serve with you, now away to home and to what lies next for us. Mr Coombes, please take us back to England if you please," said Sylvian.

The small ship erupted into cheers and the men set to with sail as the ship moved from its mooring as the breeze kissed the sails on this beautiful sunny day.

***

The explosion was not only heard but felt at the barracks north of Dinan. The group were sat to brandy and cigars and had maps across the table. The colonel moved to the window and pulled back the thick curtains whereupon the room was lit from the flames of the chateau. They stood in silence and watched such as this spectacle and without knowledge as to how it had become so.

They were some four miles in distance but the bright glare from the flames had lit the small town of Dinan. Below the room in the courtyard troops were beginning to form up and much activity had started. The colonel looked at the one-eyed Englishman with curiosity. Billings knew, he knew how this had come about and he also knew that if it was Mountjoy and he was still about then he would have news of Mary. Now was the time for him to be elsewhere, he moved back to the table and gathered up the maps and placed them in a leather pouch. The colonel had moved back to the table and again looked at Billings for an explanation, he received none.

Scrubbs came back to the table and looked at Billings. "You damn fool, you know what this means, he is still alive."

"Indeed," confirmed Billings. "Then I must be away and we shall sail on this evening's tide if we are to make the union before him. I shall leave you to explain to our hosts, it is only us now and we must make a success of this if we are to survive." He turned and walked to the door, picked up his wide brimmed hat and cloak from the stand and left the room. He made his way from the building and found their carriage and driver by the door, he threw his pouch and bag on the seat and shouted, "Au port et n'épargnez pas les chevaux." The driver cracked his whip and brought the horses to life and moving before Billings had taken his seat. He crashed down somewhat forcefully and the driver smiled. After all the little pompous Englishman had said to the port and do not spare the horses.

The carriage drew to a stop at the side of a French frigate; the port was bustling with cargo being loaded and sailors manning the rigging. Billings grabbed his bag and pouch and made his way onto the ship. The duty officer stopped him and Billings gave him the letter he had taken from the pouch. The officer having read the letter saluted Billings and started to call out orders to the ship's company. The ship was heading out of the port at the same time as Billings was unloading his bag in his cabin.

***

The not so little ketch sailed gracefully into the Solent and made a steady course for the dockyard at Portsmouth. Mr Coombes brought the ketch nicely in alongside a small duty boat as there was no room at any of the docks. It was early morning and the dawn had already passed and the dockyard was coming to life. There was some cloud in the sky but it looked like it was going to be a sunny and warm day. Sylvian instructed Mr Coombes and Mr Gant to see that the men got plenty of rest in the barracks and that he would come to the officers' mess when he had made his report to the admiral.

Sylvian reported to the admirals clerk who immediately set off to the admiral and was back in a trice. The young lieutenant took Sylvian to the grand office and announced his arrival. Admiral Lethbridge stood up from his chair with a very concerned look on his face. "So, young Mountjoy, how fared your task on foreign soil, glad you are back with us safe and sound, please give me your report."

Sylvian delivered his report to the admiral in detail causing the admiral to retake his seat quite in shock at what had taken place. He invited Sylvian to sit once he had completed. Sylvian explained that he seized some documents from the chateau which he had dropped off at the office of the translator in this very building. "Well, my boy, what!" said the admiral quite astounded at what he had heard. "My deepest condolences, my boy, most sincerely, seems like the ruse in the newspaper may have done more harm than good."

"No, sir, I think that this article had enabled us to do our duty without engaging with French soldiers. I believe, sir, that the French had been taken in by the ruse and had seen no reason to guard against any reprisal, no, sir, I believe the ruse enabled me to bring all of my men home safely," replied Sylvian.

"And Mary, young man, how are you coping. Do you need some time, it has been a dreadful shock for you and I do like to look after my young officers," said Admiral Lethbridge in a low, calm tone.

"I must yet inform my mother-in-law, sir, as she has not heard of this news. It will be hard on her after the loss of her husband such a short time ago," replied Sylvian. "I will bring this man Billings to account, sir; he shall pay handsomely for what he has brought upon me. I will search to the four corners of the earth, sir."

"I do not think you shall have to, Sylvian," the voice came from the door. "Excuse me, Admiral, for my rude interruption," said John Scott as he entered the office unannounced. He walked straight over to Sylvian who had stood at the sound of John Scott's voice. "Sylvian, my dear friend, my deepest sympathy on your loss, I cannot imagine for one moment how you must be suffering so," he said as he walked up to Sylvian and took his hand in a firm grip and looked him unfalteringly in the eyes. John's sincerity did indeed bring a little emotion to Sylvian who thanked him for his words. Both the admiral and John were affected by Sylvian's emotion. John asked Sylvian to retake his seat and with himself now in the seat next to him John continued. "Sir, again my apologies for interrupting you and Commander Mountjoy, but it would seem that some of which Sylvian has brought back for translation is indeed of great importance to all of us," he continued. "I saw Sylvian leave the translation clerk's office and made it my business to have the papers examined immediately. Sir, it would appear that the French are to fund the union in rather a large amount to build ships, on the proviso, sir, that should the invasion of the Canadas be a success, then the dominion would be evenly shared between the two countries. Sir, the documents also mention that if the union can keep the British involved in a large second front, then it will enhance Napoleon's war effort to an almost guaranteed success." He looked at the faces of the two men who were quite taken aback by the fresh news.

"Well... indeed, Mr Scott, what news indeed," said a rather shocked admiral.

"Well, sir, that's not all. It would seem that the eight men and three women that were at the chateau were being trained to infiltrate society within the dominion, mainly in the east and to work their ways to positions of authority, from such positions the puppet master Napoleon would have influence in such a way that he would be able to force their lordships to commit more soldiers and equipment away from the European theatre." John paused and turned to Sylvian. "Were you able to dispatch Billings and those that were at the chateau, Sylvian?"

"Well..." said Sylvian taking a pause and causing John to take a very slight panic. "We were able to dispatch all of the occupants of the chateau; I believe there were seven men and three women." Sylvian continued to explain exactly what had taken place and of course the absence of Billings and a man called Scrubbs.

"You are indeed a means of constant surprise, Sylvian," exclaimed John. "A thorough job no less and important papers to boot, well done, sir, although quite difficult I am glad that you saw fit to dispatch the women as they indeed may have caused us more trouble than the men. My man Bill Mitchell did eventually make it into France and I await some news on that front. However I must away to London and acquaint His Lordship of the news so far, I should think that he shall wish to see you, Sylvian. I appreciate all that you have been through but I would be grateful if you could attend the admiralty in a couple of days, if that fits with you, sir, and of course the admiral.

"Indeed, Mr Scott," said the admiral. "We have much to prepare for I feel, so young Mountjoy shall go home to his family and I will provide my carriage for his trip in two days. Gentleman, I thank you and hope to see you in a few days with an update and some papers from the first sea lord, now away the pair of you to your duties. Oh, and well done," concluded the admiral as was his way with a wave of his hand and a dismissal that no man would not understand.

John made his way quickly from the headquarters building by way of the translator's office and Sylvian made his way to the officers' mess.

The mess was undergoing a bit of a makeover and Sylvian found his officers in the temporary dining room which had been the bar. Mr Coombes and Mr Gant had been joined by Peter Selway who seemed much better when last Sylvian had seen him. His arm was still in a sling but he reported that the sling was to come off this Wednesday and that he was quite fit to resume his duties. Sylvian sat with his officers and informed them of his meeting with the admiral and John Scott. He told them a little of the letter and Mr Gant drew a sigh of relief as the task of dispatching the women at the chateau had, he explained, troubled him somewhat. Sylvian told them that he would have to attend the first sea lord at the admiralty in a couple of days, but first he must convey the bad news to Mary's mother. His officers sat silent and looked down at their empty plates for a few seconds, those that knew Mary as did Mr Gant and Mr Selway had taken very much to her kindly ways. Sylvian brought them back by thanking them for a job well done these past few days. He asked them to keep up the training whilst he was away and asked Mr Coombes to be certain to get Mr Fitzwalter and Mr Osborne to keep a careful eye on his team so as not to see them pressed aboard another ship. He asked Mr Coombes to join him as he walked from the mess.

On the way he asked Martin if he would consider a permanent place with the team. Martin was quite overcome and very eager to join with Sylvian and the fine men of Mountjoy's guerillas. Sylvian was pleased and told Mr Coombes that a requirement of his role was to ensure that no one should club him unconscious again, especially an army man. They both chuckled at the remark and Sylvian left him in command of his men.

Sylvian had asked the orderly to arrange a handsome cab which was now waiting outside for him. He climbed in and gave the address and now filled with trepidation at facing Wendy and of course, his mother with the news of his darling Mary. He was immediately brought to tears in his isolation in the cab and did not even glance at the day outside or the busy streets of Portsmouth as they headed on and up the hill to North Fratton.

The cab stopped outside of his house and he paid the driver through the pay port in the roof. He took his bag from the seat and just stood on the pavement and waited for the cab to pull away. This gave him a little time to get himself together and be ready for what he now faced. The front door opened to his key and he could hear his son being extremely vocal. Wendy had heard the door and came forth with an expectant look on her face. Sylvian stood there still in cloak and hat with bag in hand. She took the bag from him and had guessed that something was wrong but did not want to ask. She placed the bag on the hall coat stand and again looked at Sylvian's face. "So you could not find her?" she questioned.

Sylvian slipped off his cloak and placed his hat and the cloak on the stand. "Let's go into the parlour, Wendy," he said.

"Oh yes of course, I bet you could do with a nice cup of tea," said Wendy as they made their way into the parlour. There was anguish to her voice which created an atmosphere that would be intolerable to break, unless Sylvian said something now.

"Sit down, Wendy, the tea can wait," he said as he guided Wendy to the chair. Sylvia had heard her son's voice and came into the room with a big smile on her face that faded immediately that she saw Sylvian's face.

"Where's Mary?" she said. Sylvian looked at his mum and she knew almost immediately and brought the tea towel to her mouth as she gasped. Wendy stood up and faced Sylvian.

"Wendy, we… we have lost our girl. I was two days too late; I am so, so, sorry," he said as his eyes filled to full tears and his voice croaked. Wendy just stood and looked him in the eyes, first one eye and then the other, trying to process what she had just been told.

"Tell me, Sylvian, tell me what happened," she pleaded.

Sylvian told them through tears and a croaky voice what had happened to his beautiful Mary. He told them of the newspaper and her treatment at the hands of Billings. He told them of how he wanted to stay and find the man and end him once and for all. But his men were in fear of his safety and had rendered him unconscious. He told them that even if he had to resign his commission he would not rest until he found this man and put an end to him befitting his cruelty. He promised to bring Mary home when once again a peace existed between the nations of England and France.

They all sat in silence when he had finished, the two women crying bitterly and William now in his father's arms and also crying for nothing that he knew of.

Chapter Five
New Command

Sylvian stepped from the admiral's carriage and complete with his leather pouch made his way up the steps and through the double wooden doors. It was indeed a fine building and not yet twenty years old. Having conferred with the admissions clerk he was directed to the third-floor meeting room. A porter was assigned to show him the way and they made their way up the fine stone staircase that encompassed the middle of the hallway. Paintings of naval battles adorned the walls as they made their way up the three flights of stairs and down the long corridor. The porter stood outside room 317 and invited Sylvian to enter. He then returned the way they had come with his squeaking leather shoes sounding upon the polished wooden floor. Sylvian first knocked on the door and entered to the call of come. He found the same people in the room as he had last seen on his previous visit. A large long table occupied the room with a large map board on the left end wall. The first sea lord was standing by the board and looked genuinely pleased to see him. Sylvian closed the door and marched over to the first sea lord and to attention made his salute. "Sylvian, so good to see you, Commander, and safe and sound with not a man lost," he said.

Before Sylvian could answer he was turned abruptly by the Countess of Swinderby, who threw her arms about his neck and hugged him. "Can you ever forgive me, my dear Sylvian," she said and Sylvian could feel her trembling as she spoke. She pulled apart from him and with her hands firmly on his arms looked into his eyes for forgiveness.

Sylvian smiled at her. "My Lady," he said. "Please do not fret so, what is done is done and through your kindness and actions I was able to bring all of my men and those of Captain Sinclair's home safe and sound. The cruelness of the man Billings is what had taken my dear Mary from me."

She looked up at him and moved onto her tip toes and kissed his cheek. "You, sir," she said, brushing down the front of his coat, "are a credit to your uniform and to the king's navy. I am honoured to call you friend, I hope."

"The honour, My Lady, is all mine, I can assure you," said Sylvian with real affection.

"Please, Commander, take a seat," said Mr Gambier. "Mr Scott has just concluded his report and I have your report and have informed those present, something of a very good bonus what you have brought back to us following your successful mission. Damn French, so slippery the blighters, trying to force us in too many directions to gain the advantage. Seems like you may have foiled their plot a little, that is for the time being. The man Billings we are informed has sailed for the Great Lakes and is making his way to Sacketts Harbour with the coin to fund our union cousins," he stated. "The man Scrubbs was picked up by our customs boys whilst trying to land just by Folkestone, seems he had no intention of cooperation and was finished off on the end of the custom man's sword, which just leaves our man Billings acting alone. Do you think, Commander that he shall give up this useless fool hardy task, or do you think he will see it through?" he asked.

"Sir, Billings is driven by hate, for a country that turned against him and of course by his madness. Sir, he will carry on, alone if he has to, but although quite mad, is more than capable of recruiting and training new converts to his cause. His persuasion as we have seen sees no bounds. One of the traitors at the chateau was a titled man who had served in our commons. We have to believe that he will continue and we also must ensure that he does not succeed."

"Well said," said Avery Simpson. "Are you and your team up to the challenge then, Sylvian?" he asked.

Sylvian paused and looked around the table at all the faces that looked to him for an answer. He thought about the question and tried to seek in his own mind if he had any doubts whatsoever to either himself or his team having any misgivings or inability to bring this man down. "Mr Simpson, whether through this service or alone as a civilian, I shall bring this man to account. He has taken from me what I hold dear, no, sir, I have no reservations, as for my men. They all loved Mary and have suffered greatly for what this man has set upon them. They are a fine group of trustworthy servants of the king and I would trust them with my life, and indeed have," he replied.

"First class, Commander," said Mr Gambier, "well we have discussed the mission and Mr Mountjoy's involvement between us before his arrival, so lady and gentlemen it just leaves us with your approval for what I have put to you. Could we have a show of hands of those in favour?" All hands apart from Sylvian and John were raised. "Very well, carried so thank you, gentlemen. I shall talk with Commander Mountjoy and Mr Scott after the meeting, and again I thank you all for your attendance." The room stood and all present bowed their heads. Sylvian and John remained standing whilst all others left the room.

With the door closed the first sea lord asked the two men to sit. "Did you say Bill Mitchell is back in the country, John?" he asked.

"No, sir, he is currently still in France but should be with us by Friday, sir," replied John.

"Good then that gives us time to prepare. Sylvian, how do you feel about taking command of your own ship?" asked James.

Sylvian was somewhat taken aback at first but was quick to reply. "I would be honoured, sir."

"Good. Now the Colossus which you captured shall be ready to sail under the new name of Endeavour, does this fit well with you, young Mountjoy?" asked James with his eyebrows raised and a slight grin creeping across his clean-shaven face.

"Indeed, sir, I should think my men will take well to the name as they have always endeavoured to give their best, sir," replied Sylvian with a smile.

"Good, then I shall leave you to take care of the details and ensure that she is ready as soon as possible. I would like John and young Bill to be your guests aboard and you shall make for Halifax as and when you are ready. Admiral Albright will be your commanding officer and you will form part of his flotilla. However, I have added in his orders that you do have a purpose which I am sure he is most certainly aware." He handed Sylvian several folded and wax sealed papers which Sylvian placed in his leather pouch. "Your commission to captain has been approved by the admiralty board and will be posted in the gazette this week. This is as I am sure you are aware, something of an unusual event given that you have had such a short time in the service. However, the admiralty has always been given to identify good officers and has taken great pride in moving them forward as fast as we can. We need good men, Sylvian, in this time of war, and indeed war on many fronts. Do not let me down, Captain. England is relying on you to come through for her, if there is a war with the union we shall be stretched indeed, let us lessen this burden and bring any such conflict to a quick and positive ending. Now one final point," he said as he sat back in his chair, "your first task is to pick your officers and men to serve you, I have made note of such to Admiral Lethbridge as the circumstances of your task is such that you must have first choice as to who they may be. Oh, and one final point, your uniform has been ordered and should already be at the outfitters in Portsmouth on your return. Set an example, Mountjoy, now away the pair of you, John will bring you up to date on what was discussed here, and good hunting." They all stood and John and Sylvian bowed their heads to the first sea lord, 1st Baron James Gambier.

The trip back to Portsmouth was a quiet one but Sylvian's head was filled with thought. So much to take in and he just could not believe that he was now a captain. He pulled the orders from his pouch and read through them again. When they arrived at the inn in Petersfield he again read through the orders whilst enjoying his meal and a goblet of fine Hampshire ale. The landlord was indeed good at keeping his patrons' goblets filled. Sylvian had covered the top when the landlord tried to fill the goblet for the fourth time as he knew he would need a clear head for the next day. His driver Seth had joined him for supper and had already made his way to bed. He had asked Seth to drop him at his home when they got back to Portsmouth and to pick him up again on Friday morning, that would give him an evening at home with his mother and Wendy.

Thursday morning and the weather was somewhat overcast and quite cold for August. The journey to Portsmouth was uneventful and had given Sylvian some much needed alone time to contemplate this latest mission. John Scott would be in Portsmouth on Sunday and Sylvian had invited him to stay at the house so that they could discuss their plans in more detail. It was not long before the carriage had pulled to a stop outside of his house, he was eager to tell the ladies of his news and almost forgot his pouch which Seth was quick to put right. He bid Seth a goodbye and let himself into the house. His mother was first to greet him and almost straight away started fussing for her son who had just lost his wife. Sylvian protested but to no avail. He was pushed into the lounge and was forced into a chair. Wendy had the tea and some sandwiches made in a very short time. Sylvian knew that he needed to bring some sort of order to his home life, there was much to be done now that Mary was not there to organise him. Oh, how he missed how she fussed so, just her being there and how she would burst into song and always in a whisper, never singing out loud as she thought her voice was terrible, it was not.

"Mother, please quit fussing," protested Sylvian. "Thank you, I will have a sandwich. Now listen please I have something very important to tell you both, and then we shall need to discuss what we are to do about it." He paused and took a bite from the sandwich and then took some tea, all of which was very nice. "I have again been promoted by the first sea lord and now I am to captain my own ship." Both the women stood and gave their congratulations and were genuinely pleased for Sylvian. "But this does mean that I am going to be away for quite some time, this brings me to William." Again he paused and took another bite of this delicious jam sandwich.

"I don't think there is a problem, son," said Sylvia. "Wendy and I are managing quite well with our grandson; he is an absolute treasure to have in our lives."

"I know, Mother, but it is too much that I should ask this of you both, I appreciate that I am not the only one that has lost someone special in their life and I see that you both grieve so," said Sylvian as he looked into the faces of these two women who he cared for greatly.

Wendy stood from her chair and came over to the small couch where Sylvian sat. She looked down at him and had that motherly smile that he had seen so many times. She turned and took the seat beside him and took his hand in hers. "I have lost so much just this past year, but you and my precious girl have given me something else in our little William, your mother and I love him dearly and he has given us the strength to go on. We are certain that one day love will again come into your life as you are young and quite a handsome chap." She shook his hand playfully and looked up at Sylvia who was smiling. "So, I think I speak for us both when I say that you need to concentrate on this life you have chosen and that we are so proud to share in, and leave the looking after of William to us, am I right Sylvia?" she asked.

"Yes, Sylvian, listen to Wendy, we shall be quite happy to look after our little mite, you are an important man now and need to do what it is you do best," she replied.

Sylvian looked at them both and a tear had entered into the corner of his eye. He wiped it away quickly lest it should be seen, but it had. "Then you must both live here and I shall make sure that sufficient funds are here for you both to run this place and live comfortably and I shall not hear another word on the matter," he said raising his hand. "There shall be much time when I shall need to be in the mess as there is much for me to do in the dockyard and I will not have the pleasure of yours, or indeed, my son's company as I should like."

They sat for quite some time and discussed the finer issues and were soon joined by William who had announced his presence after his nap and was spoilt by cuddles from his father.

***

Seth was at the house at eight and conveyed Sylvian to the tailors in the town where he tried on his new uniform complete with gold braid to hat shoulder and sleeve. Some minor alterations were necessary but that was soon completed by the tailor. When Sylvian came to pay his coin for the work, the tailor told him that it had already been covered by the first sea lord. He left the tailors at ten a.m., where he stopped by the admiral's office, and dropped off the orders he was given by Mr Gambier. He then proceeded to the mess and found that all of his officers were in attendance at the training shed. He walked through the dockyard and made his way to the ship repair yard and into their offices, which were in themselves almost identical to the rope sheds. He was shown to the chandler's office on the top floor and found a portly man with ruddy cheeks and small half glasses at the end of his nose. He assured the captain that the repairs to the old Colossus were proceeding as planned and would see sea trials within a week. Sylvian told him of the new ship's name and was informed that they had already sent to the carver a design to replace the Col that had now been removed from the ship as a dispatch had been received from London at the beginning of this week.

Quite satisfied at the progress, Sylvian left the chandler's office and made his way back into the naval yard and to the training shed. So many salutes on his way gave Sylvian the goose bumps to think that he now only saluted admirals and above. He had agreed with the chandler that his crew could move back onto the Endeavour from this Sunday after church as work had been completed in that area. His cabin and that of his officers would be yet a few more days as the requirement to rebuild the poop deck had caused them some delays in acquiring the necessary oak to complete the job. Sylvian had already acquired an office in the headquarters building when he had left the papers for the admiral this morning. He was quite amazed at how moving to captain could so easily open doors. He had also acquired two small offices either side of his on a temporary basis for his officers as they would need to build a crew and make ready with supplies and tend to the ship as she progressed.

He entered the training shed and could see much activity taking place in this huge building. His men were training on boarding procedures using straw packed boxes as ships. He stood quietly watching for some time until he was spotted by Jacko, who himself had broken into a fair sweat.

"Attention, officer on deck," he shouted having not realised that the captain's uniform he was looking at contained his commander. The crew came to attention and Chris Thompson lost his balance on the straw and tumbled to the ground. The three officers saluted the captain. Sylvian returned the salute and moved from the dark doorway into the light of the building with a smile on his face at the predicament of young Chris as he attempted to escape from his entrapment between two boxes.

"Somebody please extricate, Mr Thompson," he said as the place erupted into cheers as they realised it was their officer. Mr Gant, Coombes and Selway approached Sylvian and again saluted him and his uniform.

"Captain Mountjoy, sir, that really does have a nice ring to it, sir," said Steven.

"Thank you, Mr Gant. Now, gentlemen, there is much to tell you all so please get the men together and we shall sit whilst I bring you all up to date," said Sylvian.

With the men gathered together and Sylvian sat on the box that Chris had been extricated from, the place was silent. Sylvian looked at all the familiar faces that sat before him and smiled at such an eclectic mix of men whom he had come to know and care for. He explained what had taken place on his trip to London and what was yet to come with their return to the colonies and what work they may have to do in the Dominion. He did not tell the men all that had gone before at the admiralty, but enough so that they understood what was yet to come. He explained about the Colossus and that it was now their ship under the name Endeavour. Albert spent almost a minute explaining to the men in that gravelly voice of his, the meaning of the word, which pleased them all. Sylvian spent a good hour explaining what was to be aboard the new ship and that although he was now their captain, he would still be at their side during missions. This was well received by the men. He also gave each the opportunity to choose whether they should continue to serve, move to another ship or retire from this man's navy with the admiralty's thanks. The place fell silent before Juno stood to his feet and looked at the men about him and asked for each who wished to stay and serve their captain to raise their hands. The whole room erupted with hands in the air. Sylvian thanked his men and told them he was honoured to serve with them. He then told them they had five days leave and to make sure that Portsmouth was left undamaged at the end. A cheer went about the shed before all of the men made their happy way to home, to wives, girlfriends and the inn.

Sylvian and his three officers left the training shed and made their way to the mess for lunch and then on to the HQ building where they were shown the offices they had been allocated. They had discussed over lunch what action needed to be taken to ready themselves and to find a crew for the new ship and their impending sailing to the new world. Now that they had the offices and had placed their belongings within, Sylvian had some desks brought up to the first-floor office and they converted the third office to a meeting room with the first meeting to take place in the morning at eight a.m. He sent his officers off to the mess for a well-earned rest and some libation. He would join them this evening for dinner at seven. Sylvian would need the rest of the day to work out how his ship's crew would be organised and in what rank structure, and whom to fill such in order to achieve this. The first sea lord had given him carte blanche to complement his ship and his team as he required so he would need a list of officers that were available for re-assignment, and with some promotions he should be able to fill the role. The ratings and ship's company he would leave to his first officer to deal with as he now needed to start delegating some of the tasks that he had always assumed.

***

The port of Brest was buzzing as so many ships of Napoleon's navy were now in port for provisions. It was a beautiful sunny day but a cool breeze from the ocean kept Brest and the busy cobbled streets that housed the many stores along the waterfront from overheating. Warehouses stood at the north of the quay wherein a multitude of goods were stored, some awaiting shipment and others awaiting pick up.

A sinister figure in a wide brimmed hat and brown leather patch to his left eye stood before the clerk's desk. He had demanded the box that had come down from Paris on the stage. The clerk assured him that no box existed in the whole of his warehouse. They had searched since yesterday when he had first enquired and the item was not found. Billings was losing what little control he had over his temper. The clerk could see this and continued to try and appease this man, he promised another search of the warehouse whereby every item would be moved and checked against inventory. Billings could do no more and as he was about to leave one of the warehousemen came into the office and said that a contingent of soldiers with a cart was at the door with the gentleman's box. Billings quickly made his way out of the warehouse and asked the sergeant in charge of the consignment to see that the box got safely stored and secured on the ship. Billings then made his way down to the town and up some narrow-cobbled side streets where he visited the armourer who had a special weapon that he made to order. The armourer welcomed Billings and took him to the back of his shop and introduced him to his new weapon. A small gun that fitted neatly up his sleeve, it would fire one shot from a pre-gun powdered cartridge. It was made of brass and slipped into a chamber. The lead ball had been fashioned to sit within the brass casing and a pin would hit the casing when the trigger was pulled and set off the charge, sending the ball from the casing and down the barrel. The man had made spare casings already filled that would just need to be put in the breech of the gun. Ingenious thought Billings, the armourer cautioned that this was just a test model and it had misfired once or twice and caused the gun to backfire. Billings was still happy to take the weapon and paid Monsieur Flobert well for his work. He thanked Louise again for his work and said he would call when next he was in Brest.

Billings made his way back to the frigate just as the cart and soldiers were leaving. The duty lieutenant reported that the box had been secured in the hold and they would be ready to sail in a very short time, to catch the tide.

They sailed from Brest and headed north west for the bay of St Lawrence. The journey was uneventful and just a little boring for Billings who was desperate to get on with his plans. His new masters would be pleased and he would be offered a very high position indeed with the States of the Union which would now encompass the dominion of Canada. They sailed close to the coast of Greenland and well away from the patrolling ships out of Halifax. Once into the Gulf of St Lawrence they again came against no foe and made good headway. The frigate had disguised herself as a French trader and flew no flags of Napoleon's navy. Citizen Billings had been treated like royalty as his papers had demanded. His cabin was extremely comfortable and he had his meals brought to him daily. He did not interact with the crew and only met with the captain daily to learn of their current location.

The passing of Kingston was a difficult time as it would seem that this town was rapidly building up in military strength, no doubt due to Mountjoy's gift of coin. However, they had sailed through without hindrance and were now sailing the great Lake Ontario and heading for Sacketts Harbour where they eventually docked at the small settlement. They began to unload their cargo, albeit not the box in the secured hold.

Billings was to liaise with the union military and ensure that this strategically placed harbour was extended and built up to become as such as Kingston had become for the British. Trade had already been suspended between the Union and the British to include Canada, although some small-scale smuggling still existed.

Billings was eventually given the use of Horse Island and he commenced to raise a small army to build his headquarters and make ready for the expansion of Sacketts Harbour. Once the army of workers had built a secure headquarters, he was able to move the strong box from the ship and under his care.

The Union were aware of the gold Billings had brought from France and were also aware that he still had control of it. This made him very unpopular with the naval and army contingent that were building up in strength. However, it had also given him a high status and quite some power in the area. He who holds the purse strings shall call the tune was almost his motto and he was not slow in reminding his Union brothers of such. They had built a natural hatred of this one eyed mean sadistic man but under orders had to put up with him. He was certainly no gentleman and assumed a status way higher than he actually was and they all knew him to be.

Billings knew it would take many years of work to build up this defensive location, build ships and make ready for war, and he had thrown himself into the task with great gusto.

***

The meeting started at 8.10 a.m. in their new meeting room. Sylvian took the head of the table with Mr Gant and Mr Coombes to his right and Mr Selway to his left. The agenda for the meeting had been put down last night over a few whiskies and now decisions need to be made as they were going to need a full ship's complement over and above the twelve good men of their team.

"Okay," said Sylvian. "I have given much thought to our complement, gentlemen, Mr Gant you are hereby promoted to lieutenant second class, as are you Mr Selway, you will serve under lieutenant first class, Mr Coombes who will be my second in command, therefore, gentlemen I shall now pass over to Mr Coombes the chair and you will discuss between you and decide how our new ship's complement will come together. The admiralty staffing office has already been contacted and will see you all at a meeting on Monday afternoon at two. There are many half pay lieutenants on the books and men who have signed to serve and awaiting a ship. It is my wish that all members of my crew be seen and interviewed as to their credit to serve with us. We have a difficult mission ahead of us, so it shall be up to you to ensure that we are correctly prepared for such." He paused and took a sip of his tea. "I expect a full list of complement by Friday of this week, gentlemen, as there is a possibility that the ship will be ready for us to sail by early next week. I wish you luck in your Endeavour." The officers smiled and stood to their feet as Sylvian stood.

He left the room and felt quite strange to delegate something that he would wish to get his teeth into. But he also knew the importance of his officers gaining experience and that Mr Coombes would be far better at the job than he would.

Sylvian left the office and his men deep in conversation as he made his way to the repair basin. The Endeavour was still in the repair basin and had not yet been moved to the rigging basin but Sylvian was curious as to her progress so he made his way aboard and enquired of the foreman. A small man came forward and touched his forelock in acknowledgement of the officer. Sylvian told the man who he was and asked if there was anywhere on the ship he should not go to, so as not to interfere with progress. The foreman reported that the ship was sound and would be moved to the rigging basin by the end of day. Sylvian thanked the man and started his full tour of the ship.

The skill of the British carpenter was very evident as the level of craftsmanship that had gone into this repair was indeed high. Sylvian was hard pressed to see where repair had joined original timber. His cabin beneath the poop deck was quite literally of all new wood and smelt so. However, it was a fine cabin indeed. The new timbers of the poop deck had been smoothed and seams were tarred. He was very pleased. The gun decks had been completely cleared of French cannon and the bulkheads that had seen cannon damage were all replaced and looking new. New fine English cannon bearing the mark of King George would be fitted when in the rigging basin.

Sylvian left the ship and made his way through to the mess for lunch where he found Mr Gant and Mr Coombes, young Peter had left for the surgeon's office to have his arm looked at and his sling removed if all was well. Sylvian told his officers about the current state of the ship and they were both pleased and were looking forward to going back to sea. Mr Coombes asked permission to take Sunday off as his wife had just arrived in Portsmouth and he would like to spend some time with her. Sylvian was happy for them all to have Sunday to themselves and apologised that he could not give them the same leave that he had given to the men.

After lunch Sylvian made his way to the chandler's shop hoping to catch the chief clerk, on his way he could see that a new ship had arrived on pier three and it looked familiar. Suddenly he was stopped by a familiar voice. "Excuse me, sir," said the voice. Sylvian turned to be confronted with the sight of First Lieutenant Henry Percy Stockwell, seventeenth Earl of Swinderby.

"Good god, sir, er… Sylvian, old chap, is that you, er, well I say, sir. I mean, sir," he stumbled with his words and saluted Sylvian at the attention.

"Bloody hell, it's Stockwell no less," said Sylvian returning Henry's salute and taking his hand in a firm and friendly grip. "How are you, old chap?" he said. The two men stood and looked at one another for a few seconds.

"Well, sir… fine, sir, I mean a captain, good lord, old boy, congratulations and all that but how, what's to do. My god, sir, just so much to ask you," said Henry in a genuine confusion.

"Do you have a few minutes for a glass or two in the mess?" asked Sylvian.

"Indeed, I do, sir, just docked and sent off on leave, Countess has sent for me, old chap, another arse kicking I shouldn't wonder," he replied.

"Good," said Sylvian as they made their way off to the mess. "I saw the countess a couple of days ago," said Sylvian as they walked. "Gave me a mighty big hug I can tell you."

"Bloody hell!" exclaimed Henry. "Not had one of those in a bally long-time, old chap, and just what did you do, sir, to deserve that may one ask."

"Indeed, one may, young Henry, your mother was on the board to sanction my last mission and even played a small part in its success, and was a member of the admiralty board that brought about my commission to captain," replied Sylvian.

Henry stopped in his stride as they came to the door of the mess. "The countess, really, well I knew she served on the commission board, what on earth role could she... well this is getting intriguing, see, leave you for a minute, old chap, and the world goes to hell," he said.

As they turned to walk in the mess Mr Gant appeared in the doorway and immediately saluted Sylvian. "Good lord," he said. "It is Mr Stockwell, how are you, sir." They shook hands and exchanged pleasantries. Henry offered Steven to join them for a glass or two. "Thank you so much but I must be away as I have a day's leave and thank you, sir, for that," he said to Sylvian. "Gives me time to spend with a certain young lady and tell her that I shall be away in Canada again."

"Enjoy yourself, Steven, you are most certainly deserving, just wished I could have given you longer," replied Sylvian. Steven again saluted the two officers and went on his way.

Having ordered some good single malt and put on to Sylvian's tab the two officers sat in the easy chairs of the mess whereupon Sylvian told Henry all that had gone on from the last time they had seen one another up to this point. Which took all of an hour and a half and, of course three good scotches later. Henry was absolutely dumbfounded and so saddened by the passing of Mary and shocked that the man Billings still lived and was indeed at it again. Henry was glad that the Endeavour was to sail back to Halifax and was sure that the admiral would be so pleased to have him back. He suggested that he should talk with Captain Jackman as they had been dispatched to load up with supplies. As the Endeavour was a much larger ship than the *Dauntless* it may serve them and of course Admiral Albright to have supplies loaded and increase Halifax's holdings to see them through next winter. Sylvian agreed to call on the *Dauntless* tomorrow and for Henry to remember him to his mother. The two parted and Henry set off to find a carriage for the journey home, leaving Sylvian to return to his office and continue his plans.

It was not until ten a.m. that Sylvian had finished his late breakfast with many a cup of tea to stave off the whisky taste still on his tongue. He left the mess in the bright morning sunlight but with a definite chill to the air. The walk down to the *Dauntless* was indeed a welcome one and had helped to clear the cobwebs of alcohol that still remained in the recesses of his mind.

He was piped aboard the *Dauntless* by the bo'sun on watch and the duty midshipman greeted Sylvian with a salute and a welcome on board. Sylvian stated his business and was shown down to Captain Jackman's cabin. A firm knock to the door was replied with a stern enter. Sylvian found Captain Jackman behind his desk and surrounded with paper.

"Good lord, it's young Mountjoy," exclaimed the captain as he stood up and took Sylvian's hand in a firm shake. "And no less a captain now, well welcome aboard the *Dauntless*, Captain."

"Thank you, sir," said Sylvian as he responded to the invitation to take a seat. "And thank you for seeing me."

"Always a pleasure, Sylvian, now tell me, sir, how it is that when last I saw you, I saw a lieutenant begad. And now look at you, newly promoted, is it?" he asked.

"Yes, sir, and one of the reasons I have come to see you this morning, you see on our journey back to England we were fortunate to come up against a Frenchy by the name of Colossus, and with some luck we outgunned her and brought her to heel for a prize. Well, the ship has been under repair following the nasty raking we gave her with the antelopes shot and she has been commissioned the Endeavour and will be under my command," Finished Sylvian.

"Well stone me begad! Congratulations, young Mountjoy, well deserved, need some good officers in this man's navy, so what are your orders, Sylvian?" he asked.

"Well, sir, we are to sail for Halifax and winter up, we shall then make for Kingston with supplies and orders. The man Billings will then be my target, sir." Captain Jackman looked confused. "It's rather a long story, sir, which I hope to share with you at your convenience. My thought is, sir, that if we are to sail then we could also stock up on supplies and maybe with your permission, sail back with you," He concluded.

"Sounds to me like a damn good idea, Captain, we hope to be back to sea by at the latest middle of next week though, how does that fit with your commission begad?" he asked.

"Should be fine, sir, the Endeavour moves into the rigging basin tomorrow, which should be no more than a week, a couple of days sea trials and she should be good to sail, sir," he replied.

They continued to discuss apportioning of supplies and with Sylvian's ship so much bigger, could take much more than they had originally thought. Captain Jackman said that he would deal with the stocking of both ships for the journey back as Sylvian had so much more to deal with in getting his ship seaworthy and crewed.

The two men parted a lot happier than they had been before. Sylvian felt happy at having another ship with him on what would be his maiden voyage as captain. With that done, it was now time to return home and join the ladies and his son for Sunday service.

***

Much had happened during the week with the ship now ready for sea trials and his officers using what was available to them to crew the ship. His team would be back from leave tomorrow just in time for the Endeavour to take to the waters. John Scott had sent a note that he had been detained in London but should be with them within a week.

Sylvian was now in the meeting room with his officers and had been given their report and recommendations. The list was quite extensive and brought much to the abilities of his officers to achieve so much, in such a short time. The list showed in full, ranks names and positions held. His team as requested were not included on the list and would have the role of overseers. Each would carry the title of master in their own area of expertise and would carry the rank of warranted officers. Fitzwalter, Osborne, Simms and Hardcastle would hold the rank of midshipman, officer class and be masters in their area of expertise and captains of parts of the ship. This would help to maintain discipline with such a large crew. Sylvian recognised two names on the list, one was Jack Robertson, ropemaker and Seth Perrin, sailmaker who was Wendy's nephew and he had known both from his previous job in the rope shed. They had managed to secure a surgeon from the medical school and two surgeons' mates. Two second lieutenants, four third lieutenants and eight midshipmen for the officers' wardroom. Two ships cooks, chaplain, purser, master at arms, gunner, bo'sun and mates, carpenter and mates plus two hundred and forty-eight able seamen.

"Gentlemen, I am damnably impressed at what you have achieved in such a short time," said Sylvian. "Do we have those on this list on complement now or when shall we expect the list to be fulfilled?" he asked.

"Sir, we have approximately three quarters of our complement already on board, the rest will be arriving tomorrow and the surgeon on Monday. Sir, I believe the surgeon has ordered his supplies which should arrive with the surgeon," said Martin.

"Good, well done all of you, my compliments, gentlemen. I will of course need to outfit my quarters which I hope to do on Monday, just been so damn busy with finances and all that is required from a ship's captain," said Sylvian.

"No need, sir," said young Peter. "I have taken the liberty, sir, to ensure that you have all that you need, including all the latest charts from the cartographer, with some bearing Mr Jones' name from the *Renown* when he charted all the coast of Prince Edward Island, you have new ship's log, new sextant and charting equipment, I hope that I have covered all sir."

"Well, thank you, Peter, a job well done by the sounds of it," said Sylvian.

"Sir, I have with the help of the two ship's cooks and the purser seen to the stocking of the Endeavour with food, water and other required livestock. It would appear, sir, that your purser, Mr Armitage, is a shrewd man when dealing with merchants and I was extremely pleased to have taken him with me. Our cooks come highly recommended and all of us, sir, have had chance to taste their preparations and I think I speak for all of us in that we shall not be wanting for good well-cooked vitals, sir," said Steven.

"Good, well again, gentlemen, you have surpassed yourselves and I now feel quite comfortable that we shall have a happy and healthy ship when we sail next Wednesday. The *Dauntless* will be joining us on our trip to the dominion so we will need to ensure that she is not left behind. We have quite a task to perform, gentlemen, in that we shall need to be ready for what lies ahead so training will be of the utmost importance. I have been instructed by the admiral to call in at Pont de la Corde in Brittany to pick up our assigned marines. The *Dauntless* will continue whilst we ferry the marines to our ship, we shall easily catch the *Dauntless* before she has cleared Southern Ireland I suspect."

"Do we know who are the marines, sir?" Asked Martin.

"No, Martin, I have been told that we have been assigned a captain, two lieutenants and twenty marines. We do have quarters on board for such so we should not have any problems. Now to uniforms, I expect discipline on my ship and will have all officers in the correct uniforms befitting their ranks, no mismatches in hats or insignia. My warrant officers will wear uniform that I have selected and right through to our seaman who will all be provided with matching uniform. At no time will anyone be out of uniform and if so, will be brought before me or Lieutenant Coombes for punishment. Now all of the uniforms should actually be on board as we speak, so, Mr Selway, if you please after we have finished check with the purser that it is so, and it shall be your responsibility to ensure that my orders are carried out," concluded Sylvian.

"Aye, sir," said Peter.

"It is not, gentlemen, that I want to have the smartest ship in the fleet, although I think we may, it is that we are the only service that does not require such, although it is in standing orders and regulations. After our visit to France and having seen the army, I noted that not one private nor officer were out of dress and discipline was indeed of a high standard, and I will see such on our ship. How say you all," said Sylvian.

All of the men agreed with Sylvian with Steven bringing a good point forward in that it would give the men some sort of pride in their service to the king. The meeting went on for another hour and with all of the officers quite happy that they were ready. Sylvian said that he would interview all of his new officers after lunch and he invited them to supper on board the Endeavour with the new lieutenants so that they may all become acquainted.

Sylvian felt quite happy and relaxed as he made his way down to pier one and the Endeavour. Martin, Steven and young Peter had again outdone themselves beyond the realms of their duty. It felt good to have fine officers to support him and he only hoped that the new officers were of the same calibre and commitment. As he approached the ship he stopped and took a long look at her sleek lines, her rigging with sails rolled and tied neatly, all new tarred ropes and everything in its place, all but one thing. He watched as a young midshipman climbed the ropes of the main mast on pier side. An officer on the poop deck was shouting at the lad to get up and over the mainstay and then up to the top. He watched a little while longer, another officer was arguing with the first and he could not hear what was being said. Sylvian slipped off his coat down to his waistcoat and left the identifying objects on top of a tie up bollard. He walked down to the ship so that he may get a better look. The shouting officer pushed the arguing officer to one side and moved to the poop deck rails and shouted up at the proceeding midshipman. The lad stopped at the second stage of the mast and held on tight with fear. The shouting officer pulled out his pistol and was grabbed by the other officer who was again pushed to the deck. He took aim at the young man and fired. A small splinter of the mast flew off just above the boy's head and he gripped tighter to the mast. The officer started to reload his pistol. Sylvian leapt onto the gangplank and grabbed the main mast rope ladder and climbed as fast as he could up to the first stage. He looked down and the officer shouted to him to get off the mast or be shot. Sylvian carried on until he reached the boy, a second shot rained just past his head. He calmed the boy down and held him tight, he was trembling with fear and his hands had gone white as he gripped the mast. Sylvian continued to talk to him calmly, he looked down and could see Fitzwalter running up the gangplank, the officer was reloading his gun. Sylvian told the boy who he was and calmly moved his hands from the mast and onto the ropes of the ladder, he looked down just in time to see Fitzwalter land a punch squarely on the officer's chin and sent him flying across the railing of the poop deck. Sylvian coaxed the frightened lad slowly down the ladder to the first stage and could see that Fitzwalter had the man down on the deck and was holding him firmly. Sylvian continued on down from the first stage coaxing the boy all the way until they reached the bottom where two of the ratings grabbed the boy and took him to safety. Fitzwalter had sent one of the sailors back to the bollard to collect his captain's coat and hat and by the time Sylvian arrived at Mr Fitzwalter's side the lad had his coat and hat which he then put on. The ship's company immediately came to attention.

"My compliments, Mr Fitzwalter, I do not think I have seen you move so fast," Said Sylvian, feeling quite relieved to see a familiar face.

"Aye, sir, after all that ale, I felt as I needed the exercise, sir," replied Fitzwalter looking up at his captain with a large grin on his face.

"Would you be so kind as to let the man up, Mr Fitzwalter, only his face seems to be going red," asked Sylvian.

Fitzwalter got up off the man and grabbed the back of his coat and unceremoniously lifted him to his feet. He then proceeded to brush him down. The lieutenant pushed his hands away roughly. "I shall have you keel hauled for this; how dare you strike a senior officer," he shouted. He had not seen Sylvian standing behind the bulk of Fitzwalter. "And where is that damn man who climbed the mast, I shall have you both hung so help me, sir."

"I am here, Lieutenant," said Sylvian as Fitzwalter stepped to one side.

"The man immediately came to attention and saluted his captain. "Sir, welcome aboard, sir, we were not expecting you until this evening. I can explain, sir, you see we needed to discipline the young…"

"Mr Fitzwalter," interrupted Sylvian. "You will escort this man to my quarters immediately, he is under arrest so please be so kind as to remain with him until my arrival."

"Aye, sir," Said Fitzwalter as he grabbed the man by the arm and unceremoniously dragged him towards the door in the poop deck bulkhead that led down to the captain's quarters. Sylvian looked around him and spotted the other officer who had been arguing with the arrested man. He was a lieutenant third class and he immediately saluted his officer.

"Lieutenant, please be so kind as to get the men back to their duties and then join me in my quarters if you please," he commanded.

Sylvian followed the route of Fitzwalter and found himself back in his quarters. Fitzwalter had the lieutenant standing to the front of the captain's desk. Sylvian walked in and removed his hat and placed it on the desk. Something he had wanted to do for a very long time.

"Sir, I can explain," said the officer.

"Silence and wait until you are invited to speak, sir," Commanded Sylvian. He sat down at his desk and looked up at the man. There came a knock to the door and Sylvian commanded, "Enter." The young third lieutenant entered the room and marched up to the desk and saluted his captain.

"At ease, Lieutenant." Both men stood to ease. "Not you," shouted Sylvian to the second lieutenant, who immediately came back to attention. "First, I need to know your names," said Sylvian as he took the complement roll off his side desk and opened it in front of him. "You first," he said to the third lieutenant.

"James William Wood, sir," he replied.

"And you," Asked Sylvian of the accused.

"Archibald Wilson-McLean, sir," he replied.

"Mr Wood, are you the duty officer?" asked Sylvian.

"I am, sir," Reported Mr Wood.

"Then can you explain why my ship was in disarray when I arrived?" Sylvian asked as he looked across at McLean who had a grin to his face.

"Yes, sir," said Mr Wood. "I observed Lieutenant McLean in a verbal altercation with young Midshipman Fowler, as I had observed him with other of the younger officers over the past couple of days. I immediately asked what was going on, sir, and Mr McLean presented himself at the poop deck and reminded me to call him sir. He explained to me in certain words that as duty officer I should have control of the ship and have discipline within its ranks. I reported that all had been well until he had come up on the deck. To which he ignored me and again started shouting at the young Mr Fowler and ordered him to get up and over the main mast. I was concerned for young Jim… er Midshipman Fowler as he had only just recently recovered from a mast accident."

"Did you tell Mr McLean this?" interrupted Sylvian.

"Yes, sir, I did, Mr McLean was already aware of this though as he has been going through the crew's records, sir."

101

"Carry on with your report," instructed Sylvian, looking at McLean with disdain.

"Thank you, sir, well, sir, at the point that I had interfered with Mr McLean's command he physically pushed me to the ground. I then saw that he had drawn his pistol and was aiming at young Fowler. I had just time to nudge his arm as he took the shot. Mr Mclean then pushed me again back to the deck with more force and I was unable to stop him from taking the second shot as I had seen you climbing the ropes, sir. That is my report, sir," he concluded.

"Thank you, Mr Wood," Said Sylvian. "Now what say you, Mr McLean?" asked Sylvian.

"The boy's lying, sir, I can assure you that was not how things took place. The boy Fowler..."

"Midshipman Fowler if you please, Mr McLean," Interrupted Sylvian. "Do please continue."

"Sir, yes, sir, Midshipman Fowler had cause to curse at me as I was walking by him. I, sir, am a great believer in discipline as are you, sir. So, I asked him what he had said which he would not repeat. I told him to get up and over the mast as punishment. I then reported the matter to the duty officer Mr Wood to which he admonished me for interfering on his duty watch. I at no time pushed him and was only shouting encouragement to the boy, Midshipman Fowler, sir. And as for the pistol shot, sir, I told the boy to come down as I could see he was somewhat distressed and used the pistol to gain his attention. Twice, sir, and then this oaf," he said, pointing to Fitzwalter, "struck an officer for which I want him charged, sir, and that, sir, is the truth and the subject of my report," he concluded.

"Thank you, Mr McLean," said Sylvian. "And thank you again, Mr Wood, you are dismissed." James replaced his hat and saluted Sylvian before leaving the office.

"Mr McLean, you are a liar and a bully, sir." Sylvian raised his hand to stop the protestation and Mr Fitzwalter took a step forward which silenced him immediately. "I watched you from on the pier before I interceded on behalf of Mr Fowler, I therefore know exactly what took place. I am indeed in favour of discipline aboard my ship so you will be taken by Mr Fitzwalter to your quarters where you will collect your belongings together, whereupon you will be escorted to the regulators to face disciplinary action for discharging a weapon on a docked ship without cause, discharging a weapon at a senior officer without regard to his or any other's safety and using excessive force on a junior rank. Mr Fitzwalter, please escort the prisoner to his quarters and carry out my instructions. At no point is Mr McLean to wear his uniform when being escorted from the ship, and please send the bo'sun to me. Thank you."

"Aye, sir," said Fitzwalter as he took the protesting officer by the arm and escorted him from the captain's office.

Sylvian took a paper from his desk along with pen which he dipped in the ink and commenced his report. Shortly there came a knock to his door which he invited to come in and was faced with the bo'sun in the correct uniform and looking very smart. He saluted the captain and stood to attention at his desk. Right now, Sylvian was wishing he was still a lieutenant.

"Mr Jackman, sir, your bo'sun, sir," he reported.

"Ah, Mr Jackman, very pleased to meet you. I have a task for you when I have completed this report, I need it to be taken directly to the regulator's office. Please assign two of your men to assist Midshipman Fitzwalter with his charge to the regulator's office if you please," he asked.

"Aye, sir, I will task the men now, sir, and return for the report, sir." He saluted Sylvian and left the office. Sylvian continued the report and signed it Sylvian Mountjoy, Captain of the *Endeavour* and set his waxed seal to the document just in time for Mr Jackman to return.

"Mr Jackman, on your return please let me know all is well and assemble the ship's company on deck, could you please arrange for Mr Wood to come and see me at his convenience if you please." Sylvian returned his bosun's salute and handed him the document for the regulators.

Sylvian then commenced to unpack his belongings and hang up his uniform in the small wardrobe. It gave him a chance to look around his sleeping quarters that were to the left of his office as you looked to the stern of the ship. The quarters were quite large and had more than suitable washing facilities along with a comfortable bunk with fresh linen. There was also a door from this room out into the gangway.

He was disturbed from his domestics by a knock to the door. He returned to his office and called enter. Mr Wood presented himself to his captain. "Mr Wood, take a seat if you please. Mr McLean has been removed from his duties so I am in need of a lieutenant second class, you will please assume that role which will be confirmed to the admiralty," said Sylvian to the now sat and quite shocked Mr Wood.

"Sir, I thank you for the promotion, sir, but there are more senior third-class lieutenants than me, sir," he replied.

"I thank you for your candor but none of those stood up to Mr McLean as you did, you will move your belongings to his quarters and assume his duties with immediate effect. Thank you, Mr Wood," Sylvian concluded. James stood and saluted his captain and left the office when almost immediately another knock came to the door. "Enter," called Sylvian and was presented with Mr Fowler.

"Sir, sorry to disturb you, sir, but I am your orderly and I have brought you some tea and biscuits, sir," he said as he placed the tray on the desk.

"Thank you, Mr Fowler, how are you now after your ordeal?" asked Sylvian.

"Good, sir, and I thank you so much for your patience, sir. I will endeavour to improve myself under your command, sir," he replied.

"Thank you, Mr Fowler, and thank you for the tea." James saluted his captain and left the office, leaving Sylvian to pour his tea and savour in its welcome taste.

Sylvian then set about sorting his office and it was not long before there came another knock at the door. Sylvian called for the knocker to enter and was presented with a short stocky able seaman who gave his name as Padraig O'Sullivan and introduced himself as the cook to the captain and his officers. He had come to ask Sylvian as to his diet and if he had any special requirements. Sylvian told him that he was a simple man and enjoyed good home cooked food. He also informed him that all of the officers would dine tonight and requested that a room be set up for them. Padraig told him that there was the captain's dining hall just next to his office and that he would set it up for all the officers. Sylvian was astounded at how little he yet knew of his ship. (Padraig was pronounced Porag).

As Padraig was leaving the captain's office, Mr Jackman presented himself and said that the ship's complement was now at muster on the main deck. Sylvian thanked him and said he would be along in a minute or two.

Sylvian went into his quarters and threw some water on his face, swept his hair back and retied his ponytail ribbon. He had flatly refused to wear a wig as was expected of captains and above. He brushed down his coat and checked himself in the mirror before leaving his quarters and making his way up and on deck. On his arrival the ship's company were called to attention and the bo'sun piped the officer on deck. Sylvian made his way up the steps and onto the poop deck where he was saluted by all of his officers including Mr Coombes, Mr Selway and Mr Gant who had just arrived having been fetched by Fitzwalter. He returned the salute and asked Mr Wood to bring the ship's company to ease. He placed both of his hands on the newly replaced poop deck rail and looked at some two hundred and fifty faces that looked back at him. "Men… welcome to the *Endeavour*, she is a fine ship and should give us a good home whilst we serve our sovereign King George. My introduction to the ship and its complement was not as I would have wished as most of you have witnessed this day." He paused and took a look at Mr Coombes who looked down at his shoes and shifted his gait embarrassingly. "However, I would like you all to know that I run a fair ship, a disciplined ship, a fighting ship and most of all a home to all of you who serve her. Tomorrow we shall take her out on sea trials and we shall work her hard and see what she is capable of. We shall test all guns and we shall then see how good your accuracy is." A small laugh went about the crew with some elbow nudging. "We shall then return to port and restock on powder and ball. Some of you will have shore leave as we shall sail on Wednesday with the *Dauntless* and maybe to sea for quite some time away from home. My officers are here for you as much as you are here for them, we shall forge the best team this navy has seen." The men erupted in a cheer and many hats flew into the air. Sylvian was not aware but there was great relief when Fitzwalter had marched McLean from the ship. They had also seen what he had done for Mr Fowler and had read his exploits in the newspapers. Most of them had volunteered for this ship and as many again had been turned away.

"I will now ask my officers to introduce themselves," said Sylvian as he stood back and allowed first Mr Coombes to make his introduction. After they had all finished, he stepped forward again. "I hope to get to know you all over the course of time so please bear with me should I get your name wrong, thank you, men."

The bo'sun stepped forward and called all the men to attention. He then turned and saluted his captain and then dismissed the men to their duties.

"I am so sorry, sir," said Martin. "I did not know the man was such an arse. I accept full responsibility."

"Good then you can buy the farewell drinks in the mess on Tuesday next," said Sylvian with a smile.

"It shall be my pleasure, sir," said Martin as he took a bow.

"So, gentlemen, we need to have a ship ready for trials on the morrow, so as you are all here can you please check through the ship and ensure that all is well. We shall dine at seven in the captain's dining hall which I had no idea of until I was informed by the cook, so whilst on sea trials we shall all get to know our ship well," said Sylvian.

"Aye, sir," said his officers.

"Sir, if I may," said Mr Gant.

"Yes, Steven."

"Should I find a replacement for the man McLean, sir?" he asked.

"No, no, I have promoted Third Lieutenant Wood to take his place, if you gentlemen feel we have a need for a third lieutenant to replace Mr Wood's position then please do so, and choose well. I shall be in my cabin and shall chart us a course for tomorrow." He started to walk towards the steps from the poop deck and stopped. "Mr Selway, could you please ask Mr Fitzwalter to come to my office."

"Aye, sir," replied Peter lifting his hand to his brow.

The knock came to the door as soon as Sylvian had placed his hat yet again on the desk. He called the knocker to enter and was faced with Mr Fitzwalter who marched up to his desk and saluted his captain. "You wanted to see I, sir," he said.

"Indeed, Mr Fitzwalter, and it is me, Mr Fitzwalter, not I, at ease and do please take a seat," invited Sylvian.

"Me, sir, I see, sir, and I doos, thank you, sir," he said, taking his seat.

"Mmmm," said Sylvian shaking his head. "I wish to thank you for quick actions this afternoon, you were indeed quick to take action when recognising the situation, although please do not make it a regular occurrence to strike a senior officer, so well done."

"Oh, no, sir, see I could thinks of nothing else at the time, sir, so's I just at to stop him from afiring that there pistol, sir. I aint given, sir, to striking no one as I is quite agin violence, sir," he said proudly and with his back straight and honest.

"Think, Mr Fitzwalter," said Sylvian.

"About wot, sir," said Fitzwalter.

"No, Mr Fitzwalter, the word is think, and not thinks. It would give me great pleasure, Mr Fitzwalter, as you are now a confirmed officer and holding the rank of midshipman that you should learn how to read, write and talk as one. Are you willing to undertake such a task along with Mr Osborne, Mr Hardcastle and Mr Simms?" he asked.

"Oh, yes, sir, I woulds like to get to writing a bit more and reading more than the little that I now dos, sir," He replied.

"Very good, then I shall task Mr Selway as he is indeed a man of infinite patience and well schooled to commence as soon as we are to sea. How old are you?" he asked.

"Oh, sir, well to tells the truth, sir, I is not too sure, sir, I aint as old as Albert and I aint as young as Chris or Colin, sir. I figures I must be near to thirty-five, sir, if all fits into place from memory, sir, which aint too good you see," he replied.

"Well, I thought you may have been such and therefore still young enough to move forward under my command, we just need you to have more education. You are not a slow man in thought so you should respond well to Mr Selway's teaching. Well thank you again, Mr Fitzwalter," concluded Sylvian.

Fitzwalter stood and saluted his captain and thanked him. He then left the cabin and back to his duties leaving Sylvian to ponder on his long-term plans and to set a course for tomorrow's sea trials.

Chapter Six
To Sea

Sylvian now had the office and his quarters looking how he wanted. Things were in their right place where he should easily find it. Mr Selway had indeed completed a fine task at acquiring all that he should need, and more. He now found himself looking around the large cabin and out of the newly replaced glazed windows of the stern of the ship. He had them open to try and remove some of the new wood smell from the cabin, although it was a smell he quite liked.

Looking to the stern of the ship and with his back to the desk, on the right were fine cabinets to hold his papers and charts and a small desk for his ship's log and report writing. Three ornate oil lamps hung from the ceiling on chains that could be lowered to enable refill. The left bulkhead that separated his sleeping quarters was complete with a world map and also a cabinet with glasses and a fine stock of brandies, whiskies, rum, gin and the like. On the other side of the right-hand bulkhead and using up the rest of the stern of the ship was the captain's dining room. A door led from his office and directly into the dining room, there was also a door from the gangway outside. Sylvian had taken a look at the dining earlier and found a fine long table suitable to seat all of his officers. Fine chairs were around the table with the captain's chair to the head. The bulkhead had pockets within which sat filled decanters, there was a serving table on the rear bulkhead by the door to the kitchen. The walls were well dressed with copies of paintings that adorned most captains' cabins.

He was disturbed from his thoughts by a knock to the door. On his call to enter Lieutenant Third Class Douglas entered the room and saluted his captain.

"Sir, I have the pleasure to report as officer of the watch that the ship is correct and in order, sir. The last of our crew are now on complement. We have two in the sick bay and no deserters, sir," he reported.

"Thank you, Mr Douglas, have all of my men as per the list I gave you this afternoon, reported for duty?" he asked.

"Indeed, sir, and have been shown to quarters," he answered.

"Good," said Sylvian. "Who has the morning watch, Mr Douglas?"

"That would be, Second Lieutenant Montrose, sir," he answered.

"Can you leave a note on the duty log for Mr Montrose to ensure that he has me woken by six a.m. if you please. Thank you, Mr Douglas," said Sylvian. John Douglas saluted his officer and left the cabin.

As Mr Douglas was leaving the office, Chris Thomson knocked on the bulkhead. Sylvian invited him in and noted how smart he looked in his warrant officer's uniform complete with tall black shiny hat. Chris however had a displeased look on his face when he saluted his captain.

"What is it, Chris?" asked Sylvian noting the displeasure on his young team member's face.

"Sir, firstly I thank you for the leave you have given us, but, sir, I have never wanted an officer's place, sir, not even a warrant officer, sir," he protested.

"Sit down, Chris," commanded Sylvian as he took his seat behind the fancy desk followed by Chris removing his hat and taking the seat opposite.

"I am aware of your desire not to serve as an officer albeit your education and demeanour state otherwise, however I have no recourse than to stand my team together as warranted officers with special regard to areas of expertise. We know yours to be gunnery as is Mr Simms. We must be ready as a team, Mr Thompson, to take on a task as and when it shall be called for, and mark me, it will be called for. This must have no detriment to this ship's company and her ability to engage with the enemy. Therefore, all of my specialist men will hold such an office until I deem otherwise. I have no wish whatsoever to lose any of you, but should your feeling rise so high then I am sure I can find you a shipboard place as a seaman aboard this vessel. You will obviously lose your position on the team, but I shall be happy to do such, if that is your desire," said Sylvian.

Chris looked shocked and confused and was obviously racing through his smart brain to find an answer that would suit him. There was not one to be found. He finally looked up at his captain and smiled, for he knew he was beaten. "Sir, I thank you for taking the time to explain to me your predicament and whilst my desire not to serve as an officer has always been with me, I can see the difficulties you face and would therefore like to apologise for protesting so. I, sir, wish to serve with you and the men I have come to trust, and, sir, would like to remain so," he replied.

"Very good," said Sylvian. "I am pleased to hear it; you will make a wonderful asset to the ship's company in the position you now hold. Thank you, Mr Thompson," said Sylvian dismissing his young protégé. Chris stood to his feet and replaced his hat, saluted his officer and left the cabin with Sylvian smiling and thinking to himself that he might not be so bad at this job after all.

The evening supper with his officers was a great time for each to get to know one another. They all stood for their captain when he entered the room as the last person to arrive, as was protocol. When he sat, they all did, food was served as was some rather fine French wine liberated by Mr Gant from the repair basin where he knew they would loot the prize ship when it arrived. He had not taken it all but left half for the workers in the basin. That way he had agreement that the *Endeavour* would come right to the top of their list for a speedy and good quality repair. There had been no objections. Mr Montrose regaled them all with his tales from Trafalgar where he had been a midshipman as had Jack Newman. It was quite evident that the two lieutenants intended the continuance of the age-old tradition for officers to stretch their stories.

All the officers had begged Sylvian to tell them of the Kingston trip and especially the confrontation with the natives in the forest. The talk went on and on well into the evening. Mr Montrose had excused himself as to his watch and Sylvian brought the meal to an end around ten thirty by dismissing the men to be on duty by six thirty at their quarters to ready the ship for sea.

Sylvian slept well that night as his bunk was fresh and indeed very comfortable and did not appreciate the wakeup call at six a.m. However, as the true officer he was and having seen to his ablutions and now dressed in his full uniform made his way to the poop deck. It was a fine day and the ship buzzed with action. His lieutenants had gathered and came to attention and saluted their captain on his arrival.

"Mr Coombes if you please, report as to the ship's readiness," he asked.

"Sir, the ship is ready and we are in a position to lower gallants and to cast off, sir," he replied.

"Seems we have a fine wind, gentlemen, and the sun beats its way on the horizon. Mr Coombes if you please, cast off and take her out," he ordered. Mr Coombes shouted his orders and the lieutenants moved to their posts. Within minutes the *Endeavour* pulled from her moorings with Jason Baker at the wheel and Mr Coombes more than able instructions saw the ship into the Solent and heading for the Isle of Wight.

The wind blew nicely and the ship moved steadily through the waves. She was of a size as to not give much quarter to roll. As they sailed steadily past the coast of Southampton and on out into the English Channel, the sun was now up and behind them.

"What heading shall we make, sir," asked Mr Coombes.

"We shall stay coastal, Mr Coombes, and shall round the Needles and into the Bristol Channel where we shall test our cannon. Mr Simms," he called out loud.

"Aye, sir," shouted Albert in that unmistakeable gravelly voice of his from down on the main deck.

"Lieutenant Wood shall take charge of the gun deck and you shall assume the role of gun commander, please use this time to sharpen up your gun crews and let us have some good accurate cannon fire as I know you can," said Sylvian.

"Aye, aye, sir, we shall make it happen," Said Albert.

"Mr Wood," he shouted as James was at the far end of the main deck close to the forecastle steps. One of the ratings brought the officer to the attention of his captain and James made his way quickly to almost stand beside Albert.

"Aye, sir," he said on his arrival.

"You shall take charge of the gun decks for practice and Mr Simms shall be your gun commander. We shall test our cannon when on the approach of the Bristol Channel," said Sylvian.

"Aye, aye, sir," said James as he looked at Albert and smiled.

"Mr Coombes, the ship is yours. Please call me when we have rounded the Needles and into the channel," said Sylvian.

"Aye, sir," said Martin as his smile grew larger and he saluted his captain.

Sylvian returned to his cabin and sat to the rear of his desk just to enjoy the slight roll of the ship and the sound of the waves as they beat on the side of this wonderful ship. He took out his watch from his waistcoat pocket and was reminded of this gift from Admiral Albright and noted the time at 9.50, a good start he thought.

***

It was nine thirty on the dot when the door opened to the large house of colonial style, and the black cloaked man in the large brimmed hat walked out and onto the cliff path that went around this island. The day was warm and sunny, a little windy perhaps, but he was on an island. Since the completion of the house Billings enjoyed his morning's walk around the cliff tops of what he considered to be his Horse Island. Just a start for eventually he would have this half of the dominion at his personal disposal once the British had been removed, and of course the natives tamed.

He stopped at the top of the highest cliff and looked down some one hundred and fifty feet to the waves that crashed on the rocks below. He envied the waves the power that they held so as something as tough as the granite cliffs could not fight the power of the waves. Parts of the cliff had already given way to this mighty force. He checked his time piece, ten thirty and his first appointment with Colonel Farraday. He turned and walked slowly back to the house whilst taking in the beauty of his surroundings. His soldiers knew not to be in sight at this time of the day when he took his walks. He needed to feel that all was well and he was just taking a walk along the English cliffs without a single soul around to spoil it. His new little gun had worked well when one of the soldiers had forgotten his orders. He had landed at the bottom of the cliffs. No one had made this mistake since.

On his arrival back at the house, his Caribbean slave greeted him at the door and took his coat and hat and told him that Colonel Farraday was in the study. He told his man to bring coffee as he made his way to the double doors past the sweeping staircase. He found the colonel in his usual place in the chair in front of his desk. The colonel stood when he entered and Billings waved him to sit.

"How do we proceed, Colonel, are we on target as set out in my plans," asked Billings

"Sir, we have come to a halt on pier three as the lumber yards are asking for their pay," answered the colonel. "And we need more lumber for the third ship as we are at a crucial point in the build. I have received $5,000 from my government, sir, but that is not enough to pay for what lumber we have already consumed."

"What do you require, Colonel Farraday, from me?" asked Billings.

"With another 50,000 I could complete pier three and at least two more ships, sir," replied Mr Farraday.

Billings stood and walked to the window. "I shall need receipts and as usual my account's man is very thorough, I shall authorise $25,000 in gold, you will come back to me when we are up to date and are ready to build the ships." He turned and sneered at this proud colonel and made him feel like a beggar. He walked to his desk and took pen to parchment and passed the completed order to the colonel. "You know what to do with this, now please leave I have much to prepare."

The colonel knew exactly what he would like to do but was under orders. He took the parchment and left the room just as the man servant entered with a tray of coffee. He placed the coffee on Nathaniel's desk and turned to leave. "Pour it out, man, damn you. Next time have the coffee ready as soon as any guest arrives, I have told you this before, next time you will be whipped," he shouted.

"Yas, sir, masah," said the slave as he poured the coffee carefully and then turned to leave the room.

"And Jacob, shut the damn door as you leave," barked Billings.

"Yas, sir," said Jacob as he pulled a sneer to his face and then smiled as he walked out, closing the double doors behind him.

There was not a man, nor woman on this island or in the harbour that liked this pompous Englishman, except one, Messie, Jacobs's twenty-year-old daughter. She was fascinated by him and did not mind what he did to her, she thought it was only foolin as she put it, and after all he did own her when he bought her parents and her at a slave market. She didn't understand him yet, but she sure as hell was gonna try. She would walk around doing her chores thinking about him and would often smile and shake her head and say, "Wots I gonna do's about my masah, he a funny cuss, that's fer sure." He had never shouted or cussed at her or brought the whip to her back, yet she had argued with him over small things even when he was 'doin it' as she put it. It had got to such a point that people would come to her when there was a problem and young Messie would put it right by talking to the masah. She had sometimes accompanied him on his twice a day walks along the cliffs where he had never laid a finger on her and they had both enjoyed the walk and scenery together. Some folks had got to calling Messie Mrs Billings, only in fun and never to her face.

Messie was a pretty girl, a little chubby but well proportioned. She had a happy way about her and took to her housekeeping chores as if the house was her own. She was at the point where she would make sure that her mother, the cook, and her father, the butler, were kept to their place, as with the other slaves that worked in the house and indeed, those that worked on the land clearing the trees for the animals. Messie was in her element and being only young, was given at times to go beyond herself and was often threatened by her father to a whipping. She would just run away laughing as she knew she had the upper hand.

Nathaniel sat behind his desk making out his report to his French fathers. He reported on progress against his plans. He was yet to recruit suitable candidates to replace those lost by Mountjoy's exploits at the chateau. Jacob knocked on the door and was bid enter where he introduced Mr Courtney, a small man from New Hampshire in his late fifties and riddled with gout to his right foot, requiring him to walk slowly and with a stick. He was Nathaniel's account keeper. He finally made it to the chair recently vacated by the colonel and groaned as he sat down. He was however, very good at his job.

"What is it, William?" Barked Nathaniel.

"Tis the gout, sir, does trouble me something awful…"

"Not your groans, man, I have no concern for your troubles, what do you want, can you not see I am busy," interrupted Nathaniel.

"Indeed, sir, I will not take up your time… no not at all," he said as he shifted his leg to a more comfortable position. "I have tallied what is left in your vault, sir, and can report that after the release of this morning's gold to the good colonel, you have precisely one hundred and eight, ten-pound bars remaining." He checked his figures from his notebook. "That, sir, equates at today's prices to around \$328,000, sir. A quite healthy amount considering your budget against your plans sir," he reported.

"Very good, William, we must continue to be economical on our spending and ensure that what moneies we issue are spent where they are meant to go. How is that progressing?" he asked.

"Ah that, well, sir, it is going according to plan, the man Jackson you employed to enforce that has indeed been doing his job, with what I may say some degree of enjoyment. The mill owner who overcharged the colonel for his lumber on pier two has been dispatched and the word spread. It would seem, sir, that many discounts seem to be coming our way," he chuckled.

"Good, William, let's see it stays that way, pay the man Jackson a bonus for his good work will you. Now get on, man, I have work to do," barked Nathaniel.

"Sir," said William as he struggled to his feet and made his way slowly to the door which he left open.

"Jacob," shouted Billings, and the door closed.

***

The captain's dining room set well to its task as the ship's meeting room, with Sylvian at the head of the table and all of his officers sat around the table in positions of seniority. The room was lit from the beautiful sunny day that now streamed through the open stern windows and surprisingly the noise of Portsmouth dockyard did not penetrate the room.

"So, we are all agreed, gentlemen, HMS *Endeavour* has passed her sea trials and is ready to sail?" asked Sylvian, with all about the table indicating their agreement.

"Good, although I do feel that we shall need some more in-depth training in our gunnery, Mr Wood, what say you, sir?" asked Sylvian.

"Yes, sir," said William. "Damn poor showing I'm afraid, sir. However, the marvelous Mr Simms with that voice of his is even now holding school on the gun decks, as we have heard throughout this meeting. My feeling, sir, is that Mr Simms and myself shall have a fine gun crew when next we practice," he answered, with a confidence that was rapidly growing.

"Good," said Sylvian. "And Mr Montrose, how goes your training on the mast and rigging, sir?" asked their captain.

"Again, sir, I have to say that with Mr Gant's fine work, the men are coming into shape, sir. We yet have a few more tactics to discuss and will drill the men when we have set to sea, sir," he answered in that mild Scottish brogue.

"Excellent," said Sylvian. "Well, gentlemen, it is Monday morning and we shall sail with the first tide on Wednesday. Mr Scott here has informed me that his colleague Mr Mitchell will be ready with our marines at Pont de la Corde. We should be there by late Wednesday and have the men aboard and to sea that evening, all being well. Mr St John, could you please arrange with the purser, Mr Armitage, that all budgets are brought aboard by tomorrow latest. Mr Coombes, could you please post a note to all crew of the officers aboard this ship and their areas of responsibility, this should only be temporary until all have been acquainted with one another. Well, gentlemen, I think that shall be all for now, thank you," said Sylvian concluding the meeting.

"John, can I see you for a moment in my office?" asked Sylvian.

"Indeed, Captain," said John as they made their way through and into the office.

"Take a seat, John, drink?" asked Sylvian.

"I could murder a cup of tea, sir, long drive from London," replied John.

"Padraig," shouted Sylvian and within seconds the door opened.

Padraig poked his head around and said, "I am just bringing tea, sir, if that's what you wanted, sir."

"Indeed," said Sylvian. "So, John how was your business in London," continued Sylvian with Padraig having closed the door.

"Mmmm, eventful, sir. Our people have managed to track the vessel that Billings left on, which called in at Brest and was loaded with something that was obviously important to require an armed guard. My men were unable to find out just exactly what that was, but we do believe that it was either coin or gold. We..." they were interrupted by a knock on the door and Padraig entering with a tray of tea and biscuits. He poured the tea to their requirements and then left the office.

"Where was I?" continued John whilst taking a sip of his tea. "That's good tea, anyway, yes, we believe that the ship then headed for the dominion."

"I see," said Sylvian. "Do we know where Billings went to in the dominion?" asked Sylvian.

"Well, that's where our intelligence is a little vague, I'm afraid, sir. However, I feel that the intelligence regarding Sacketts Harbour would be an ideal base for him whilst he sets about the French interest in assisting the Union to build up its military strength," he concluded.

The two men sat and consumed their tea and biscuits and pondered the many questions yet to be answered.

"Well, thank you, John, we shall need to think long and hard on how we deal with this intelligence, now I must away to the admiral's office for pre sailing orders and to bring him up to speed on our sea trials. I will see you for supper," said Sylvian as he stood and shook John's hand firmly. He then put on his coat and hat and together with John made their way up and on deck. Sylvian received his report from the duty officer Mr Fitzjohn and informed him that he was leaving the ship. The bo'sun piped his captain from the ship and Sylvian headed off for the admiral's office.

His meeting with the admiral went well and he was given more dispatches from the admiralty. He called in at the purser's office and cancelled his requirement for the office they had used. The purser stated that as a posted captain of a Portsmouth vessel the office would be kept for him when in port. Sylvian then headed home in a handsome cab to spend the rest of this day with his family before returning this evening and making ready to sail on Wednesday's first tide.

He was shocked and very pleased to find Jack was home on a two-day leave. They shared a great deal between them and more than one tear was shed. Jack was doing well on his course and had already progressed beyond the first year's course because of his experience. He was now studying diseases and was finding the latin names for such, very intriguing. He hoped to have all completed within eighteen months as he had a real desire to get back to his wife. Sylvian had told his mother of Jack's wife's sister Sarah Bennett and the feelings he had experienced, she scolded Sylvian as she was already aware. She had been told by Jack when first he arrived, and that is why she and Wendy had suggested that there may be someone else in his future. Sylvian was greatly relieved by this news although he had boxed his brother's ears for being such a tell tale.

The day went well and Sylvian spent a lot of time with William, he was a fine boy and was growing so fast with the spoils of his grandmas. Sylvian knew that he would be away for quite some time and both Wendy and his mother had been given to tears when it came time for him to leave. The brothers shook hands and Sylvian promised to give Abigail a kiss when he saw her. Jack had insisted that it should only be on the cheek, and just a small peck at that. Sylvian was sad yet again at having to leave all of this behind and took a long look at his house as the cab pulled off and headed back to the dockyard.

***

The call came early and Sylvian was up and dressed and he was so ready to get back to sea. It had been nice to spend time with his family but this was his life, this was his calling. As he left his cabin, he found the ship to be a hive of activity. He found Mr Coombes on the poop deck and after their good mornings Mr Coombes reported that the *Dauntless* was being towed out of her berth and she could pick up no wind. The *Endeavour* however had lowered partial sail which had brought the tie ropes to a taught that was taking six mateys to pull back on to remove the loop. Sylvian looked out and across to the *Dauntless* on this Wednesday's first morning light. It was dry but the sky looked cloudy. He could see two row boats with lines attached to the *Dauntless* and the rowers pulling for all their might. They had pulled the *Dauntless* into the wind and were now furiously making their way back to their ship.

The *Endeavour* was slowly pulling from her berth as she had let out small amount of sail from her mizzen that was enough to move the ship. Jason Baker had the wheel and Jacob Stubbings was with him under tuition. The *Endeavour* glided gently from its berth and nudged its nose into the Solent until Jason under command from Martin brought the ship about twenty-five degrees to port, the wind died on the turn but the momentum of the ship kept her on course. Mr Coombes commanded all sails to be let loose and within minutes the ship had picked up the wind and was gaining in momentum. The *Dauntless* was already some quarter mile ahead of them and had picked up the full wind in the Solent.

With all sails now picking up the wind Sylvian asked Martin to bring in the foremast sails and leave the main mast to do the work. He wanted to keep the *Dauntless* at its current distance. They enjoyed the open sea and were now just passing with Southampton on their starboard and the Isle of Wight to port. Daylight was now with them but as yet no sun. The wind had reminded them all of the chill of the sea and to Sylvian that as captain he had no need to be there. He gave command of the ship to Mr Coombes and repaired back to his cabin for breakfast. The privilege of rank, but with that came the responsibility of one of His Majesty's ships.

Sylvian enjoyed an excellent breakfast prepared by Padraig and was attended to by Mr Fowler who had responsibility for his captain's wellbeing and needs. It was James who had the responsibility of ensuring that his captain was awake at the time requested and that his uniform, bedding and all that was personal was in tip top condition.

Sylvian decided to go up on deck and then do a tour of the ship to make sure that all was well and also to start to get to know his crew. Down on the first gun deck Sylvian found Mr Simms well into his training and had his men running out cannon to a count. Sylvian remembered well when he had been so schooled by Mr Simms, and felt a little for the men that now fell to Mr Simms' rigorous training.

He moved further on to the lower deck and found Mr Wood carrying out the same with the lower gun deck crew. Mr Wood had most certainly found himself in the past few days. He called the crew to attention and saluted his officer as had Mr Simms, and received the same instruction, to carry on. Sylvian spent a good hour and a half to explore the ship and although built by the French, he was very impressed at its layout and construction standards.

Having returned to the poop deck he found Mr Gant in command who reported all correct and maintaining an even distance to the *Dauntless*. When questioned Steven reported that they were now ten minutes from taking a fifteen degree to port turn to align themselves with the Pont de la Corde and their rendezvous with the marines. Sylvian remained on deck during the manoeuvre and Steven sent Mr Watts to inform Mr Coombes of the turn. Mr Coombes was met on his way and dismissed Mr Watts back to his duties. Martin attended the poop deck with charts which he spread on the chart table and took his spyglass to the horizon and around. He reported no enemy ships and commented that he would like it to remain so.

"Mr Coombes I have the command," said Sylvian. "Mr Gant, please send a flag to the *Dauntless* that we are stopping to pick up passengers and that we shall see her somewhere south of Ireland, if you please," commanded Sylvian.

"Mr Baker, you will come a further fifteen degrees to port and when close to coast but not so close as to find rock, please bring her back on course," asked Sylvian.

"Aye, aye, sir, fifteen degrees to port and maintain coastal sail, sir," repeated Jason.

"Martin, I feel we shall be safer if we sail closer to land as our outline shall not be too visible against the horizon," he said.

"Yes, sir," said Martin. "The cliffs are quite high and should give us some cover, thank you, sir."

"A lesson I learnt when we avoided contact with a French vessel off Anticosti Island." Sylvian took his spyglass to eye and could just make out the headland of their destination. Jason brought the ship back on course and announced the manoeuvre. Sylvian figured with this wind and their current speed that they should prepare to bring in sail in about fifteen minutes and allow the *Endeavour* to slow down naturally. He checked his pocket watch, five fifteen on this fine September evening. All was going well and they had not seen sign of ship or even fishing ketch.

Sylvian checked his watch, five thirty, he did not need his spyglass as they were just coming around the headland.

"Mr Coombes, take in sail and let's see her drift into the Pont de la Corde, Mr Baker, when we have the Pont to our portside bring her about and into the wind if you please." The ship jumped into action with monkeys manning the rigging and Jason repeating his order. The ship glided into the small bay and Jason brought her about with just enough speed to bring her to a slow.

Mr Coombes gave the command to aweigh anchor and the ship came to a stop. All boats had been made ready by Mr Gant and the rowing crews stood by. Martin and Sylvian used their spyglasses to look to land where they could see the massing of the red coats on shore. Sylvian gave the command to man the boats and pick up passengers.

It took just over two hours to ferry twenty men, two lieutenants and a captain from shore to the ship. The boats also picked up Mr Mitchell and twenty fusiliers and their captain, who presented himself along with the marine captain to Sylvian on the poop deck, First came the marine captain who stood to attention and saluted Sylvian and reported his name as Captain Peter Albert Wood, older brother of James Wood second lieutenant on the *Endeavour*. Peter asked his captain as to whether he should excuse himself of this duty owing to a family member being aboard.

"Not at all, sir, I have served with my brother who is a fine ship's surgeon so I see no need for you to excuse yourself from my ship. You are most welcome, sir," said Sylvian. "Please make yourself familiar with the marines' quarters on board, and let me know if there is anything that you need. Mr Wood, if you please, escort the captain and his marines to their quarters, oh, and captain, I shall be pleased if you and your officers would take supper with us at seven."

"Thank you, sir," said Peter as he took a step back and saluted the captain before leaving with his brother to the marines' quarters.

"Sir," said Lt Douglas. "Beggin' your pardon, sir, but the boats have returned with a small contingent of army, sir, they are just coming aboard, sir."

"Very well, Mr Douglas, have their officer present himself when they are aboard," said Sylvian.

"Aye, sir," said Mr Douglas as he turned and left the poop deck.

Sylvian and Martin were consulting the charts as there were reported sandbanks on this inlet and they had decided that they should follow the same route out as they had used coming in. Mr Coombes then suggested that they sail directly across the channel until closer to the English coast and then head with full sail towards the Atlantic. Sylvian requested that they go with full sail when they were completed here.

"Sir," came the voice. "Captain Sinclair, Royal Regiment of Fusiliers, sir, my orders."

Sylvian swung round to face his friend. "Robert, what the damn hell are you doing here?" he asked returning Robert's shocked salute.

"Sylvian, my god, sir, captain, really, but it was less than a month and you..." he was lost for words but the two men embraced as old friends. "So is this your boat, sir," he asked.

Sylvian smiled and cocked his head to one side. "Ship, Robert, this is a ship and I am indeed her commander. There is a lot to tell, dear boy, for which you, sir, are the one I owe all of this to. It is so good to see you. Now what of your orders." Sylvian broke open the seal and read the parchment. It was from Major General Farquason, Royal Regiment of Fusiliers and stated that Captain Carlisle and his squad required passage to Halifax whereupon they were to move into enemy territory and dispose of a munitions store in the state of New York.

"Good lord," said Sylvian as he passed the papers back to Robert. "We shall of course give you and your men transport to the Dominion. Mr Coombes, could you please find suitable quarters for Captain Sinclair and his men. Robert, please join us for supper at seven, we shall talk after," said Sylvian. Martin and Robert saluted Sylvian before they left the poop deck. Both were in deep conversation as they had gained quite a friendship at the chateau.

"Mr Gant, please prepare to take her out, sir."

"Aye aye, sir," said Steven as he started to bark orders and soon the men had the anchor back on board and the sails full of wind as Jason took the ship at Mr Gant's command out of the bay and back into the channel.

Sylvian excused himself from the poop deck and returned to his office. He placed his hat on his desk and poured himself a glass of port and sat down to ponder his first day as captain of this beautiful vessel.

With the ensign flying high in the wind the *Endeavour* cut her way neatly through the waves and out of the channel and into the Atlantic Ocean. The wind had held well and required no tacking to pick up speed. With all sails now employed the *Endeavour* had the speed and would soon catch the *Dauntless*.

The dining room although large was now quite full and extra chairs had to be found. Padraig had excelled himself at his catering to this great number in such a small kitchen, and the food was excellent. The room was full of colour with the blue and gold of the navy, the red and blue of the marines and of course the red and gold of the captain of fusiliers. Captain Wood and his two lieutenants Roger Pettifer and Philip Wilson soon felt welcome and part of the ship's company, stories had been shared round the table by all and many a joke made in that greatest of British humour. Robert had regaled them with the destruction of the chateau and of Sylvian's man Fitzwalter who could bring down a place, well single handed. Much fun was had by all which engendered to Sylvian a happy ship. If only he could keep it this way.

Sylvian ended the evening at ten thirty and thanked the officers for their attendance. They all stood up and saluted their captain and thanked him for the invitation before they left. Sylvian and Robert retired to Sylvian's office where a whiskey was enjoyed by the two men. Sylvian expressed his concern at Robert's orders as that would be quite a trip into what would be unknown Union territory. Robert was unconcerned as he would try to find a good and reliable guide to lead them. Sylvian suggested that he knew of such a man and would see to it that they both should meet. Sylvian told Robert of the time him and his men had ventured into the Union to destroy a band of cut throats led by Billings that were out to capture the coin they had taken to Kingston. They discussed the merits of what Sylvian had learnt on this trip and what maybe, Robert could employ.

The two men spoke for an hour before the day caught up with them and they said their goodnights, and retired for the night.

Morning came oh too soon for Sylvian, he was already up and dressed when Mr Fowler put a knock to his door. He made his way up and onto deck where Mr Selway, duty officer reported the ship all correct. He reported that the *Dauntless* had been spotted by the lookout at 3.30 a.m. and sail and been taken in to maintain the distance. Sylvian thanked Peter for his report and asked him to carry on. They were soon joined by Martin who suggested that today as they were passing the south west of Ireland that they should commence cannon practice. Sylvian agreed and asked Martin to flag the *Dauntless* and let them know what they were doing before the *Dauntless* should come about and make ready for engagement. They both laughed at the thought and Mr Selway set off to make the *Dauntless* aware.

It was not long before the cannon roared under the instruction of Albert and James Wood. Sylvian was impressed at the improved speed to reload guns. Martin and Sylvian had stood with watches and timed the reloads. Impressive, unfortunately accuracy still needed to be achieved, but they were sure that Albert would have it done in no time.

Peter had his spyglass set on the *Dauntless* and interrupted his officers. "Sir, the *Dauntless* reports ship or ships dead ahead, sir."

"Thank you, Mr Selway," said Sylvian. "Do we have identification?"

"No, sir, she reports that they are too far distant, sir."

"Mr Gant, my compliments to Mr Simms and Mr Wood and ask them to desist with gun practice if you please."

"Aye, sir," said Steven as he set off at the double to the lower gun decks.

"Mr Jackman, please ask the crow to keep a sharp eye dead ahead and when he has an identity on the ships to report immediately," called Sylvian.

"Aye, sir," answered the bo'sun.

Sylvian moved forward to the forecastle deck to see if he could gain a better look but could see nothing on the horizon. He was joined by Mr Coombes with spyglass who also could see nothing.

"It's possible, sir, they are the same tack and direction, although somewhat slower than the *Dauntless*, sir."

"Indeed," said Sylvian. "We shall maintain course and speed and see what we come up against in a few hours. The ship is yours, Martin; let me know if we have a sighting."

"Aye aye, sir," said Martin.

Sylvian returned to his office and was served his tea and breakfast. He then spent time plotting from their current location what was around them. They were now in open sea with Ireland some forty miles to their stern. Sylvian continued with his paperwork and recorded in the log the report from the *Dauntless* of a sighting giving longitude and latitude at the time of the report. He spent the rest of his time pondering on possible methods of engagement should it be necessary. Captain Jackman would have seniority and would call the battle plans but he may give this over to Sylvian as the *Endeavour* was a class two vessel of eighty-four guns after her reconfiguration. The *Dauntless* was only a class three with sixty guns at her disposal and not the speed of the *Endeavour*.

Sylvian did not have long to find out.

Chapter Seven
Engagement

Sylvian called enter to the knock at his door. It was Mr Fowler. Mr Coombes had passed his compliments and requested that the captain attend the poop deck at his convenience. Sylvian grabbed his coat and hat and headed up to the poop deck where Mr Coombes reported that the ships had been identified as French. Martin reported that the ships were first identified by the *Dauntless* but our own crow had reported that the ships had turned and were sailing towards us in line.

"Do we know how many, Mr Coombes?" asked Sylvian as he took up his spyglass.

"Two, sir, we think, from what we could see when they took to port, sir," replied Martin.

"Mr Newman, please send a flag to the *Dauntless* and ask her how she wishes to proceed," asked Sylvian

"Aye, sir," said young Jack as he headed to the Forecastle.

"Lieutenant Wood and Mr Simms," shouted Sylvian. "Make ready the gun decks for port and starboard fire if you please."

"Aye, sir," was the reply from both with the gravelly voice of Albert almost drowned out by William's.

"Sir," said Jack Newman rather out of breath after his run from the Forecastle. "The *Dauntless* reports that the *Endeavour* should take the lead, she awaits your orders, sir."

"Thank you, Lieutenant," said Sylvian, deep in thought.

"Martin," said Sylvian after a pause to think and having taken up his spyglass to see how far the two French men of war had gained. "Let out full sail and take us in front of the *Dauntless* if you please. Mr Newman, semaphore the *Dauntless* to follow close to our stern and to remember Mr Pepys."

"Sir," said Jack quizzically.

"Away to it, young Jack, and all will be explained," said Sylvian, hurrying the boy on.

"Pepys, sir," asked Martin, having completed full sail and the ship pulling hard in the wind.

"Mr Stubbings, bring her fifteen degrees to starboard as we pass the *Dauntless*, please," commanded Sylvian.

"Aye, sir, fifteen degrees to starboard, sir," repeated Jacob.

"Yes, Martin, the two French frigates are sailing as ships of the line as shall we, however we shall give them the thought that we are about to flee by steering to port, when they take action, we shall come back to starboard and come between the two-line astern. That will give us the advantage of full broadside," explained Sylvian.

"Indeed, sir," said Martin giving the manoeuvre a great deal of thought.

"Sir, the *Dauntless* reports understood, sir, I wish I did, sir," said young Jack.

"Then watch Mr Newman, and you may learn," said Sylvian as they completed their sail past the *Dauntless* and Jacob brought them fifteen degrees to port.

"Mr Ottershaw," shouted Sylvian to his lieutenant of the deck. "Have the sails taken back in if you please, we have no desire to lose the *Dauntless*."

"Aye aye, sir," said Walter who at forty-two was a career lieutenant and would not advance past third class. He was however good at his task and had a wonderful rapport with the crew, who responded to him well.

Sylvian watched carefully as the two frigates started to turn in response to the *Endeavour*'s move to port. "Mr Gant, have Mr Wood and Mr Simms aware that we shall be cutting the two frigates and will require both broadsides, if you please?" asked Sylvian.

"Aye, sir," replied Steven as he made his way quickly from the poop deck.

"Mr Stubbings bring the ship hard to port fifty degrees on my command, let us hope and with God's good favour we shall maintain wind, gentlemen," said Sylvian.

"Aye, sir, fifty degrees to port on your command," repeated Jacob.

The four ships closed in on one another and there was less than a quarter mile between them but Sylvian's manoeuvre and the response by the French had taken the two English ships in an arch past the French.

"Now, Mr Stubbings," shouted Sylvian as they all held tight as the *Endeavour* took a lean hard to starboard as the wind chased the sails from one side to the next. Sylvian glanced astern to the *Dauntless* and she had done the same. The French had maintained their course as they must have been confused at the move made by the British.

"Bring her straight, Mr Stubbings," Sylvian shouted and the bow of the ship was now some fifty yards and facing two French frigates to their port sides. The frigates commenced firing and their cannon shot found only water on each side of the *Endeavour*. Sylvian glanced back and could see that Captain Jackman had brought the *Dauntless* close and had moved slightly to port. The frigates were now both firing furiously at the approaching British causing some superficial damage to deck railings and glancing blows to the side of the ship.

"Mr Stubbings, take me right between those two ships and be precise on distance," commanded Sylvian.

"Mr Ottershaw, take in sail," his captain shouted.

The *Endeavour* had slowed her pace through lack of wind but sailed straight between the two frigates and unleashed a broadside on port and starboard guns that filled the air with smoke and noise, the two frigates had no reply as they had only two cannons on their stern and two on their bow. One from the port ship took a direct hit on the *Endeavour*'s upper gun deck, but the thick bulkheads held well to the small cannon ball and she skidded down the side of the ship, however the shot from the *Endeavour* had found her powder store which caught and lifted the ship into the air. The *Dauntless* repeated the scathing attack and brought down the stern mast of the frigate to starboard and almost immediately they raised the flag of surrender.

The *Endeavour* came alongside the French ship gently and grappling hooks were sent over and the boarding ramp was laid across. The marines boarded in a well rehearsed manner and encircled the deck of the French frigate and its crew, and took possession of the vessel. The *Dauntless* attempted to pick up survivors from the portside ship that had taken a direct hit to her powder store, just as their ship gave herself to the waves.

The day was overcast and the air smelt of sulphur as the wind had now turned to a breeze. The *Endeavour* buzzed with action as the officers had the men to their duties and Captain Wood had his marines lined around the deck of the French frigate and its crew.

"My god, sir," said Martin. "My compliments, sir," he said rather astounded at what he had just witnessed.

"Thank you, Martin, our ship's company did very well indeed, now will you please join me on the Frenchy so that we take her as prize. Mr Gant, a report on casualties and the condition of the *Endeavour* if you please, Mr Selway the same for the French frigate if you would be so kind," said Sylvian as he replaced his hat which he had removed during the battle.

"Aye, sir," said the two officers as they raced off to their duties.

Sylvian and Martin made their way down the highly glossed new wooden steps from the poop deck and to the port side gate. The frigate was somewhat lower than the *Endeavour* and required the two officers to take a few steps down the bulkhead ladder to reach the boarding ramp. Once on board the frigate Sylvian was presented to Captain Flo'rence Dessault of zee free French Navvy as he put it. He had no command of English and Martin was able to translate. He was not sure that such a manoeuvre was as a gentleman on the seas should behave, however he now surrendered his ship and her company. Sylvian thanked him for the compliment which absolutely infuriated this pompous little French man, and accepted his sword and his ship. Sylvian told him that he would be a guest on the *Endeavour* and his men would be shared between the two British ships until their arrival in Halifax in the Dominion of Canada, where they would be held until a prison ship could carry them back to England.

Sylvian tasked Martin with ensuring all of the French officers and crew were transferred to the *Endeavour* and *Dauntless* and had a quick look around the frigate. She would make a fine prize as she was newly constructed and had been quite well appointed. Mr Selway reported that the ship was well stocked for what seemed a long voyage. He said that the aft cargo hold was well secured and he had Mr Caxton and his men working on the locks. Sylvian asked Peter to let him know what had been found within when they had succeeded. He then made his way down to the captain's cabin. He found it to be about a quarter of the size of the *Endeavour*'s. He searched around in the captain's writing desk and found his orders and some sealed parchments wrapped in a leather folder. They unfortunately were all in French but one word on the front of the sealed parchment caught his eye immediately. 'Messrs. Billings'. A shiver ran through his body and try as he might he could not translate the words within. Nonetheless that name again was here to haunt him. He continued to look around the room and found the captain's charts and pulled a few from their round cubby holes and laid them on the desk. The second one down had a clear route marked out for Lake Ontario and most especially Horse Island off Sacketts Harbour. He was joined by Captain Wood who reported that all was correct on the ship and did Sylvian wish him to dismiss his marines back to the *Endeavour*. Sylvian asked him to leave a lieutenant and ten men aboard the frigate and by all means dismiss the rest of his men back to the *Endeavour*. Sylvian gathered up the charts and carried them back up and onto the main deck where, he was met by Mr Selway. Peter informed him that they had found sealed boxes and he would like the captain to attend before they were opened. Sylvian handed the charts and leather pouch to Midshipman Aitchinson and asked him to ensure they got to his quarters. He then followed Peter down to the lower decks and to the store room. He found Master at Arms Robert Caxton and his men in the room.

"Mr Caxton, such a small room and so stuffy, do you think that your men could wait outside whilst we take a look at these boxes?" asked Sylvian, as he thought he knew what might be within and did not wish it to be common knowledge. Mr Caxton dismissed his three men to outside the room and Peter closed the door and stood in front of it. "Go ahead, Robert, and open one of the boxes as I think all three will contain the same," said Sylvian.

Robert worked his jemmy on the lock and soon forced out the rivets that held it tight. The lock came away and Robert looked at his captain in the light of the oil lamp. "Open her up and let us see if I am right," he said.

Robert opened the box and just stood and glared at the contents. He looked up at Sylvian and the look on his face was amazement.

"Mmmm," said Sylvian. "More money than you or I will ever see. This money was intended for the Union to build a port and ships so that they may invade the sovereign Dominion of the Canadas Robert. What we have discovered in this room must remain only with us and not to be repeated outside of this room. There are many who would wish to lay their hands on such a find. It shall go to our cause and will fund our defence of the Canadas from any invasion from the Union, do you agree, gentlemen?" he asked.

Robert closed the lid and banged the rivets back into place. He then stood and looked at his captain and saluted. "You have my word, sir, on my life."

"Thank you, Robert, you shall not be forgotten for your work here this day," said Sylvian as he returned the master's salute. "Now if you please could you escort your men back up on deck and ask the good lieutenant of marines to attend here immediately. We shall say, when asked, that we have discovered what appears to be a new type of explosive and we believe it to be highly volatile, is that clear, gentlemen?" concluded Sylvian. Both men said aye and again saluted their officer before Mr Caxton left the room.

Sylvian and Peter took to the outside of the room with the oil lamp, closed the door and awaited the arrival of the lieutenant of marines.

Back in his office on board the *Endeavour* Sylvian was joined by Captain Jackman, Lt Stockwell, Martin Coombes and Steven Gant. Sylvian explained to them all what had been found on board the French frigate Nantes. He told them that he had tasked his marines to guard the hold around the clock and no one but himself and Mr Coombes were permitted entry. Sylvian explained that except those that were currently in the office and Mr Caxton and Peter Selway the story had been spread that they had discovered a new type of explosive substance and that it was quite volatile.

Captain Jackman asked if the crew on board his ship needed to know and it was agreed that no more was to be said on the matter. Sylvian had asked Martin to translate some of the documents that he had found in the captain's cabin on board the Nantes, but without rush, as they must get to sea. Sylvian asked Mr Coombes to captain the prize with Mr Montrose and John Douglas as his lieutenants, and with men to be ferried from the

Dauntless, and also some of Sylvian's complement. They should make haste to get under way soon. Sylvian asked Mr Gant to take over as first officer on the *Endeavour*.

With Captain Jackman and Henry piped off the *Endeavour*, and on their way back to the *Dauntless*, Sylvian asked Robert Carlisle if he and his men would mind transferring to the Nantes. Sylvian confided in Robert concerning the find and said that he would feel much safer if his team were aboard to assist the marines. Captain Wood was more than happy for Robert to assume command under Lieutenant Coombes of his marines and their officer.

With makeshift repairs to the minor damage of the *Endeavour* and repairs ongoing on the Nantes, Sylvian instructed his carpenter and mates to remain aboard the Nantes and make running repairs as they were underway. With that done, and all men where they should be, Sylvian asked Mr Gant to get them underway and behind the Nantes, with the *Dauntless* taking the lead. The ship came alive to the called commands, and Sylvian remained on the forecastle deck and watched as slowly the three ships came into line.

The wind was good and, in their favour, and the *Endeavour* cut through the waves with ease. A swell had built up and the Nantes was running quite well although somewhat disabled with lack of sail. It would be slow going until they had rope tied the mast back into place and winched up the yardarms and back into place to take sail.

They had been three weeks to sea and the weather had been kind but changeable. The early cold chill of the coming winter in this northern hemisphere was starting to make itself known, and coats and sou'westers were now a common sight. The crew had thanked their captain for their uniforms which had kept them warm against the chill. Most now wore shoes that Sylvian had purchased as a bulk purchase from the purser's store. They were comfortable, flexible and had been fitted with rubber soles. They were manufactured in the Union and had been acquired before trade had been stopped.

Young Midshipman Rupert Watts, had set too and plotted their position by sextant and was within three miles of Sylvian's plot. Admirable work and was commended by Sylvian but was reminded that mathematics was the most part of the lieutenant's exam. He pushed the issue with all of his midshipman that he had been sea training since the engagement, on a daily basis.

However, it did show them to be only two days out from Halifax. Sylvian found himself quite excited to be getting back to the port and the Dominion and seeing the now Admiral Albright as he had the orders from the admiralty in his folder. He had also seen in the London Gazette that King George had honoured him with a knighthood for his service to the Dominion of the Canadas. He would say nothing of this as he was sure that it would be contained within his pouch. He had worn his naval medal for gallantry with pride since it was awarded to him. Sylvian and his team were presented with the medals at a ceremony at the admiral's building in Portsmouth, by the first sea lord himself, First Baron James Gambier. The ceremony was quite some to do and had humbled Jacko to the point that only a stiff rum afterwards brought him back to his senses. Sylvian could not remember a time in his life when he had been filled with so much pride for his fellow man. He was proud of them all.

Two days had passed and the bell had been rung to call the ship's company to order. Sylvian was just completing his log entry for yesterday and put down his quill and made ready to go on deck. Mr Fowler had brushed down his coat and hat and had put it on the stand that the carpenter had made to keep his coat in shape. On his arrival on deck, Mr Gant reported the ship all correct and indicated the port of Halifax. They had taken in sail and slowed to give the other two ships time. The Nantes had dropped anchor in the basin as instructed by flag. The *Dauntless* was already docked leaving just one pier free. Sylvian was shocked at the growth of the port. He could see three new piers and what looked to be a dry dock for repair and ship building. He could see the *Renown*, Antelope and Hampshire but not the Sheffield.

"Mr Gant, take her into dock if you please," asked Sylvian.

"Aye, sir," replied Mr Gant. This being the first he had taken a ship into port. He had the men scurrying about the rigging and deck with Jason Baker at the helm the ship cruised in to dock perfectly. The mateys had her tied and secure in a trice.

"Sir, I am pleased to report the *Endeavour* is docked and secured to port, sir," said Steven.

"Thank you, Mr Gant, well done to you, a fine first docking," said Sylvian. "And well done to you, Mr Baker, for your helmsman ship. You are dismissed, gentlemen." Jason secured the wheel and made away quickly to his bunk for a fine quart of beer is what he had promised himself at the local inn.

Sylvian looked down at the dock at the amassed townspeople who had been fascinated to watch the three ships come into port. He did not see what he wanted to see.

Sylvian returned to his cabin to retrieve his leather folder and piles of parchment for the admiral. With all now secured in his captain's case he made his way back on deck. The ship was quiet with all rates below deck and some getting ready to have shore time. Mr Newman reported that the prisoners were being brought up by the marines and would be transferred to the fort. Mr Newman was officer of the watch and was informed by Sylvian that he would be at the fort reporting to the admiral. The bo'sun piped him from the ship with the duty watch lined up to attention and Mr Newman giving the salute.

He found himself uneasy on his sea legs and just stood on the dock for a couple of minutes. The row boat from the Nantes had arrived at the pier ladder and Sylvian was joined by Mr Coombes. They were happy to be back on land but were already missing the sea. Mr Coombes excused himself with a salute and a report that all was well on the Nantes. It was now 4.30 p.m. and they would meet for supper in the officers' mess at the fort.

Sylvian headed for the fort and was greeted by a few friendly faces and many congratulations on his promotion. He was stopped by a hand that grasped his arm and when he turned, he saw the smiling face of Abigail his sister-in-law. They hugged and Sylvian asked as to her health. She reported that he was an uncle to a fine boy called Jack and she could not wait to introduce him. She asked of her husband and Sylvian gave her all the details of Jack and how well he was doing at medical school. She passed on her father's invitation to dinner tomorrow evening which he gracefully accepted.

Sylvian found the fort quite as he had left it, with little change. It was now a bright sunny day with a chill in the air and the leaves on the trees changing colour and spreading their beauty across the hillside. On his arrival at the fort, he found good security and was booked in by the rounders which was obviously as a result of Henry Stockwell's changes.

He made his way up to the commodores office and found that he now had a clerk. He presented himself to this unknown man and was asked to wait. He knocked on the commodore's door and entered, Sylvian could not hear but a mumble until he heard quite clearly, "Captain Mountjoy, tell that man to get his arse in here on the double, man." Sylvian heard and started for the door and passed the shocked clerk as he exited and shut the door behind him. James was up and out from behind his desk as fast as his legs would carry him and had Sylvian's hand in his and his other hand on his shoulder in no time.

"My dear boy, Sylvian, it is so good to have you back and after all that had gone before in Kingston. And captain no less, and damn well deserved I am sure. Come, come sit down you obviously have much to tell me," he said as he moved around his desk and bellowed for his clerk. The door opened and his clerk was immediately informed that he had precisely two minutes to have two large glasses of brandy on his desk before being hung from the yardarm. Sylvian was so pleased to be back with this man he so respected.

"So, damn it, sir, you are just one rank below me for god's sake, no stopping a good man I say," said James.

"Two sir, well actually three, sir," said Sylvian with a smile to his face.

"No, sir, just the one... what are you smiling at, young Sylvian Mountjoy," asked James.

Sylvian pulled the commission parchment from his case and handed it to the admiral. James took the parchment and broke the seal, settled back in his chair and started to read. His clerk returned to the office with two glasses and a full decanter of brandy. He poured two large glasses and James picked his up whilst not stopping his read. He put the paper down on his desk and looked at Sylvian. "Did you know of this?" he asked.

"Yes, sir, and might I say I have so been looking forward to this moment when I should see your face as it is, for I know of no man who I would wish to see so, sir," said Sylvian as he stood up and saluted his admiral.

"Missed out the vice and moved me straight up to rear admiral, young Sylvian, with military responsibility of the dominion no less," he said in total shock.

"Mmmmm, that's not all, sir," said Sylvian as he pulled out another parchment from his case and handed it to James. James took the parchment and opened it as he had the other and then just shot to his feet.

"Did you know this too?" he blustered.

"I saw it in the London Gazette, sir, when I was at the admiralty." Sylvian picked up his glass and stood up, raised his glass and said, "To Sir James William Albright KCB, Rear Admiral of His Majesty's Royal Navy," and took a long drink of the sharp liquid.

"To Captain Sylvian Mountjoy, Medal of Gallantry, His Majesty's Royal Navy," said James taking a large sip from his glass. "Now, sit-down, boy, and tell me all I need to know, and that's everything, Mountjoy."

They sat for the next hour and Sylvian told James all about his mission and the outcome. James was shocked at the news of Mary and they both raised their glasses to her. James was particularly interested in the papers Sylvian had found and the news from Mr Scott on the possible whereabouts of the man Billings. Sylvian told James what he had found on the prize ship and they agreed to move it to the fort to be secured whilst the prize went in for repair. Sylvian gave James the rest of the orders that he had brought with him and they discussed the contents and what action might be taken. Sylvian made recommendation to his admiral regarding the prize and who he thought should captain her. They were both pleased to see that Huw Jones had received his posted captaincy and would continue as captain of the *Renown*. They were disturbed by the admiral's clerk who announced that the admiral's captains and first officers were now assembled in the meeting room. Sylvian asked if he may go first and greet his fellow officers as he had not seen them for some time, and most had seen him last as a lieutenant. He would then love the honour of introducing his admiral to the officers under his command that is if the admiral would not mind waiting for ten minutes, and then send his clerk when he was ready. It would mean so much to the men.

James agreed and sent Sylvian on his way. When Sylvian entered the room there was much conversation going on but the room fell silent when they saw him. Andrew was the first to greet his friend and they shook hands and hugged; Andrew was indeed so saddened by the news of Mary. Richard was the next to congratulate Sylvian and there were so many questions fired at him that he was finding it so difficult to keep up with his answers. He was really pleased when the admiral's clerk entered the room and nodded to Sylvian.

"Gentlemen, gentlemen," said Sylvian. "May I please have your attention and would you join me in welcoming Rear Admiral Sir James William Albright KCB, of his Majesty's Royal Navy." The faces about him were an absolute picture as James walked into the room. The place erupted into applause for this popular and well-respected man.

"Gentlemen, thank you all," said James as he moved to the head of the table and waved his arms to indicate for them all to sit. "My grateful thanks to you all, it is only through all of your efforts that I stand before you so today. We again have within our merry band, now a captain and with a fine ship I am told, Sylvian Mountjoy. Join with me in my congratulations on his promotion, and well deserved it is, as is, gentlemen, Mr Jones my trusted commander is now a posted captain and shall captain the *Renown*. Now young Mountjoy has brought much news from home not least of all which I sadly ask you to stand and share with me the very sad news of Sylvian's wife Mary. Some of you knew her and have given great account of what a fine woman she was. We shall take a minute." They all stood and bowed their heads. It was too touching a moment for Sylvian as he allowed tears to roll from his eyes and took his handkerchief to them but not without notice.

"Now to more news, our friend and fellow captain, Mr Richard Swain, is hereby promoted to commodore and his first lieutenant young Gordon is now the captain of HMS Hampshire and shall hold that post as captain until posted." The room erupted into applause to which Richard and Gordon stood to a bow.

"Furthermore Captain Jackman has been promoted to vice admiral to serve as my second in command." Again, applause to a well-chosen appointment. Caruthers Jackman was a good solid man and was well respected for his fairness and firmness. "Lieutenant Stockwell will serve as Captain of the *Dauntless* and will remain so until posted." again applause took the room and Henry's face was an absolute picture. Eventually he looked over at Sylvian and a broad grin shot across his face.

"Captain Mountjoy has increased our dominion fleet with a prize today, she was called the Nantes but she is to be commissioned as the *Bedford* and Sylvian has suggested that she should be captained by Lieutenant Martin Coombes who is new to our group. Mr Coombes, you will in the first instance be promoted to the rank of commander until I can have the ship accepted into the fleet and have you posted as captain. Mr Mountjoy has spoken very highly of you and we welcome you to what is now known as the Dominion Fleet. The first sea lord has seen fit to create this fleet and to put myself at its head. We shall have need of more ships and ports, gentlemen, to protect this sovereign land of His Majesty's. Please join me in welcoming Mr Coombes to our ranks." Another round of applause went amongst the group and Martin stood and took a bow to those assembled before leaning across and taking Sylvian's hand in a firm grip.

"We here at Halifax have been given the duty to ensure that the Dominion of Canada, her land and seas as well as her people are protected from foreign invasion and domestic threat. Now, gentlemen, this is quite a task, as you know Britain is defending itself against the tyranny of the French and Spanish, therefore this command will be engaged solely in the defence of Canada and what is believed to be the interests of the Union in securing this soil for her own purposes. We shall therefore be engaged in building our own ships, recruiting and training our own men and building and training an army of Canadians for Canadians, and gentlemen, this task starts now and you all shall be the forefathers of this *Endeavour*. I am sure that after this is all done the outfitters in Halifax will be very pleased to receive our coin," said the admiral raising his voice as he concluded. The room erupted into applause as all who now stood and clapped for their admiral looked at one another, some in trepidation and some with excitement at the prospect. Sylvian fitted firmly into the latter.

As the applause died down and the men retook their seats the admiral continued. "Each one of you shall be granted land to build your home, if it is to be within the bounds of the city of Halifax then the size shall be apportioned as per your rank. You may choose land outside of the city and will be granted land as per your rank and station. You may if you so wish bring your families over to the Dominion and choose to settle here. If that is so then we shall have them transported here. At this time, gentlemen, the Dominion of Canada is a growing new world and we have been chosen as her protectors to make it our homes and bring up our families here. Commodore Swain, it shall be your responsibility to take on the task of assisting our men in becoming more settled and at home, funds and manpower will be made available to assist you and of course the office of my vice admiral is there if needed. Vice Admiral Jackman will have the duty of building up Halifax's defences and building new ships and recruiting men. You will have your own staff for which some of you may be chosen. Mr Mountjoy has been tasked by the admiralty to root out the traitor Billings who is believed to be back here in the Canadas or working for the Union in the area of Lake Ontario. I am sure if Mountjoy can cause some damage to the union effort during the course of his tracking down the traitor, he will do so. It has been ordered by the war department that our good Colonel Gage shall head the Canadian land forces under my authority. He will form a defensible regiment from what military strength he has and those he shall garner from the good settlers of the Dominion. Now one last thing, gentlemen, before we shall all retire to the mess for supper. We have a long and arduous task ahead of us. Our intelligence tells us that the Union is close to having the men and ships to invade our colony, and we hope that Mr Mountjoy and his army compatriot Captain Carlisle can be successful in giving us a few more years to prepare for such. However, we must now work hard to prepare ourselves to defend the Dominion and her people," he concluded and took his seat. The room was silent as each mind processed the many questions that they had. For here they were and, as it looked, here they would stay.

All of the men stood and applauded the admiral although still unsure of what it all should mean to them; however, they were one hundred percent behind Admiral Albright.

The meeting continued for another half hour with many questions asked and it was agreed that each captain would inform his crew of what had been ordered and each ship would have a liaison officer to Commodore Swain's office. They would have the winter to put these plans together and to make a start on recruitment, training and ship building. The carpenters of Bedford Basin would be increased in number and apprentices and labourers taken on. Special crews would be put together to fell trees and create lumber mills to process the wood for ship and house building.

***

Sylvian enjoyed his meal in the mess and Admiral Albright requested a meeting with him tomorrow after lunch. Sylvian then returned to the *Endeavour* to find Mr Newman on watch who reported the ship all correct with a complement of one lieutenant second class, two third class and three midshipmen with a total of one hundred and forty crew members. He reported that Mr Selway and Mr Gant had taken his crew of special ratings to the fort at the top of the hill. Sylvian thanked Mr Newman for his report and retired to his cabin.

Mr Fowler had lain out his shirt and under garments with new stockings and fresh breeches. Sylvian poured himself rather a large single malt and sat to his desk. The thought of his home in Portsmouth, his son and of course the two ladies in his life, his mother and Wendy. What to do he wondered. He wished Jack was here so that the two could discuss his dilemma, he knew he would have to make some sort of commitment to the admiral on the morrow and wondered what he should say. He loved what he had now with his career and this damn fine ship, however the thought of being away from his England and permanently residing here in the Dominion was not one decision he was sure he could make. As fine as Canada was and indeed a beautiful country, unfortunately it was not England. He decided to sleep on it and so he completed the consumption of this very fine malt and made his way to his welcome bunk and settled down for the night.

The morning on this Sunday the twenty seventh day of September in the year of eighteen seven was a fine one indeed. The sun was low in the sky but the temperature was remarkably warm. Sylvian was on the forecastle deck and was checking on the condition and cleanliness of his ship. He had decided to do a full and unaccompanied inspection and he had thus far completed most of the ship except the poop deck which would come next. Mr Douglas had the watch and had done well to stay out of his captain's way. He had seen that his captain had been preoccupied with thought after giving his report. Sylvian had a restless night and had risen early. He had managed to clear quite a bit of his paperwork and had completed his inspection of the purser's accounts, which were admirably in order. A fine English breakfast had been enjoyed but without tea as they awaited the rather in demand tea leaves to arrive, he endured coffee instead which he just had not gained a taste for. Now having completed his inspection he asked Mr Douglas to pass his compliments to the ship's company on a well-kept ship.

Having completed his paperwork and inspection Sylvian made his way to the fort to ensure that the gold had been stored securely in the fort's vaults. He met Martin at the gate office who had been given charge to take the gold on inventory. Martin and Sylvian made their way down to the vault which even now was quite heavily guarded. The weighing process was near completion and the fort's purser was tallying up the figures. "Sir, we have four boxes, there are fifty bars in each box. They are ten pounds in weight, sir. They have quite some value, sir; I would need to work out that value in dollars, sir, as that would be the currency, we do use for our trade here. We are getting in the region of $20 to the ounce so that would be $320 to the pound, sir, you have let me see." He paused and looked at his notes. "Five hundred pounds in each box, so a total of two thousand pounds in weightm sir," he concluded.

"Phew," said Martin.

"So, what monetary value in dollars does this equate to, good purser," said Sylvian.

"Well, sirs, which does come to about $640,000, sir. That is a sizeable sum and no mistake," replied the purser as he scratched the black area above his eye with his charcoal, which was obviously his habit.

"Very good, purser, please ensure that your numbers are committed to parchment and sent to the admiral with some haste," said Sylvian.

Martin and Sylvian left the vault and headed up to the officers' mess along the stone corridors of this fine building. On their arrival they found

Andrew and Richard with a mug of ale each. The two men joined them and ordered their own ale and gave their order for lunch.

"So good to see you back safe and sound, Sylvian, our deepest condolences on what has happened to the sweet Mary. Her memory shall remain with me forever," said Andrew. "It does not seem but a short time that we had all just met and enjoyed such a fine meal in the rose garden of the Rose and Crown. That is the memory that shall stay with me forever."

"Yes, such fond memories we have, the one that keeps coming to me is when my dear Mary went after Juno after the trial and kissed his cheek. She could always see the good in a man," said Sylvian.

Richard lifted his mug and said, "To Mary Mountjoy, one of the pure ones snatched from us before her time and to be avenged." All four men took up their mugs and raised them to Mary Mountjoy.

They were soon joined by Captain Sinclair who whilst sharing a drink with them asked Sylvian if he and his men could make use of the fort on the hill alongside his men. He felt that for his men to share some of the training with Sylvian's crew it would enhance their capability when soon they will enter the Union to commence their mission. Sylvian agreed wholeheartedly and asked that he should go ahead and move his men in, however their first task would be to improve the lodgings to home the extra men. Robert thanked him and said that they would start this very afternoon.

Neither Sylvian nor Martin mentioned anything of the fortune in gold that sat in the vaults of this fort during the meal as they thought it better that if the admiral wished to share that information it was his privilege to do so. After the meal the five went their separate ways and Sylvian presented himself to the admiral's clerk. He soon found himself in front of the admiral's desk and invited to sit.

"So, young Sylvian, did we get this elusive coin moved from the *Bedford* and into the vaults?" he asked.

"Indeed, sir, it was dealt with first thing this morning and the *Bedford* has been moved into the repair basin, sir," reported Sylvian.

"So, what was the number of boxes that we had and in what form do we have this coin, Captain?" asked Admiral Albright.

"Well, sir, there were four boxes in total, when opened they were found to contain fifty, ten-pound bars of gold, sir."

"Good lord, sir, let me see sixteen ounces to the pound at around $20 to the ounce gives us three hundred and… let's see… $20 per pound, and each bar weighs ten pounds, would give us $3,020 per bar, sir. Good God, Sylvian, you say fifty bars, sir, well that gives us one hundred and, no wait a minute, oh yes that is right, $160,000, sir. My God, man, we could build ten ships and a whole port with that money and still have change to boot," he concluded slamming his pen to the desk and looking at Sylvian in awe.

"In each box, sir," said Sylvian. "Fifty bars in each box sir, four boxes," said Sylvian.

"In each box, sir, well, young Mountjoy," he said picking up his pen and dipping it in his inkwell and putting a shaky hand to paper. "That makes a total of $640,000, sir. What on earth are we to do, I surely must report this to the admiralty, and at the very least the governor general…"

"Sir, might I suggest that we should leave out the governor general and the admiralty at this time as they would have no idea that this amount has come into our possession, and indeed from the French, sir. This money should be put to good use in defending the Dominion against the French and the Union as is your total remit, it seems rather apt, sir, if you agree, that they should pay for us to defend against them," exclaimed Sylvian. "And, sir, I am so sure that this money was intended for Nathaniel Billings to give out to the Union and further build up his credibility with his new masters. Let alone build up the Union's capability to attack the Dominion and its people, sir."

The admiral sat back in his chair and looked long and hard at Sylvian. "You are absolutely right, young Mountjoy. We must put this coin to good use and defend this new country; we must help to build her as she becomes our new home and her people our neighbours. I shall report to the admiralty that we have taken on the *Bedford* as part of the Dominion fleet and nothing of the assets that she carried. Good, well that is decided then. Now then, young Mountjoy, what are your plans for this winter and your team," he asked.

"Well, sir, Captain Sinclair and his men will be joining us at the fort and will undergo training with my men. That is, sir, until they set off on their mission," answered Sylvian.

"Mmmm," said the admiral with caution to his voice. "What do you know of this man, Sylvian?"

"Well, sir, I would not be here today if it was not for him, firstly, he took a musket ball for me at Kingston and secondly, sir, he knocked me out in France," he replied.

"Ahh, so he was the lieutenant that came to your aid at Kingston when you had come against the traitor colonel and his men. But what of this knocking you out in France?" he asked.

"Well, sir… when I had learnt of Mary's death, I had taken to a mind that I would not normally accept as my behaviour and had decided to go on a lone pursuit of the traitor Billings. Captain Sinclair persuaded me otherwise with a cosh to the back of my head, and had me contained until I had regained my mind, sir," he explained.

"Then I should thank this man, he obviously thinks quite highly of you, dear boy. In that case I think it would be good for you to work with the army and show them some of the ropes that you and your men have perfected. Now what of your mission in the spring?" he asked.

"Sir, shall I remain as captain of the *Endeavour* or would you wish me to take on a lesser ship and allow a more senior captain to take her or, indeed no ship at all?" asked Sylvian.

"I have not given thought to this, young Mountjoy. It would seem quite the right thing if one of my more senior captains should take her," he said again sitting back in his chair and pushing his fingertips together in great thought. "It would seem to me, Sylvian, that the very purpose of the missions we set you is at the very least daring and downright dangerous, therefore I feel it prudent that you should have the tools to do the job, sir. The *Endeavour* I grant is a fine ship and most obviously a class two vessel, however you shall need the power she offers in both armoury and speed. Now be that in pursuit or, making well your freedom on completion of your mission. No, sir, I feel it necessary that you keep your command and let that be an end to it."

"I thank you, sir," said Sylvian, "then this winter my men and I will concentrate our efforts in forming our plan on our search for the traitor

Billings. We have some good intelligence from the Nantes now *Bedford* after her capture. Commander Coombes shall brief me this afternoon on his translation of the documents, but from what I have seen thus far, we believe he may be on Horse Island. That is in Lake Ontario and just off the port of Sacketts Harbour which, if you remember, sir, from my report, was indeed the firm favourite for the base of the Union's planned invasion."

"Indeed, Mountjoy, well I shall also have need of you at the fort as and when we start to run some of these midshipmen through the exam for lieutenant. We shall need to build our complement and as new ships come online, we must ensure that we have only the best and well-trained officers and men to complement them. That sir, shall fall to you," replied the admiral.

"How, sir?" asked Sylvian.

"We shall have need of a school for training our officers and men and from what I have heard from my men, you are one of the best candidates to make this happen. Now you shall work under the auspices of Commodore Swain for this task and you may choose what men you intend for this position to aid you in your endeavour to get this thing up and running," replied the admiral.

"I see, sir," said Sylvian. "I shall need to juggle a little, sir, but I will give it my all."

"That place on the outside of town, you know the place, where your men trained, you had the area cleared by the tree fellows. Now I should think that would make an excellent place to build a training school would you think," said Admiral Albright.

"Indeed, sir, far enough from town to not cause too much disruption to the daily lives of the town's folk, and yet close enough for convenience. I shall ask around, sir, and see if I cannot find a surveyor and some builders who may wish to take on the task. Sir, what budget should I put to this?" Sylvian asked.

"I shall send a note to the fort purser that you shall have funds as you need them, obviously all of the bills and such must go through the purser who will see to their payment and accounting, which, young Sylvian, you know so well having sorted my accounts on the Antelope. So much has happened since, my boy, so much," he concluded.

"Then, sir, I must be about my duties, I need to get up to the wooden fort and see how my men settle, sir, and of course Captain Carlisle's team and then I shall return to the ship for the night, sir, unless of course you have need of me," said Sylvian as he took up his hat and stood before the admiral's desk.

"Not at all, young Sylvian, it was good to talk and set our paths a little more clearly. You should also take time to think about where you would like to set your home. We shall talk of that when next we meet. Now away with you," he said with that dismissive gesture he always had.

Sylvian found the fort in a good state and was piped through the gate by Mr Hardcastle before doing his inspection. He found that Robert and Sergeant Strong had organised their men well and together with some of his team had made a start on extending the accommodation block and also the mess area. Mr Fitzwalter had come forward with some good ideas on the extension and had assumed the foreman's role in setting the men to their task. Sylvian made his way to his office and had asked Mr Gant and Mr Selway to join him in his office at their convenience. The two men had presented themselves almost at the time Sylvian arrived. Sylvian placed his hat on the desk and asked the two men to take a seat.

"Gentlemen, I have a conundrum to solve and will need the help of my two lieutenants. The admiral has seen fit to confirm my captaincy of the *Endeavour* with the crew I currently have, now Steven, Peter, I do not have a first lieutenant now that Mr Coombes has command of the *Bedford* so, it must be either one of you. I have the utmost faith in you both, so which one shall it be?" asked Sylvian looking at the two faces before him. Both now had concerned looks and sent darted looks to one another and ended almost in embarrassment between the two.

"Sir, with respect, I think it should be Mr Gant as he has seniority and experience and would make an excellent second in command," said Peter.

"No, sir, I do not agree. Mr Selway is an excellent candidate for the role, he is young and extremely knowledgeable and has an enviable relationship with the crew, sir," responded Steven.

"As I thought," said Sylvian sitting back in his chair and looking at the two fine men in front of him. "You have a great deal of respect for one another and indeed, work well together." He paused and took in the two faces that had smiled at one another. "So, as I do not wish to lose either of you from my team you shall remain so and I shall find another. However, you are now promoted to lieutenant first class with special roles within the team and also in the new training school to be built overlooking Bedford Basin. We are to build up our team of special servicemen, there will be two groups, group A which, Steven, you shall command, and group B which shall be your command, Peter. Each group will have twenty men selected by yourselves and your officers, those you will find and make your presentations to me within the week. These men will be the core for any special services to our king and will also form the instruction staff for the new training school. I need you both now to spend some time and come up with a plan that will set us comfortably on this road to success. Am I clear so far, gentlemen?" Sylvian asked the two men sat in front of him with looks of shock yet excitement on their faces.

"Yes, sir," they both answered together.

"Good, now I shall be returning to the ship this evening as I have a dinner to attend at the Bennett's but shall return tomorrow. Is there anything that you need right now?" he asked.

"No, sir," said both men, again together.

"Okay, thank you, gentlemen, now I must be away if I am not to be late."

Sylvian left the fort and made his way back to the *Endeavour*, it was quite some walk but with a sea breeze and a sunny early autumn day, he found it quite pleasant. He stopped at the fort and had a brief conversation with Mr Scott and Mr Mitchell who were preparing to leave, they were going in the first instance to Kingston and would then enter union territory in search of some more intelligence to add to that which Sylvian had retrieved from the Nantes captain's possessions. Sylvian wished both men a successful trip and a speedy return.

He continued on to the ship and was given a full report by Midshipman Barrett Fitzjohn the duty officer. He asked Mr Fitzjohn if he would add a note to the watch log that Mr Montrose attend his office at nine a.m. in the morning. He told him that he would be off the ship for this evening but would return later and asked him to arrange for a carriage for six thirty. He then went to his cabin and prepared for his evening. It would be nice to spend some time with his brother's family; he knew Jack would be pleased that he had.

Chapter Eight
The Sheffield

Sylvian looked resplendent in his full-dress captain's uniform, young Fowler had done a good job when he steamed the garment using Padraig's pot of water boiling on the stove. James had explained that his mother often did the same for his father's coat before he gave sermon on a Sunday. Young James poked his head around the corner of Sylvian's door and told him that the carriage had arrived.

He soon found himself walking up the steps of the Bennett house and was indeed looking forward to an evening of fine food, wine and conversation. He was shown as he always had into the drawing room where he found Abigail with her baby in her arms and Mr Bennett looking resplendent as always in evening coat and a fine ruffled shirt.

"Ah, Sylvian, my dear boy," said William as he came forward and took Sylvian's hand in a firm grip. "It is so good to see you safe and sound and back with us, and please accept my most sincere of condolences on the death of your good lady. We all felt so bad for you when we heard."

"Thank you, sir, it is very much appreciated," said Sylvian wondering just how they had heard the news.

"Young Jack wrote in his letter of the absolute awful circumstances of Mary's death, I cannot begin to understand such a loss," he said releasing Sylvian's hand and making his way to the decanters. Abigail stood with the baby and walked over to Sylvian, she had tears in her eyes and on her cheeks. Sylvian leaned forward and wiped the tears from her cheeks and kissed her cheek with a brother-in-law's affection.

"Please, young lady, cry ye not, for I have shed all of my tears and hold Mary now in my heart forever. But I thank you for your empathy, as do I for all of you such good people whose family I feel honoured to be a part," said Sylvian. Abigail smiled and offered the child Jack up to his arms. Sylvian took him with such skill and had the boy cradled like a professional. Jack was a little over a month and already had his father's mouth but unmistakably, his mother's eyes.

"Well, young nephew, I am so pleased to meet you as I am sure your father will be on his return, you are indeed a very handsome young man, and not unlike your cousin William who grows so fast," said Sylvian, as he handed young Jack back to his mother and accepted a drink from William. "And what of Mrs Bennett, sir, will she not be joining us this evening?" he asked.

"Good lord yes, dear boy, they were in St Johns and when you arrived Abigail sent a message that you were here and they took the very first stage back, just got here an hour ago, my dear fellow," he said indicating Sylvian to take a seat of which he was just about to take when Annie Bennett came into the room. She marched straight up to Sylvian and threw her arms around his shoulders and kissed his cheek, it made Sylvian blush slightly but he really enjoyed the affection.

"So so good to see you back here and safe, what news we heard of you sent me almost to a faint I can tell you. Such dangerous things you do that I cannot understand why or how you should put yourself in such harm's way," she blurted not once taking her eyes from his.

"He is in the service of the king, my dear, we know young Sylvian deals with what normal men would find." He coughed. "Well, damned difficult, me dear."

"Oh, I know, I know, William, but why does it have to be Sylvian. Anyway, you are back with us and safe,," she said

"For now," said William and received a very scolding look from his wife as she was steering Sylvian to the couch that he had almost seated upon before her arrival.

"You are looking very well, Mrs Bennett, and may I be so bold as to say quite beautiful," said Sylvian as he took her hand whilst she took her seat. William again coughed and Sylvian looked up and smiled at him whilst William raised his eyes and smiled.

"As do you, Abigail, my brother is a very lucky man and I shall make sure that he hears it often," continued Sylvian.

"Why thank you, sir," said Abigail with a giggle.

"Will you please sit down, Sylvian, before I fall into a deep sleep from boredom," said William. Sylvian reached down and took Jack just as he was starting to cry. He gently cradled the boy in his arms and rocked him back and forth and the boy quietened at the rhythm and the feeling of security.

"Now there is a sight, I wish I could paint and hold forever." Sylvian turned and looked up and saw Sarah standing by the door, she wore a regency blue dress with white frills to the collars and neckline, her long fair hair was curled and ran in ringlets down each of her shoulders and onto her breasts. Her piercing green eyes were full of tears and shiny bright. The electricity of attraction filled the air.

"Sarah.!" exclaimed Annie Bennett in a scolding nature, and then she looked at her daughter's face and her eyes which had not left Sylvian's and she knew.

William stood up and looked back and forth at Sylvian and Sarah and drained his glass. "Anyone for port," he said, breaking the silence and the mood.

Sarah walked over and put her hand on Sylvian's arm and leaned forward and kissed his cheek passionately then walked to her father and calmly said, "Yes please, Father." William looked into his daughter's eyes as she wiped away her tears with her back to the room.

"Careful, daughter," he whispered as he kissed her forehead.

Sylvian cleared his throat in utter embarrassment and did not know what to say or how to react. He looked down at young Jack and saw that the boy was sound asleep. Jack's nanny, Elizabeth, had come into the room and she looked at Sylvian and smiled and offered to take the boy. Sylvian gave him up reluctantly and turned back to the group. William stood with a full glass of port in his hand and put it into Sylvian's hand with a smile to his face and a quick wink to his eye.

"Seems the boy has taken to you, Captain," said William as he retook his seat on the sofa next to his wife. "And perhaps not the only one," he concluded, taking a sip from his port.

"Father," scolded Sarah. "I am just pleased to see Sylvian safe and sound and back with us."

"Yes, dear," said William. "As we all are, now, Sylvian, pray tell us in your words of your deeds and how indeed you came to be the captain that sits with us?" he asked.

Sylvian finally took his seat next to Abigail and Sarah took the arm of the couch opposite to him and next to her father. He explained all that had taken place since last he had seen them, with his trip to Kingston, the Indians and of course his incarceration by the false colonel. There were many ohhs and ahhs as he continued with his story. Even Jackson the butler who had come in to tell them that dinner was served stood with mouth wide open and his big eyes staring at the shock of it all. Finally, he stopped them at a pause in Sylvian's most interesting story and announced dinner. They all repaired to the dining room with Abigail taking Sylvian's left arm and of course Sarah on his right. Once dinner had been served Annie implored Sylvian to continue on although it had been her that ohh'ed and ahh'ed the most and clasped her hand to her breast during the violent moments. William was the one to ask most questions to clarify the points of most interest, and also as they were the ones that gave Annie most discomfort.

Sylvian continued on with his story, the taking of the Colossus and what he had found when arriving home. He told them in detail and without too much embellishment of his trip to France and his meeting with Robert Carlisle from Kingston, the attack on the chateau and the traitors they had found. William wanted more detail on how they were dispatched, but Sylvian refused to divulge in the presence of such fair ladies. William was certain that Annie blushed.

With the first and second course cleared away and as they were waiting for their dessert Sylvian had just started on his journey back to England when Jackson entered the room closely followed by Midshipman Fawkes from the *Endeavour*. "Sir, ladies and gentlemen, please do excuse this intrusion on your evening," he said.

"Hat, Archibald," said Sylvian as the nervous young midshipman quickly removed his hat and gave his apologies. "What is it, sir?" asked his captain.

"Sir, the rear admiral has asked me to find you and to give you his compliments, sir, and his apologies to you Mr and Mrs Bennett, but he requires you on a matter of some urgency, sir," reported the young officer.

"Very well, do you have a carriage, Archy?" asked Sylvian.

"Yes, sir, I thought it expedient, sir," he replied.

"Good," said Sylvian as he stood and removed his napkin from his lap. "I shall be out presently." Archy bowed to the family and took his leave.

"Sir, ladies, I must ask you to excuse me as it would seem my admiral has need of me, please accept my deepest apologies," said Sylvian.

"Not at all, dear boy," said William. "Jackson, please bring the captain's coat and hat," he concluded. Sylvian said his goodbyes and received a kiss to the cheek from the three ladies and was soon on his way, having promised to return soon.

He arrived at the fort and made his way directly to the admirals office where he found Admiral Albright and Admiral Jackman and Commodore Swain. Sylvian presented himself to the group and saluted his officers.

"Sylvian, I am so sorry to take you from your evening at the Bennett's, only something has come up that may require your skills and that of your men. I have taken the liberty to send a runner to the fort and asked all of the men to return to the *Endeavour*. Now come around here and look at the chart please," said the admiral as a space was made for him to share the view of the chart that was laid out on the admiral's desk. The admiral had ringed around an area with a small port town called Sebasco in the center. "It would seem that Lieutenant Crumb has himself and the Sheffield either captured or boxed in, he had been on a routine patrol of the New England coastline with strict instructions to report only and not engage with any enemy ships, we do not know as yet what had taken place to find him so. Now our spies tell us that the Sheffield is intact and sits in this small harbour here," he said pointing to the map. "Now I do not think that with this topography and the fact that there are two French ships in the harbour that we shall have much chance of rescuing the Sheffield, however I should like to get Mr Crumb and his crew back to Halifax. And that, sir, is where you come in. What are your thoughts, Mountjoy?" he concluded.

Sylvian studied the map and also the topography further on down the coast. "I think it possible, sir, daring but possible, sir. We could move across land and see how things lie before making our final plan, however I think it prudent to set off immediately," he replied.

"What ships shall you need?" asked the admiral.

"Just the *Endeavour*, sir, too many ships would so easily be spotted by coastal watchers. One ship they will think is just on patrol. Sir, by your leave I would like to set about this task with some urgency as I think time may be in our favour," said Sylvian.

"Very good, Sylvian, well, Godspeed, and get back to us safely," said the admiral.

Sylvian was back to the *Endeavour* as fast as the admiral's carriage could get him. The ship was already alive with activity. As he arrived on deck, he was greeted by Lieutenant Montrose who reported that the admiral had sent an order to make the ship ready. His team had returned from the fort along with Captain Carlisle's and were below decks making ready, all the ships complement had returned from shore, some a little inebriated and the ship was ready to move on the tide. Sylvian thanked him for his report and told him to get the ship underway and out to sea with as much speed as he thought necessary.

It was dark and they only had the port lanterns to go by. There was chill in the wind that with its dampness forced its way through clothes and skin to reach the bones. Sylvian made his way to his cabin where he found Mr Fowler who he tasked to find lieutenants Gant and Selway and ask them to come to the cabin with Captain Carlisle and Mr Fitzwalter at their earliest of conveniences. He felt the ship pull to sail as the *Endeavour* moved gracefully from port and out into the harbour. Sylvian stowed his coat and hat in his room to the side of his office and called for Padraig who arrived instantly to his call. He asked him to bring some brandy and six glasses.

The first to arrive was Mr Fitzwalter closely followed by Lieutenant Gant and Mr Selway. He asked James to find Mr Montrose and if he was free to please attend also. They retired to the dining room together with some charts from Sylvian's office. Sylvian laid out the charts on the table and looked around at his officers. Mr Montrose soon arrived and joined the team.

"Gentlemen, I am sure you are all curious as to why we are finding ourselves back to sea so soon. Well, it would seem that the Sheffield finds herself and her crew captured and being held here," said Sylvian pointing to the map and particularly Sebasco. "We as of yet have no idea as to her current state or that of the crew, however our intelligence leads us to believe that there are two French ships and what would appear to be a Union vessel in the port. The Sheffield had been tasked to patrol and report on the New England coastline and it is my belief that she had been outrun and taken by the two French vessels. As for the Union's involvement we are not sure. We shall however use that fact to our advantage as any destruction or invasion of union property would not escalate a diplomatic situation due to the embarrassment to the Union, well that is the embarrassment of having a British ship in their harbour guarded by French vessels, and possibly indeed, one of their own. We shall not know the exact situation until we indeed see so for ourselves. Now my first instinct is for our teams, including Captain Sinclair's to land here, some way down the coast and make our way on foot to the location and reconnoitre the situation as it stands. What say you?" asked Sylvian.

"Beggin your pardon, sir," said Mr Fitzwalter. "Should we not when we land, sir, take what provisions we may require just in case we is able, sir, to deal with the situation as we do finds it, sir."

"Good point, Mr Fitzwalter, and quite well said, your language lessons are coming on admirably. We shall have to pack quite a bit as we do not know what we are to come up against," replied Sylvian.

"Sir, I think it might be prudent if the *Endeavour* was to anchor up here, sir." Steven pointed to the map quite close to Sebasco. "There is quite some protection from sight at this point as it would seem that the cliffs are quite high and all of these small islands would give ideal cover to the *Endeavour*," he said as he pulled out the chart showing land topography. "We could then make use of the ship's boats, sir, and row our way along the shoreline and as close to the port as we may get without being seen. This could be completed during the hours of darkness, sir," he concluded.

"Mmmm," said Sylvian as he studied the two maps. "What say you all to Mr Gant's plan?" he asked. There were a few minutes silence whilst the officers mulled over the charts and gave it some thought.

"I think that might work, sir," said Robert. "That gives us the possibility of cover from the *Endeavour* and her guns should we need it."

"Mr Montrose, as first officer of the *Endeavour*, what is your opinion?" asked Sylvian.

James received a few pats on the back and took the news humbly. "Well, sir, thank you, sir, for your faith in me for such a task. I believe that the plan holds merit, sir. I believe that we should need some form of signal that should bring me to your aid should you need it," he replied.

"Sir, might I suggest that we have a man on the cliff top here," said Peter pointing to the map to the east of Sebasco. "Who could send a signal to the *Endeavour* should we need to."

"Good idea," said Sylvian as he responded to a knock to the door. It was Mr Fowler reporting that they had reached the end of the estuary and required further orders.

"Very well, gentlemen, we have a plan, First Lieutenant Montrose, take us to our destination if you please." With the men dismissed and a plan formulated Sylvian retired to his cabin with the maps and another brandy to consider their position.

He was woken by Mr Fowler who reported that they were off the coast of Maine and would be navigating towards the coast and inlet within the next half hour. Sylvian thanked Mr Fowler and was soon up and having seen to his ablutions was now ready to go up on deck. Mr Montrose greeted Sylvian on his arrival with a salute and a report on their exact location. They examined the chart table and decided to take the ship into a small cove called Bald Head Cove and anchor for the day before setting off for the rest of the short journey once in the hours of darkness.

Sylvian headed off below decks and found his crew in the officers' mess which they had borrowed for preparation of their equipment for the mission. Mr Osborne reported that the crew were ready and willing to get on with this rescue. Mr Gant and Mr Selway had briefed the crew on the mission and reported to Sylvian that all eventualities had been discussed and that Mr Carlisle's soldiers had also come up with some good ideas to deal with the ships in the harbour if they had a need too. They had suggested that grappling hooks and rope as they used for their tall building or cliff assaults would help them to gain access aboard a ship should there be no boarding ladder or ropes. Albert Simms had been detailed to the task of cliff top signaller if it were required. There was a definite excitement to the air as Sylvian looked around at his crew and their faces which revealed their excitement to get on with the mission.

Their captain stopped them from their tasks and called them in front of him. It was a little tight in the mess but they all managed to get around him. "Here we are again, gentlemen, it would seem that the captain and the crew of the Sheffield need our help, we have been here before and I have no doubts that we shall be here again and again. It is what you do best, you are an elite team some of you new members will need to stick close to our more experienced members and learn from them. I apologise that I have not had the time to get to know you all but I will during this mission. Gentlemen, we leave at two bells on the dog watch, which will be seven p.m. for our army friends. I shall see you then," he concluded.

Sylvian returned to his cabin quite buoyed by the enthusiasm of his men and also to the thought of getting into some form of battle, albeit hopefully only with the French and not the Union. He opened his desk drawer and took the locket that Sarah had given him and placed it in his trouser pocket. He had changed his uniform to more suitable clothes for battle and had again and again gone over the charts. On the east side of Sebasco was a high cliff that overlooked the settlement. He would reconnoitre the place with his spyglass from this position, before he made settlement on his plans. He had told Mr Montrose to lift anchor at six p.m. and make the two-mile journey along the coast and nestle the ship to anchor close to the island known as Harbor Island.

Mr Gant reported to Sylvian at fifteen minutes before seven that they had now anchored and the boats had been lowered. Sylvian thanked him and threw his cloak about his shoulders and with two pistols in his waistband and his sword to his side, made his way up on deck. He returned the salutes of his officers and instructed the men to start loading the boats. Mr Montrose wished them luck and with practiced ease they were all in the row boats and making their way to shore.

As they came close in to shore Sylvian who was at the helm of the leading boat steered her along the coast. He could just make out the white caps of the waves as they rolled upon the shore. There was not a star to the sky as the clouds were thick and threatening. They could feel small spatters of rain which by the time they pulled the boats ashore by the peninsula, was now raining hard. With the boats secured on the beach the men made their way with a small amount of their equipment up a rough animal track and onto the cliffs above. They found some shelter in a small wooded area that overlooked the small settlement below. Sylvian studied the settlement with his spyglass along with his officers. Robert pointed out the long building at the east end of the quay where they could see that it was heavily guarded by French marines. The marines were obviously not enjoying this weather and the rain being driven at them from the sea. Sylvian noticed to the centre of the quay and close to some buildings that looked to be an inn and some houses, where some twenty boats had been tied up to the quay. He pointed this out to Robert who looked and could see also that the quay was not guarded. They were not expecting anyone.

A quick scan to sea showed two French class two ships and one class three Union ship anchored in the bay. The Sheffield was anchored to one side of the first French ship. So, from their position the ships lined up with the Sheffield first, then the two French ships with the Union ship off and a little further to the west and away from them. Sylvian could see a little action on board but all four seemed to have only a skeleton crew. The officers made their way back to the woods where the rest of the men were sheltering from the rain.

"I think, gentlemen, that our crew from the Sheffield are being held in the long building at this end of the quay. Mr Fitzwalter, could you and ten of your men make it to the building unseen and crack a few necks?" he asked.

"Most definitely, sir," replied Fitzwalter, quite eager to get underway.

"Good, then you shall take Juno, Will and Colin and pick seven of the best from the new men. Now, Albert, I need you to get back to the *Endeavour* and tell Mr Montrose with my compliments to sail into the sound and between the French and Union ship and bow facing the Union ship with broadside and guns run out to land, is that clear?" he asked.

"Aye, sir," said Albert in that gravelly tone.

"Take five of the new men with you so that you can row quickly, now away with you," said Sylvian. "Mr Fitzwalter, please take four of Captain Sinclair's men with you, including Sergeant Strong, if that is okay with you, Robert?" he asked.

"Indeed," said Robert. "Sergeant Strong, you know which three to take, so away with you."

The two teams set off and Sylvian asked Robert if he could have his men ready with grappling irons to board the two French ships. Sylvian and his team would make their way down to the quay and make ready with the boats as soon as Fitzwalter had done his deed. Sylvian sent twenty of the men under the command of Robert to secure their boats and bring them around and behind the French vessels from seaward and board them as quietly as possible and neutralise the skeleton crew. Robert set off with his team and grappling hooks wrapped across their shoulders. The remaining men with Sylvian made their way slowly down the cliff and onto the gravel beach. They slipped into the water and swam along the quay front and up to the boats where they waited.

Fitzwalter and his men had come down the cliff on the rear of the long building where they observed eight French marines with lanterns marching up and down the front, sides and rear of the building. They crept through the long grass to as close to the building as they could get. Four of the men took to the left and right of the building whilst three had made their way through the bushes on the left of the building to be level with the front. From the time they had left each other and on Fitzwalter's instructions the one that could count would start and when they reached one hundred, they would make their move. Fitzwalter had got to ninety-three, two of the guards thought they heard something and stopped to take a look. Ninety-seven, seeing nothing they carried on their march. One hundred and they leapt into action almost exactly at the same time and with precision had the eight guards receiving their last rites.

Fitzwalter opened the door to the front of the building and found Lieutenant Crumb with a wooden board in his hand and just about to bring it down on Fitzwalter's head.

Sylvian's men had stealthily climbed into the boats and were making ready when a bright light from an open door lit the quay briefly before closing again. They had not been seen. The sailor commenced to relieve himself against the wall. Sylvian could see that along the quay Fitzwalter had been successful and was now leading the men out of the building. He did not need this. He took his knife from his waistband and crawled from his boat onto the pontoon that led to the quay. The man was no more than fifty feet from him and he would need to crawl to get to him. Suddenly the man gave a little shake and redressed himself before pulling up his collar before the bright light bathed the blackened quay for a second time. They were back into darkness; within minutes the boats were loaded and the crews started to row their way back out of the bay and towards the ships. Sylvian could just make out the shape of a moving object way behind the two French ships and then pass behind the Union ship, still no sign of action. The rain was now biting into them with such force that it was kinder to dip one's face down to protect it, but Sylvian kept watching. They were now far enough out from land that Sylvian called quietly to Jonas to put half his crew on the first French vessel. He told Mr Gant that his boat and him should board the first French vessel and make her ready to sail. Sylvian called over to Peter and told him to make his way to the second French vessel with his boat load and more would come from the *Endeavour* and then make sail. Both officers acknowledged their orders with a smile.

The *Endeavour* had come into the bay around one hundred feet to the rear of the French ships and had noticed the little boats and men with ropes climbing up the sterns of the ships. Lieutenant Montrose smiled and told his helmsman to circle the Union ship and come around her bow to face her bow on to her starboard side. The gun crew had already run out the guns and were on standby. As the *Endeavour* drifted around the bow of the Union ship James noticed the small flotilla of boats nearing the French ships. With spyglass he could see that the two French ships with skeleton crews had been completely surprised and taken quite easily. They were obviously not expecting this. One of the row boats came alongside the *Endeavour* and Sylvian came aboard. No sooner had his feet hit the deck than he ordered the bo'sun to get fifty men to the two French ships.

The guard on the Union ship called out a warning to the *Endeavour* that she would fire if they did not identify. They remained silent. Men were now pouring over the side some into the boats and some swimming to get to the French ships which were already starting to lower sail. A musket shot rang out from the Union ship and hit Sylvian directly into his right arm and sent him spinning from the forecastle and down onto the main deck. Montrose shouted, "Hold your fire, we are British and not at war with the Union."

He heard a shout from the Union ship. "Hold your fire damn you. State your business," came the reply.

"We are here to rescue our British ship the Sheffield, sir, which seems to have lost its way in your harbour," shouted Sylvian as he pulled himself to his feet and holding his arm to stop the blood and try to curtail the pain he felt.

"State your name, sir, for the record." came the voice back from the Union ship.

"I am Captain Sylvian Mountjoy, sir, of His Majesty's Navy and this is the ship *Endeavour*. State yours, for the record."

"I am Lieutenant William Montgomery of the United States Navy and this is the Charleston sir… did you say Sylvian Mountjoy, sir?" asked the lieutenant.

"Thank you, Lieutenant, and yes I did," replied Sylvian. "Do we know one another?'

"Oh, I know you, sir, and we do now," replied Montgomery.

Sylvian looked around and saw that one of the French ships was making good ground from the bay and the second had sail lowered and was making slow progress.

"Then, sir, I bid you safe sailing and hope that we shall meet again under somewhat better circumstances," replied Sylvian.

"Indeed, sir, the same to you and I hope that our shot did not cause any damage," replied the lieutenant.

"Just a nick, but I shall be fine, Lieutenant." Sylvian called back.

"Oh my god, I shot Sylvian Mountjoy," came a voice from the rigging just as Sylvian lost conscious.

The *Endeavour* made her way slowly from the bay and soon caught the two French ships. It was still heavy rain and very dark but they decided to follow the *Endeavour* which had overtaken them and out on to the Atlantic and a heading north.

Mr Waverly the ship's surgeon had Sylvian taken down to the captain's cabin and his wet clothes stripped from him. Mr Fowler had hot water brought in by Padraig and the three set to sewing the holes in Sylvian's right arm to seal the wound. Padraig was apt at using the alcohol to clean the wounds as the ball had found its way through his upper arm and had thankfully missed the bone. The muscle damage would slow him down somewhat but should heal in time.

At ten a.m. Mr Montrose reported to Sylvian's cabin and to his ailing captain that they were about four hours out from Halifax, the two French ships were sailing side by side and the Sheffield was between and to the stern of the *Endeavour*. Sylvian thanked Mr Montrose and succumbed to the laudanum that the good doctor had given him.

He next woke in the surgery at the fort and was surrounded by his men and of course Jonas Crumb who had stayed with Sylvian since they arrived back in port. His men were pleased to see him and Sylvian noticed that Albert had a bandaged hand. When he enquired as to why, Albert's head dropped and Jacko explained that he had broken his finger when climbing aboard the *Endeavour* and slipping on the deck. Albert looked at Sylvian with that stupid dopey look he could use and Sylvian burst into laughter as did all of the others, including Albert. Sylvian winced at the pain in his arm which set the men off again.

"Right come on, you lot, off and leave my ward in peace," said the doctor as he started to herd the protesting men from the ward.

"Thanks, Sylv, said Jonas, I thought we were done for. They came out of nowhere and the Sheffield just did not have the pace so we tried to find a hiding place and ended up right where they wanted us," said Jonas.

"Well, all that matters, dear friend, is that you are safe, and of course your crew and the Sheffield," replied Sylvian.

"And to boot, much to the admiral's pride, two fine French frigates to add to the flotilla," said Jonas as he sat down on the bed beside Sylvian.

"Hey, Sylv, I have been here these last three days since we got back and, well some lady has been by each day, beautiful and with the most penetrating…"

"Green eyes," interrupted Sylvian.

"Yes, is she, Jacks sister-in-law?" he asked.

"Yes, you pest, that is Sarah Bennett and we are good friends," replied Sylvian.

"Oh, look, Sylvian, I have to say I am glad because I was so sad to hear of Mary's passing, I did so love her, my friend," said Jonas looking at the ground and twirling his Lieutenants' hat in his hand.

"I know, old friend, but you must do as I have done and lock her away here." He brought his hand up to Jonas's heart. "And never forget her, that way she will live forever in all of us," said Sylvian as he grabbed Jonas's hand. "Now, my friend, my body says I must sleep again and you must come back soon and get me out of this place."

"I will," said Jonas as he got up and put his hat on and saluted his officer before leaving the room. Sylvian laid still and ignored the numbing throb from the top of his arm and thought of Mary and what plans they had shared, no longer to be. He fell into a deep sleep.

He awoke to the pain in his arm and looked up into a beautiful face with green eyes and a big smile. The face came down to his and kissed him on the lips sending a sensation through him and totally numbing his pain. If it was a dream then he never wanted it to stop. Then he realised that it was Sarah and that nice feeling went right throughout his body. "Sarah," he said.

"Yes, my love, you scared me you know," she scolded lightly.

"Sorry, I had a disagreement with a Union bullet and it won," he replied.

"Well next time can you just crouch down a little lower so that it misses altogether," she said whilst squatting down and finally taking the chair beside him.

"Deal," he said with a large grin on his face.

"Ah, Mountjoy," said the admiral. "I er I can come back, so sorry."

Sarah stood up and smiled at Sylvian. "No, Admiral, that is quite all right he was starting to bore me so I shall go now," she squeezed the admiral's arm as she walked past him.

"Good lord," said the admiral as she closed the door behind her. "So sorry, dear boy, didn't know see."

"That's quite all right sir, nor did I for sure, not until now that is," replied Sylvian.

"Good lord, well I say, um look how are you, dear boy, hear you took one from the Union by all accounts. Do you need me to escalate this? I cannot have Union Johnny's taking a pot shot at my captains now can I," he exploded.

"It's fine, sir, a matter of mistaken identity I feel, sir, and after all they took no further action even though we stole two French ships from under their noses. I think that way, sir, we may have avoided an international incident of some degree of embarrassment. I think it may be the French that shall have something to say if we keep taking their ships, and so easily, sir," said Sylvian.

"Easily, goddamnit, sir, I have read your lieutenants and Captain Roberts' reports, damn feat of brilliance and bravado to say the least. And just you on the injured list, what say you to that, young Mountjoy? Shouldn't be surprised if you do not have my job next," he blustered.

"Well, sir, I do not want it. I am very happy where I am," replied Sylvian.

"As am I, dear boy, now what about this arm, doc tells me some muscle damage and you may need some specialist work done to repair it," said James Albright with compassion.

"Well, sir, it sure hurts but I think I shall give it time to see how it heals and then maybe if I need to undergo a surgeon's attention, well then so be it. But for now, I shall just keep it rested. I have the whole winter to get it back and working," Sylvian replied.

"Very well then, dear boy, now before I am away is there anything you need?" he asked.

"No, sir, I am fine thank you, looking forward to getting back to my ship, sir," replied Sylvian.

"Well, that will not be long," said the admiral as he turned to walk to the door where he paused and looked back. "Er the girl Sylvian, anything I need to know?" he said quietly.

"No, sir, but if there is, you shall be the second to know," he replied.

Chapter Nine
Winter

For such a beautiful country it could be so harsh, with temperatures quite often below zero Celsius and winds cutting that temperature even lower. There was much to learn about the Dominion and its seasons. Those who had been born here handled such extremes with ease, yet enjoyed each of the seasons with what they brought. The warmth of spring, the heat of summer and the cool evening breezes of autumn that blew at the multicoloured leaves, and teased them from the branches to give coloured carpets that littered the land. Children wrapped in scarves and woolen hats played in the leaves as they were brought into piles by the swirling breezes. The cooling nights that caused the breath to mist and fingers to chill, and then came the winter. The deep freeze where from late November and through to April kept this land in a blanket of frozen white. The trees bare, and their branches like fingers pointing to the cold cloudy sky.

The carriages had their wheels removed and long wooden bars fitted in their place, these sleds would slide through the snow and not become bogged down as would wheels. The men would strap boards to their feet and use balance poles to push themselves through the snow and when traveling the countryside, they strapped what looked like tennis bats to their feet to widen their footprint, this enabled them to walk on the top of deep snow. Sylvian had tried these things and had great difficulty in keeping his legs wide enough so as not to step down on his other foot. Colin Bates had mastered these snow shoes and had been a great teacher for the men. The amount of times Albert had found himself face down in the snow and with the curses emanating from his snow muffled face was of great humour to the men. Special shoes had to be made for Midshipman Fitzwalter's very large feet which made him look like a large hairy monster with the way he had to walk.

The men had taken well to their winter training and the mix of army and navy men had worked well. They had trained well and both Sylvian and Robert had pushed their men hard. Combat tactics in the frozen wastelands had been a far more daunting challenge. How to be secreted and unnoticed when tracks in the snow were so easy to follow. The men had been quite ingenious in their inventions of how to become invisible. Will Armstrong had an idea and needed to prove such so he had his lady make him a two-piece suit in white cotton with a hood that covered his head, she had also knitted him a white woolen hat that came down over his face with only two holes for his eyes. He had challenged the men to give him one half day starting early in the morning, and if they found him before dark, he would allow Mr Fitzwalter one punch and would buy all of the men one glass of ale. The challenge was on.

Will had left early in the morning and when out of sight had tied a pine branch to his belt and dragged it behind him, he had guaranteed the men he would not go further than one half mile from his leaving point and he would only go north. The pine branch was very effective in rubbing out the signs of his snow shoes. He found a place between some trees and dug himself into the snow and waited.

The men struggled hard to find his tracks but had spread out in a line going north and searched for any sign. They had doubled back and tried again but only found signs of their own and some animal tracks. The evening was closing in around four p.m. and still they had not found him.

It was Jacob Stubbings that eventually, sort of found him when by torchlight at almost dark he felt something grab his ankle and down he went face first into the snow with a surprised shout that brought the others. Even then with their torches they were unable to see him until he stood up and removed his woolen face hat. Fitzwalter still had his punch because Will had stood behind him when he removed the hat and tapped Fitzwalter's shoulder. When he turned and saw him, he instinctively lashed out in fear at this white monster in front of him. They carried Will back and to the Inn as their hero, and Molly his girl was kept very busy with her lucrative trade in snow suits for the military.

Sylvian had spent Christmas with the Bennetts and had grown closer to Sarah during his visits, although his training regime and his duties to the fort and the design of the new military training school had kept him busy. January would see the first lieutenant's exam and board, so their time together had not been long. They were both adults and they knew what their feelings meant, although Sylvian was at odds with his heart as Mary still took up a large part. He knew he loved Sarah as much, but in a different way to Mary, but he would need time to finalise his grief. He owed that much to Sarah and her family. Sarah and Sylvian had discussed it at great length and were both agreed. She loved him dearly and was quite prepared to wait forever if needs be. The Bennett family however, had quite made up their minds that Sylvian was already a member of the family and marriage was just a formality.

The architect that Sylvian had been working with was so glad of the trade he was receiving from the military, at the docks and with the new training school that he had sat with Sylvian and Sarah and had drawn up plans for a home for them, should they ever need it of course and he was quite pleased to act on their behalf to see the build through quite free of any charge of course, and only if they need it.

The admiral had insisted that only local trades should be used for all the builds under his command. He was quite pleased when Sylvian had brought the costs for the new training school in at $22,000. The tradespeople preferred to be paid in gold with a value of the Union dollar as most of their trading in materials was with the Union. The first building to be put in place was a small mint where the gold from the fort was smelted and turned into tradable dollar value coins. The mint could only have two bars at a time and each bar made thousands of the small coins. They had attached the stone-built mint to the stone fort with a direct access to the fort for the transfer of the bars. Entry to the mint was only through the fort and was strictly secured by the rounders.

They had broken ground on the new training school before the winter freeze had started. They were able to erect scaffolding and prepare the site for when the freeze lifted in the spring. They had used the site Sylvian had selected as the ground on top of the hill was quite flat and leant itself so well to the building they had designed. Recruitment had commenced and they were using the hill fort built by Sylvian's team as a temporary seamen's school. The team had adjusted well to training the new recruits as well as their own training. They had extended the fort to accommodate the new use and had built classrooms and practical training areas. Sylvian was pleased with how all of this was slowly taking part and was very proud of his men, they had really thrown themselves into this new task wholeheartedly and with a disciplined approach.

The first week of January had seen Robert and his team leave on their mission to the Union. All of the men had got together to load the two farmer's carts they had acquired to carry their stores. Peter had made up some of his small casket bombs and given Sergeant Strong a length of saltpetre fuses and taught him how to cut them, each length taking a certain time to burn. They were to travel in separate groups to avoid detection as they had done in France. Robert had spent a great deal of time with Sylvian going over the plans for his mission. More Bowmore Islay Scotch whisky had been devoured on occasions than was absolutely necessary, but Robert had gained much from these planning discussions, certainly that he now felt quite confident on his approach to make the mission a success. It had been quite some farewell as the teams had left in small groups with Robert taking the last cart. They had wished each other well as they would not see them again for some time. After the mission Robert was to make his way across country to Kingston and report to Colonel Gage. They hoped that in the spring with the *Endeavour* making its way to Lake Ontario that again they would meet at Kingston.

January had been unusually good with little snow and some decent temperatures, certainly unusual as January and February were well known as the worst two months. The exams had gone well at the fort and Sylvian was part of the marking panel and together with Vice Admiral Jackman and Captain Young saw service on the boards. It had brought many memories flooding back of his time in that hot waiting room waiting for the board, the nerves, the sweat and the anxiety he had felt and knew that these candidates felt the same. Of the eight midshipmen that had passed the exam only five lieutenants were required at this stage. Two of Sylvian's midshipmen, Mr Fawkes and Mr Watts were successful at the board with each to serve on the *Endeavour*. They had discussed moving the men around the fleet but had decided that the *Endeavour* complement had not been together for long enough to require such action.

Third Lieutenant Jack Newman had succumbed to a bout of pneumonia just before Christmas and had passed away through complications of a lung problem. John Douglas had moved up to replace Mr Montrose as second lieutenant. So, he had two vacancies for third lieutenant that had now been filled nicely. Interviews would commence in February for the place of midshipman in the fleet. Quite a few of the affluent members of the Dominion's Society had put forward their sons for service. Some had even offered to pay for a guaranteed place but that practice had recently been stopped, and Admiral Albright would not have that within the Dominion fleet.

The two French frigates had been through the repair basin and had been renamed the Bristol and the Exeter. So, the admiral had tasked his officer selection team to find a full complement for each. Lieutenant Crumb had been selected as posted captain for the Bristol and Lieutenant Sefton St. Peter from the *Dauntless* would command the Exeter as posted captain.

Lieutenant Brian Baldry from the *Renown* would move to commander and captain the Sheffield. Each of the frigates would require five lieutenants and four midshipmen. The Sheffield already had her complement and would continue with Commander Baldry from the first day of February 1808. A new lieutenant's exam and board was scheduled for the last Thursday of January and fifteen applicants had applied and the three midshipmen who had passed the last exam applied for the board. The board called lieutenants Crumb, Baldry and St. Peter before them on the last Wednesday of January. Mr Baldry was the first to be called in front of the board and was informed by Vice Admiral Jackman that he had been selected for promotion to commander and would take command of the vessel HMS Sheffield on February first. Brian was delighted by the news and favoured telling his family as soon as he could. He stood and saluted the board and then proceeded to shake each one's hand, as Andrew said after, "Such a really nice character."

Lieutenant St. Peter was called into the room and was informed by Andrew that he had been selected for promotion to posted captain and would assume command of HMS Exeter with immediate effect. He was informed that his crew would be selected by this panel and he would be notified in due course. Sefton again was pleased and needed to shake the hands of the board.

Lieutenant Crumb was next in the room and was informed by Sylvian that he had been selected for promotion to posted Captain and would assume command of HMS Bristol on the first day of February, his officers and crew would be selected by this board and he would be notified on completion. Jonas was stunned as he thought that he had been called before the board to face punishment for the capture of the Sheffield. He was almost brought to tears and again took the board's hands in a very firm shake.

This work had kept Sylvian from his team and their training and that of the new recruits which was going well. Young men from all over the Dominion had been making the long trip to join the service and the four-week training course had proved well structured and implemented by his team. By the close of February and the beginning of March had seen some three hundred and eighty passed recruits. Sylvian's board had worked hard to place the recruits. This task was taking up too much of these senior officers' time, so as part of their duties they created a selection and recruitment division at the fort. This division had the responsibility of selecting which passed recruits would serve on what ships and also which applicants were sent to the training school and when. The division was headed by Lieutenant Walter Jarvis on his retirement from the service and was staffed by some of the local civilians. Meanwhile Sylvian's team under the command of Lieutenant Gant had selected and were training new instructors to take over from them. They had taken serving men from the fleet and had put them through a training system to enable them to continue the good work started by the team.

The structure of the new training school would start with Sylvian as overall commander and a commandant that would be filled by Lieutenant Jack Abrahams who on retirement from the Hampshire would take the honorary rank of commander and serve as commandant of training. Albert Simms had been promoted as honorary lieutenant to serve as second in command on his retirement in March. His wife and family were already on their way to Halifax where they would all settle. Sylvian was sad to lose Albert from his team but it had been his request and he had said in that oh so loveable gravelly voice of his that he was starting to struggle with the rigours of training with Sylvian's fairly young team.

They had sent him off with a party to excel all parties and even Fitzwalter had a tear to his eye.

Sylvian was starting to look at the structure of his enlarged team; it was just but two weeks before they were scheduled to sail for Kingston and the Lake Ontario and he had given great thought to what he might find at the end of his journey and how his team would best be suited to what lay ahead. Admiral Albright had suggested that he wait for the return of John Scott and Bill Mitchell to gain more intelligence before he departs, however they had heard by messenger that John Scott was due to arrive in Kingston during the first week of March and would remain there until Sylvian's arrival. No further information would have been sent of a sensitive nature owing to many of the messengers waylaid on their journeys and robbed or murdered for what they carried. Sylvian had agreed with the admiral and had set his journey for the first week of April and would give great attention to the icebergs that would be found on his journey.

It being late March and with much to prepare, Sylvian set off to the wooden fort to make final decisions on the organisation and structure of his team. He found them hard at work preparing weapons and equipment for transfer to the *Endeavour*. Midshipman Fitzwalter was the first he came across and he asked him to find lieutenants Selway and Gant and with himself and Jacko, Juno, Chris Thompson and Jacob Stubbings to report to his office in one half hour so that he may sort himself before seeing them. Fitzwalter saluted his captain and set off on his task, whilst Sylvian made his way to his office. On his arrival he found it had been moved when the accommodations had been extended. He found his office had been enlarged and now contained two beautifully crafted desks, one for his use and one surrounded by chairs for the use of meetings and such. A fine fire burned in the grate and the windows crafted into the walls gave much natural light to the room.

Once settled in he found many documents on his desk pertaining to the training school and its recruits and teachers which he shall have to spend the rest of the day dealing with. It was not long before he answered, "Come," to a knock to his door. His team as requested presented themselves to him and Mr Gant took the salute. He invited the men to sit to the table in front which had been set as the bottom of a 'T' to his desk that formed the top. The men took their seats and looked to their captain.

"Thank you, gentlemen, for coming, we have much to sort through, but before I start, I would ask Mr Gant to bring us up to speed on the progress of the training school and its staff," said Sylvian.

"Sir," said Steven as he stood. "We have this last week completed our training of the instructors and under the command of the commandant, Commander Abrahams, and his deputy Lieutenant Simms we have handed over all the running into their capable hands. The system seems to be running remarkably smoothly, sir, and Mr Fitzwalter has been overseeing on the discipline front. Work has commenced on the new training center and should be finished and occupied by this time next year. It is their intention to have the stone exterior completed during the summer giving protection to the workers during the winter to complete the interior, sir. That is my report, sir," said Steven as he retook his seat.

"Excellent work one and all, I am very proud of what you have achieved in such a short time and with such exemplary results. I know you have all worked hard to make this training school happen and I thank you," commended Sylvian.

"Sir, one other thing," said Peter. "We have had word from Colonel Gage, sir, in Kingston. He asked if he could supply some of his men to work with ours and to form a joint service training center. The note is on your desk, sir. I think that this would be an excellent opportunity to have the services train together in the same place so that a greater understanding could be engendered between the services of the tasks faced by each, sir."

"I think it should be an excellent opportunity and I shall write such to Colonel Gage. I think we shall take Lieutenant Simms with us in two weeks and drop him at Kingston to discuss the matter further, thank you, Peter," said Sylvian. "Now that brings us nicely to our sailing on the next full moon on April the tenth. We shall need to make our plans soon and I think this room should serve us well to do so. Now on to the matter of our team, we have increased in size and now stand at what, Mr Fitzwalter?" the question took Fitzwalter totally off guard.

"Oh, sir, me, sir," he said as he moved his bulky frame from the seat. "Yes, sir, er… we have twenty men in each team sir, and each team has been working as individual units or as one team, sir, we as spent quite some time with the new men, sir, and have filtered out twenty-two during training, sir. I as been basing standards on what you have set us in what you as come to expect, sir," he replied and remained standing.

"Good, Mr Fitzwalter, so you are certain that our teams are now sufficient in skills, fitness and ability to perform whatever we shall ask of them?" asked Sylvian.

"Aye, sir, and just as an aside, sir, they are quite a nice bunch of youngens, sir, I think that they should do us proud, sir," he concluded as he retook his seat.

"Excellent, Mr Fitzwalter, now it is time we should sort our team out as far as its officers and senior ratings so that we are ready when we go into the unknown, as we most definitely will do when again we find ourselves in Union territory. Now Mr Montrose has been promoted to the post of first lieutenant on the *Endeavour*, which will leave our team clear to act as a unit without endangering the operational ability of the ship. Any questions so far?" he asked and paused looking at the faces before him.

"Sir, shall Lieutenant Selway and myself revert a rank, sir, when aboard?" asked Steven.

"No, Steven, the ships complement although includes you and the team, and we shall most certainly take part in her day to day running, will operate as a separate entity to our team. Training will continue when we are aboard and Captain Wood has kindly agreed for his marines to take part in our exercises. Now the structure of the team as she has grown in strength will need to change. We now have a corps of nearly fifty men to manage and that shall fall to you my initial team taking more of a responsible role in the structure." He paused and looked at Peter. "Before I go on, Peter, see if you can get us some tea if you please?" he asked.

"Aye, sir," said Peter as he was up and through the door and calling to someone to get the tea sorted for the captain in a trice.

With Peter now sat back at the table Steven was the first to speak. "Sir, we have a lot of good men and I think we may need to make some decisions regarding promotions and areas of responsibility."

"Thank you, Steven, that has brought me, nicely to my next point. A little over two weeks ago I asked Mr Thompson and Mr Stubbings to take an exam that had been devised to see how or where that exam could be used in our selection process. I apologise, gentlemen, for being less than honest in my reasoning for having you sit the exam. I chose you both as I knew that you are both well educated and have mastered seamanship with exemplary standards. The exam you sat was indeed the current lieutenant's exam that all midshipman candidates are required to take before sitting the board. Now I am well aware, Chris, that you have no desire whatsoever to hold a rank of responsibility as you have told me many times, but for the last six months you have done so as an honorary midshipman whilst we built the team and the training school. And you have done a mighty fine job. Now you both passed that exam, and you also were the two top scorers of all the candidates we have tested. I shall not reveal your individual scores in this meeting but I will tell you in private, if you so wish. So, having spoken to the other members of the promotion board who know you both, it has been agreed that you be offered the position of lieutenant third class within this team. You will each be assigned to either squad 'A' or squad 'B'." Sylvian was disturbed by a knock to the door and two of the men carried in mugs and tea, with some mess made biscuits. With the tea poured and the men now enjoying the biscuits Sylvian continued.

"Now where was I, gentlemen, yes indeed, Chris and Jacob you have had a little time to digest what I have told you and although I appreciate it has come as something of a shock, could you please give us some idea as to your thoughts on the matter."

"Sir, if I may be so bold, I am not sure that I am up to such a task, sir. I have come from quite a lowly class of people in Essex, sir, mostly farmers, and a few poachers, sir. We are church going folk but none has had the education to grammar school level, sir. I feel that I would be insulting such as Mr Gant and Mr Selway if I was to presume to hold such a rank, and that I should never wish to do," replied Jacob.

"And you, Chris?" asked Sylvian.

"Sir, I could not have put it better than Jacob, only to add that my service with you, sir, has been the best years of my life and I should not wish it to end. I have never felt so welcomed by so many good men as I have since we started out as a team, sir. But I do have to agree with Jacob, sir, and that's a fact," he replied.

"Oh, I see, well I do understand, but I shall ask Mr Gant and Mr Selway to give over their opinion as to what they have just heard, Peter?" asked Sylvian.

Peter took a large sip of his tea and then stood up. "Sir, well I am the son of a farmer, he is middle class and I did not attend a grammar school, sir. In fact, most of my education was as a midshipman, green behind my ears and, I must say, gentlemen, without not an ounce of sense common or otherwise. I have learnt much from those around me and continue to do so, including my two colleagues Chris and Jacob. Just the day before yesterday Chris was teaching a group on helmsmanship and course plotting, he taught them a way with the sexton and calculations that I had not heard of before. So, I can say that it would be an absolute honour for me to share a rank with two fine individuals such as these, sir," he concluded.

"Steven." asked Sylvian.

Steven stood and looked at the men and paused. "My father died when I was three and my uncle made my career possible for me, partly because he wanted to get rid of me, and partly because he thought it would make a man of me. I too would feel it would be an honour to serve with Chris and Jacob as fellow lieutenants in our team, sir," he concluded.

"Sir, can I if you please, sir," said Jacko.

"Go ahead, Jacko," Sylvian said.

"Well, sir, I just wanted to say that I as always known, sirs, that these ere two was summink different to the rest of us only in that they was good wiv there brains, sir, and I woulds be equally honored, sir, to takes my orders from thems two, sir, thats alls I as to say, sir," said Jacko retaking his seat.

"Thank you, Jacko," said Sylvian. "I too can say that if it had not been for Jacko, Manny, Albert and Fitzwalter then I would not have been here today. All of what I needed to learn about the sea came from these men. And if it had not been for Juno, I would not have been talking to you now. So, we all owe much to each other which is what shall make this team better as time goes on, now do you both wish to be a part of that?" concluded their captain.

Chris and Jacob looked at one another and stood up and addressed them all. "Sir, I think I can speak for Chris, we shall both be honoured, sir, to accept," said Jacob.

"Aye, sir, and thank you sir," said Chris.

"Good then that is settled, you shall both take yourselves to the tailors in town tomorrow and get yourselves suitably attired. It has all been paid for, now to the rest of the team. Mr Fitzwalter, I should like you to take the title of master at arms, senior midshipman for both Groups 'A' and 'B' if you please," asked Sylvian.

"Aye, sir," said Fitzwalter.

"Juno, you shall serve as midshipman group 'A' and Jacko you shall serve as midshipman group 'B'. I would like Will Armstrong and Colin Bates as warrant officers of group 'A' and Sefton Marnier and Jason Baker as warrant officers in group 'B'. Mr Gant shall command Group 'A' and Mr Selway group 'B' with me in overall command. Good..." he said, taking a pause and looking at the faces in front of him. He finished his tea which had become quite lukewarm and continued. "I shall leave the assignment of each group's complement to my lieutenants and shall hope we are well balanced and ready for our next mission. I will give a briefing on the mission gentlemen, when we have set sail on the tenth. Any questions?" he asked.

"Sir, appropriate uniforms for the warrant officers, sir, as they shall need blue coats and breeches, sir?" asked Jacob.

"Ah yes, thank you, Lieutenant, please ensure that those ranks we have just discussed and assigned are suitably uniformed at the tailor's, he has a good stock so it should not cause a problem and we should have all, suitably attired before we sail. Well, thank you, gentlemen, I have somewhat of a mountain of paperwork to get through so I shall dismiss you all and see you for supper this evening," he concluded. The men stood and put on their hats and with Mr Gant taking the salute, left the office.

Sylvian sat back in his chair somewhat exhausted, his right arm had pained him much and although healed, was not yet fully back to working order. He then glanced at the pile of papers, pushed his cup to one side and commenced his work.

Chapter Ten
Kingston

Anger and frustration show differently in many men. Some will punch a wall and scream and shout. Some will silently sit and fume. Some will take their anger out on others and vent through violence, others vent through violence against property and will destroy tangible items around them, sometimes even to their own detriment. Billings was one such, although given the chance he would vent against any other person that should be stupid enough to come close.

The library in this beautiful colonial house was a wreck. Not a stick of furniture was left unbroken or undamaged. He sat on the floor in the middle of this mess, his hands on top of his head and his elbows resting on his knees. Blood dripped from his right elbow and onto the wooden floor. A small piece of glass from the bowl of the oil lamp was embedded in his forearm, but he did not care. His face was red and the veins on his neck protruded almost to bursting, and there he sat amongst this ruin of what had been a beautiful room. He felt that his life was ended, he had failed and failure was not a word he would ever accept, not from others and certainly not from himself. He sat this way for twenty more minutes before calming down.

The group on the other side of the door to this wreck of a room stood silently and shaking for they knew when their 'massa' got this way it would be oh so bad for them.

They waited.

All of them wide eyed and shaking. There was the butler Jacob, his wife Celie the cook and their daughter Messie, the two footmen and the three young housekeepers all remaining silent and waiting.

They all jumped in fear when suddenly a voice shouted loud from inside the room and echoed around the house. "Messie," was the cry and the wide-eyed servants all looked at Messie.

She pulled down on her dress and apron with her nervous hands and looked at her father. "Go's on, Messie, der massa needs ja," he said whilst pushing her on from behind.

She smacked his hands away and glared at him with a snarl. Her hands were sweating along with her brow as beads of nervous perspiration rolled down the sides of her face. She had seen this before and had got a whoopin for her trouble. She reached for the ornate door handle and turned it and jumped back six inches when he shouted again. "Messie."

This time she grabbed the door handle and went straight in. The door pushed aside a pile of books and stopped her in her tracks as she took on such a sight. There were probably just three books left on the walled bookcases and as for the furniture, well not one piece was upright, and in its place, not one piece, from what she could see, unbroken. This would take some clearing up she thought.

"Massa, wot you'd gone done t'dis room, wot is took you so dis way, massa," she said as she moved over towards him. She looked down on this sorrowful creature before her. A man she feared greatly but loved passionately. She knelt down on the floor in front of him and looked at his bloody arm but did not touch him. "Wot ails you so, massa, wot all dis mess fer and you done gone hurt yourself, massa," she said quietly and with compassion.

"It's all finished, Messie, we are all finished," he said, and then he sobbed like she had never seen him this way before. She looked back at the door and all of the staff were struggling to peek around the door.

"Shuts dat damn door," she shouted, and as if the command had come from their massa they all disappeared and the door banged into place.

"Wat dat you say abouts it all finish, massa, wot finish?" she asked.

"We are, Messie, all of us, it's all gone, and the money has all gone," he sobbed.

"Wells we alls gona finds it, massa, jus donts go like dat, massa. Now ju gets up and lets ole messie fix dat arm, ju gots blood all over der floor," she said as she stood up and walked over and started to right the upturned chairs. She moved back and took him under the arm and lifted him into a chair. She lifted up his chin with the palm of her hand and looked into his eye.

"Now wiles I do fix dis arm, you tells ole Messie jus wot ails you so," she said and then smiled. She tore off a strip of cloth from her apron and walked to the upturned liquor cabinet and took out an unbroken bottle of whiskey and a glass that she found on the floor. She blew the debris from the glass and wiped it with the cloth from her apron. She poured a very generous amount into the glass and handed it to Nathaniel in his left hand. He took a large swig of the amber liquid and felt the burn as it found its way down to soothe his troubled stomach. She quickly gripped the piece of glass and pulled it from his arm. The blood poured from the wound and Messie put the cloth to it straight away. Nathaniel screamed at the pain and thought to strike out, but did not have the energy. Messie took the cloth away and poured the whisky into the wound and Billings screamed again. Messie tore another length from her apron and folded the first one into a pad and placed it on the wound, using the second one as a bandage to hold the pad in place.

Nothing was said between them.

***

The day had started with the usual cliff top walk. It was a beautiful day, cool with blue clear skies and a warm early winter sun, so nice for the end of October. When he got back to the house his butler told him that the colonel was back and was not looking happy. Billings went into the library and found the colonel standing by the window, his hat behind his back and being rapidly tapped on his legs. Billings walked over to his desk and saw a parchment on the desk that he had not left there. He didn't touch it. The colonel without turning around said. "It's from New York, our spies tell us that the man they captured was an English spy, there were two of them, the other got away." He paused and turned back to Billings who was still standing behind his desk. "He told our men quite a few things before he died. Our boys were able to make up a report which they sent to the state department who in turn sent it on to me." He came away from the window and stood in front of the desk.

"So, what does this have to do with me?" asked Billings with a smirk to his face, but feeling a little worried at what was to come.

"A lot as it turns out, seems the English have been somewhat busy," he said as he sat down. "Seems that gold you were expecting got picked up already, and to think you told me that the ships must have been caught by the early winter ice." He snarled, enjoying every minute of what he was about to say, and drawing it out after months of this little pompous bastard making him suffer.

"What the damn hell are you talking about, Colonel," snapped Billings as he was coming to the end of his tether.

"The money, Billings, the money to finish the harbour and the ships, the money that you no longer have because you have frittered it away on this house, this Island. But not to worry, you are expecting four boxes of gold and a ship load of spies and workers to make it all work," he said with growing sarcasm. "Well, it ain't coming, Billings, because half of it is at the bottom of the sea and the other half is in the hands of some god damn captain in the god damn British Navy," he said with anger.

Billings slowly dropped down into his seat without taking his eye off the red-faced colonel. "Did your man say… who this captain was?" said Billings calmly.

"What the damn hell does it matter what the damn captain's god damn name is, you pompous little prick, the money's gone and we have bills to pay and ships to finish, I have made promises and I have a damn job to do, and all based on you and your god damn French government's promise, now tell me Billings… just what the goddamn hell are you gonna do about that," he shouted, now standing and leaning over the desk glowering down at a fractured pompous little prick.

"I asked you… did they say what the captain's name was?" asked Billings menacingly and pointing his little pistol directly into the shocked face of the colonel. The colonel leant forward a little more and picked up the parchment, read a little and then put it back on the desk. "Mountjoy," he said and the word came out like a bullet as Billings's gun lowered and he turned his face to one side all screwed up with the pain of hearing yet again that name.

The colonel sat and took a long look at Billings and finally said, "You know this god damn son of a bitch… don't you?"

Billings squirmed a little more before looking back at the colonel and saying, "Yes… yes, I know him, I killed his wife… and now I am going to kill him. Now get out, you faceless ignorant foul-mouthed poor excuse for a military man. I need to be alone," he snarled with a very bitter twist to his face and still with the pistol in his hand. The colonel wisely said no more, picked up his hat and left the room. By the time he reached the front door and the butler had given him his cloak, he heard a blood curdling scream and the crashing of glass and wood. The colonel smiled at the butler and left the house, almost with a skip to his step, but definitely one of the better days he'd had in a long time, and certainly since he had been given this assignment.

***

The day was indeed a fine one with the sun just mustering across the hills to the east and the early spring warmth in the air. The port was busy with sailors rushing about to their duties and officers calling out their commands. The seagulls had filled the rigging in the hope that there may be food around with all the activity. The last of the carts of supplies now empty made its way up the pier and a carriage made its way past and on towards the ship. Sylvian recognised the carriage and looked to Mr Montrose and made his leave. As he descended the gangplank she was elegantly climbing from the carriage where she stood and waited. She looked absolutely beautiful her wide brimmed bonnet sheltering her eyes from the sun, the small green cloak around her shoulder to keep off the early morning chill and her resplendent dress of light green silk trimmed in ermine of white and black to the hem, collar and cuffs. Her small little clutch type purse held by a gold chain to her wrist with folded hands to her front. She did not take her eyes off her captain as he made his way through the men and towards her.

"I thought we said our goodbyes last night," he said as he swept her into his arms and kissed her cheek.

"We did, I'm sorry, I just had to know that you had it," she replied.

"What, have what?" he asked.

"I need you back safe to me, Sylvian Mountjoy, and it brought you safe back to me last time. The locket, I'm talking of the locket, silly." Her eyes had filled with tears at the sadness of their parting.

Sylvian put his hand into his breeches pocket and pulled out the locket. "Would I go anywhere without you, my darling Sarah." They hugged tight until he had to pull away and just turned and ran up the gangplank without looking back. He made it back to the poop deck and returned Mr Montrose's salute. The carriage was pulling away as he looked back and then she was gone.

"Mr Montrose, take us out to sea and set a course for Kingston if you please, and make sure to post iceberg watch in the crow."

"Aye aye, sir," answered James as he barked orders at his lieutenants who in turn had the crew up the rigging and on to the yardarms. The ship now untied, slowly made pace from the dock as the sails picked up the breeze. Sylvian headed for his cabin and his charts, and hopefully Padraig had a nice breakfast for him.

***

The dining room was full as all the officers had now gathered just leaving Midshipman Conte at the helm. Sylvian now feeling full and fettered after his good breakfast started the briefing. Mr Montrose had reported that the *Endeavour* was now in the Atlantic and was taking a north westerly heading and the ship was cutting the swell with ease.

"Gentlemen, thank you for your attendance, I am sure you all wish to know what is to take place on this mission. Well, we are to head for Kingston in the first instance where we shall take on some more supplies and drop off one or two of our passengers, and then, gentlemen, we shall move on and into the Great Lake of Ontario, where we shall head for and into Union territory. Our objective is Horse Island, which is right here." He pointed to the chart that sat open across the table.

"Sir, that is right into the heart of the Union, did we not hear that the Union is building a large military presence in Sacketts Harbour, sir." asked Captain Wood.

"Indeed, sir, it is," replied Sylvian. "Let me explain, I hope that our call into Kingston shall give me more intelligence however, we already know that the Union intends a further strike on our territory of Canada, both upper and lower is our belief. We think that they have all intentions of conquering the whole of these Americas even though we had an agreement with the Union after the uprising. At this time, we also believe that the traitor Billings is the occupant of this Horse Island and with French coin is helping to build the size of the Unions capability to attack. Therefore," he paused and took a sip of his coffee and pulled a face of discomfort. "Therefore, gentlemen, it has fallen upon us to slow down this build up as much as is possible," he concluded.

"Are we to attack the Union, sir?" asked Mr Douglas.

"No, Mr Douglas we are not. It is our orders that we shall take Mr Billings and whatever he has to supply the Union out of the picture and to do as much damage as we can in doing so, but not to the Union directly, but just to the French interest that we find," said Sylvian as he looked about at the faces at the table. He felt that there was some degree of relief at what he had said as none of his men wished to go back into battle with the Union so soon after the last conflict. "Therefore, I propose, and please, gentlemen, bring forward any issues you foresee with my proposal as I do so. I think that we should be somewhere near to the island but not within easy sight by late day. When darkness comes and the lake allowing that my teams shall row out to the island under the cover of dark. We shall need to neutralise any guards that we find and then move onto any headquarters that we shall come across and destroy it. I will deal with Billings personally," he concluded. He had pointed to the map and any possible landing places for the two separate teams to disembark on the island. "Our charts show quite some current in the area of the island and moving out into the lake, and with melting ice and a general rise in the lake because of that may give us some problems. We shall know more when we have better intelligence. In the meantime, that is my plan and that, gentleman, is our objective. Any comments?"

"Sir, I know we shall need more intelligence that you hope to get at Kingston, but what if we should find the island with a heavier guard than we anticipate, even with the additional intelligence?" asked Steven.

"A good point, Mr Gant, if we do encounter a greater number than we anticipate then we shall need a withdrawal plan. I would be extremely grateful if you and Mr Selway could come up with one and let me have a look, we can then share it with the team during training. Let's say day after tomorrow," said Sylvian.

"Sir, looking at these currents, sir, we might be able to use them to our advantage if we come in at the north of the island," said Chris Thompson, as he moved the chart over towards Sylvian. "You can see, sir, as the current moves north and hits the island it is forced to move around the island, and then join again at what looks like, let's see, maybe half a mile off coast. If we come in just to the west of that we could use the centre to be dragged on and into the island, also… for a withdrawal plan it may be prudent to hit the current right here," as he again pointed to the chart, "which would carry us faster than we can row and back to the *Endeavour* sir… maybe our way home after our success too, sir," he concluded.

"Very good, Mr Thompson, I see," said Sylvian pulling the chart more towards him. "Then Lieutenant, I think you should take the lead boat and navigate us to and from our destination. Well done, Chris. Well, I think that is all we can do for the time being, gentlemen, so I shall leave you to your duties and we shall discuss this further when we get to Kingston," said Sylvian as he dismissed his men.

Sylvian sat in the dining room going over the charts when Padraig came in and asked him if he would like his lunch, and he had found a whole casket of tea and now had some brewing. Sylvian did like his tea and told Padraig that some fresh bread and ham would go nice with his tea. As Padraig was leaving Mr Fowler came in and asked the captain if he would like the charts put away. Sylvian thanked him and gave him permission to remove the charts to his office. He walked over to the bulkhead windows and sat on the seat at their base and looked at the sea and nothing beyond. He loved the sea for this very reason. Nothing but sea as far as the horizon could be seen, no birds no land no people just the sea. The waves were building and gave evidence that they must be approaching the north of Nova Scotia and about to enter the Gulf of St Lawrence.

***

Sylvian was on the poop deck enjoying the warm afternoon springtime sun as the *Endeavour* under full sail was cutting through the waves at a good pace. The wind had been kind and was now filling the sails to capacity. Mr Montrose was proving to be a good choice as first officer and had the ship well organised and under a good head of sail. The crow called out ship sighted to the nor nor west on the horizon and headed in their direction. Sylvian asked for confirmation on nationality and the crow reported possibly Spanish man of war or possibly men of commerce under the Spanish flag. Sylvian could not see the ship from the poop deck and asked the crow to keep an eye on her direction. Within minutes the crow called that she had sighted them and had turned about to flee. Mr Montrose asked Sylvian for permission to pursue the ship and was refused. Sylvian explained that they had a task to fulfill and could not risk an engagement at this stage, although he really would like to it was not possible as they must keep to their mission and sail for Kingston. James Montrose was obviously keen to pursue the pirate but would not question his captain's orders. He asked the bo'sun to tell the crow to keep his weathered eye to see if the ship should alter course and to remind the crow about iceberg watch. They had passed two icebergs as they had altered course to west on entering the gulf. It was always a sense of amazement when passing such a gigantic floating piece of ice. The colours were dazzling and from the obvious white through to a deep blue.

Sylvian asked Mr Montrose to look for a place close to land where they might anchor for the dark hours and to let him know when the ship had been secured and where so that he may complete his log. He then left the poop deck and made his way below decks to the training area, where he found Captain Wood instructing the men on cliff climbing and methods of assault when arriving at the top. Peter was demonstrating the use of the grappling hook and how to actually throw it using the swinging motion when Peter suggested that they should try it on the yardarm when the ship had raised sail and anchored for the evening. Sylvian was keen to see for himself and gave permission but only when it was dark as that would simulate the assault on the island in the early hours of the morning when it was still dark, or even half light.

The men had gathered on the main deck and the ship's company after mess time were interested to see what these special sailors were doing. So, the main deck and the forecastle deck were full of sailors. The only light came from the ship's lanterns which did not reach as far as the yardarms. Fitzwalter was the first to try, with Captain Wood standing to one side of him he swung the hook in a large arc and sent the thing skywards and out of sight in the darkness. The sharp eyes of Juno shouted at the crew to get back as the metal hook clattered to the deck narrowly missing fleeing sailors. After that the crew moved over to the opposite side of the ship and Fitzwalter tried for a second time, remembering what Peter had told him and giving the hook the direction of the yardarm, or where he thought it might be before letting the rope go. It sailed up into the air and did not come down. Peter told Fitzwalter to pull on the rope to see how secure it was and after a few feet of loose rope Fitzwalter was able to put his whole weight on it. Juno came forward as always, the brave one he pulled the rope and feeling it firm started to climb up the rope and into the darkness. After a few minutes they could no longer see the whiteness of his breeches against the dark sky but they heard his voice when he shouted watch out below as the hook came hurtling down and landed at Fitzwalter's feet causing him to jump back at the shock. Juno came down the rope ladder with a huge smile on his face and as soon as his feet touched the deck Fitzwalter had him in a head lock and gave him a fist screw to the top of his head. The crew bellowed with laughter at Juno's screams.

Each member of the team took a turn and they practiced for three hours with a great deal of success, both at throwing the hook and also climbing the rope. Sylvian was impressed and declined to take a turn and said that he would do so when required on the island. All of the men were given an extra ration of rum and retired below decks. It was not long before Sylvian, who was still on the forecastle deck, could hear Sefton Marnier on his hand organ and regaling the men with one of his sea shanties. He had the perfect voice, a little gravelly in singing just as Albert had with his talking. Albert was in the centre of it all and Sylvian could see by his face when the men were practicing that he was missing all of the camaraderie from his old team.

Their trip to Kingston had been without issue and it was good to see the place so much more than when Sylvian had last been here. The port now stretched well out into the fast-flowing wide river and had many docks with trading ships, and at one end he could see the *Fawn* that had carried them all here last year. She was much improved by the looks of it and set Sylvian to thinking. Mr Montrose brought the *Endeavour* into port with skill and ease and soon had the ship tied up and secure. Sylvian went down to his office and retrieved his leather folder with all the documents for Kingston and Colonel Gage, secured within.

He made his way up to the poop deck and took Mr Montrose's report and congratulated him on a well manoeuvred docking in such a swift current. He left the ship having been piped off by the bo'sun and made his way to the headquarters building.

Colonel Gage was very pleased to see Sylvian and welcomed him into his office with a firm handshake, he was pleased that Sylvian had been promoted but was not surprised having witnessed his bravado at Kingston last year. He was very sad at the news of his wife's passing and the two sat and discussed what had happened since they had last seen one another.

The conversation soon came around to his current mission. "Well, sir, I am glad you have asked as we are here to cause as much disruption as we can to the Union's efforts to build up its ability to invade the Dominion. Without, I stress to add, actually attacking the union itself," explained Sylvian.

"Now you have my interest, young Mountjoy, and how on earth do you propose to achieve this?" he asked.

"Good question, sir, I and my officers have put some initial plans together and do intend to discuss the matter further whilst we avail ourselves of your facilities, which is of course, sir, with your permission?" Sylvian asked.

"Whatever you need, dear boy, shall be at your disposal, I shall assign my adjutant to the task to ensure that you get what you need. Now how or what can you do to bring discomfort to our cousins without initiating an all-out war?" replied the colonel.

"We know that the French are engaged in an enterprise to assist our cousins with financial and intelligence aid, the man Billings is at this very moment we believe, acting as a banker for the French, and providing the coin for the Union to build its ships, and also enhance the small port of Sacketts Harbour as you have done so with Kingston," replied Sylvian.

"The same man Billings that was involved in the kidnap of your good lady wife and her demise damn it," snorted the colonel.

"Indeed, sir, one and the same, we know he left France with considerable amount of coin and may have already achieved a great deal since the late summer of last year," reported Sylvian.

"I see," said the colonel thoughtfully. "Then I think you must have a visit with our Mr Scott who is currently in the infirmary. I do believe he may have some answers for you on the intelligence side. Our group under Captain Sinclair came across him on their return from a mission in Union territory, he was quite badly injured and had done well to make it as far as he had," said Colonel Gage.

"My good lord," said Sylvian. "So, both John Scott and Robert Sinclair are here in Kingston, well that is indeed fortunate," said Sylvian thoughtfully.

"Indeed, you should find Robert in the officers' mess I shouldn't wonder, dear boy, and of course John is in the infirmary and continues to make good progress. Both have given good reports of yourself; I believe they both travelled with you from England," he replied.

"Indeed, sir, well if I may give my leave and see if I can root out these two and find out what they know that may help me in my mission. I would be pleased, sir, if once we have put together our plan if I may discuss it with you to see if we have any floors that we have not considered," asked Sylvian.

"Of course, dear boy, I would be pleased to get away from this desk even if it is only to live your plan for a short while," he replied.

Sylvian stood and replaced his hat before saluting Colonel Gage. He stopped by the door and turned back to the colonel. "Oh, sir, I have brought one of my men Lieutenant Simms to discuss the army's use of our new training facility which should be completed by autumn, sir," he said. "Should I get him to meet with your adjutant?" he asked.

"Jolly good, dear boy, yes please if you would and we shall talk on the matter before your return to Halifax. Exciting times, young Mountjoy, for this new land," he replied.

Sylvian did indeed find Robert in the officers' mess bar, and he was indeed enjoying a good Islay single malt. He saw Sylvian enter the mess and the two greeted immediately with a firm handshake and smile of two good friends.

"So how went the mission my friend?" asked Sylvian, as they sat down at the same table as they had used when first they met.

"Well, Sylvian, it was a success and I must say down to your Mr Fitzwalter who shall enjoy a good drink when I see him!" exclaimed Robert.

"How so?" asked Sylvian.

"His lessons in concealment were amazing, and indeed worked much to our advantage. The French armaments dump in New England I can now say, and along with many French soldiers, no longer exists. I did however loose two of my best men, one was Sergeant Strong I'm sorry to say. A very heavy loss to the group, French sniper had him from a tree top. My men very nearly cut down the tree with their return fire," he explained.

"I am sorry to hear that, Robert, the sergeant was a good man, and I had much to thank him for. My men shall be sad to hear of his passing." The two men sat in silent thought for a minute before Sylvian raised his glass and the two men saluted the memory of Sergeant George Henry Strong.

"Have you spoken with John Scott?" Robert asked.

"Not yet, my friend, he shall be my next call and I would be extremely grateful if you would accompany me and give me the way to the infirmary and join me in my conversation with John?" asked Sylvian.

"Indeed," said Robert. "Are you ready now or did you wish to have another?" he asked holding his glass up.

The two shared another drink and more conversation on Robert's first mission and Sylvian could see that he was just the same and now had the bug of adventure.

They found themselves at the infirmary having passed Mr Simms on the way with Mr Fowler and Mr Ottershaw who Albert had asked to assist him with his boxes of training material and parchments that he had prepared. Sylvian told Albert to report to the adjutant who was expecting him. They found themselves on the first floor and found John lying in his cot in a single room. The orderly was just leaving the room and asked them not to keep Mr Scott too long in conversation. Sylvian sat in the chair beside the bed and Robert stood to the end of the bed. As soon as John recognised Sylvian a smile spread across his face and he reached out his hand, which Sylvian took in a firm grip.

"Old friend, how do I find you so?" asked Sylvian with a very concerned look to his face.

"Well, Sylvian, if not for young Robert here I would still be in the Union territory," he answered in a very frail voice. "I have much intelligence for you, but it shall have to wait as I feel the laudanum starting to take my mind and voice," he said with his eyes starting to close.

"Then I shall return on the morrow, you take the sleep, John," said Sylvian as he felt John's hand give a squeeze before falling limp.

Sylvian returned to the mess with Robert where they parted until supper. Sylvian was able to book the mess meeting room for Thursday seventh of April and then left for the ship. On his way through the harbour, he took a small diversion to the *Fawn* which sat tied up to the wharf and was looking good with her extra sails. He thought she would hold forty men with room to spare and might just be the answer he was looking for.

On his arrival back at the ship Mr Montrose made his report that Mr Simms, Fowler and Lieutenant Ottershaw had left the ship for the headquarters building. Sylvian told him they had met on the way. James also informed him that the sailmaker and carpenter had left the ship for the chandler's office to secure more equipment. He also asked if he may be permitted to give some of the crew shore leave as many had not been to Kingston before. Sylvian thought that the men should have some leave but must be back on board by twelve midnight and no later, he already had four disciplinary cases to hear on the morrow without more to add to that. Sylvian thanked James for his report and asked if he could ensure that himself and the officers involved in the mission for Horse Island were made aware that there was a meeting to finalise plans for the mission. The meeting was to be held in the officers' mess meeting room at nine a.m. on Thursday. The two officers saluted and Sylvian returned to his cabin to catch up on his log entries and reports. This part of his rank he was not enjoying but knew of its importance to the welfare of the ship and its complement.

The evening went well with most of Sylvian's officers dining in the mess and not on-board ship, which should give Padraig some time ashore. Robert and his two lieutenants Roger Pettifer and Phillip Wilson joined the crew of the *Endeavour* and exchanged stories on their expedition into Union territory. Of course, the stories were much expanded to what had really taken place. But it had been good fun for the young men to relive their adventure, which with honesty, was indeed quite scary at the time. Robert had approached Sylvian with a proposal that his men join Sylvian on the Horse Island mission as it would give them a better feel for the area that they would be most engaged in should the war with the Union come to fruition. Sylvian told him he would give it much thought, although the size of the joint force would give him logistical problems, he could see the benefit to the army in gaining experience in this area.

"Sir, I was wondering if you had been able to give much thought to our discussion earlier today?" asked Robert as the brandy and cigars had arrived.

"I have given it some thought, Robert, my main concern is of course the logistical side of such a large force in Union territory," replied Sylvian.

"I see," said Robert looking rather disappointed.

"However, I do see the benefit to your team in gaining some experience and indeed intelligence in this area, which after all could become our theatre of war, should that unfortunate situation come about," said Sylvian.

"Indeed," said Robert. "And that, sir, is why I asked to join you on this mission. I think it imperative for my men to get back out there after such a difficult mission as we have just endured. It will not only be good for moral but also, as you have said it will serve well for my officers and men to gain some intelligence of the area," Robert replied.

"I concur, Robert, however I do still need to consider the logistics of such a mission which such a great force shall require, but we shall discuss that on Thursday next, can you and your officers attend the planning meeting in the meeting room of this officers' mess?" he asked.

"We shall be there, sir; what time are you starting the meeting?" Robert asked.

"Nine a.m. Robert, that shall give us tomorrow to both put our thoughts together and see what we may come up with, do you need to clear this with Colonel Gage?" asked Sylvian.

Robert looked down at the table and swirled the brandy round in his glass before taking the whole contents and feeling the burn of the liquid as it flowed to his stomach. "I rather pre-empted the possibility of joining you, Sylvian, and asked the colonel prior to your arrival," he replied.

"You, sneaky little toad," said Sylvian. "And what was his reply?"

Robert squirmed a little in his seat and looked over to the waitress and raised his glass for a refill. "I know and I do so apologise, but I do feel that you would have done the same in my position. The colonel thought it a good idea but would leave the decision to you," he answered.

"Then I shall make well your request to your colonel as soon as we have decided what, or indeed if, your team's involvement shall be," replied Sylvian with a smile that said it all.

The two men continued to discuss the mission and agreed at the end of the dinner to meet again at noon tomorrow to see John Scott and see what intelligence they may derive from him. Robert was pleased with the chance for him and his men to contribute to what he saw as partly their failure in not getting the man Billings during the French encounter at the chateau.

***

Sylvian and Robert met up at the infirmary and found John Scott in a much better frame of mind than the day before. He was resting up in bed and although quite ashen to the face, he had a smile when he saw the two men enter his room.

"So, John, still resting I see, that's good," said Sylvian.

"I do hope to be out of this bed soon, my friend, although this time I may have cut it close to the mark, is there any word on Bill Mitchell?" he asked, looking at both men.

"I'm not sure what you mean, John," said Sylvian looking at Robert with a queried look to his face and Robert responding with a shrug to his shoulders.

"Bill and I were captured by Union soldiers as we left Sacketts and were making our way back to Kingston. I managed to jump and roll down an embankment and found myself in a fast-flowing river and then into the lake," he said. "I thought Bill had done the same but when I searched for him, I could find no sign, have you heard anything?"

"No, John, we were not aware of your capture or escape, when we found you in the woods some twenty miles from here you were unconscious," said Robert.

"I see," said John thoughtfully. "So, it's possible that Bill is still captured or, at the very least perished in the river or lake. I must get back and see..." he said climbing from the bed. Both Robert and Sylvian gripped hold of his arms and pushed him back into the bed.

"You would not make it a mile," admonished Sylvian. "You need to stay where you are, sir, you are exhausted and need to recover. We shall find what has happened to Bill," he concluded having got John back into bed and laying back on his pillow. His brow was furrowed and he was showing great concern for the safety of his friend.

"We need to know what you know, John, to help us on our mission and to find Bill," said Robert.

"Arghhh," said John as the pain of his effort was starting to surface. "Yes, yes of course you do, well Bill and I spent two weeks observing the port of Sacketts and also Horse Island, we did see your man Billings, he has quite some setup and is well guarded. There is a large colonial style house where he lives with many slaves at his disposal. The place is guarded like a fort with his own guards, not Union soldiers." He leant across and took a glass of water from the side table and emptied the contents which Sylvian refilled from a jug.

"So, he has his own men, what of the island, John, how does it look for cliffs and access?" asked Sylvian.

"Bring me some parchment and charcoal," he said. Robert headed off to the infirmary office.

"You have to get this man, Sylvian; he has enabled Sacketts to build up far superior to Kingston, and they are building ships in a boatyard, quite quickly from what I have seen," he continued.

"I have every intention of doing so my friend, even should it kill me, I will have my revenge by taking his life away from him," replied Sylvian with his teeth gritted. Robert returned with some parchment and a piece of charcoal and John began to make a plan of the island and its proximity to Sacketts Harbour.

"Now, this is how we saw the island, there are cliffs to three sides and quite steep and somewhere around seventy-five to a hundred feet in places. The east of the island has a landing stage for the small service boats and a walkway has been built into the cliff side. The main residence is somewhere near the centre of the island with a small soldiers' barracks nearer to the east side walkway. This has been built into the trees so that it is not seen from the big house," explained John. He had drawn a good map of the island and was now placing trees and possible cover areas on the small island.

"Is there much cover, John, I mean once our men have scaled the cliffs and dealt with the guard?" asked Sylvian.

"Well, that's where it gets tricky, both I and Bill got onto the island and we were able to secrete ourselves here." He pointed to a small area to the west of the island. "There is a small quarried out area which gives seclusion from sight. Now we managed to get onto the island when we heard that the Englishman takes a walk twice a day around the cliffs, once at nine thirty a.m. and again at four thirty p.m. He has instructed his guard to not be in sight when he takes these walks, so now they remain in their barracks until he is back in the house, which on average takes about forty-five minutes," he said as he wrote the information on the top of the map.

"So, he is regular with this walk, no exceptions, not even weather?" asked Sylvian.

"Not as far as we could tell, the locals told us that even in driving winds and snow he had been seen on the cliff tops," said John.

"So that would give us ample time to scale the cliffs and make a secure hideaway until his next walk. I thank you, John, for this information. It will greatly aid in our planning. Now I see that you are growing tired so Robert and I shall leave you in peace for a sleep and shall let you know our plan when it is fixed," said Sylvian. John handed the map to Robert with a nod of thanks and slid down into his bed and let the tiredness come over him.

***

"So, what is the total sum of our funds remaining?" asked Billings of his ledger man William Courtney.

"Well," said Courtney as he glanced over the top of his half spectacles and read from his book. "We have but just $36,000 left, sir, it was good that your man was able to get back the fraudulent sums taken by the woodcutters," reported William.

"Indeed, so we have sufficient sums to continue for this next month, good then we shall await an answer to my request for more funds owing to the theft of the last consignment," said Billings. "It was also good that you had put aside that large sum of gold into the reserve, however I am still curious as to why you had done such, and indeed why you had not told me about it," queried Billings as he rounded his now repaired desk and sat upon its edge in front of Courtney and glared down upon his nervous person.

"I explained such, sir, it is always good practice that accounts should hold a reserve for such matters that may become pertinent, as we have found, sir," he explained nervously twitching his pencil between his fingers. "I did not find it necessary to report such as it is common practice and I thought such as a learned person as you, sir, would of course be aware."

"Indeed," said Billings in a sarcastic tone as he stood and made his way back to the far side of his desk and retook his seat.

The two men were interrupted by a knock to the door and Jacob informing them that some Union soldiers were at the dock with a special consignment and needed the attendance of the 'Massa'.

Curious as to the reason for such an intrusion both Billings and Courtney made their way from the house and down to the jetty. Courtney had been somewhat delayed by his gout but had eventually hobbled his way to find Billings and a young Union lieutenant at the pier.

"So, you say this has come across land and is intended for me, Lieutenant?" asked Billings.

"Yes, sir, all the way from the harbour at New York, sir. My colonel told me to get it straight to you, sir. There are two very heavy boxes, sir, as you can see, we needed two boats to bring it across. The colonel has asked for your signature, sir, before I may release same to you, sir," explained the young lieutenant in a southern drawl.

Billings signed the form as it was presented and the two boxes were unloaded from the boats and onto the wharf. The young lieutenant handed Billings a sealed parchment before saluting him and making his way back to the boats. Billings took in the size of the two boxes and looked at Courtney with a curious look. He opened the parchment and its folds and proceeded to read the French text as it was scribed. The letter was from General Lascelles who was in no uncertain terms very angry about the British acquiring the vast sums that he had sent last year. He explained that this was indeed the last supply of gold that would be sent and that Billings needed to ensure that the agreement with the Union by the emperor was upheld and seen to its successful conclusion. Any further failings in this endeavour should see the recipient before the guillotine.

Billings lowered the parchment and unconsciously run his hand around his neck. He looked at Courtney with his glowering one eye and told him to get the boxes to the cavern and get it counted and weighed and have a full report before him by dinner. He turned and walked back up the cliff path as he heard orders flying to the guards to get the boxes to the secure cavern. It was just starting to snow yet again and Billings had forgotten his hat when he left the house. His mood was changing rapidly back to his mean demeanour as he now had the control of more funds and could once again rise to the heights that he once held, no more contempt from the colonel.

Jacob opened the door as Billings approached and received a slap across the face sending him to the floor as Billings marched through the door and pulled his cloak from his shoulders and threw it down on the now cowering servant. "Next time I leave, have my hat ready with my cloak damn you," he snarled.

"Yas, suh, massa," said Jacob as he pulled himself to his feet.

Billings slammed the door of his office as he made his way through. He poured himself a large brandy and sat down behind his desk with a huge smug grin occupying his ugly scarred face.

***

All the officers had gathered in the meeting room at the officers' mess, including Fitzwalter, Jacko and Juno Hardcastle. On the table were some charts and John's map, they had discussed the route to the island and how they would transport themselves to the island using the *Fawn* and some of the *Endeavour's* boats. The *Endeavour* was to anchor two miles out to sea and would hopefully remain unseen as the island would shelter her outline on the horizon. The row boats would leave first followed by the *Fawn*, Lieutenant Chris Thompson would take the helm of the *Fawn* and Lieutenant Jacob Stubbings would lead the boats in to shore. The boats would take the north and east side of the island with the *Fawn* beaching on the west side, after dropping off half the crew to the southern side. Billings always took his walk starting from the southern side of the island heading west. Sylvian would command the boat crews and land on the north side of the island and remain on the beach until daylight. The rest of the team would on landing make their way up the cliffs using the hook irons and rope and take out the guards. The row boat team to the east would have Mr Selway and Fitzwalter with four of the crew carrying some of Mr Selway's magic gunpowder kegs. They would then make their way to the garrison of guards and take out those that are resting and then set two of the kegs. They would then move onto the main house along with the crew landing to the south and west of the island and free any slaves and then demolish the house. They would all then meet at the old quarry and make their way back to the ship.

"Sir, what about the man Billings?" asked Mr Gant.

"That, Steven, shall be my job," he answered. "Now we must be certain that each crew leader which is Mr Gant, Mr Selway, Robert and Lieutenant Stubbings have watches that are synchronised to exactly the same time. The action will commence with each of the crews remaining on the beach in concealment and then ascending the cliffs at ten a.m. to commence your action. The guards will have returned to the barracks and therefore, your discovery whilst climbing the cliffs should be avoided. Now, gentlemen, we know that Billings leaves the house at nine thirty every day, so it is imperative that you remain out of sight and secluded until ten, which is when I hope to have Billings secured," he explained. Sylvian looked around the table at the very attentive faces before him. "One final matter, we know that there must be coin somewhere on the island that Billings uses to keep his masters build going, however where that is kept is a mystery. Steven, your team will attack the house and free the slaves, I would think that there must be some sort of account keeper for all this coin so find him and find where the coin is kept, it is of paramount importance to locate this coin and get it off the island and back to the *Endeavour*, so Chris, you will take the *Fawn* to the pier on the east of the island and await Mr Gant, his crew and the coin. You will then make your way to the north west of the island and pick up the team from the beach and myself and Billings. Mr Selway and Mr Fitzwalter along with their team will set the barracks with their barrels charged and make their way to the house where they shall lay the remainder of their charges. Mr Fitzwalter, I shall need you to search the house and gather all parchment that may give us some intelligence as to what the Union may have planned for us. Now, gentlemen, any questions?" asked Sylvian.

"Sir," said Jacob. "Apart from Billings, do we take any prisoners?"

"No prisoners, gentlemen, we shall leave the slaves if they do not wish to take their freedom and return with us," he replied.

"Sir, will you have a time by which we should all be back to the beach and the boats, sir," Asked Chris.

"No, Mr Thompson, we should only ensure that the time of the attack is synchronised, as for your escape that shall be at your individual team choice dependent on the circumstances that you find yourselves in. We must all try to get home safe, gentlemen; I want no casualties apart from the enemy. Each team leader must nominate a second in command to take over should he be unable to continue, is that clear?" asked Sylvian.

All the men in the room replied with a strong and resolute, "Aye, sir," to the question. Minor issues were then dealt with as to who would be in charge of grappling hooks and who should be first up the ropes. Mr Gant asked about how long the fuses would be set on Mr Selway's munitions and it was agreed that the barracks would have a thirty-minute fuse as would the house. They should all be off the island when the barracks went up, and on their way, back to the *Endeavour*. Martin ensured the group that at nine thirty he would have the *Endeavour* under short sail and would head for the north of the island to pick up all the teams.

They were all happy with the plans and of their individual roles within the action. Sylvian again went over the plans and timing and then each of the individual commanders went over how they expected to execute their individual parts. With the meeting completed Sylvian dismissed the men to their duties and then set off for the infirmary.

John was sat up in his cot with a plate of food and some tea on his side table. He looked much better and was pleased to see Sylvian. They went over the plans that had just been concluded and John was impressed with the detail. "What have you planned for the man Billings on his capture, my friend," he asked.

"Mmmm, good question, John. I know what I should like to do, however I think that my admiral would like to see him tried and hanged for his offences," he answered, rather unsure of his feelings.

"Well, I can see some merit in the admiral's wishes, it would send out a strong message, however, I do feel for you and also all of the men, myself included in what they would like to see," he commented. "If I were you, I should think that you need to deal with what presents itself at the time. If it looks like he may put to flight or to harm you then you have no choice but to take his life," he said.

The two men looked at one another as they both knew that on a mission such as this, it was impossible to plan for all the variables that may present themselves. But Sylvian knew for this mission to be a success, and it must be, then he would need to try, at least try and cover as many probables, as possible. He knew that John had given him good information, with this intelligence he could see a way of making the mission work to his and his men's favour. However, it would be even more guaranteed if he could make one more variable count.

"John, how are you feeling now?" he asked cautiously.

"I don't like that look on your face, Mountjoy, what, sir, are you asking of me, come on, sir... say what is on that mind of yours," replied John.

"Well," said Sylvian as he slid himself into the chair beside the cot. "If you were to come on the mission, just as an advisor I mean as I would not wish to put you in harm's way, not so soon after your ordeal…" Sylvian paused as John held up his hand.

"I was wondering, and I might say was quite hoping that you would ask me such, Sylvian. I am not sure just how much I can help and my current fitness is not at its best, but it would please me greatly to be a part of this mission," he replied. "However, I do not know if the doctor will give me leave to join you, when are you planning to sail?"

"One week from today, John, that should see us to the island by the weekend and I was hoping to make landfall on the island early on Saturday," Sylvian replied. "That should give you time for rest and also to get some fitness back into your muscles."

"Indeed, my friend. Well, that should suit me fine as I hope to be out from this cot by Sunday at the latest. A little training with Fitzwalter should see me back to some fitness before we sail," he said with excitement. The colour had most definitely returned to his cheeks. The two men shook hands and Sylvian left for the colonel's office to make his report.

He was delayed by the doctor as he left John's room who asked him to come into his office. Sylvian obliged as he thought it might have some bearing on John's condition and his recovery. The office was small and dark with no windows and just an oil lamp hung from the ceiling above a small wooden desk loaded with papers. The good doctor asked Sylvian to sit as he made his way around the desk and took his seat.

"Captain Mountjoy, I am Dr Richard Smallbone the army surgeon for the garrison of Kingston and have the responsibility for the army as well as the civilian population. I see that you are good friends with Mr Scott, he seems to enjoy your visits and is responding well to his rest and recuperation. I have however, noticed on your visits that you favour your right arm somewhat, please forgive me if I am intruding, but would this be the result of some injury?" he asked.

Sylvian looked over this young doctor who spoke with a very educated accent and vocabulary. He was tall and rather thin for his height but carried himself quite well nonetheless.

"I thank you for asking, Dr Smallbone, and commend your power of observation, sir. It is indeed an injury sustained from musket ball sir; may I ask, sir, why you ask me so," answered Sylvian.

"A doctor's curiosity, Captain, just observed your rather slow and apparently painful movement when giving exercise to your right arm, would you object, sir, if I was to take a look?" asked the doctor.

"Well, the wound is quite healed now, sir, the ball passed directly through my upper arm and I have with perseverance and exercise gained more use as time has gone, sir," replied Sylvian.

"I see, well that is indeed progress, Captain, how old is the injury, sir?" he asked.

"It is indeed some six months now, sir, that I sustained the injury, maybe a bit longer," replied Sylvian. "I have no objection, sir, if you would like to take a look," replied Sylvian.

"The curiosity of a doctor, sees no bounds, Captain, and I would deem it a privilege if I may examine you. Could you please slip off your coat and shirt," he said as he stood and moved to a tray of tools to his left. Sylvian removed his coat, waistcoat and shirt and stood before the surgeon. Dr Smallbone examined the wound and used a small rubber hammer upon his elbow very lightly and prodded in and around the wound before telling Sylvian to redress. "Interesting, Captain," he said as he re took his seat. "Your brachii bicep at the short head has been severed and will lay to waste if we do not attend to it."

"And pray, sir, ignore my ignorance but what is that?" asked Sylvian.

"Of your bicep muscles at the top of your arm, Captain, one has become severed, that is the top from the bottom of the muscle and needs to be reattached. The longer this remains then it will start to waste with lack of use and the usability of your arm will severely degrade. I already note that the top of this muscle has indeed already rescinded towards the bone," he answered and explained his meaning by pointing to his own upper arm in the areas he was indicating.

"Oh," said Sylvian. "So, I should prepare for the arm to lose its use after time, Doctor, is that your meaning?" asked Sylvian. Looking rather worried as he had seen this as just a minor inconvenience which, over time would right itself.

"Not at all, sir," said the doctor as he pulled a book from his desk drawer and opened it to a drawing of the skeletal and muscle mass of the human body. "Here is where your problem is, this muscle here has been severed and needs to be reattached. It is this part at the top that is already starting to waste towards the bone, this is due to blood flow and lack of use. It would require a small incision here and the two parts to be sutured together. Modern medicine, Captain, has brought us a long way in our understanding, and of course the battlefields of Spain and France have given us more knowledge. The muscle when reattached will fuse and become working again in time," he explained.

"I see," said Sylvian deep in thought. "So how long would this process take, Doctor?" he asked.

"The procedure is quite short in time to perform however the recovery can take some time as the arm cannot be used for some months whilst the muscle tissue fuses," he answered.

"Well, sir, whilst I see the benefit of such surgery, I would not be able to do so until I have concluded my mission which would be at least two weeks before we are back in Kingston. Would this be too long, would the muscle have wasted beyond repair by such time?" Sylvian asked.

"No, I should think that would be fine but no longer or the procedure would not be possible," he answered.

"Then, sir, I thank you for taking this time with me and I shall promise to make you my first call on our return," said Sylvian as he stood and picked up his cloak and hat, shook the doctor's hand firmly and painfully and left the office and infirmary.

***

The colonel was quite pleased with the plans that Sylvian presented and was doubly pleased that both Captain Carlisle and John Scott would be on the mission. One point that Colonel Gage was curious about was what would be the plan if they were to encounter any French or Union ships in the area.

"Sir, it is not our intention to engage with any Union vessels unless we are fired upon. Our intelligence from Halifax tells us that the Union is yet to build anything more substantial than their clippers and small frigates which are of no match to the *Endeavour* however, if we are to come upon a ship of the French or Spanish Navy then we shall most certainly engage," he replied.

"Good then we are safe to assume that no war shall be started by us, what about the Horse Island whereby you intend to destroy property, this is Union territory you will be acting upon is it not?" he asked.

"Indeed, sir, but again our intelligence tells us that the buildings on the island were at the behest of Billings on behalf of the French government, sir," answered Sylvian. "Any property destroyed would then arguably be part of the war we are engaged in with the French, sir. Also, it is my orders that I should cause whatever damage I may to the Union's ability to bring war against us in the Canadas, sir."

"I see, very well then, Captain, I wish you good luck in your venture and hope that you shall be back to us with yet another victory to your name," he said.

"Sir, the matter of the *Fawn*, may we make use of her on this mission. I feel she will enable us to move more swiftly than our ship's shore boats, sir, although they have sail, it is only one and the *Fawn* is of much better a size to carry more men and faster to the south of the island?" Sylvian asked.

"Indeed, Sylvian, you must take what you need, my adjutant shall make sure you have what weapons and powder you require," he replied.

The two men parted with a salute from Sylvian and some kind words from Colonel Gage.

***

Mr Courtney was just finalising his briefing with Billings on their current state of finances and the full account holding of the gold that was received two boxes each containing fifty ten-pound bars with a value of $320,000.

"So, what does that bring our current holding to, Courtney, with no reserve?" Billings asked.

"Well, sir, we had $36,000 before the delivery so that would be $356,000, sir," replied Courtney.

"And how does that align with our plans?" asked Billings as he stood and moved to the small table in the corner that housed the decanters of his fine whisky, port and of course cognac. He poured himself a good measure of cognac.

"Mmmm," said Courtney eyeing the recently poured cognac and feeling the warmth of the liquid as Billings took a large sip from his glass. "It would, well, sir, we were expecting twice as much last year sir, so we are behind and shall need to revise our plans somewhat."

"Indeed," said Billings as he moved back to the desk and retook his seat. "I will need your revised plans by the end of the week, William. Jackson, do we still have need of his services?" he asked.

"I believe so, sir, as we move into our next phase. The man has instilled fear in our suppliers, so much so that I feel they would breathe a sigh of relief if we were to dispense with his services, and should probably go back to their thieving ways, sir," William answered.

Billings took another sip from his glass and sat back in his leather chair. William watched and felt every last drop.

"You are right, Courtney; we shall keep the man on for the time being. See to it and make sure you have the revised plans before me by week's end, now away with you, man," he commanded with a wave of his hand. William struggled to his feet and retrieved his walking cane and made his way through the door, again leaving it open but Jacob had it closed before Nathaniel could shout. William smiled as he crossed the hall, just his way of revenge.

Chapter Eleven
Horse Island

The ship heaved in the wild Atlantic Ocean throwing those below decks not sitting or contained within their hammocks, cleanly off their feet. The wise had found purchase against the storm and bucking and bowing of the ship. The timbers creaked and groaned under the pressure of the crashing waves and water ran down and between the timbers and stairways. It was cold, dark and wet giving a totally miserable feeling to all those who dwelled down there.

In the corner near the stern and rope locker was a figure curled up against the bulkhead, his arms wrapped about his knees. The swinging of the oil lamp gave yellow light to him for a split second before he was back in the dark. He had on no shoes and tattered wet clothes as his life had befallen him. Once a great man of importance and stature, now just a deckhand on a merchantman out of Southampton.

He sat wide eyed and contemplating his lot and filled with hatred to the man that had seen him so. First his trial and then imprisonment and his dishonourable discharge from the service as his commission was stripped from him. His wife had disowned him, his family had turned their backs on him. Such dishonour he had brought to a seafaring family who had served for centuries as officers to the crown with pride and honour. His brother, a captain had often warned him of his temper and bullish temperament. He had told him on many occasions as they had grown to curb his anger, but no, he had known best, discipline was the way forward and God help anyone who should not obey him. He had been discharged from four ships and finally shelved until a new ship had been commissioned and was desperate for officers as she was to sail within a week.

He had found on his arrival that discipline was indeed lapse and that he needed to bring these young useless officers to book. He had started with the midshipmen and intended to bring them smartly in to shape but the other lieutenants did not share his views that the ship could only be successful if they bred fear into their juniors and brought them into line. So, it was a task he was willing to fulfill on his own. He had made a good start by raiding the captain's files and learning as much as he could of the officers on the ship. Knowledge to him was power and power was what it was all about. He would make first officer when the captain saw how good he was at handling the men, and then just one more step and he would be on his way. That would show his brother who was best at this game.

Now here he was cold, wet and hungry and this hovel for a home. He had lice and fleas that he had picked up from this motley crew in just the first two weeks of their sailing. At least he was not chained as he had been at Portsmouth gaol for these past four months. Having nowhere to go he only had what he knew and that was his life at sea. First, he had tried to sign on as a merchant officer but his record had come before him. He was physically thrown off two ships and the third offered him a place as deck hand. Having nothing else and already half starved and robbed of all his possessions when he had taken too much ale one night, he signed on, and here he found himself in this rotten rat-infested hole with only one person to blame.

He Second Lieutenant Archibald Wilson-McLean of His Majesty's Navy had so unjustly been treated by that pompous bastard of a newly promoted and no nothing Captain Sylvian Mountjoy.

He would have his revenge.

***

The *Endeavour* was full of life and action as the crew readied her for tomorrow's sailing. Sylvian could hear the running of feet and the calling of commands as the ship was alive and happy at the prospect of going back to sea. He was going over his charts for Lake Ontario as this was his first incursion onto a lake, which was in itself as large a sea as any. He had plotted his trip to Horse Island which should take about eight hours. They would anchor up in Sherwin Bay until night and then sail on to the north of Horse Island. This would give him time to go through with his officers the final plans for the mission. It was now close to supper and he should wash and dress as all of his officers and Mr Scott would dine with him this evening.

The dining room was full and all the officers stood when Sylvian entered the room. "Please, gentlemen, as you were," he said as he took his place at the head of the table. To his right was his first lieutenant, James Montrose and next to him James Wood, John Douglas, Steven Gant and Peter Selway. At the far end of the table was Marine Captain Peter Wood. To Sylvian's left was Robert Carlisle and next to him was his lieutenant, George Cole, John Scott, Marine Lieutenant Roger Pettifer and Marine Lieutenant Philip Wilson. Wine had been served and the conversation was flowing when Sylvian entered. Padraig poured Sylvian a full glass of red wine and asked if he may start the first course. Sylvian told him to go ahead and looked around him at the silent table.

"So, what was the conversation, gentlemen, that I so rudely interrupted?" asked Sylvian.

"Mr Montrose was asking us all a question sir, and was indeed part way through," said Robert.

"Indeed, well, Mr Montrose, pray continue, but from the start if you please, sir," said Sylvian jovially.

"Well, sir, I thank you, but I merely asked of my learned colleagues a question of some concern to myself and that is in which of Shakespeare's plays would be the greatest chicken killer, sir?" asked James.

"Well, I am not sure that any chickens were killed in any Shakespeare play that I am aware of, but pray tell, Mr Montrose," asked Sylvian.

"Well sir, I have come to the conclusion that it would of course be Macbeth, because after all, sir, he did murder most foul," said James as the room erupted into laughter and James received some small snippets of bread thrown his way as he too laughed heartily.

"Very good, Mr Montrose," said Sylvian as he regained his composure.

"Thank you, sir," said James. "But I know not why I laugh so heartily as I have heard this story before." The room again erupted into laughter and Mr Montrose's face had gone quite red as he tried to compose himself. This fact was indeed exacerbated by Padraig entering the jovial room with his platter of six roasted chickens which he placed in the centre of the table and could not understand why all of his officers had now been brought to tears with laughter.

The evening was indeed a good one with great food and laughter a plenty. The wine had flowed well and the stories had grown and grown as the wine dulled their minds and loosened their tongues. Even Marine Lieutenant Pettifer who was a most serious man had been given to share a story which again had the table of men in tears of laughter. Sylvian was pleased to see such a good group of men such as these, becoming quite settled and comfortable together. It would be important in the coming days that they should all feel that they know and could rely on one another on this next mission that they faced.

***

It was dawn when Mr Fowler woke his captain from a deep sleep and into a heavy headed wakefulness. Padraig had already laid out some tea and some bread, eggs and bacon under a platter on Sylvian's desk where he had preferred to breakfast. Sylvian wrapped himself in his smoking jacket and took his breakfast quite heartily for the way he felt. The tea had helped to rehydrate him from last night's wine and brandies. And the food had made him feel more human and ready to face his day. With his ablutions complete and in fresh shirt and uniform, he picked up his hat and made his way to the poop deck where he found Mr Montrose looking quite pale. He sent him off for one of Padraig's breakfasts and stood to watch his ship come to life. The lieutenants and midshipmen had the men up the masts and the ship was loosed from its moorings at Kingston wharf. Mr Douglas had the duty to take the ship out and was doing a fine job of it. The ship gave a jolt when it hit the current of the river and with the sails now unfurled the *Endeavour* began to pull against the current and head out towards Wolfe Island, named after Major General James Wolfe. They would round Simcoe Island and then take an easterly heading towards the Union border of this great lake.

Mr Montrose returned to the poop deck looking much refreshed and back to his normal pallor. Sylvian handed over command to him and he then returned to his cabin. He had been deep in thought whilst on the poop deck and what he might feel when finally coming face to face with Nathaniel again. He must control his anger, but he knew that every time he heard that man's name, he could see Mary's sweet face. He took up the map that he had laid out with their route now pencilled upon. He looked at the small almost ellipse shaped Horse Island and knew as he looked that Billings was at this moment making ready to take his morning walk. This would be his last morning walk that he will complete of this island. Sylvian could not plan how he would deal with this beast when he confronted him, there were far too many variables in play for him to come to any fixed plan, other than the one that would see Billings either captured or dead, he knew not which it would be.

The *Endeavour* had found a secluded part of Sherwin Bay and had dropped anchor. They had come across no other ships on their journey, not even traders. It was a warm and very sunny evening and the crew were making the ship ready for the night when they would aweigh anchor and make for the north of Horse Island. Sylvian had called his officers to the captain's dining room where the table was strewn with charts and hand drawn plans. "Gentlemen, it is imperative that each team knows what they are doing and where they must be at attack time. We have the advantage as we have just learnt from Mr Scott that if we wait for Billings to take his morning walk, then the guards will be at their barracks. The full force of our attack will be at the barracks when they will least expect it," he explained.

"Sir, can we run over the changed plans one more time as there is one part I am concerned with, sir," said Steven.

"Well tell us the part that concerns you, Steven, and we shall address that first," said Sylvian.

"Sir, the changed plans allow that the four teams shall now concentrate on the barracks and house with Mr Carlisle and his marines seeking out the gold if there is any," he explained.

"Indeed, go on," prompted Sylvian.

"Well, sir, that leaves you alone on the cliffs with the man Billings, without any support. And whilst I am certain without any doubt whatsoever that you shall deal with the man, I do however have concerns that he may not be alone. If it is such and with your arm as it is, would not some support be appropriate?" asked Steven.

"Yes, Steven, it would and I thank you for your concern, what suggestions have you?" he asked.

"Sir, I would suggest that yourself and Captain Carlisle would be a formidable foe for any man to face. You would still have the advantage over Billings and I am sure that the good captain would give you leave to deal with the man, in whatsoever way you should deem sir," Steven replied.

Sylvian looked at Robert who was already looking at his friend. He nodded and pulled himself upright. "I think he is right, Captain. You must have some support even if it is just as lookout for any other person that may come along or guard that may have hidden from view," said Robert. "With John taking the lead on the house and barracks and in search of any coin, and with my two lieutenants and Mr Gant and Mr Selway and your team, then I think we have all other covered well."

Sylvian took great thought to the suggestion. He needed to get Billings alone, he needed to know why he had done what he had done to Mary. A woman he had professed to love, and then he must make the decision as to whether he would go back to face charges or whether it would all end there. But he understood the concern that had been showed and indeed his own knowledge of how bad his arm was. It was worse as the good doctor had predicted and he wasn't sure that he would be able to draw his sword let alone make use of it. Damn Union shot.

"You are right, gentlemen, and indeed I do thank you for your concern. Mr Scott, you will take charge of the land assault if you would, sir," said Sylvian.

"Indeed, Captain, it shall be an honour," said John.

"Robert, I thank you for your offer and I gratefully accept. So back to the plan, we shall leave the *Endeavour* at four a.m. and reach the island in darkness. We shall then seclude ourselves from the guards at the bottom of the cliffs here, here and here," Sylvian said pointing to the charts. "Point 'A' shall be Mr Selway's Team. Point 'B' shall be Mr Gant's team and at the point of the island 'C' shall be Mr Scott's team on the *Fawn*. You must ensure that you pull your boats from the water as fast as possible and as silently as possible. If you come across a guard then he must be dispatched quickly and silently. Is that clear, gentlemen?" All present indicated their clarity. "Now, Billings should leave the house at nine thirty so we must be in place by ten to start our attack. Robert and I have no cliff to ascend as we shall meet Billings at the north west of the island where he should be at around ten, by that time, gentlemen, you should be at your places and making good your mission. Any questions, gentlemen, before we ensure our timepieces are synchronised?" asked Sylvian.

There being no questions the team leaders synchronised their timepieces and were all dismissed to their duties.

The ship slipped from her moorings as soon as the anchor was raised, the sky was black and the wind was building quite fiercely as a storm approached. The first drops of rain spattered on the heads of the sailors as they made their way down from the rigging. The lake water was already building up and the *Fawn* towed behind the *Endeavour* was let out on its rope to ride the waves. The *Endeavour* stayed level and true as the waves began to crash her bow as they left the protection of Sherwin Bay.

Sylvian gave great thought to cancelling the mission should the storm come and be greater than she was. Although it would give his team a greater protection from spying eyes on the coast as they would seek shelter from the cold driving rain.

The ship sailed on with Mr Montrose having command. The teams were below decks preparing what they needed for the mission. Tar covered canvas had been wrapped around the gunpowder barrels to keep them dry. The crew had made good use of the oilskins that Sylvian had purchased. They were black and long and came with hoods attached and drawstrings to bring them tightly to the face against the wind. Their muskets had been sleeved in tar covered canvas slip bags that had been made by the sailmaker. They had long strips attached at each end so that they may carry them across their shoulders. The sailmaker had also prepared some pouches and belts to hold them for their musket balls and powder horns to leave their hands free for rock climbing and defence against attack.

When the ship reached her place of anchor and the team was now gathered on a windy rain-soaked deck, Sylvian and Robert looked them all over and were proud at what they saw. Forty men all in black with musket bags slung from their shoulders and bags for grappling hooks and ropes hung from their backs. The *Fawn* had been pulled alongside and would be difficult to board as she bucked high and low in the raging water. But these men had practiced time and time again for boarding and disembarking from a vessel in all weather. Sylvian looked at his watch, three minutes to four. He looked at Robert and nodded. "Mr Scott, get the teams loaded if you please," he shouted.

"Aye aye, sir," shouted Mr Scott against the wind. The men were quickly on their way lined up on the starboard side of the ship and making their way onto the *Fawn*. Sylvian, Robert, Jacko and Juno climbed into the ship's longboat and were lowered via the transom davit into the water. This was a perilous task and would see them in the water at one point and then halfway up the ship at the next. Juno waited until the water took the weight of the boat and then cut the davit ropes before the water fell again. He quickly pushed the boat from the side of the ship before they were sucked down by the fall of the water. Jacko had the mast raised and the sail deployed in seconds as the small boat bobbed in the heavy water. The oilskins were doing their job at keeping the men dry and with hoods raised keeping the water from their backs.

The lake was indeed rough and the little boat rose and fell with bumps and jolts. Juno had taken the helm and Jacko was manning the sail, they could not see the *Fawn* with her two sails she must be well ahead. The landscape was briefly lit blue as a bolt of lightning flew across the sky. Jacko was sure he had seen the *Fawn* well ahead and the island dead ahead. The crack of thunder rattled their very souls as the storm reported she was directly overhead.

It took them an hour and a half to get to the shore of the island and they hoped that the *Fawn* had found her place on the beach. The early light of dawn was coming in the east but was late and the sky was still angry with heavy rain and almost gale force winds. The four men dragged the small boat up and onto the gravel beach. Sylvian went off to find her a hiding place and was soon back directing the men to the right and a tall rock that stood proud from the beach next to the cliff. Sylvian was aware that they had come too far to the east and Robert and he would need to make their way west until the land fell to the beach as John had told them. Sylvian left Juno and Jacko with the boat and well secluded from prying eyes from the cliff above. The spot they had chosen was indeed perfect to secrete the boat and the two men from the weather and would not be seen from above.

Robert and Sylvian kept close to the cliff as they made their way west and soon came to where the land dropped towards the beach. They had found cover and were well secluded from the weather and any prying eyes. Now it was time to wait.

The *Fawn* with Chris Thompson at the helm and Peter Selway at the sails had made good headway from the ship, she had picked up a good wind and was soon away into the choppy lake water. The men had found their space and were well placed giving the boat good balance and ballast. With their heads bowed against the wind and rain and their hoods giving good protection against the cold rain, they settled down.

The sailors fared well with the bucking of the *Fawn* as she was tossed from wave to wave, however the soldiers were not faring that well and a few were already given to take to the side of the boat and give way to their suppers. Chris deftly kept his eye to the sails which gave him the way of the wind and made it much easier for him to steer the *Fawn* into the swell. He had a compass to his front which he could not see, that is until a blue flash of lightning lit the sky and he stole a look. He was dead on course and had also seen the outline of the island in the brief flash.

After a little over an hour the *Fawn* beached herself on the gravel of the island. The men were quickly out of the boat and dragging her ashore. The two teams worked in silence and worked extremely well with one another as they got the *Fawn* into cover of some bushes at the bottom of the tall cliff. They then separated into their groups and moved east to find cover.

With a hundred yards between them the teams had found good cover and hunched down in silence for the night. The wind was blowing from the north and right at them. The rain was cold and hands had been tucked well into their oilskins. Now it was time to wait.

***

"Massa, is you shaw you is wantin to take yowa walk dis monin. Shaw has bin da nassy stowm, massa," said Jacob as he was clearing away the breakfast things.

"It's fine now, Jacob," said Nathaniel as he wiped the residue of corn muffin from his lips. "The sun is about to shine and it will be a marvelous day, where is Messie?" he asked.

"Oh, Massa she dun gon to der market, Massa, we's needin vitals bad, suh. She tooks the boat wid two o der guards right early, Massa," replied Jacob from the door.

"Damn," said Billings. "When will she be back, I could wait I suppose," he asked.

"Oh, Massa, I donts thinks she gon be back for safternoon massa, she gots lots to git, Massa, we dun got no vitals, suh," Jacob replied.

"Very well," said Billings. "I shall take my cloak and hat, oh and my cane, Jacob, see to it."

"Yas, suh, Massa," said Jacob as he made his way from the door and towards the kitchen, cussing as he went.

Billings stood outside the front door and took his watch from his pocket and flicked open the cover, 09.32, perfect. He looked up at the sky to see that the clouds were breaking up and the sun was pushing its way through, casting rays of light that lit up the bushes and trees as it passed over them. He wondered if he should go left today instead of right, but as Messie was not with him he decided to go his usual way to the right. He wanted to catch Messie out and take a turn to the left as he had not been that way with her before. He reached the cliff top and took a minute as he often did to look out across the lake. This time he watched as the sunbeams danced across the now calm water and made it glisten like diamonds. He really loved this place, and once he had dealt with Mountjoy he would settle here. He was still waiting for Jackson to report back on that situation. He had sent him to Halifax to capture Mountjoy and bring him to the island where finally he would make him suffer, and realise who he had wronged was not to be done so. Then he would slit his throat and throw him from these very cliffs. He took a deep breath and sighed as a grin spread across his scarred face. He turned and carried on his walk along the cliff path. He would not go down to the beach today on the north west side as time was against him and he had to do some report writing to the French on how progress had exceeded plans. They would be pleased and hopefully would send some more money. The cloud was breaking more as he continued on, stopping in places where he could see the view. His favourite place was on the north of the island where the cliff path went up to the edge with the woodland behind. He felt like the master of all that he surveyed when he stood and looked out across the lake. Sometimes he would go down to the beach and see what the lake had washed in but this morning he would just stay on the path. He must get those reports done.

***

Sylvian looked at his watch for the tenth time in as many minutes, 09.58. He looked at Robert and they both nodded. His legs were stiff as they crawled from their hiding place and out onto the gravel beach. Sylvian checked around and could not see any sign of guards or movement. The two men made their way stealthily along the bottom of the cliff until it dropped to their level. This was where they were most exposed; there were no trees or large bushes to hide them, just scrub grass and a steep hill to climb. That should put the life back into their legs.

They reached the top and the cliff path, and turned to their right and followed the path up and onto the cliff top. The path at this spot ran close to the edge with trees quite close and inland. A perfect place for an ambush thought Sylvian. Robert said that he would scout in amongst the trees to make sure they were alone. Sylvian sat himself on a log just into the tree line and waited in the sunshine and enjoyed the beautiful view.

***

He was glad that he had worn his cloak as the breeze of the north part of the island was quite chilled and brought tears to the eye. He had just finished what he called the fish tail of the island and was now standing looking down the hill to the beach. He was in two minds whether to go down or not. He really wanted to, certainly after a good storm like last night had served them. He took out his watch and flipped the cover. It was already ten fifteen; he would need to raise his pace. He set off on the upward stretch of the cliff path to his favourite spot where he stopped and looked out across the lake.

"Beautiful view is it not," said Sylvian. Billings swung round and jumped at the voice behind him.

"You," he said snarling.

"Indeed," said Sylvian as he jumped to his feet and drew his sword with his left hand. Billings stepped back a pace and then stopped himself as he was now close to the cliff edge.

"Mountjoy, how…" he said looking around him for a place to run or hide. He reached for his pistol but before he could put his hand to the grip, Sylvian was upon him.

"No no, old friend," he said as he brought the point of his sword to Billings' throat. Nathaniel pulled his hand away from the grip and raised his chin to the blade. Sylvian reached forward with his right hand and could barely grip the pistol with the pain, but he had it and threw it into the bushes.

"Now what?" said Billings, and then looked to his left as he heard gunfire from the direction of the house and barracks. "So, you didn't come alone, how disappointing, I would so prefer a one on one."

"Just tying up loose ends, the same as me," said Sylvian as his blade drew a small trickle of blood and Billings took a half pace back.

"Well go on, kill me and be done with it," demanded Billings.

"Not so fast, you need to do some talking first, and then I shall decide whether you are to go back to face trial and hanging, or if I finish you here," said Sylvian with as much venom as he had ever used.

"Talking, what the hell do you want to damn well talk about, Mountjoy, I have nothing to say to you," snarled Billings.

"Alas, I have plenty to say to you. Firstly, why Mary, why a woman you professed to love and yet you set out to destroy her?" asked Sylvian.

"I never set out to destroy Mary, it was you I wanted, and succeeded in destroying. I took the one thing you cared about and I played with her until she could take no more. I played with every inch of her body, when she squirmed, I slapped her. I had her every day, sometimes in the garden over the bench, sometimes twice a night, and do you know… I think she was really starting to enjoy it; she had a real man for a change, someone who could satisfy her…" Billings choked as the point of the sword bit a little bit further into his throat.

"You bastard, you took a mother away from her son, a son who will never know who his mother was. You are pure evil and a traitor to your country." Sylvian took a step back and looked at the sorrowful sad expression of a failed man, evil and mean. He lowered his sword. "You will be taken back for trial and I will watch you swing from the gibbet and then I will spit on your remains, you are forever damned, Billings, I..." Billings raised his right hand and a small pistol sprang into his grip and as soon as he felt it secure, he pulled the trigger. Sylvian flew back a few feet at the force of the explosion as the small pistol exploded and took away Billingss' right hand and lower arm. The force of the explosion sent him over the cliff edge and away from sight. Robert ran out of the trees further down the path and saw his friend lying on the ground. He ran as fast as he could not knowing what he would find, looking all around him for the cause of the bang as he ran. He found Sylvian alone and, on his back, a small amount of blood was on his cheek but his chest was covered in blood and his eyes were open. He dropped to his knees and picked his friend up by the shoulders as he shouted his name over and over again.

"I am fine, friend, somewhat dazed and a little deafened, but fine," said Sylvian.

Roberts's relief was instant and he helped his friend to his feet. "What the hell happened, Sylvian?" he asked.

"Billings," said Sylvian trying to make sense of what he had seen. "His hand exploded and threw me back, old friend."

"Well.... Where did he go?" asked Robert looking down the path he had not come from.

"I have no idea, Robert, I was busy flying backwards with my eyes closed," answered Sylvian as he moved closer to the cliff edge and looked over. He saw a black cloak on the rocks below. But was it just a black cloak, he felt sure he could see a foot? Robert joined him and they looked at one another and set off in the direction they had come.

They reached the beach and started to make their way east and towards what they had seen. An almighty explosion came from the east end of the island and they both stopped and looked up where they could see billowing smoke climbing its way into the now blue sky. They continued on their way and found the twisted body of Nathaniel Billings missing one left eye and one right hand and lower arm. With one leg tucked under his back and the other with the foot facing the wrong way. His one eye was open and blood was trickling from his mouth, he coughed and more blood came. Sylvian looked at Robert who nodded to his friend and made his way on and down the beach leaving Sylvian alone. Sylvian sat on the rock in front of Billings and looked at this twisted frame of an evil man. "Why?" he said. "If you had just come with me... why, Nathaniel?"

Billings' mouth moved into a smile and his eye blinked, he then coughed for the last time and his relaxed body slid from the rock and onto the gravel beach. Sylvian stood up and stepped over the corpse and made his way sadly down the beach. He found Robert, Jacko and Juno pulling the boat from cover and into the water. Not so far to go this time.

***

John Scott looked at his watch, 09.59. He looked around at his team and indicated for them to get up and get moving. As they came out from the bushes, he looked down the beach and could see Steven Gant had his men already climbing ropes up the cliff. John sent half of his team under the command of Peter Selway up the cliff face to come into the barracks from the back. He and the other twenty made their way towards the small harbour and pier and then with Fitzwalter having taken out the single guard, they made their way up the path and to the front of the barrack building. A guard stood to the front of the building and was at first shocked to see all of these men coming towards him from the pier. He took aim and loosed his shot which missed and he had no time to reload. By the time the rest of the guard had come out of the building Peter's men had stormed the back and was wreaking havoc with pistol and musket. John's team had used front rank, rear rank firing and loosed their shots at the men who were exiting from the fracas that was behind them. Within minutes the whole thing was over. Peter appeared at the door of the barracks and raised his thumb.

Meanwhile shots could be heard from Steven's team as they stormed the house. They had easily made their way up the cliff face and through the trees to the side of the house. Steven sent half of his men to the rear and he and the rest attacked through the front door, a guard stood at the right of the door with musket ready and fired at the party as they entered, one of the soldiers fell by the door but Steven brought the guard down with his pistol with a direct shot to the man's head. A second guard had rushed up the hallway at the left-hand side of the staircase and was taken down by Jacob Stubbings with an amazing shot on the run straight to the heart. The female slaves had been rounded up along with the footman and butler and brought up to the entrance hall. Steven spoke to them and knowing that the butler normally held the senior role addressed old Jacob directly. He told him that they were English and would give the slaves their freedom if they wanted to accompany them now. If they stayed then they would be sold off again by the Union. Jacob said that they would go with the English to Canada where they at last could be free. Steven asked Jacob if he would show him where his master had kept all his papers. Jacob was only too pleased to show him where they all were and even the key to the safe which was hidden on the bookcase. Jacob told him that the massa also had a lot of money which was hidden in a cave at the barracks. Steven searched through the papers and found the letter that the colonel had left about Bill Mitchell. He placed it into his inside pocket and collected all of the other documents into his canvas bag. Chris Thompson came into the library with a skinny man limping quite badly, he told Steven that he had found this man in a cupboard by the back door. Chris reported that he had told him that he was William Courtney, Mr Billings' book keeper. Steven told Chris to take him down to the barracks and give him over to Mr Scott.

John left Peter and Fitzwalter to do their job and headed for the house. When he arrived, Chris Thompson had hold by the scruff on the porch of the house, a skinny man with glasses that looked like a book keeper.

"Is this what you're looking for, Mr Scott?" he called.

"Well bless my soul, Lieutenant, I do believe it is," said John as he took hold of the man by his lapels and with a grin said, "I bet you know what I am going to ask you," he dragged the man down the path towards the barracks and stopped halfway down.

"Mr Thompson, I will need ten men and some rope if you please, oh and make them strong," he said.

Chris turned and went back into the house and picked ten men and sent them after Mr Scott. With the house cleared of servants and all the papers Steven could find he headed out onto the porch where he was met by Peter and Mr Fitzwalter. "It's clear," he said, "go and lay your charges. Oh, and Peter, make sure you bring the house down, we shall see you back at the boat."

Lieutenant Wilson ran up the path shouting at Steven that he could see movement of boats from the mainland. Steven looked back at Peter. "And you might want to be quick about it."

The men made their way back to the beach and found that the *Fawn* was already in the water which the army team had been tasked with doing. As Steven passed the barracks, he saw his men carrying two heavy boxes from the building and joined them as they made their way as quickly as they could to the *Fawn*. With the boxes loaded and all the men aboard the *Fawn* was well down in the water, but she was a good boat and with sails filled with wind was making good her way from the island.

It was Jason Baker that called their attention to a two master that had come from the lea of the island and was heading straight for them. She was a good two miles away but would most certainly catch them before they made the *Endeavour*. Chris Thompson also called out to the fore that the *Endeavour* was on a course towards them. Mr Montrose had weighed anchor and was heading straight for them.

There was an almighty explosion that brought ringing to their ears as the house and barracks took to the powder kegs. A large plume of smoke was heading in a swirling pattern together with chunks of wood up and into the clear blue sky. The slaves in the boat just stared wide eyed at the spectacle of their home filling the blue, blue sky.

Within ten minutes the *Endeavour* which had closed on them fast let loose with one of its long cannons. The ball whistled as it passed over the heads of the *Fawn*s crew and they later watched it land in the water just in front of the Union clipper. She immediately came about and headed back towards the mainland with a huge cheer from the *Fawn*.

It took some time to pick up the crew and its bounty from the *Fawn* and then secured the boat to the stern of the ship. The *Endeavour* then set sail to the east and soon came across the long boat with Sylvian, Robert, Jacko and Juno on board. The transom davit was lowered and the men were soon winched aboard. Sylvian and Robert immediately made their way to the poop deck where they found Mr Montrose who was obviously very pleased to see them. John Scott and Steven Gant were also there and all the officers gave their salute, however Mr Gant was first to show his concern at the blood on Sylvian's face and chest."Sir, are you injured, shall I call for the surgeon?" he said with concern.

"No, no, but I thank you, Mr Gant, for your concern. It is indeed the blood of Mr Billings that I find myself decorated with," answered Sylvian.

"Sir?" said Steven questioningly as they were joined by the rest of the officers from the mission who were also curious at the outcome of their captain's mission.

"Well Steven, gentlemen, I can report the traitor Billings has indeed met his end, and by a twist of fate, by his own hand," explained Sylvian.

"So, he is dead, sir?" asked Fitzwalter from the main deck.

Sylvian turned to see all of the crew had mustered on the main deck and were trying hard to listen to what their captain was saying. So Sylvian raised his voice so that all could hear. "Nathaniel Billings, the traitor and murderer of my wife and good friend Simon Collins is dead, and he died by his own hand and fate that had served me when I should have been killed. Mr Billings took it upon himself whilst I was about to arrest him to pull a small pistol from his sleeve which he aimed at me and pulled the trigger. The pistol failed by backfiring causing it to explode and send both of us backwards at the force. I was sent onto the path and Billings over the cliff edge, where gentlemen, he died upon the rocks in the most painful of ways for one to perish," answered Sylvian.

There was a long pause and then the crew erupted into cheers and threw their hats into the air. Juno stood in the front next to Fitzwalter and had tears to his eyes and running down his cheeks. He had loved Mary for the good kind person she was.

"Mr Montrose, please take us back to Kingston, I must wash this vile stench from my body," said Sylvian as he made his way from the poop deck and onto the main deck where he paused and smiled at Juno Hardcastle, one of the hardest men he had known, now stood in tears for Mary, there would always be a bond.

Chapter Twelve
The Operation

The *Endeavour* allowed the current of the river to drag her stern first into the dock of Kingston Harbour. The officers of the ship had gathered in the captain's dining hall for their mission debrief and were sat in the same places as they had occupied two nights ago. The smell of eggs, bacon and potatoes wafted in the air causing more than one stomach to rumble at the thought.

John Scott had started his report on the barracks capture and was pleased to report that only one man, Captain Carlisle's new staff sergeant had sustained injury during the skirmish. There had been no survivors from the guards who had put up a good fight although outnumbered and caught by surprise. The boxes that they had recovered from the cavern had been secured in the ship's hold and should be inspected by the captain with a view as for him to decide what should become of them. John gave Sylvian a ledger book that he had acquired from Mr Courtney the book keeper.

Steven stood and informed the room of what had taken place at the house and the seizure of all the documents with the help of Billings' butler, Jacob. "Sir, with that in mind and by your leave, sir, I would like to pass to Mr Scott a document that I found in Billings' safe," said Steven.

"By all means, Steven," said Sylvian.

John read through the letter, folded it up, and gave it to Sylvian.

"With your permission, sir," said John as he stood up and left the room in total silence. Sylvian opened the letter and read the contents. He then folded it up and placed it before him.

"Gentlemen, it would seem that Mr Bill Mitchell a close friend and colleague of Mr Scott has perished at the hands of the Union. He was also inspirational in our recovery of the gold from Billings and his Indians. A sad loss to us all indeed," said Sylvian sadly.

The men hung their heads as even those present that had not been on the mission all here had read or been told of that epic mission against all odds to get the gold to Kingston. They were brought back to reality when Padraig and his two helpers entered the room with platters of fried eggs and bacon with fried cubed potatoes accompanied with tea and coffee. The room of hungry men made good work of Padraig's fare and were soon fed, watered and back to their duties.

Sylvian returned to his office and started to wade through the paperwork that Steven had brought from the house when a knock to his door was greeted with, "Enter." Mr Fowler stood in his doorway and asked Sylvian if he would see the slave Butler from the house, Jacob. Sylvian told him to show the man in.

Jacob stood before Sylvian and saluted him. Sylvian was quite taken aback and asked Jacob to take a seat. He removed his flat hat from his head and sat in the seat with it wringing between his hands. "Now what can I do for you, Jacob?" asked Sylvian.

"Well, sah, I does thanks yous for seeing me, sah, and fawr rescuing all us peoples from the cruel massa, sah, but sah we dus has a problem now, sah, we dun gon from der only home we dus has, sah, wat is we alls to do, sah?" asked Jacob meekly.

"Oh, I see, Jacob, yes well now you have your freedom and may go where you please, but I do see your dilemma. Please leave it with me and I will see what I can do, please you and your people remain on the ship whilst I see what can be done," replied Sylvian.

"Yas, suh, I does thanks you sah for our freedom and fur wat you is doin fur us now, sah, you is a kind man, sah, yas indeed a kind man, sah," said Jacob as he stood up and made his way to the door.

As the door closed Sylvian called out for Mr Fowler who almost instantly entered the room. "James, will you ask Mr Gant to come and see me at his pleasure if you please?" asked Sylvian.

"Right away, sir," said Mr Fowler as he closed the door behind him.

It was not long before a knock to the door saw Steven Gant in front of his captain. "Take a seat, Steven," invited Sylvian. "It would seem through our kindness we have somewhat of a problem. The slaves we rescued from the island are quite at a loss as to what to do with themselves, and quite frankly, so am I. Any suggestions, Steven, would most gratefully be accepted," said Sylvian.

"Oh, I see, sir, yes I had not thought of that, they are quite obviously so used to being told what to do and when," answered Steven. "Sir, might I suggest something as a thought has just come to me."

"By all means, Steven, please do," Pleaded Sylvian as he was quite concerned that these poor mistreated people should find a home and a life.

"Before we left Halifax, sir, I heard that the officers' mess in the castle was to be moved to a new building just outside of the castle of greater size, to cope with the greater number of ships and officers that would now be in Halifax," said Steven with excitement in his voice.

"Yes, indeed, Steven, the foundations to the building had already been completed when we left, but what is your point, sir," said Sylvian still not understanding where his lieutenant was going with this.

"Well, sir, surely the mess will need good staff to make it work, I believe that Jacobs's wife is an excellent cook and the footmen and maids would fit so well into the picture as waiters and maids, sir. I'm sure the admiral would be pleased to have such a dedicated team in his new mess. Old Jacob could manage the place with some training," concluded Steven.

"What an excellent idea, Steven, and as the mess chairman I shall have responsibility for staffing and the running of the mess. Good, then so be it. Please be so kind as to tell Jacob and his people of your plan and see if that is what they would like to do," said Sylvian.

Steven stood and saluted his captain and left the room with a large grin on his face. Sylvian then opened the ledger book that Steven had given him and was astonished at the figures before him. The money that had gone into Sacketts was phenomenal. But what was left and had been retrieved by his men was also outstanding. There was the better part of $350,000 in gold bars. He sat back in his chair and contemplated such a large sum and what it could mean to the efforts of building the colonies military force as the admiral had foreseen. He would split the total into two and leave one box at Kingston in the care of Colonel Gage and for his use and take the rest back to Halifax to add to the admiral's already sizeable bounty.

Sylvian looked at his watch and saw that ten thirty had crept up upon him and he must away to headquarters and brief Colonel Gage on the mission and of course the gold to be added to his coffers.

He soon found himself at the headquarters building and had remembered on his way that he must see the good surgeon who had offered to look at his arm. He would do this on his way back to the ship; he should also call on the good staff sergeant who had taken a musket ball to his leg at the island. The colonel's clerk was glad to see him and had been told by the colonel to show him straight in. The colonel came around his desk and they exchanged a firm handshake and both took their seats.

"So Sylvian was the mission a success, I mean a complete success?" asked Colonel Gage.

"Indeed, sir, and maybe more so than we first anticipated. My orders to cause as much disruption to the Union effort as possible has been achieved," replied Sylvian. He then went on to make his full report of the mission. The colonel was obviously enjoying and may have been living every minute of the report. When Sylvian told him of the gold that had been liberated from, well technically, the French and that he would leave half with the colonel to continue with his build, the colonel was over the moon with the excitement of it all. He invited Sylvian and his officers to the mess this evening to celebrate their safe homecoming and the success of the mission.

Sylvian told him of his appointment with the surgeon and was not yet sure if he would be able to attend as the doctor had not indicated whether he would operate immediately on his return. Colonel Gage was very concerned that the injury Sylvian had sustained at the hands of a Union musket had caused so much damage. He told him to get away immediately to the surgeon to see if it can be put right. The two men exchanged salutes and Sylvian made his way to the infirmary.

He found Doctor Smallbone in his office where last they spoke. The doctor was pleased to see him and invited him to sit. "How was the arm, Captain?" he asked.

"As you said, Doctor, it would get worse and indeed it has," replied Sylvian.

"Let's take a look," said the doctor as he commenced to examine him. "Well, you're right the upper part of the small end has receded further; I think I shall operate straight away. That is if you have nothing pressing, Captain."

"Please call me Sylvian and no nothing is more pressing than my concern for my arm, Doctor, will it be painful?" asked Sylvian.

"A little, we do have a leather strap for you to bite down on whilst I perform the surgery so you will feel pain, however I shall be as quick as I can and I will give you some laudanum to ease the pain after the procedure, now come with me and we shall get you prepared." The doctor escorted Sylvian from the office and down the long corridor and into a white painted room with a flat bed and multiple oil lamps burning above making the room very bright indeed.

"Please remove your coat and shirt, Sylvian, and then lay on the bed on your back if you please," the doctor instructed.

Sylvian felt strange but he did trust this man and he did need to get this arm seen to before it got too bad. He lay down and was blinded by the light but a cloth was soon put over his face and then he felt the pain before he lost consciousness.

***

Mr Montrose had received word from headquarters that one of the boxes in the hold was to be taken to headquarters and handed over to the colonel's adjutant. He tasked Jacko with the job and told him to make sure that it got to the adjutant in one piece and for the adjutant to give him a receipt for it. He also told Jacko that the captain was in the infirmary and was getting some work done on his arm and that he might appreciate seeing a familiar face when he was done. Jacko need not be told as his officer was more important to him than life itself. Jacko arranged for six men to carry the box on a litter from the ship. When they arrived at the headquarters, they found the colonel's adjutant waiting for them. He had eight of his soldiers take over from Jacko's crew and carry the box away to the armoury. Jacko insisted on a receipt as he had been asked by his first officer and one was given to him. His reading and writing were now perfect thanks to Mr Selway and he checked over the

Essex Library Services

Great Wakering Library
Renewals/Enquiries: 0345 603 7628
Visit us online: libraries.essex.gov.uk

Customer ID: **********6629

Items that you have borrowed

Title: Inquisition
ID: 30130215673616
Due: 26 August 2023

Title: Mountjoy : to catch a spy
ID: 30130304090433
Due: 26 August 2023

Title: Robert Ludlum's The blackbriar genesis
ID: 30130304565269
Due: 26 August 2023

Total items: 3
Account balance: £0.00
Borrowed: 5
Overdue: 0
Hold requests: 10
Ready for collection: 0
05/08/2023 16:21

Items that you already have on loan

Title: Alibi
ID: 38040012073468
Due: 12 August 2023

Title: Yankee mission
ID: 30130304644015
Due: 19 August 2023

Thank you for using Essex Libraries

receipt thoroughly thanking the adjutant as he left with receipt firmly in his pocket.

Jacko arrived at the infirmary just as they were reviving Sylvian from his unconscious state. The doctor had given him some laudanum and he was feeling quite sleepy but the doctor let Jacko in anyway.

"Well, well, sir, Ole Jacko is always a finding you just lazing away in yer cots, sir," said Jacko as he pulled the wooden chair to the side of Sylvian's bed. "How is you feelin', sir?"

"I have felt better, old friend," he croaked. "My arm feels like it is afire Jacko and I feel like sleep may take me sooner than I should wish. Please tell Mr Montrose with my compliments that he shall be in command until such time as I am back to fitness." His last words were slurred and old Jacko knew his officer was drifting away. He sat there for a good fifteen minutes just watching over Sylvian and remembering their first meeting in the rope locker of the Antelope. They had both come far and had some adventures such that had made him so glad to feel alive, and to have being pressed that night.

***

Sylvian had spent two days in the infirmary and was now back in his cabin on the *Endeavour*. The operation according to the good doctor had gone well and he had found that part of the muscle was still attached and had kept a good blood supply to both the lower and upper portion of his muscle. This would give a greater chance of the arm regaining full use, given time and rest. Lieutenant Richard Waverly the *Endeavour's* surgeon had attended Sylvian on his return and given him a little more laudanum and told him that he must remain in his cot without disturbance for a couple of days. Richard was a man slightly older than Sylvian at thirty-six and was a studious looking fellow. He wore little round wire rimmed spectacles and sported a pointed goatee beard. He was a man of kindness in the way he spoke and dealt with his patients, knowledgeable in his field but was given to the study of botany and how plants may help in healing and medicine. Sylvian and Richard had spent many an hour discussing the way of the world and what yet science has to learn from nature.

Sylvian had settled back in his cot as the good doctor was finishing off his administrations. He told Sylvian that he had spoken with Doctor Smallbone and was indeed impressed at the young man's knowledge and skill with the knife. He had admired Sylvian's wound and the techniques used by the good doctor to mend the muscle and according to Richard, the way in which he had sutured afterwards was almost an art. Sylvian joked that maybe he should swap these two doctors over and leave Richard at Kingston, to which the good doctor agreed stating that he may find someone knowledgeable to converse with on his botany in Kingston as to find such aboard a ship was indeed trying his patience. Sylvian giggled and asked the doctor to close the door on his way out.

***

The explosion could be heard many miles away as the sound carried across the lake and buffeted the shoreline, bringing people out of their homes and offices in curiosity. For it was a fine day and there was no sign of thunder clouds as was the night before. Colonel Farraday came out of his office and looked across the lake divide to Horse Island where a large plume of smoke rose into the air, like the smoke from a volcano. He looked around and saw that a clipper from the harbour had set sail and was heading towards the island. The colonel ran down to the port and jumped onto the island ferry which sat with two passengers from the island, the slave that lived there, a smart gentleman with a large bag thrown across his shoulder and the ferryman and his boy. The colonel instructed the ferryman to get underway immediately and the boy saw the boat free of its moorings and they headed out towards the island. The trip was unbearably slow as the colonel needed to get there with some haste, he asked the ferryman to loosen the sail and get more speed, the ferryman who was not fond of the military told him to sit down and be patient as they would get there when they did. The colonel glared at the man and took his seat as instructed.

As they approached the small dock of the island, they turned their heads to the north of the island as they heard the sound of a cannon fired, they saw the clipper not too far from them turn abruptly to starboard just after a plume of water was raised in front of them. She had been fired upon by the large ship in the distance. They could also see what appeared to be a small sail boat heading towards the large ship.

The ferry pulled into the island dock and the colonel was off before it had been tied up and was racing up the coast path towards the smoke. The slave waited for the well-dressed man to leave the boat before she grabbed her sack and put it across her shoulder and made her own way out of the ferry. She climbed slowly up the hill and could see that the barrack on her right was completely destroyed; bodies and bits of bodies lay all around, only recognisable by their light blue uniform with yellow trimming. She continued on and up towards the house and dropped her sack and fell to her knees at the sight before her, lots of smoke and flames and bodies spread all around. She covered her eyes and mouth and then let out a terrible scream. "Massa, oh, Massa, wot dey gone dun to you," she sobbed.

The colonel tried to get into what was left of the house which was just the front porch and columns but was beaten back by the acrid smoke and flames. The rest was spread all around and burning fiercely. He took some steps back and looked at what was before him, total carnage and not a single living soul. He turned and walked slowly back towards the barracks and saw Messie on her knees sobbing.

"They have all gone, Messie, blown to the four winds and not a soul left," said the colonel. Messie just looked up at him and then slowly something dawned on her. She stood up and took the colonel's arms.

"Der massa gone take his walk at dis time, Colonel, sah. He woulds be out dare someplace," she said wide eyed and pulling the colonel's arm.

"Show me where he goes, girl," said the colonel as they both set off on to the cliff path that ran around the island. Messie couldn't stop talking all of the way, she was excited to think that her massa was still alive and taking his walk. They covered the path on the south and west of the island and passed the point where Sylvian had met his adversary. The colonel stopped and walked back to look at the path. The gravel was scrubbed as if someone had lain upon it, he looked towards the cliff edge and saw that the grass was well trodden down. Messie came up to him with a worried look to her face.

"Wot is it, Colonel, sah, you looks powerfully worried sah, wot you seen?" she said inquisitively. The colonel moved to the cliff edge and looked down upon the twisted remains of the man he had come to hate. He turned and stopped Messie who was moving towards the edge and grabbed her arms.

"Don't look, girl, god dammit," he said as he pushed her back.

"Wot is it, Colonel, you is frightening me, sah, is it da massa, sir," she cried out.

"Yes, it is and you don't want to see, go back to the house," he commanded as he pushed her towards the cliff path. Messie stopped and dodged around him, as was her way, and looked down upon the man she loved, twisted and torn and lying on the rocks. She ran along the path and down onto the beach and ran to the rock where she stopped and took in the sight so close. Her eyes welled up as she looked upon his one eye still open but lifeless. She walked up to him and she leant forward and kissed his dead lips and closed his eye.

The colonel left Messie and made his way back to the barracks and found the well-dressed man coming from the cave that was the vault for the French gold. "It would seem, monsieur, that again we have been robbed of what is ours, and it would also seem that our partnership is, ow you say, disol ved," said the Frenchman. He turned and walked back towards the dock and the ferryman. Farraday watched from the top of the cliff as the ferry made good its way from the island with one man aboard. He looked back at the barracks and the smoke from the house, raised his arms in the air and screamed, "God dammit."

***

They had now been in Kingston for little over a week and during that time Sylvian had found his feet and was feeling fit enough for the *Endeavour* to get underway and back to Halifax. His one last visit to Doctor Smallbone was encouraging as the wound had healed nicely and the sutures were removed. They had formed a strap type of sling that went around his neck and supported his arm keeping him from making use of it until it was much better. The doctor had said maybe two weeks and he could start to exercise his arm.

With all of their goodbyes said and Robert and his crew now back in their barracks at Kingston and of course, Albert back aboard having completed his mission for the new training school. The *Endeavour* slid from her moorings with skill at the hands of Mr Montrose and Chris Thompson supervising the helm. There was a good wind and the current had carried them well along and into the main swell of the St Lawrence River.

Sylvian spent as much time as he could with Mr Montrose on the poop deck and the forecastle deck enjoying the view of this Great River and vast country which was now well into spring. The beauty of Mount Royal and the undulating countryside of this part of Upper Canada was breathtaking. The new green of spring with the colours of early wild flowers had Doctor Waverly almost constantly glued to his spyglass. He had persistently pressured Sylvian to put into shore so that he may better study the flora and fauna of this great country, but to no avail. Sylvian was keen to get back to Halifax, not least to make his report and to see Sarah but also to relieve himself of the responsibility of the vast wealth that they had liberated from the Union.

It took two days and some good running until they entered the Gulf of St Lawrence and headed east and past the Isle of Anticosti. Icebergs were still around so navigation and the crow were important on this part of the journey. It was as the *Endeavour* was passing on the east side of the isle that crow shouted his warning of ship to the port bow. The wind was good and the sun was now high in a clear blue sky with clear visibility to the horizon. Sylvian had just made it to his cabin and was looking forward to his lunch when he heard the cry from the poop deck for all hands-on deck and to stations. He replaced his hat and made his way up to the main deck and then to the poop deck where Mr Montrose was ready with his report. "Sir," he said as he saluted his captain. "Crow reports ship to the port bow, sir, no reports from the forecastle yet, sir."

"Very good, Mr Montrose, I have the command. Mr Fitzjohn," he called. "Take a good spyglass to the crow if you please, I shall need constant reports, sir."

"Aye, sir," said midshipman Barret Fitzjohn as he made his athletic way to the side of the ship and was up the shroud in a trice. The forecastle lookout called out the sight of the topsail of what appeared to be a

Spanish flag and may have a privateer flag at flight. Within minutes Mr Fitzjohn had placed himself at the crow and together with the duty rating they conferred that the ship was indeed a Spanish privateer of maybe forty guns and she was on a heading towards us. Sylvian's thought of the privateers that Admiral Albright had encountered and destroyed may have already been replaced. His memory of how they had been fooled at the sight of one ship when in fact two were employed in their capture had come back to him. He shouted up to the crow to check both port and starboard along with bow and stern was soon met with Mr Fitzjohn's report.

"Sir, mastheads spotted at Shiphead point, sir, off the starboard bow, looks to be privateers, sir, three masted, possibly... forty guns, sir. None other sighted and no icebergs, sir," he shouted his good report.

"Mr Montrose, it would seem that we get to test out our new ship's guns and manoeuvrability in battle, sir. Gun decks to be made ready if you please and then we shall take in sail so that we do not have the two to our stern, rather to our port and starboard," said Sylvian as he removed his hat and placed it in the poop deck locker.

"Aye, sir," said James as he started to move his officers into action. Sylvian was pleased at how he handled the officers and his foresight in who would be needed where. He thought him not long to remain his first officer.

After an hour at a slower pace the two ships were still off to port and starboard bow and could now be clearly seen. They would need to make this precise and not give leave for either vessel to come to a firing position before the *Endeavour*. She was well equipped with the latest long barrel cannons and indeed some grapeshot that Mr Selway had been experimenting with to good effect. The two privateers would not be aware of the cannons' range that they had and would come closer before they would turn to put their cannons in range. This could work to their advantage.

"Mr Montrose, my compliments to Mr Selway and ask him if he would load all top deck cannon with his grape shot on the starboard side, if you please," said Sylvian as he looked hard and long at the starboard privateer. She was a much older vessel and he could see repair to her main mast. Her crew from his observation at still a great distance did not seem to be as fluid as his. However, the ship to his port bow was completely the opposite and may give them a good run. She looked fairly new and in good condition and with luck and God behind them would make an excellent prize.

The ships were gaining on the now slowed *Endeavour* and would soon come into range. The starboard side ship would come into range first and Sylvian hoped to dispatch this one fairly quickly and before the port side privateer came into range. The sea was quite calm with a swell no more than a couple of feet. All posts reported ready and Mr Fitzjohn reported that the starboard ship would be in range in five minutes. Sylvian checked with his glass and confirmed Mr Fitzjohn's assessment but would give it seven minutes. He took out his watch just as Mr Fitzjohn shouted out ship to stern on the port side coming from the lea of Anticosti. A privateer, sir, and she is coming fast under full sail. Sylvian swung his glass to stern and could see the ship was just a little further than the starboard ship.

"Mr Fitzwalter," he called. "Have your men ready with the port anchor if you please. If I should call release then she must be away with no friction."

"Aye, sir," said Fitzwalter and although others were questioning this action, he would not as he knew full well to trust his captain's judgement at whatever command he should give.

"Mr Ottershaw, have the mainsails full if you please," he said as he glanced at his watch. "Mr Douglas, have Mr Selway fire on my command to the portside if you please."

"Aye, sir," said John as he moved to the hatch and called down to Mr Selway.

"Sir, I am somewhat confused," said Mr Montrose. "To aweigh anchor when we are under full sail could sink us sir."

"Indeed, it could, Mr Montrose, we shall see if it works. We are under attack from three lesser class vessels, sir, and need to be canny in our approach," said Sylvian as he looked at his watch. "Mr Douglas, have Mr Selway fire top guns in one second intervals if you please."

The guns fired off in one second intervals and Mr Selway's aim had indeed been good. The ship to starboard had no masts and no sails except those that now dragged in the water. The bow of the ship had been disintegrated by the grapeshot and she looked to be slowly sinking. Sylvian took his glass to port just as that vessel let go with her bow cannon which did not have the reach. The ship to stern was gaining fast and would be in range of their guns shortly.

Mr Douglas, have Mr Selway ready with upper gun and lower gun decks port and starboard to fire at one second intervals when both ships present themselves to his guns, and have him ready for the turn of the ship if you please," shouted Sylvian as again the port side ship fired her bow guns which were much closer this time. Sylvian could see that she was starting to tack to her starboard. Perfect.

"Mr Ottershaw take in all sail and have your men hang on, Mr Fitzwalter, port anchor aweigh if you please," Sylvian shouted. "Crew brace for the turn," he commanded just as the *Endeavour* bit to her anchor and Mr Thompson spun his wheel to port.

Everything appeared to be in slow motion as the ship groaned and seemed as if she would come apart at the seams as the anchor dragged on the seabed and would hopefully not catch a rock. One poor man on the mizzen top rigging had not held tight to his line and flew from the mast and into the sea on the starboard side. The stern of the ship in its motion to catch the now stopped bow slew the ship to port and came around at a fast rate of speed. The starboard guns let go both decks in one second shots as the ship came back to a level and Sylvian watched as his port bow ship lost her mizzen and the upper deck and gun deck were raked with shot. The *Endeavour* recovered quickly to roll back to starboard and as the ship rose the port side guns let flight their ball. Sylvian turned his head from the starboard rake and just in time to see the stern vessel with timbers flying high amongst the smoke and her foremast fall slowly with men flying and into the sea.

Mr Fitzwalter and his team were quick to cut the anchor loose just at the right time for the *Endeavour* to right herself. Men lay everywhere as the wind started to take the smoke away and the devastation around them became evident. One shot had hit the *Endeavour* and had raked her side on the turn with very little damage to her thick timbered side. The port bow ship had been unable to stop her motion as her mast and sail had hit the water on her starboard side and dragged her around and against the side of the *Endeavour*. Mr Wood and his marines along with

Fitzwalter and his team were over the side in a trice and had the ship tied to the side of the *Endeavour*. The marines fought hard and valiantly against the remaining crew who had not been prepared to be boarded. Sylvian looked to his stern from the action on the tied ship and saw that the first ship had succumbed to the waves and her stern was just going under. He looked to the port and saw that the third ship that had been to their stern was now listing to port and her crew were abandoning the decks in favour of the sea.

Mr Selway and Mr Gant along with their teams were soon on deck and were over the side in a trice and aboard the second vessel to join the fight. Sylvian cursed his rank and his right arm as he would love nothing more than to be engaged in the battle, but it was soon over now that Peter and Steven had joined the fight along with a great number of the crew. Mr Montrose was amongst them and accepted the surrender of the ship by its captain.

Mr Montrose returned to the *Endeavour* with the captured ship's captain and presented him to Sylvian. The two captains saluted one another and the prisoner introduced himself. "Capitan, I am Duke Juan Manuel Alphonso Alonso of his Spanish Majesty's navy, Capitan of za sheep Phillipe Da *Cartagena*, may I geve me complemente to ju on dis victory," he said in poor English.

"I thank you on behalf of myself Captain Sylvian Mountjoy of his Britannic Majesty's Navy and my crew for your compliment, Duke Alonso. Yourself and your crew will be well treated as my prisoner and will be taken back to Halifax, Nova Scotia. Mr Montrose, see to the duke's accommodation and that of his men and report to me on the condition of the prize *Cartagena* when she is examined if you please," said Sylvian. The Spanish crew were removed and placed in the lower hold and the captain and his officers were taken to the officers' hold at the stern of the *Endeavour*. Sylvian moved to the poop rail and the crew were called to attention by the bosun.

"Gentlemen, my compliments on a well fought battle, you showed bravery and perseverance under fire, now we must secure the prize which Mr Gant shall captain and take back to Halifax. Now set to it and let's get under way," said Sylvian to a loud cheer from his crew. He indeed had a happy ship and was proud of everyone aboard.

The crew searched the ocean for survivors from the two now sunk ships and found only one boat with seven men aboard, one was the captain, a very scruffy unkempt individual who was incarcerated with the rest of the pirates. The sea at this time of the year was far too cold for a man to survive being in the water for more than a few minutes. The rest of the crew had set to on the prize and cut away the damaged rigging and prepared her for sail. Sylvian had returned to his cabin and had asked to see Mr Selway and Fitzwalter. He poured himself a large brandy and filled two other glasses which he placed on his desk and then took his seat. A knock to his door and the two officers entered. He invited them to sit and partake of the brandy he had poured.

"Well, Mr Selway, that was indeed fine gunnery, I could not have done better. Well done. And Mr Fitzwalter, I do believe it is you that has saved this ship with your precise handiwork. Your timing was impeccable on the anchor release and when you chopped the hemp free to stop us from being dragged down. Well done indeed," complimented Sylvian as he raised his glass to the two men, who acknowledged their captain by raising their glasses and with huge smiles to their faces. "I would like you both to join with Mr Gant in taking the prize back to Halifax, gentlemen, we shall sail as soon as you are ready. I await a report from Mr Montrose on her condition but I would be pleased if you would go and see to the crew and make her ready as fast as we can." Both men acknowledged their captain and downed the good brandy and made their leave.

Within five minutes Mr Montrose presented himself and reported that the prize was in good shape and would be ready to sail within the hour. A search had found papers in Spanish and some bounty in the hold. It consisted mainly of gold, silver and jewels that must have been liberated from other ships. There were fruits and other tropical goods aboard that would suggest she may have sailed the Caribbean.

"So, you think she may be a pirate, James?" asked Sylvian.

"I would think that there is every chance, sir, that she was. It would appear not only from the tropical produce that the amount of coin, gold and silver that we have found must surely have been plundered from many ships," he answered.

"I see, then we shall indeed need to talk at some length with the duke and his officers when we are back in Halifax, please ensure that they are guarded well, James, for if they are pirates, they will be the most slippery of thugs we have yet had aboard. Please brief Mr Wood on our fears and have his marines take over the guarding. We are still three days from Halifax with a fair wind and need to make sure we get there in one piece," said Sylvian.

"Sir, should I move the captain and his officers back to the prize in order to separate them from the crew?" asked James.

"No, no, Mr Montrose," said Sylvian thoughtfully. "That may indeed be what they want us to do. No, they shall remain confined, and I think chained in the prisoners' hold on the *Endeavour*," Sylvian answered. "If it is proved that they are indeed pirates, then they shall hang for their crimes so we are justified to chain them all."

"Aye, sir, I will see to it immediately and have Mr Wood informed of our suspicions." He saluted his captain and left Sylvian alone in his cabin where he could now endure the pain from his arm as the sudden turn of the ship, on his command, had wrenched his arm. Padraig had provided him with a cup of tea and some ham, cheese and bread which he picked at.

The *Endeavour* got underway in just under an hour from the *Cartagena*'s capture She had main mast foremast intact and her mizzen had been cut free and left to the sea. She had sustained damage to her upper gun decks and forecastle deck but was now under sail with Mr Gant in command. James Montrose had command of the *Endeavour*, and now with reduced sail to keep up with the *Cartagena*, moved out into open sea of the Gulf of St Lawrence, on a heading for Halifax and home.

Chapter Thirteen
The Pirates

The *Endeavour* and *Cartagena* sat in the estuary to Bedford Basin and Halifax and waited for the *Dauntless* and Hampshire to make their way out and to sea. Sylvian watched their progress from the forecastle deck as Captain McLeod and Captain Stockwell headed their ships past and out into the open ocean. The two ships gave their salutes as they left the estuary and the *Endeavour* returned her salute with a five-cannon fire.

With the two ships now clear the *Cartagena* lowered sail and made her way slowly down the estuary and into the shipyard at Bedford Basin. The *Endeavour* lowered sail and made her way slowly into the wharf side of Halifax and was skillfully helmed by Jason Baker nicely into place. The dockyard mateys moved into action with skill and precision and had her tied and secured quickly.

It was a nice early summer day with a warm breeze and cloudy skies stopping the sun from filling the harbour with its glorious light. Crows and rooks filled the sky above the abattoir looking large and black against the white clouds and hoping to pick up a tasty treat from the butchers below. Canada did not have the birds that Britain enjoyed. No dawn chorus to greet you to your conscious state. No song in the back garden that lulled you to want to sit and enjoy, except for the chickadees and other small birds that flitted from tree to tree and bush to bush and the redwings with their strange unmistakable call. However, it did have its other beauties, the mountains and the rivers, the sun dogs on those really cold days when three suns would grace the sky inside a perfect arc, the snow and the ice guaranteed every year preceded by the wonder of colours presented by the trees in autumn, and followed by the warm, warm summers that sometimes could be so hot and humid. Sylvian missed a lot of what he had at home in England but there was so much more here to explore and the vastness of a country still yet untamed. He knew in his heart that this was his new home and he would make it so, but in a different way to that he had before, as now he was a different man to what he was before.

Sylvian watched with pride as his command was handled with great skill in order to bring her home safely and secured to the dock. He called on Mr Fitzwalter to take command of the box that was in the hold and make sure of its safe removal to the fort. He also tasked Robert Caxton his bo'sun to form a prisoner escort party and have the captured crew escorted to the gaol and handed into secure custody. Lieutenant Wilson of the marines and his team would accompany the prisoners in an armed escort. Sylvian then returned to his cabin where he completed his log and reports for the admiral and then left the ship for the fort.

Sylvian gave over command of the ship to Mr Montrose and made his way down the gangplank and onto the quayside where a rather beautiful woman ran up to him and threw her arms around his shoulders and kissed him passionately on the lips. He returned the kiss just as passionately and received a round of applause from his ship's company for their effort. Sarah blushed uncontrollably but cared not as she had the arm of the man she loved once again securely in her hands. Sylvian looked down at her beautiful face and gazed into her emerald green eyes and felt the passion in him rise. "Oh Sarah, you are so beautiful, I have missed you so much," said Sylvian with passion.

"What is wrong with your arm, my love?" asked Sarah as she backed away from his embrace.

"The good doctor at Kingston found that it was not mending well and had cause to do some surgery to put things right. I feel it is much better now, than it was," replied Sylvian.

"Oh, Sylvian, shall you lose the use of your arm?" she asked.

"No, no, my love, fear not the good doctor tells me that I should recover full use in time, now what of you, my sweet Sarah. What news do you bring since we had parted?" Sylvian asked.

Sarah tucked her arm in his and swept her long skirt to one side as she turned to walk alongside him to the carriage that had brought her. "Not much, my love, except Abigail has sailed with Jack to England so that she may be with Jack whilst he completes his medical training and Father has travelled to St John's on business, so… Mother and I were wondering if you should like to come to dinner and then we can talk…"

"Oh, my darling, I cannot, I have to report to the admiral and then I must deal with a matter of most importance as it would seem we have a pirate problem yet again," said Sylvian.

"Pirates, oh my!" said Sarah as she looked over at the *Endeavour* as the first of the prisoners were being led off by the marines and Fitzwalter.

"We shall talk, Sarah, long and hard, when is your father due back to Halifax?" he asked.

"He is due back by week's end, Sylvian, why do you ask?" she replied.

"Two reasons," he said as they stopped at the side of her carriage. "One is that we shall need the services of our judge when we come to bring these vagabonds before him, but most importantly... I need to ask him a very serious and personal question."

She swung round and looked straight into his eyes to search for the answer she wanted. It was there. A tear slowly grew in the corner of her eye. She swung back and took his hand as she climbed into the carriage.

"Then I shall tell him of your desire to see him as soon as he is home, and not a minute longer," she said as she indicated for her driver to carry on. He stood and watched the carriage disappear up the hill and turn right at the park and out of his sight. He felt such a love for Sarah, not the same as he still felt for Mary, but deeper and one that belonged in a different world.

The admiral's clerk was quick to knock upon the admiral's door and announce Captain Mountjoy. The admiral greeted Sylvian as he always did, like a long-lost son that he cherished. But he was good at hiding such and keeping their meetings on a more military and correct footing. "Please, Sylvian, sit down, dear boy, and tell me all," said Admiral Albright.

"Thank you, sir, and there is much to tell," said Sylvian.

"First tell me about your arm," said the admiral as he pointed to Sylvian's arm in its sling.

"Well, sir, it would seem that the Union sniper was good at his shot as the damage he caused could have indeed rendered me with a useless limb. The good doctor at Kingston recognised such and was given to operate on me to put the matter right, well we hope so anyway," replied Sylvian.

"Upon my soul... operate you say, and do we know if any success was achieved by such action?" he asked.

"Well, sir, I do think so although it is early days and one needs to wait and see, but I have been noticing an improvement almost daily sir," replied Sylvian.

"That is good news, Mountjoy, now what of your mission, did you capture the man Billings and bring him back here for me to hang?" asked the admiral.

"Mmmm, no, sir, I am afraid I did not," said Sylvian just as the clerk entered the room with a tray with two glasses and a decanter of brandy.

"Well give me your full report, young Mountjoy, and I mean full report," said the admiral as he poured two generous brandies and handed one to Sylvian.

Sylvian spent the next hour and two glasses of brandy giving his account of the mission to the island, what had taken place with Billings and the finding of the gold. "How much!" asked the admiral in some astonishment. Sylvian told him again and also told him that he had left half with Colonel Gage which he was not sure how the admiral would take that news.

"Very good, would have done the same myself, Mountjoy, check with me in future though, if you don't mind."

"Indeed, sir, only I knew of your wish to build up the strength of military in the Canadas and thought that is what you would wish me to do," explained Sylvian. "But that is not all, sir," Sylvian continued with his report and the meeting of the three ships in the Gulf of St Lawrence and the action that took place.

The admiral sat back in his chair and was aghast at the explanation his officer was giving. Then Sylvian told him of the treasure that they had discovered in the hold of the prize which would easily have a value the same as the gold he had brought with him from the island. He explained that the captured crew had been removed from the ship and taken to the gaol and would hope that he should have a chance to interrogate the officers to establish if they were indeed pirate privateers. The admiral was again shocked at this news and said that he had sent out the *Dauntless* and the Hampshire to search for pirates in response to information from a merchant ship that had recently docked in Halifax.

The ship had been chased by three ships but their close proximity to Halifax had afforded him a good escape.

The two men discussed at great length Sylvian's mission and what they might do with the additional funds that he brought back with him. They had decided on naming the new ship *Halifax* as the *Bedford* had already been commissioned. The admiral asked Sylvian to decide who should captain the new ship and to let him know by the weekend when the repairs should be close to complete.

Sylvian advised the admiral that he would like to wait until Captain Young returned before he commenced his questioning of the suspected pirates. Andrew had a way of asking questions that would reveal hidden answers which he would pounce on to confuse the interviewee. He had no idea how he did it. They agreed to wait as Sylvian had much to do in sorting out the treasure from the prize and trying to set a value to it and just what they should do with it.

"So now back to Billings," said the admiral. "You say he took his own life, how so, and do not skip the details, Mountjoy."

"Well, sir, I had him trapped on the cliff top at the end of my sword, and indeed wished to run him through, however it was in the back of my mind that you had wanted to take him prisoner as a sign to all what would happen to traitors to the crown." The admiral nodded and showed an agreeable face. "So, I lowered my blade and told him that he was under arrest. Billings then raised his arm and a small pistol dropped into his hand which he fired at me. The pistol exploded as it backfired and took off his hand and threw me back onto the cliff path. Billings was too close to the cliff edge and was blown over. I found his dying body on the rocks below."

"Pray tell me you remained until he expired..." said the admiral worryingly.

"Yes, sir, he died slowly and in a great deal of pain, I could not help the pleasure and relief I felt at this gruesome sight and have questioned myself since," said Sylvian.

There was a pause between the two men. The admiral sat forward in his chair with his arms resting upon the desk top. "Damn it, Mountjoy, question yourself not. This man took your wife from you. I will not hear of you questioning your actions against this man. I am only sorry that I shall not have the pleasure of seeing the man squirm upon the gibbet," said the admiral.

"Indeed, sir, for that you have my apologies," said Sylvian sincerely. "Sir, if I may bring us back to the *Halifax* and who might command her, sir, and of course her place in the North American Fleet. I may have one or two suggestions that I should appreciate your opinion."

"Oh, sounds ominous, well out with it, Mountjoy, let's hear what you have to say," said Admiral Albright with some curiosity.

"Well, sir, I would like to put forward my first lieutenant Mr Montrose as a candidate, sir. I have found him during this trip to be a man of vision and well able to command a ship of the line. He is brave in the face of the enemy and certainly does not shy from bravado when it is required, he had the gumption to up anchor and make his way towards Horse Island and just in time I might add as a Union ship was making good ground on the *Fawn* as she made her way from the island. He showed restraint and correctness when he loosed a shot at the proceeding Union ship to land some one hundred yards to her bow. It was that action, sir, that took her away and allowed my men safe passage," suggested Sylvian.

"Well, he does sound like a good candidate, quite young, but how should you feel at losing a good first officer, especially given the circumstances that you often find yourself in, young Sylvian?" asked the admiral.

"It would be difficult, sir, I grant. However, I, like you were yourself, sir, not going to let my needs override the overall need of the service and the advancement of one of my officers, sir," replied Sylvian. "Apart from that, sir, the second part of my suggestion brings that somewhat back into line. May I propose that the *Halifax* serves as a support ship to the *Endeavour*, you see, sir, one of the problems we endured during our last mission was space, with both personnel and munitions required for our task. It was rather overcrowded, sir, to say the least," Explained Sylvian.

The admiral sat back in his chair and as usual put his fingertips together as he gave great thought to Sylvian's proposal. "I like the idea, Captain; it would make me feel better too in the knowledge that you shall not be sailing alone on these crazy missions that you and your men so successfully perform," he said still in thought. He leaned forward and placed his elbows on his desk as he had concluded his thought. "Yes, Sylvian, go ahead with your proposal. Now do you wish Mr Montrose to serve as a temporary captain or perhaps, commander or is it your intention that we should make him posted. If so, I shall prepare the necessary paperwork for the gazette." The admiral studied Sylvian for his reply.

"Well, sir, I would prefer that he is posted, however that does cause some issues if he is to remain under my command," said Sylvian giving the matter great thought. "I think, sir, that initially we should appoint him as commander and see how things progress."

"Well done, Mountjoy, as indeed I would do. I shall leave the details to you to see to," said the admiral with a smile on his face.

"Now to another matter that has come to my attention, I have received word from the admiralty that we have quite a sharp increase in pirate activity in the Caribbean. We have so far lost forty-two ships and their cargos to these devils. The admiralty has informed me that they are quite tied up with Napoleon and this damned war, with ships in the Mediterranean and also in the south China seas. So, it has been passed to us to send out patrols to put a stop to this damnable practice once and for all. So, I shall need you ready to sail when the *Halifax* has completed her repairs. The *Renown* and the *Bedford* will be leaving on tomorrow's tide and I would like you to join them in a week or two. Now, Sylvian, these pirates are damnably smart and treacherous so watch your back, sir," said the admiral as he again sat back in his chair with a concerned look to his face.

"Yes, sir, as my recent engagement has proven with the most unusual and unexpected three prong attack," said Sylvian with a little concern. "I will start preparing for our departure, sir. There are two other matters, sir, firstly I have rescued a number of slaves from Horse Island and have given them their freedom, which has given me quite some conundrum as they now feel no place of belonging. Might I suggest, sir, that we give them employ in the new officers' mess that I see has progressed well since I left. There is a man and wife whom I believe would be ideal as cook and mess manager, there are three maids and two footmen who would make good as the staff we shall need, sir," asked Sylvian as he looked at the admiral's face which had a smile at least.

"Captain Mountjoy, do you not head the committee of the officers' mess?" questioned the admiral.

"I do, sir," replied Sylvian.

"Then I see no problem as you now seemed to have solved some of your staffing issues. Now you said two points, Mountjoy," replied the admiral.

"Indeed, sir, um," said Sylvian as he shifted in his seat. "I should like to ask Mr Bennett for his daughter's hand when he returns from St John's and I should like your permission for me to proceed with such," said Sylvian rather sheepishly.

The admiral smiled and stood up and walked around his desk and took Sylvian's hand in a firm grip. "Nothing would please me more, dear boy, you must sweep this beautiful young lady off her feet and make her yours, and you do indeed have my blessing. Such good news," said the admiral with a pride he could not hide. "Now away with you, sir, you have a ship some treasure and prisoners to deal with," he concluded as he walked back to his desk waving Sylvian away.

Sylvian stood and saluted his admiral and gave him a very kindly grin that showed their mutual respect for one another and then left the office, feeling a lot better than when he had gone in.

The armoury led on to the secure vault area where the colonies' gold was stored and made into Canadian coin for use by the military. Sylvian was partly in charge of this area as part of his land-based duties and was well known by all of the guards and staff that worked here. He was welcomed by the fort's purser Lieutenant Archibald Winstanley a broad clean-shaven Yorkshire man who was used to speaking as he finds. He was the senior fleet purser and all ships' pursers answered to him and woe betide those that had not done their duty in the way Mr Winstanley required. He saluted Sylvian on his arrival and reported that the gold had been taken on stock. Sylvian asked if Mr Montrose had seen the treasure into the vaults and was told that he had and now was in the officers' mess for lunch. The bounty retrieved by the pirates was being assessed by two of *Halifax*'s finest jewellers. He hoped to have a value ready for both the admiral and Sylvian by end of day.

Sylvian found James in the mess and joined him for ale and some ham, fried eggs and potatoes. James reported that the captured ship sailed well and would be a good addition to the fleet. Sylvian asked about the repairs and how long it would keep the ship in the repair basin. James told him that he had spoken with the yard foreman who said that they would attend to the ship tomorrow and it should be ready within a week. They would then move it to the commissioning basin where it would be stocked with provisions and equipment and taken on stock as a ship of the line. The foreman had asked what name she should be commissioned as. Sylvian told James that the admiral had suggested she be named HMS *Halifax* and asked James to inform the foreman so that the signage could be made before she sails.

"Sails, sir, where to?" asked James.

"It seems, Mr Montrose, that the pirates we encountered were just a small party with treasure bound for somewhere we do not know and that the situation has grown quite grave in the Caribbean," replied Sylvian. "The *Renown* and the *Bedford* are to sail on the morrow's tide and we are to join them when the *Halifax* is ready to sail."

"I see, sir, what do we know of the pirates, I mean where are they operating, do we know how they are led and by whom, sir?" asked James, rather excited at the prospect of some action.

"We do not, James, and that is why we are being sent. It would seem a great many cargo vessels have been waylaid by these pirates and relieved of their valuable cargos which are then being traded for gold and jewels, it is possible that what we have captured may indeed be the gains of such and will be put into good use to fund our mission to destroy these thieves," Sylvian answered.

"Well, sir, with the *Renown*, *Endeavour* and the two frigates of *Bedford* and *Halifax* we should be able to make some impression on these thieves," said James.

"Indeed, Mr Montrose, but it is not my mission to create an impression as you say, but to capture these pirates and see them hung and then destroy whatever setup or system they have in place, and of course, the people they use to get such ill gotten cargo to market and earn their bounty. We shall see them captured and hung. We must destroy this evil trade, however long it takes us," replied Sylvian with conviction.

"Then, sir, we shall need to recruit a crew for the new ship and some officers to ensure that the ship is well equipped and ready to sail in a couple of weeks, sir. Would you like me to go up to the training school and see what we have in the way of officers and men to crew the vessel?" asked James.

"Indeed, Mr Montrose, please give my compliments to Lieutenant Abrahams and tell him of our mission and select only the best and strongest for such a tough mission. You will need to ensure that you have good officers to serve you, and freshly trained men ready to serve their country. Oh, and you shall need to stop by the tailors and ask him to sew the correct rank to your coat, commander," said Sylvian with a broad smile on his face.

"Sir, you mean me, sir, to command the *Halifax*," said James with an extraordinarily wide grin and excitement fit to burst. "I am indeed honoured, sir, and I thank you for this opportunity. I shall not let you down, sir."

"Indeed, Commander Montrose, you shall captain the *Halifax* and you are to become my support ship so that you may still have a part in the action of our specialist team. Now away with you, sir, and mind that you do as asked, and when next I see you then you shall look a commander and present yourself as such," said Sylvian, whilst sad to lose his first officer but again very pleased to see a good man move on in his career. Mr Montrose set off from the fort to see to his errand with a new vigour in his step. Sylvian made his way back to the *Endeavour* in what was now sunshine and broken clouds that filled the sky. Halifax looked so much better when the sun graced her streets and harbour, the *Endeavour* looked splendid as he approached causing him to pause and stand awhile to take in this vision. He still had to pinch himself to see that this was no dream and that he did in fact captain such a beautiful vessel.

Two more traders had docked at the port and were unloading their wares, the dock bustled with horses and carts and seamen going about their business of loading the carts. The noise was intent with calls to get men working and the clatter of the hooves upon the cobbled center of the port approach. Sylvian could see that the new naval dock was well into its construction on the other side of Bedford basin. This would give a better access to the naval ships that were increasing in number and would free up this port for the commercial vessels to ply their trade.

Sylvian was greeted by the bosun who piped him aboard and then set the men back to their duties. Mr Douglas made his report to his captain and stated that all the prisoners had now been removed to gaol and shore leave had been granted to half of the crew. He stated that the holds were now empty and they were awaiting delivery of supplies. Sylvian thanked John for his report and asked him to report to his cabin when he had concluded his duty. The two saluted one another and Sylvian made his way to his cabin.

***

"Get to it, you lazy scurvy dogs, see to that davit that man and don't you be slow about it," shouted the ship's master at arms as he tried to speed his men to their tasks. The SS Robin out of Southampton was unloading her precious cargo of wool and whale oil along with other textiles for the Dominion and would then load up with skins and pelts, maple sugar and other delicacies. But first the master needed to get this ship unloaded and these scurvy useless lice ridden scoundrels were slowing him down. He cracked his whip above their heads which brought a few of them who had felt the whip to attention. One who had not, stood by the portside rail and glared at the officer who stood amongst the conundrum of horses and carts, men and loose women on the bustling port approach. He stood tall and proud and stared at the warship that sat at the end of the wharf. A warship that he had been in charge of as first officer. A warship that he would have eventually had command of had it not been for this man, this officer that stood and looked.

A sharp crippling pain ran down his back and sent him to his knees. He looked up to see the huge frame of the master at arms standing over him with whip in hand. "What makes you so special, you lazy scurvy poor excuse for a man, get to your work before I have you flayed before the mast and the skin taken from your back, you lazy scum," shouted the master as he bent down and spat the words into the man's face. McLean was up and on his feet in a trice with bale hook in hand he put his aching muscles back into his work but the anger inside had only grown fiercer through hatred. He would have his revenge.

***

It was now early afternoon and Sylvian had cleared his desk of paperwork at last, this was definitely one part of his command that he had not taken well to. He had dealt with two disciplines which the master at arms Mr Caxton had brought before him. One was a seaman who had consistently been fighting with his crew members. Sylvian gave him five days in the brig and no shore leave. The other had taken a knife to Midshipman DeWitt and threatened his life. He had pleaded guilty but had said the midshipman had been riding him ever since coming on board and he had just had enough. Sylvian sent for the midshipman and asked him to answer the allegation. Mr DeWitt stated that he had cause to get on to the man as he had found him lazy and given to loitering at his task. Sylvian dismissed the two men from his quarters and called for Midshipman Fowler, Aitchinson and Roberts who were still aboard to come to his office. He asked the three officers if they had cause to rebuke seaman Cardew over his tardiness. None of the officers had any problems with Cardew or had been given to rebuke him, Midshipman Andrews stated that he had found the man to be quite a hard and diligent crewman to his tasks and was indeed impressed with his gunnery skills. Sylvian cleared his office of all but Mr Fowler who stood before his captain and stated that Mr DeWitt was not a popular officer with the men and was given to bullying. Mr Fowler had need to put Mr DeWitt on report for his actions which Mr Montrose had dealt with by means of a fine and restricted privileges. Sylvian thanked and dismissed Mr Fowler and asked him to send in Mr DeWitt and the master at arms.

Sylvian sat for some time looking at the man DeWitt before he finally spoke. "Mr DeWitt, you have been aboard this ship since we sailed from Portsmouth and you are aware that I do not suffer bullies or ill treatment of my men in any way. This, sir, is a happy ship and can find no place for those who make it not so. You have been before my first officer and have been reprimanded for this action before." DeWitt started to protest his innocence and was soon silenced by Sylvian who most definitely now had his dander up. "Silence when I am talking and remain yourself to attention, Mr DeWitt. Now, I will neither tolerate one of my officers being threatened with assault as I will neither tolerate my officers being less than fair to their juniors, is that clear, sir?" asked Sylvian.

"Yes, sir," said DeWitt, feeling that he might yet again just receive a reprimand.

"So, sir, you will be stripped of your rank and you will be reduced to seaman and will serve the rest of your service in that rank, you will be taken to the training school where you will undergo retraining and will then be assigned to another ship where your conduct will be closely monitored. Take him away, Mr Caxton, and see that Cardew is before me," commanded Sylvian with a wave of his hand dismissively.

Cardew was shown into the office by Mr Caxton who stood back in his usual place by the door. "Now then, Cardew, I find you guilty of assault of an officer of His Majesty's Navy, now although with mitigating circumstances this behaviour cannot be tolerated aboard a fighting ship. You will be taken from here to the gaol where you will serve a term of five years and will then be dishonourably discharged from the service. Take him away, Mr Caxton," Sylvian commanded.

With the office now clear he sat back in his chair and thought about the punishments he had given and was sure the admiral will have something to say when he reads his report. It was normal in the service when a man assaulted an officer that he would be hung on conviction. However, he was happy that with the mitigating circumstances he had acted fairly and had seen justice done.

Sylvian had asked for Jacob and the slaves from the island to come to the captain's dining room. Just before he went in Mr Douglas reported to him that he had concluded his duty and was reporting as requested. He asked John to take a seat and relax. John looked nervous; he was young not yet twenty-five in years. He was always smart and had shown good judgement when the *Endeavour* had been under fire from the pirates. Sylvian had watched his progression and had seen that all of his actions had been well thought through and had needed no direction from Mr Montrose or himself; he worked well with the crew and was well respected for being fair. His fellow officers had a tendency to defer to him when they were faced with a problem for which he always seemed to have an answer.

"John, thank you for coming to see me, there seems to be a slight dilemma which I am hoping that you may be able to assist with," said Sylvian in his very serious voice.

John looked even more concerned. "I will try, sir, er what is the problem, sir, that I may help with?" he asked.

"Well, Mr Douglas, it would seem that I have no one to deal with my staff and operate as my right-hand man in running this ship," stated Sylvian, as he taunted poor John.

"Oh, sir, I well, I'm not sure I can be of assistance as Mr Montrose would normally have that in hand, and, sir, he does do a very fine job indeed," replied John.

"Oh, I'm sorry, John, have you not heard of Mr Montrose, he is no longer with us I'm afraid," continued Sylvian with his taunt.

"Oh, my, sir, what has befallen Mr Montrose, sir, I saw him but this morning as he left the ship for the fort, sir," said John in a panic of concern for his first officer.

"Well, it seems that Mr Montrose has got himself into a predicament, John, and now finds himself as captain of the prize ship, and so you can see it leaves me in a dilemma as to having no first officer," stated Sylvian as he leant back in his chair watching the changing faces of young Mr Douglas.

"Oh, dear, sir, well that's awful, I mean gosh, sir, oh I see well that's excellent news and so well deserved for Mr Montrose, I am sure all the officers will be sad to lose him, sir," stumbled poor John.

"So, Mr Douglas, you shall now take his role and position aboard the *Endeavour*, your promotion to lieutenant first class is approved with immediate effect, see to the transfer of Commander Montrose's effects to the *Halifax* if you please, that is the prize, Mr Douglas, and sort out your uniform and get to work. Congratulations, sir, on your new appointment," said Sylvian.

"Oh my, really, sir, me, sir, as your first officer, well thank you, sir, it will be an honour for me to serve," he said with great gusto and standing to take Sylvian's hand in a firm grip. "Thank you, sir, indeed, well I shall be away, sir, to my duties and will report when all is done. Oh my," he said as he saluted Sylvian and left the office.

Sylvian sat back in his chair as he had enjoyed what had just taken place and was so happy when his crew were happy. This part of his command he enjoyed.

His deep thoughts were very soon disturbed as Mr Fowler reported that the island people were now in the captain's dining room as requested. Sylvian thanked Mr Fowler and asked him to ask Third Lieutenant Watts to attend his office in one half hour if he was aboard, and to also attend with Mr Watts. James Fowler looked quite worried but saluted his captain and left the office.

Sylvian stood to the mirror checked himself and retied his hair. He entered the dining room and all of the freemen stood up, he told them to all sit down and he took his seat at the end of the table. He looked at all of the faces before him wide eyed and clearly very nervous as to their futures.

"Jacob, may I talk through you as I am unsure as to whether your people speak English?" asked Sylvian.

"Why yas, suh, but my wife Celie speak dat better dan wot I is, sah," he replied.

"Yes, sah, I was lucky to goes to school, sah. I speak better dan my Jacob, sah," replied Celie.

"Good," said Sylvian as he looked at the chubby wide-eyed lady in front of him. She was proud that she could talk well and had been to school, she had a smile that could dazzle with her perfect white teeth, she was a lady to whom you could immediately take a liking to, a mother figure who wanted to mother every child, boy or man she would meet. "So, Celie, when I spoke to Jacob about what is to be done with all of you, I mentioned that we might find employment and accommodation for you in our officers' mess. Well, I am pleased to say that I would like to offer you the position of cook and Jacob as our mess steward with the rest of you in positions as waiting staff, how do you feel about such an offer?" asked Sylvian.

Celie looked at her comrades and turned back to Sylvian. "Well, suh, is we free now, suh, or does we still belongs to the massa, suh?" she asked.

"The master is dead, Celie, and when we rescued you we gave you your freedom as we did not purchase you but rescued you, therefore you no longer have an owner and it is not my intention to sell you on. I have given you your freedom so you get to choose now what to do with your life," answered Sylvian as best as he could.

"Well, suh, we has spoken bout dis afer Jacob did say, and tho we is still not sure why der massa aint owned us no more, we all did say dat we woulds like to work for der captin, sah, in dis mess, sah. I is der good cook, sah, and dees girls Jessi, Sori and Judit is good at keeping tings clean, sah, oh yes, sah, and yung Abraham, sah, well he strong and can doos most anyting, sah, but I doos thing dat Jessy wants to be a ship man, sah," said Celie.

"That right, captin, and I as bin schooled too, captin, and I woulds like to be in dis navy, sah, iffin that possible sah," said Jessy as he sat and wrung his hat around in his hands.

"Then so be it," said Sylvian. "Jessy, you shall report to my master at arms and he will see you to the training school, the rest of you can report to the fort where we shall find you temporary accommodation until the officers' mess has been completed. Celie if you could come to my office in an hour, I will give you a letter to present to the guard at the fort which shall explain all that we have spoken of. Thank you all and I wish you well in your new lives," said Sylvian. They all insisted on shaking his hand and thanking him for their freedom and new lives. Abraham said that he was now so glad to be free from the massa who had treated them so badly and now he had a life to look forward to. Celie mentioned about her daughter Messie who had not been on the island when they were set free and wondered if she could come too, if she was ever found. Sylvian assured her that if she was found then he would make sure that they were reunited.

He returned to his office to find Mr Watts and Mr Fowler outside his door. "Come in, gentlemen," he said as he walked into his office and took his seat. "Please sit down," and indicated the two chairs in front of his desk. "Now, gentlemen I find that I am short on officers now that Mr Montrose and Mr Douglas have been promoted so, Mr Watts, I am moving you up to lieutenant second class, and Mr Fowler, you to lieutenant third class with immediate effect, any questions?" Sylvian asked.

The two men looked at one another with smiles on their faces and thanked Sylvian for their promotions. Sylvian asked them to see to their uniforms and to charge it to the ship. He told Mr Watts that he would assume Mr Douglas's area of responsibility and likewise for Mr Fowler. Sylvian told James that he would find a replacement to cover his duties as his assistant and sent them off to their duties.

Sylvian spent the next hour writing his letter for the freemen and passed it onto Celie when she called for it. He was also able to complete his discipline reports for the admiral and would drop them off when he returned to the fort to see the purser Mr Winstanley.

Sylvian then spent the rest of the afternoon on the poop deck with the duty officer Mr Wood and was able to garner some suggestions for a candidate for midshipman. James was indeed very knowledgeable about the ship's crew and was able to suggest a young gentleman who had been apprenticed to the master at arms and had held such on his previous ship for three years. He had come from a good family although he did not hold the king's letter. The lad was fourteen years and was well schooled, his name was Arthur Blaketon and was currently ashore. Sylvian asked James if he would pass on these details to Lieutenant Douglas and ask him to promote the boy when he returned to ship.

Sylvian then left the ship and made his way up to the fort, he stopped briefly at the entrance to the park as he had this funny feeling that he was being followed, but when he checked he could not see anyone that looked faintly out of place or seemed to be observing him. He shrugged his shoulders and moved onto the fort.

He found Mr Winstanley in his office and the two exchanged salutes. The office was small and dark without windows and served only by one oil lamp that sat upon the desk. The desk was old and somewhat rickety as were the chairs. When Sylvian sat down at the bequest of Archibald he found the chair that sat before his desk almost gave way causing him to stand quickly.

"Damn it, Mr Winstanley, you need to provide yourself with suitable furniture in this office, tis perilously close to dangerous, sir," rebuked Sylvian.

"Beggin your pardon, sir, nowt wrong with the chair, sir, it'll take yon self and many more to come, can't be frivolous with the king's penny, sir," he said as he wobbled on his chair and opened his book. "Looks like most of this treasure, sir, has come from Russia so as me jeweller's report."

"Russia you say?" answered Sylvian with a wry look to his face.

"Aye, sir, and some as come from the Orient and even India, sir, 'appen its good quality the lot. They have given me two figures to run with, sir, one is as they are sold on to jewellers, sir... at a fair market price I do add. And tother is jewels removed and gold and silver smelted down, sir. Done it by weight they have, sir, so as we should know the true worth," he stated.

"Indeed, Mr Winstanley," said Sylvian curious to know what the two figures might be so that the treasury can decide on a suitable way forward. "And pray tell what are the two figures?" he asked.

"Well, sir, would you like it in pounds or dollars sir?" asked Winstanley as he looked over his half spectacles at Sylvian.

"I think as most trade is carried out with the Union, we should say dollar amounts and be done with it. We can convert back if in the unlikely event the admiral decided to return it to Britain," replied Sylvian,

"Very good, sir, then smelted it would have a total value, including the sale of recovered precious stones at $280,000, sir," he said as he looked up at Sylvian with a smile on his face.

"And as it is, what would the jewellers be able to raise from a sale on the market?" asked Sylvian.

"Well, sir, tis just an estimate appen, but they have said that it should make around $400,000, sir. Some pretty items and well made indeed, sir," he answered.

"Very well then, Archibald, have you informed the admiral?" asked Sylvian.

"No, sir, we have only just finished with the appraisal, but I do have the report here, sir," said Archibald as he handed over the two parchments that he had been reading from.

"Do we know of, or even have an agent that can act on our behalf, should need arise?" asked Sylvian.

"Indeed, sir, we have the finest in the Dominion, most trustworthy man by the name of Walter Smithers. He has been a trader for many years in fine art and jewellery," replied Winstanley.

"Good, well thank you, Mr Winstanley. I shall take this to the admiral and see what it is he wants to do, we shall let you know," said Sylvian as he took his hat and the two men saluted as Sylvian left his office.

The admiral's clerk told Sylvian that he would be out for around an hour. Sylvian told him that he would be back and to please tell the admiral that he had called. He then left the office and the fort and headed back to the ship. As he entered the wharf, he saw that the Antelope had just docked so he made his way there and aboard. Mr Seagrass first lieutenant of the Antelope greeted Sylvian warmly and with a salute, he told him that Captain Young was in his cabin and to go straight down. A quick knock to the door brought Andrew's to normal, "Enter," and Sylvian found him sat behind his desk. He was quickly up and the two officers greeted each other warmly and as the old friends they had become.

"So, what news from your mission, Sylvian, please tell me the damn man is dead or is here to be hung?" asked Andrew. The two men sat to Andrew's desk and the good captain dragged out a bottle and two glasses, they both saluted one another with their glasses and downed a good sip.

"I can confirm, Captain Young, that the scoundrel who has plagued my life, and yours is indeed dead," said Sylvian raising his glass again.

"So, tell me, old friend, you have my attention without doubt," said Andrew leaning forward on his desk in anticipation. Sylvian explained the whole story from start to when they fought the pirates and Andrew did not speak a word. He concluded with the capture of the pirate's treasure and the ship now called HMS *Halifax*.

"My dear Sylvian, you must now be so relieved to put aside that nagging chapter of your life. I must say that it makes me feel somewhat relieved and good in myself to know the traitor now rests in hell, what now my friend?" asked Andrew.

"Well, I was waiting until your return as I had hoped that you would join me in interrogating these captured pirates, we have them locked up in the gaol at the fort," stated Sylvian.

"Indeed, I will," said Andrew. "But what service would it do us to learn any intelligence from these thieves, my friend?" he asked.

"It would seem that the Caribbean is yet again seeing increased pirate trade and I have been tasked to join with the *Dauntless* and *Bedford* to seek out, as you say these thieves. But I feel we must go one step further and find their trading partners and what system they have in place that feeds their dirty deeds, and finally put a stop to the whole pirate thing, once and for all," replied Sylvian with excitement.

"Quite some task, my friend, quite some task," said Andrew thoughtfully. "What chance do you think that the admiral should include the Antelope in such a quest?" he asked.

"I was hoping you would say that, Andrew. I do believe if we should put forward such a plan to the admiral, a plan that should only give us maximum chance of success he could not possibly refuse. It would leave the *Sheffield*, *Exeter* and *Hampshire* in Halifax to continue our North Sea patrols. That would give us the Antelope, *Dauntless*, *Bedford*, *Halifax* and *Endeavour* as the task force to combat the pirates," replied Sylvian.

"Then best we get to these pirates in the fort and learn as much intelligence as we can, sir, might I suggest that we make a start first thing on the morrow," said Andrew raising his glass which Sylvian clinked with his as they found the bottom of their glasses in one final gulp.

Chapter Fourteen
Death Comes To One

The early morning sun was warm but a cool breeze blew in from the ocean indicating the early arrival of summer still had a chill to the air. This early June morning was bright and full of colour as the trees around the port had already started to emblazon themselves with the colour of new greens, and shades in between would soon become full, and the trees would fill out and give shade from the hot summer sun to those who sought it.

Sylvian stood on the poop deck and looked around at this beautiful scenery set out before him. The calm waters of Bedford Basin and beyond the hills that stretched all around the basin to the east. The fort that stood proudly on the hillside was slowly being surrounded by the growing town of Halifax, Nova Scotia.

Nova Scotia, Latin for New Scotland was settled in the 1600s and with a climate so changeable and not unlike the highlands of Scotland from where she got her name. The hills to the west of the town rose proudly and gave the area a protected feeling. The hills on the other side of the basin were not so high but did afford the basin protection and made it the perfect place for this growing port. The admiral had mentioned that the naval area would be called Dartmouth as the area so resembled where he was born and raised. It was located on the opposite bank of the estuary from Halifax and would give some protection to the naval ships from the commercial ships that came in and out of the port on a regular basis. The training school was being built there along with a new naval headquarters building being built from brick and quarried stone being brought in from Britain. The new docks were already in place and Sylvian could see the vast activity that was going on with new buildings sprouting up all over the place on the far shore. He had not given much thought to where Sarah and he should live once they were married, close to the dockyard would be good but he did not wish to be far from Sarah's parents when he was away at sea. He would ask her and see what she would have in mind.

He was disturbed from his thoughts when Andrew arrived from the Antelope. He stood on the dock looking resplendent in his uniform and called up to Sylvian. The two men made their way to the fort and Sylvian told Andrew about his intentions with Sarah. Andrew stopped him in his stride. "Well, my friend, I so wish the two of you well. It pleases me greatly, Sylvian, to hear such news, she is a fine woman, my friend, and the two of you were most certainly made for each other without a doubt in my mind, sir," he said, quite excited by the news.

"Thank you, Andrew, your words mean much to me. I er, I was wondering, old friend, if you would be so kind as to stand beside me and give me the honour of your presence as my best man?" asked Sylvian.

"It would be an honour, sir, one that would please me greatly, and I, should be the honoured one, my friend," said Andrew as he slapped Sylvian's back as they again commenced to walk towards the fort and gaol.

They found the duty lieutenant and a room was arranged for their interrogation, they asked for the pirate captain to be brought before them in the first instance, and he duly was. Before his arrival Andrew had briefed Sylvian on what technique he would like to use, he had asked Sylvan to be kind and sympathetic and he would adopt the opposite. He was indeed curious to see how such a process would work on an individual under stress. The duty lieutenant escorted the prisoner into the cell room and sat him down at the table. Sylvian and Andrew just stood on the other side of the desk looking at the man. Andrew walked around behind him and stood for a short while. The prisoner shot his gaze between the two men getting more nervous by the minute.

"What's your name?" barked Andrew from behind the man.

"No entiendo, no entiendo," screamed the man as if he was under attack.

"Cuál es tu nombre, what is your name?" Sylvian asked nicely as he pulled up the chair and sat down facing the man.

"Capitan Raul Sylvestre, senor," he answered with shooting looks behind him to Andrew.

"Raul, si?" asked Sylvian nicely.

"Si, si, senor, Raul, mi nombre," answered the scared Spaniard.

"You see Raul, I know you speak English, you spoke to my lieutenant when your ship was captured. So why do we not speak English as that is much easier for us, understand, entender, senor," said Sylvian as he lent on the table and looked directly at Raul.

"I speak a little of the English, senor, not much," answered Raul.

"That's good, Raul, we shall get by with that, now where are your ships from, Raul, where do you sail from?" Sylvian asked slowly.

"I am Spanish, senor, we are coming from Espana. We are jus traders, senor, nusink more, senor, jus traders from Lisbon," he said feeling far more confident.

"So, you're not pirates, Raul?" Sylvian asked.

"Pirates senor," he spat to the side of the table. "Pirates, senor, I spit on dem. May all dare mutters rot in hell, senor, and dare padres too senor. Dah!" he said with disgust and raising his hand in the air.

"So, you are a trader, a trader from Lisbon, and yet you sail a warship with thirty-six guns, senor, tell me why?" asked Sylvian.

"You jus said it, senor, deez pirates, senor, day is averywhere," he answered.

Sylvian sat back in his chair and smiled. Raul smiled back with black and dirty teeth showing through his bearded and scarred face, a very unpleasant man indeed. Andrew had stepped back and away from the pungent smell of the man.

"You are a pirate, senor, you fly no flag from your ship and you had treasure aboard as your cargo. Now where had you come from, and where are you heading to?" asked Sylvian with more grit to his voice.

"I do not understand, senor. I is not zee pirate as ju say," Raul said nonchalantly.

Andrew moved in a flash and had the man out of his seat and against the wall, and as unpleasant as it was, was almost nose to nose.

"The captain asked you a question, dog, now give him the answer or I will slice out your liver," shouted Andrew. He could take it no more and threw the man to the floor.

Sylvian got to his feet and picked Raul up and felt him trembling from the shock and fear of the sudden movement. Sylvian brushed down his coat and helped him back to his seat. Raul sent Andrew a frightened look and then looked back at Sylvian.

"Tell me, Raul, I think he means what he says," pleaded Sylvian.

Raul put his hands on the table and looked at Sylvian. "I know not of deez pirates, senor, I cannot tell you, I is telling der truta, I swear, senor," Raul pleaded. The speed of Andrew even caught Sylvian off guard as he brought his knife down and through the back of Raul's right hand.

"Tell the captain what he wants to know," shouted Andrew as Raul stood and screamed at the same time. Andrew pushed him back into his chair and started to twist the knife.

"Okay, okay, I will talk," Screamed Raul. Andrew pulled the knife from the back of his hand, wiped off the blood on Raul's shirt and put it back into the scabbard.

"So talk, Raul," said Sylvian with a little more grit to his voice.

"It is true, senor, we is as you is saying der pirates, so we help a little with der ship that we stops, and der cargo, senor, it is nussing," cried Raul whilst holding his injured hand.

"That is not what I asked, Raul, maybe I should go and leave you to Captain Young," said Sylvian standing up and making moves to leave.

"No, no, senor, please, I is talking to you, senor," said Raul as he shot glances back and forth to the two men. Andrew had his hand on his knife hilt and put his other hand on Raul's shoulder.

"I am waiting," said Sylvian as he retook his seat.

"We is coming from Port Au Prince, senor, many ship, many ship, senor, I is jus uno in der many, senor," replied Raul rapidly.

"And who leads you all, Raul, who is in charge?" asked Sylvian leaning forward on the desk.

"Senor, please I cannot, senor, Raul will be no more, senor," stated Raul with fear in his voice. Andrew pulled his knife from its scabbard as he stood to the side of Raul.

"Who is in charge, Raul?" shouted Sylvian.

"Capitan Freado, senor, he is der man. He runs us all, senor," said Raul in blind panic.

"And, where is he?" demanded Sylvian.

"Tortuga, Hispaniola, senor, he dare, senor, he go nowhere, senor, never leave, he as ship which take what we bring and sell to Georgia in der Union for trade," he answered.

"And who buys it there, Raul?" asked Sylvian.

"Der man call imself Mr Jackson, he live in big houses in Charleston, senor, I know not more, jus dis, I only been twice," stammered Raul whilst holding his hand and bending forward with the pain.

"Guard," shouted Andrew. The door unlocked and a burly man entered that they both recognised from when they interrogated the spy.

"Sir," said the guard.

"Take him back to his cell if you please, and find a cloth for his hand, and then throw a bucket of water over him and perhaps he will not smell so bad," ordered Andrew.

"What of Duke Alonso of the Phillipe De Cartegna, shall we interrogate him too at a later date?" asked Sylvian.

"I do not think it matters much, my friend. His association with this Raul fellow merely by being in battle alongside the man, should prove his fate as being guilty by association," answered Andrew.

"Should I bring another one, sir?" asked the guard. Andrew looked at Sylvian and Sylvian shook his head.

"No, thank you that will be all for today," dismissed Andrew. The guard left with the smelly Raul and the two men looked at one another and smiled.

"Time for lunch, Andrew," said Sylvian as he replaced his pocket watch back into his coat pocket.

"Indeed," said Andrew. "A good morning's work I think."

The two men made their way to the mess hall and sat to a fine lunch of tomato soup followed by chicken, potatoes and vegetables. All washed down with a fine locally brewed ale. They spent this time working through their plans to present to the admiral for Andrew's inclusion into the trip to the Caribbean.

As they were completing the meal Mr Blaketon his new midshipman came into the mess rather nervously as this was his first time of entering an officers' mess. He made his way over to Sylvian and saluted his captain. "Sir," he said, "beggin' your pardon for this interruption but

Lieutenant Douglas sends his compliments, sir, and says that I am to deliver this message which was just delivered to the ship, sir."

"Are you my new midshipman, Blaketon is it not?" asked Sylvian.

"Yes, sir," said Blaketon shyly. "May I, sir, thank you for giving me this promotion, sir."

"Indeed, Mr Blaketon, you are most welcome, now to this uniform you wear. Is it borrowed, young man?" Sylvian asked.

"Yes, sir, it is, I have use of it until I have enough coin to purchase my own, sir," he replied.

"Well, Mr Blaketon, this will not do I'm afraid. It is somewhat too large for a lad of your size and as an officer on board my ship, shall not be tolerated," said Sylvian quite sternly. The lad looked down at his uniform and could clearly see that the pants were well below the knees and his hands could not be seen below his sleeves. His hat had been packed with paper to keep it upon his head and he felt ashamed now that he had presented himself so to his captain.

"My apologies, sir, for presenting myself so," he stated.

"Mr Blaketon, present yourself to the tailors immediately and give him my compliments and ask him nicely to fit you as you should be fitted, sir. Tell him to place the cost upon my name," said Sylvian.

"Sir, yes, sir, and thank you, sir," said the excited lad as he turned to walk away.

"Oh, and Mr Blaketon," said Sylvian stopping him from his exit. "Be quick about it, no dawdling, and it is customary to salute your captain and other officers when you have been dismissed." The lad brought himself to attention and saluted the two officers before again turning to leave.

"Mr Blaketon," called Andrew.

"Sir, yes, sir," said Arthur as he again stopped and turned to the call.

"The note, Mr Blaketon," exclaimed Andrew.

"Oh yes, sir, sorry, sir," he said as he reached into his coat and pulled out the note which he gave to Sylvian. He was about to turn away but remembered and saluted the two officers before he made his way from the mess. Sylvian and Andrew burst into laughter as the boy left the mess.

"Twas me just a little while since Sylvian. Such memories," said Andrew.

263

Sylvian opened the note which was from Sarah. It would appear that her father was home and they had invited him to dine this evening. Sylvian felt nervous but also relieved that he would now, hopefully secure his future. Sylvian passed on the news to Andrew and the two men then finished their ale and made their way to the admiral's office, only to be told by his clerk that the admiral was on a visit to Dartmouth to check on progress. The clerk suggested that the two officers should return in the morning as the admiral was free. Sylvian left his discipline reports with the clerk for the admiral's attention.

Back on board the *Endeavour* Sylvian had a meeting with Mr Gant and Mr Selway regarding the upcoming trip to the Caribbean and asked them to get to work on the men's fitness as it would be hot and humid where they were going. Mr Selway requested permission to move the teams up to the wooden fort for the duration of training, this was duly given and Sylvian asked him to leave behind Mr Fitzwalter as he would have need of him with the prisoners at the fort when they come to trial. Sylvian then spent the rest of the afternoon on deck and enjoying the goings on of the port of Halifax. He had sent a message back to Sarah accepting her kind offer and confirmed that he would be there at six thirty.

It was now five and Sylvian had chosen to walk up to the Bennett's on such a fine evening. The sun was still gracing the sky which was blue and uncluttered, although it had reached the top of the hill now and was starting to move towards night. Sylvian turned the corner of the park onto the main street of Halifax where all the traders had their stores, long since closed and now quite peaceful with few people around. As he was passing the park gates, he thought he heard a call for help across the street. He stopped and listened and yes, there it was again, coming from an alleyway between two of the stores. Sylvian made his way across the street and down the alleyway where upon he found himself in a courtyard created by the rear of the shops and a long wall and some buildings. The light was really starting to fade but he could not see anyone.

He was about to turn to leave when a voice echoed in the courtyard. "Sylvian Mountjoy I see before my very eyes," said the voice tauntingly. Sylvian went for his pistol. "Ah, ah, no, no, no, Mr Mountjoy leave that right where it is," said the voice. Sylvian could still not see anything only the shadows at the side of the building at the end of the courtyard.

"Show yourself," said Sylvian as he moved his hand away from his pistol.

He heard a shuffling noise and then saw a scruffy long-haired person emerge slowly from the shadows in front of him. Sylvian looked long and hard at this vagrant that stood before him. "Do I know you?" he asked.

"Know me, why yes, Mr Mountjoy, you know me well as it is you that has taken my life from me, do you know me you say. Destroyed my life and sent me to the gutter as I now stand as witness to," he said grating his teeth as he spoke and moving slowly more from the shadows. He had two pistols, one in each hand and pointing at Sylvian.

"How so," said Sylvian. "How so have I wronged you?" he asked.

"My, my, Mr Mountjoy, you don't even recognise who I am do you?" asked the voice.

"I am afraid, sir, you have me at a disadvantage," Sylvian replied.

"In more ways than one, sir," he said waving his two pistols around to make his point. "Does the name McLean have any meaning for you, Mountjoy?" he asked.

"You?" said Sylvian questioningly.

"Yes, me, Mountjoy, the man you cast from your ship and into the gaol at Portsmouth for five months, to see my rank and commission stripped from me, and then to watch my family turn its back on me and leave me to rot like a rat in the gutter of society. Yes, Mr Mountjoy, the once mighty First Lieutenant Archibald Wilson-McLean, who all I ever wanted to do was have a disciplined ship to command, and you, sir, yes you, sir, are the one that took it all from me, and now I shall take the only thing I can from you," he said as he took three steps closer.

"I did not take that from you, McLean, you took it from yourself with your cruelty in the name of discipline, you are the only one to blame McL…"

"Silence, Mountjoy, silence as I am the one that holds the pistol that shall send you to where you belong." He moved to the side and raised the pistol and took aim carefully at Sylvian.

The shot echoed around the courtyard and the pistol ball found its mark right between the eyes and he fell, face first to the ground... dead before he arrived.

Chapter Fifteen
A Murder Most Foul

Sarah was getting concerned as Sylvian was now half an hour late. Her father was trying to calm her saying that he was probably delayed at the fort or on his ship, but his wife was little help in suggesting that all sorts of things may have become him. William gave up and sat down on the couch and quietly drunk his sherry. Things only got worse when the butler entered the room and announced that the town constable was here to see His Lordship. Sarah very nearly died and her mother stood in grief suddenly believing all the things she said had befallen poor Sylvian. William told the butler to show the constable into his office and he would be there presently. Sarah grabbed her father's arm and started to pull him from his seat insisting that he needed to go and find out what was happening.

William gave up and went to his office followed by his two women. He stopped in the hall and ushered them both back into the library. He found the town constable Silas Willoughby in his office pacing the floor. The judge closed the door to his office and sat down behind his desk.

"Now what's to do, Silas?" he asked.

"Well, Your Honour, you see there has been a shooting in the town and a man is dead, sir, there has also been a killing on one of the merchant ships, sir, which the regulators are seeing to, but you see, Your Honour, the killing in the town also involves a senior naval officer, sir," said Silas rather hurriedly and obviously quite out of his depth.

"I see," said the judge looking down at his desk top and not wishing to know the answer to his next question. "Do we know who this officer is, Silas."

"Yes, sir," said Silas opening his small pocket notebook. "Captain Mountjoy of the *Endeavour*, sir," he answered nervously.

"Is Lieutenant Fleming of the regulators in attendance, Silas?" asked the judge.

"Yes, sir, he is, should I let him take charge, sir, only this is city property and not military, you see my quandary, sir," said Silas.

"Indeed..." said the judge thoughtfully. "I think as they are naval personnel, we should leave this to them but give them what assistance we can. I shall come presently, where is it, Silas?" asked William.

"At the rear of Jones's dry goods, sir, in the courtyard, sir. I told everyone to leave the body alone and that I should be back presently," said Silas.

"Okay, Silas, well you cut away now and I shall join you there presently," said the judge as he ushered Silas from the office and to the front door. He then turned and looked at the two faces that stood in the library doorway and did not know for the first time in his life, what to do or say.

He called to the butler for his coat and hat and for the carriage to be made ready. He then ushered the two women into the library and sat them down and stood to the front of them. "There has been a shooting in the town, it would seem that it is a naval officer and the name given was our Sylvian," he said. Sarah fainted and fell to the floor just as the butler entered the room to tell the judge that his carriage was ready.

"My dear, I have to go at all haste, I must leave you to deal with our Sarah," said the judge as he took his hat and cloak from the butler and made his way hastily out of the house and to his carriage.

The butler and Annie had the unconscious Sarah up onto the couch from the floor and lying comfortably. "Bring me the smelling salts please, Jacob," asked Annie and with the smelling salts soon had Sarah awake and alert. She remembered what her father had said and jumped to her feet.

"I have to find out, Mother, I must go," said Sarah as she made her way quickly to the door.

"No, Sarah, you must stay here your father..." but she had already gone and was making a fast pace down the hill towards town with the tears flowing freely from her eyes.

William arrived at the alleyway and was allowed through the blockade of regulators and into the courtyard where he saw the body lying on the cobbles. The back of the head was missing where the ball had found its way out. William looked at Lieutenant Fleming who he knew well from the characters that he had brought before him in the court. "Do we know what happened here, Michael?" he asked.

"Yes, Your Honour," said Michael Fleming as he explained what he had been able to find out.

"What of the man on the SS Robin?" asked the judge.

"Dead, sir, stabbed through the heart," replied Michael.

Sarah made it to the alleyway somewhat out of breath and out of place in her long evening gown and no shoes. The regulators were taken by surprise but would not let her enter much to her protestations. The judge heard his daughter's frantic pleading to be allowed to enter and made his way back to the entry to the alley. "You cannot come in, Sarah; go back home I will tell you all when I get there," he said with compassion.

Sarah, with tears flowing from her eyes could not believe what was happening to her, she felt as if her whole life had fallen apart, she could never love again as she had loved her Sylvian.

A hand gripped her elbow and a voice said, "Come, let me take you home," she turned and looked up into the face of the man she loved and threw her arms around his neck and held him oh so tight as to never let go. Sylvian hugged her hard and was glad he had this love in his life. They kissed passionately. The judge had stopped his walk up the alley and turned to see his daughter in the arms of the man she loved, and smiled. Only a father knows such feeling when he sees his daughter so happy.

Annie was so relieved when Sylvian walked Sarah back into the house, she too threw her arms around his neck and hugged him just as tight.

"I am so glad it was not you, please come in and sit, you must tell us all what has happened to you," she said leading him into the library and to the coach. Jacob asked him if he would like a sherry and Sylvian asked for something stronger and was given a large glass of Scotch. Sylvian explained to the two women what had happened to him on the *Endeavour* just before they left Portsmouth and that he had McLean jailed for his bullying.

"Well it would appear that this man had fallen on hard times and now found himself as a seaman on a trader out of Southampton. He saw me when he docked here to unload produce and made up his mind that he could rid himself of the cause of his predicament. He decided to follow me after seeing me with Sarah I believe, and has been following me since. This evening he had decided to deal with me in the most horrendous way and stole two pistols from the armoury. He was caught in the act by his master at arms so he killed him with his knife and laid in wait for me to leave the ship," said Sylvian taking a short pause, but he could see from the ladies' faces that this was not enough and they would need to know the whole story. He took a large sip of the good single malt and continued.

"So, he made his way to the alley and into the courtyard and hid himself in the shadows, from there he could see the street at the end of the alley. When he saw me, he called out for help, which I heard the second time he called, which is when I went to see. He then held me at gunpoint whilst he serviced his need to tell me how I had been so cruel to him. I was not aware that the body of the master had been found and a search for this man had commenced. They found paperwork by his hammock area which had my name and the name of the ship upon it. The bosun of the Robin then reported to the *Endeavour* what had happened and asked to see me, luckily my man Fitzwalter, who has saved me many times was the recipient of this information and was able to put it all together. He then set off to find me. Fitzwalter is an expert shot with both musket and pistol and saw that the man McLean was about to shoot me and had him dispatched in a trice. Lucky for me," said Sylvian taking a long drink from his glass.

"And me," said Sarah as she gripped his arm with absolutely no intention of letting go.

"So, this man McLean was sent from your ship for this cruelty he had done to your men?" asked Annie.

"Indeed, from what I had seen when I approached the ship was obvious that the man was unstable," answered Sylvian.

They were disturbed from their conversation when William came into the room and shook hands with the now standing Sylvian. "My answer is yes, young man, for I have never seen my daughter so distraught over anything in her life such as you, please take care of her as she is as precious to me as is her mother," said William. Sarah jumped to her feet and hugged her father hard and then kissed Sylvian.

"So, another wedding to plan. I am glad I kept the tablecloths and some of the wedding regalia from your sister's wedding, my dear. What shall I do, my dear, when you have all left me?" said Annie with her eyes full of happy tears. "When shall we plan this for?"

Sarah looked at Sylvian for some guidance.

"I shall be sailing for the Caribbean in just a week Annie and will be gone for some time, so I think then you shall have much time to plan. Sarah shall also have to plan our home and have it built where she pleases, the architect has drawn us some good designs, he just needs to know where and he will then find a builder," said Sylvian.

"Caribbean, why there, Sylvian?" Sarah asked.

"Pirates, my love, we intend to stamp them out once and for all," said Sylvian

"Oh my!" exclaimed Annie.

"Pirates!" exclaimed Sarah with some worry to her voice.

"It's his job, ladies, and you shall both need to get used to it, it is what he does and he does it well," said William looking at Sylvian and giving him a wink of the eye.

"Well, if I am to take charge of this house where should you like it built, darling," said Sarah with a huge smile on her face. The smile of life where you know it is all new and things are just beginning.

"Wherever you shall please, I would like to be fairly near to the new dockyard but I shall leave that to you, my love," said Sylvian.

Jacob interrupted proceedings by announcing that dinner was served.

The evening was spent with further wedding discussions and then they were all regaled with Sylvian's battle on the return from Kingston. The capture of the pirates had fascinated them and many questions were asked but were not all answered. Nothing was said of the treasure that was found or the gold he had relieved from the French and Union coalition on Horse Island. Annie had wanted to know in great detail what had taken place on the island and how was the evil man Billings dealt with. Sylvian kept his answers to a standard to suit ladies which did not go amiss by his father-in-law-to-be.

With the evening ended Sylvian and Sarah said their romantic goodbyes and whilst not wishing to part, there was yet much for Sylvian to do. William had made his carriage available and the ride back to the ship was quick and the report he received from the duty officer Mr Watts was one of all is well and the ship was happy to have her captain back aboard safely. Sylvian thanked Rupert for his comments and made his way to his cabin where he sat with a large glass of whiskey and started on his reports for this night's events.

***

The morning brought yet more sun and Mr Blaketon as Mr Fowler's replacement. He looked resplendent in his new uniform which the tailor had already produced for another but could see the young lad's needs. Sylvian commented on his smartness and told him that he would be leaving the ship for an appointment with the admiral this morning. He asked Arthur to let him know as soon as Captain Young was aboard.

Sylvian enjoyed his breakfast and complimented Padraig on his cooking and being able to make the most perfect cup of tea. Padraig was so happy to receive this compliment from his captain and it had made his day so much happier.

It was not long before Andrew himself was knocking on his door and with his hair tied up and coat on the two men made their way to the fort.

The admiral's clerk showed the two captains straight into the admiral's office who asked them both to sit. He asked Sylvian to give a full report on last night's events for which Andrew had not heard a word and sat there in shock at what had taken place. The admiral suggested that the gift of Fitzwalter to this man's service was ever so more evident, he explained Fitzwalter's role in getting their release from the privateer's camp in northern Canada and all that he had achieved since, and now this. He tasked Sylvian to find a way to thank this man properly as the service owed him a great deal, as did the admiral and Sylvian. Sylvian suggested that Fitzwalter had not seen his family in quite some time and that they should consider bringing them all to Canada and building a home for them all. They were indeed a poor family and had depended on

Fitzwalter's naval pay to exist. They all agreed that it was a fine idea and that Sylvian should assign one of his finest to get the job done.

Sylvian then laid out to the admiral the plan that Andrew and he had come up with since interrogating the Spanish pirate and gaining the intelligence they now had. The admiral was concerned for their safety and the incursion on Union territory. He agreed without reservation that Andrew should go and help bring this pirate problem to a completion. His trust for his officers was without question and he wished them both luck to their task. He said that he had received reports that the British frigate Redoubt had been sunk just off the coast of Jamaica by three pirate ships and the men that had swum to them for rescue had been shot in the water and left to drift with no survivors. It was indeed a difficult and dangerous task these men were embarking upon.

On Sylvian's return to the *Endeavour* he found Commander Montrose in his office. James stood when Sylvian entered and gave his salute. Sylvian put his hat on his desk and removed his coat to the hook by the bookcase. He complimented James on his appearance and asked him how things were progressing with his command.

"Sir, I have good news; the carpenters have completed their work this day and the ship has been moved to the commissioning basin. She should be ready by Sunday this week, sir," he reported with a great deal of pleasure in his voice.

"Good, James, then we shall plan to sail on the evening's tide on Monday, will you kindly inform Captain Young of such as he will be joining us on this mission. I will ask Mr Fitzwalter to ensure that all of the team's equipment is loaded aboard. I should like the 'A' team under Mr Selway to sail with you, James, if that pleases you?" asked Sylvian.

"Indeed, sir, it will be good to have them aboard, good news that Captain Young is joining us too, that should help greatly in our task," answered James.

"Now did you find yourself good officers and crew, James, and what of your first officer?" asked Sylvian.

James sat a while and gave thought to his answer which concerned Sylvian a little. "Sir, I think I have found good officers but none that shall serve me as my first officer. I was wondering if you may have any suggestions, sir," said James.

"In fact, I do, James. Second Lieutenant Michael Fleming who currently serves as our head of regulators and is just itching to get back to sea and see some action. You must approach Commodore Swain with your request, James, and please tell him that it was at my suggestion that you make such an approach," said Sylvian.

"I thank you, sir, I do believe I have met Michael, seems a damn nice chap and pretty handy in a tight spot I have no doubt," said James. "Well, sir, if that is all I shall beg your leave and see to my duties."

After James left, Sylvian took the time to sit back and mull over his plan for the Caribbean mission, to see if there was anything Andrew and he had missed.

***

Monday the twenty sixth of September eighteen eight at four thirty post meridian three ships made ready to leave the confines of Halifax Harbour. All goodbyes had been said and many tears had been shed. A final briefing from Admiral James Albright and under the command of Captain Sylvian Mountjoy the three ships, *Halifax*, Antelope and *Endeavour* slipped gracefully from their moorings and sailed slowly up the estuary and out into the Atlantic Ocean and after one hour of sailing time all three ships took a forty-five degree turn to starboard and headed south. They would not all come back.

The End